MW01139845

Sophisticated Seduction Series

By L. L. Ash

ISBN: 9781671757202

Prologue

"Georgia, what am I going to do?" I sighed, pressing my head into my hands as we sat across from each other on her childhood bed.

"Ok, so it's not the end of the world," she told me, patting my back with a hopeful expression.

"You don't get it. If I can't find a place to stay up there, then I can't go. And you know how much I need to go to college!"

"I have an idea. Just give me a second," she told me, holding up a finger as she pressed a few buttons on her phone and put it on the bed, ringing on speaker phone.

"Sup baby girl?" a deep, gruff man's voice came through the phone.

"Hey Daddy. I hope you're not too busy."

"Just riding ass like usual." He chuckled, a loud metallic clink in the background booming through the speaker.

"That's not what bosses are supposed to say these days, Dad." Georgia frowned into her phone. "It means something completely different now."

"I'm not that ancient. Now, what's up?"

"Well, I was just thinking. You have that big ol' house up in Seattle and I was just thinking that maybe you had room for one more tennant."

Silence.

"She can help me clean and everything. But her dad just lost his job and she was counting on them to help get an apartment and stuff. She's earned scholarships for college but..."

"She cleans up, she can stay," her dad said with a sigh. "Hey, I gotta go though, the drywallers are f-uh messing up again."

"Ok, thank you daddy!"

"Mhmm," he hummed, the sound erupting goosebumps over my skin as the line cut out.

"See?" Georgia turned to me with a grin. "Daddy gives me anything I want."

"But, I don't want to be a burden..."

"It's fine. You have a car and everything. No big deal. Dad won't care."

For once, her having a spoiling dad actually worked in my favor. Now the hard part was convincing my parents that I should live with my friend's dad instead of putting off college for a semester. We'd see which turned out to be the bigger problem.

Chapter 1

Bay

"And if you ever feel uncomfortable, you just call and we'll drive on up there and go get you," Mom said in a rush as I dragged out my last suitcase.

"I'll be fine!" I smiled at her, trying to fight back the tears.

It'd been a month now and Dad was still trying to find another job, and adding the stress of my moving in with a grown man who was a complete stranger to them and me, well, they were at their last emotional straw.

"I'm going to be just fine," I told her again, dropping the bag to give Mom another hug.

"Ok," she nodded, wiping up her makeup-blackened tears.

"I'm only a few hours away, and I'll be home soon for Thanksgiving, ok? Fall break will be awesome! And you don't have to worry about me at all!"

Dad came up and hugged me too, squeezing me almost to the point of pain.

"Now, why did you have to go and grow up on us?" he asked with an emotional laugh, voice cracking under the weight of his unshed tears.

"I'm not dying," I groaned. "I'm just going to college! I promise to move back home and live with you until I'm forty. Deal?"

The joke had done what I wanted, making them both laugh away their sadness.

"Ok, sweetheart," Dad nodded and took up my bag, bringing it the rest of the way to the car.

"I put some money in your account," Mom blurted. "To make sure you have plenty of gas money."

"Mom," I chastened.

She just smiled again at me and followed me to the car.

They didn't have money to give me, which was why I was going to Georgia's dad's house in the first place. Being nineteen, I really was done being a burden on them.

"Love you," they both told me, giving me hugs and a kiss on the cheek each before I managed to slide into the driver side of my car, getting in.

They waved from the driveway of my childhood home and I felt a heart-wrenching sadness overtake me for just a moment as they disappeared in my rearview mirror. I would miss them. A lot.

Heading over three streets to Georgia's house, I parked in her driveway and got out to help her with her bags.

"C'mon Mom! Dad will be just fine."

My friend didn't sound so enthused as she talked to her mom on the other side of the door. Lifting my hand to knock, I barely rapped on the door when it swung open.

"Your father is smothering and controlling. There's a reason *I* got custody when we got divorced."

"You got custody because you cried in court." Georgia frowned over her shoulder as she waved me in. "Bay is here, by the way."

Georgia's mom looked at me around her with a frown on her face that was almost identical to her daughter's.

"I can't believe she roped you into this, Bay!" Tiffany puckered her lips in disgust. "I count on you to be the smart one to keep her from doing stupid stuff like this!"

Now, I knew the divorce was nasty. I knew that Georgia's parents didn't talk, which was why I'd never met her dad. I heard stories from the summers she spent with him on the west coast, but that was all. Not a single picture on the wall had him in it, and only a blurry snapshot or two over the years had given me a small idea of what to expect. That, and Georgia's emphasis that he was tall.

"We're going to be fine," I told Tiffany with a half smile. "We have each other, no matter what."

She grunted at that, not quite appeased, but not as worked up as she'd been earlier.

"Just keep an eye on each other. And don't hang out with his friends."

What kind of man was he, that his ex-wife would be worried about her daughter around his friends?

Georgia rolled her eyes and hugged her mom.

"Call you when we get there," she told her. "Don't have too much fun without me."

At this Tiffany laughed.

"Nothing you wouldn't do, honey," she told her daughter, then walked us out, each of us with a bag or box in our arms.

We stuffed it all in my sedan and after another round of hugs, we were on the road for the start of our college career.

"Do you mind if we stop for coffee?" Georgia asked with a sigh, scrolling through her phone as I got onto the freeway.

"Well, you could have asked me like, ten minutes ago!" I told her, slapping her on the arm.

Georgia laughed at me before nodding.

"Fine. When we stop for gas, I need a fillup too."

"Whatever." I smiled at my friend.

There was absolutely nothing that could stop me from enjoying my newfound freedom.

"And donuts. Those too."

Laughing, I agreed and kept going toward the Pacific Northwest.

"DAD!" Georgia called as she began to get her bags out of the trunk.

Me? I just started yanking and pulling until I had one out and was able to drag it out of the backseat and toward the cute little blue bungalow that her dad lived in. That *I* would live in.

"Here, let me get that," I heard suddenly, the bag being lifted with ease out of my grasp with large, tanned hands.

My eyes dragged up worn and stained jeans, up a gray t-shirt and ending at the face of someone who was definitely not old enough to be Georgia's dad.

"Daddy!" Georgia called again and this beast of a man called back with a dismissive run of 'yeah's' accompanied by a big smile.

Oh my God... This is Blake?

"You're just down the hall and to the left, that-a way." Blake pointed toward the door and motioned to his right.

"T-thanks." I choked as he gave a half nod, dark hair falling over his face in a boyish sort of way, brushing against thick eyebrows above deep blue eyes.

Georgia's eyes.

"Sure," he grunted out, then went around me to my friend.

"Where's my big strong Daddy?" She teased her dad with a grin, waving at the bag half out of the car already.

"Hey baby girl," he said, slipping his arms around her waist and hefting her up over his shoulder like she was five years old.

"Put me down!" she yelped between laughs, slapping his broad shoulders.

He chuckled, this deep, gritty sound that hit me like punches to the gut.

Wow.

"When did you become so lazy?" Blake sighed at Georgia, popping the bag out of the back like it was nothing. Then three more bags lined up on the driveway before he hefted up a box. *My* box.

"In. Left. Right." Blake nodded with his chin toward the door that I was effectively blocking.

"Oh right. Shoot. Sorry," I said, dragging up my bag with three thumps up the steps into the house.

It was immaculate inside. Not what I was expecting at all, especially after what Tiffany had said.

I followed his instructions and found myself in a bare room, nothing there but a bed, a side table, and a dresser. It was absolutely *perfect*.

"You give her the guest room?" Georgia asked as she pointed her dad toward me.

"Yeah, that's mine," I told him, holding out my arms for the box.

"I don't care whose it is, just tell me where to put it," he said with a half smile that I was starting to think was his go-to.

"That's mine. Just on the floor is fine," I told him and he did just that.

Crouching, he gently put the box down with a little grunt before taking off back out the door.

"So? What do you think?" Georgia asked and I almost let the words I was thinking burst out of my lips.

Beautiful. Hot. Yes please.

"Do you like your room?" she specified.

"Oh! Yeah! It's great. I love that we're going to be housemates!" I gushed, hoping she wouldn't notice how weird I was acting.

No chance. She was way too perceptive and we'd been friends way too long.

"You ok?" she asked, brows crinkling with worry.

"I'm fine," I forced a softer smile onto my face. "I'm just excited and I...I can't believe I'm here."

She snorted and nodded.

"Oh, believe me. I didn't think I'd be living with my dad when I went to college. At least he's not *your* dad."

God help me. It's a damn good thing he's not my dad, because that would be weird with how hot I was getting over him.

"Right!" I laughed as Blake came up with two more suitcases.

"Pink yours, baby?" he asked Georgia.

9

"You know it!" She nodded at her dad and took the bag from him into her room across from mine.

"So this is yours?" he asked me next, motioning to the old, threadbare blue bag that had been my grandmother's before I had stolen it from my mom to use for the trip. "Ok, where do you—"

The bag picked that *exact* moment to not just break, but absolutely explode all over the room.

"Fuck," I heard Blake grunt, staring at the beaten up leather handle still in his hand as the bag laid splayed open over the floor.

He dropped to his haunches again and tossed the handle over his shoulder into the hall. He grabbed handfuls of clothes and tried shoving them back into the bag that had split at the zipper.

My face burned beet red when I saw the underwear and bras that he fisted back into the bag.

"Sorry, Bay," he started, then froze with a few thongs in his hands that had been hiding...

Oh God...

"I'll just uh..." Blake choked on his words a bit, but the grin that spread over his face told me he was holding back a laugh as he stood again and put out his hands. "I'll leave this to you."

I quickly grabbed the thongs and saw the little black bullet and hot pink dildo wand that I had packed just so that my parents wouldn't find it in my room while I was gone. Georgia and Tiffany had gotten them for me at graduation, insisting that it was better than making a mistake on a bad guy. And honestly, I agreed with them. I just hadn't broken those little things in yet because I was too afraid Mom would burst into my room unannounced and catch me red handed.

And he *saw it.*

Georgia's smoking hot dad saw my bullet and dildo massagers, and he left the room with a laugh.

God? Just kill me now. Please?

I pressed my hands over my face and fought back the urge to cry—slash—laugh over it when Georgia found me.

"Whoa, what happened here?" she asked, dropping to her knees and scooping up a few things.

Then her eyes found the sex toys.

"You brought them?" she asked me, all excited.

"I couldn't leave them at home for my parents to find!" I whispered-yelled. "And your freaking *dad* just saw them!"

She shrugged. "Dad's cool. Believe me. He doesn't care if you masturbate."

I pressed my hands over my face again and gave in to the half laugh, half cry that was forcing its way out.

"Pizza?" I heard Blake call into my room, but he didn't enter.

I would never be able to look the man in the eyes again.

Ever.

"Hawaiian!" Georgia called.

"Pineapple does *not* belong on pizza. We've talked about this," Blake told her, pushing the door open a little more to argue with his daughter.

"Just because you don't have my sophisticated tastes doesn't mean that I am wrong."

"Your mother has ruined you," he said with a chuckle, shaking his head.

"True." Georgia nodded with finality before grabbing the toys and holding them up in the air. "You don't care, right Dad?"

I lunged for the things, knocking my friend onto the ground as Blake belly laughed.

"Hell no," he said, still laughing. "We all gotta get off somehow."

"Oh my *GOD!*" I shrieked and pulled at the roots of my blond hair. "Freaking *shut up* Georgie!"

The two of them just laughed at me for a minute before Blake pulled out his phone and started ordering pizzas.

"You're the worst!" I yelled full out at Georgia as her dad left us. "I can't believe you!"

"See? Nothing to worry about!"

"Oh my God, I hate you," I growled, pressing my hands to my cheeks while they continued to burn up.

Was it possible to get a fever from embarrassment? It certainly felt like it.

She plopped the devices into my bedside drawer before following her dad out of the room and slipping into her own.

"You'll forgive me eventually," she called over her shoulder.

Of course she was right. I always forgave her, no matter how freaking embarrassing the things she did were.

I managed to sort through the disaster of a bag and put things in drawers. I hung things in the closet and neatly stacked my shoes at the bottom. Last, I opened my camera case to check that everything was still in perfect condition.

My lenses sat comfortably in their foam-padded pockets while the body of it was still packed neatly. I was worrying about nothing.

Satisfied that it was safe, I changed into some leggings and a tank top before stalking out of the room and back the way I had come just as the doorbell rang.

Blake almost ran me over as I approached the front door from the hallway at the same time as he did from what I assumed was the living room.

"Oh, sorry," he said, waving me by before he opened the door and held out some cash to the delivery kid.

"Thanks Blake," the kid said, tilting his logo hat to him before handing the pizzas over.

"Got supreme and disgusting. Uh, I mean Hawaiian," Blake told me as we went to the living room together where Georgia was already in pajamas and cuddled up in one corner of the couch.

I sat beside her while Blake left to the kitchen just in the other room, and I took a moment to look around.

While it was clean, the house was also pretty barren and sparsely decorated. It was obvious that a bachelor lived there.

Tasteful wood furniture and a comfortable couch were the main parts of the living room, all focused on the huge TV on the wall.

"Where's my dinner?" Georgia called out like she was three years old before winking at me.

"Hold your horses," Blake called back and Georgia giggled to herself.

"What are you, five?" I asked her, digging down into the unusually comfortable couch.

"He loves it," she said in a whisper. "And it's so much fun to mess with him! He's so *not good* with girls!"

I shook my head and tried not to laugh as Blake came out with paper plates and napkins and a parmesan shaker.

"You didn't get into praying or anything since you were here last, did you?" he asked Georgia with a quirk of his eyebrow.

She just made a serious face and shook her head.

"Good. You do something like that and I should know. Right? We had a deal."

"I know. No big life events without calling you."

"Which means...?" He rolled his hand for her to continue.

"No dating a guy more than three times before bringing him to meet you."

"Good girl." He winked at Georgia before giving up the plates and napkins, plopping that shaker on the coffee table.

We each took one and dug into the pizza.

I took a piece of each and settled back as we watched a show about some motorcycle club.

Chapter 2

Blake

I hadn't expected Georgia's friend to be so...*cute*. From what I'd heard of her over the years, I imagined some buck-toothed, hicksville girl with a camera in her hands. The last time I'd seen pictures of them together was a few years ago at some camp they went to together. Greasy hair and nose sunburn weren't exactly becoming...

But this girl? I was going to have to watch myself around her.

Rolling my eyes at my own thoughts, I shoved my jeans down and crawled into bed.

Not that it mattered anyway. I was old enough to be the girl's dad. Literally. Didn't matter that I was only thirty-five. She was my daughter's best friend and that's all she would stay.

Fuck...I needed to get laid if even some teenaged girl seemed like good pickings.

Flopping over to my side, I just tucked away the thought to maybe make some kind of online dating profile that was just for hookups. Yeah, that wasn't bound to backfire at *all*. Besides, I wanted more than a hookup. I wanted a relationship. Love, even, if I could swing it.

A thousand things ran through my head of what needed to get done over the weekend, and sleep eluded me because of it. Running my own construction and renovation company left me with heavy weight on my shoulders, and I was really feeling the pressure. The timeline we'd bid for was almost up and we were still a couple weeks from completion. Working on the weekend was a must at this point, and I wasn't any exception. Except tomorrow. Being the boss had some benefits, at least. I had Georgia all to myself for the first time in months and I was going to enjoy it, even if it was with her friend trailing along.

The image of the poor girl's cheeks about ready to burst a blood vessel was hilarious when Georgia held up her little toys. And who knew teenage girls had sex toys? I thought I had a few years at least before having to come to terms with that, but judging by the ease with which my daughter picked them up and displayed them to her own father, she was comfortable with them. Thanks a whole hell of a lot, Tiffany. Just one more way you fucked up our daughter with lies and judgements and manipulations. It was kind of her M.O. and I should have been used to it after so many years. But no, I was pretty sure I never would. Teaching a kid to be ok with their sexuality was one thing, but teaching them to spread it around like it meant nothing was something else entirely.

Giving up on sleeping, I grabbed my crinkly pack of cigarettes and pulled on some sweats before heading to the back porch. The door was already cracked open.

"Oh, sorry," I heard a light voice say after a bright flash blinded the fuck out of me.

Bay.

"The hell?" I groaned, rubbing at my eyes.

"Oh, I just couldn't sleep," Bay said, voice high and edgy and almost scared. "I came out to take a few pictures. I hope you don't mind..."

"I don't mind," I told her, pressing one of those demon cigarettes between my lips, contemplating whether I should light it around her or not. I'd been so careful over the years not to smoke around Georgia, but this girl was an adult. If she didn't like it, she could leave.

"You smoke?" she asked, face shadowed and highlighted by the faint street light coming from the other side of the house.

"Not really." I gave a weak chuckle.

I'd been trying to quit for-fucking-ever, and I was down to just stress cigs at this point, but it still wasn't gone from my life.

And unfortunately, I was really fucking stressed lately. Adding Georgia and her little friend to the picture didn't help any, either.

"I don't mind." She shrugged, then turned to look through her viewfinder at the trees outlining the low, almost full moon.

Fuck it all...

I dug through my sweats pocket and found a lighter there, where it typically stayed since nights were usually when I'd give in to the temptation to use it.

The stick lit up with a cherry end in the darkness while she snapped picture after picture of the trees against the night sky.

"I-uh," she said suddenly, breaking the quiet of bugs and the whoosh of her camera shutter with her words. "Thank you. I mean, I really appreciate you letting me stay here. I know you don't know me or anything..."

I nodded even though she couldn't see it.

"I don't mind," I told her. "Georgie has been talking about you for years. I might as well know you from all her stories."

She sighed with a chuckle under her breath.

"Still, I couldn't be here without your generosity. And I want to help where I can, so don't hesitate to give me chores and things so I can pull my weight."

"I'm sure you'll have plenty. Georgie never liked doing her chores."

She laughed a little fuller this time, her head bobbing in agreement in the faint reflection of the moon on us.

"I'm sure I will," Bay agreed before dropping her camera on the neck strap, letting the thing hit her chest.

Nope, Blake, eyes off her chest.

I turned away and took another drag, lighting up the cherry end as I inhaled.

"Guess I should get some sleep," she said after a few seconds of awkward silence.

I just nodded, not turning back to her as she went toward the sliding door and slipped into the house.

16

Breathing out in relief, smoke drifted between my lips, lifting toward the sky as I closed my eyes and just tried to relax.

Since I wasn't sure how much relaxing I'd be able to do with the girls in the house, I would have to savor the moments of silence and stillness where I could get them.

Quirking a half smile on my lips, I thought for just a moment how good it felt to have kids in the house again. To have *Georgie* in the house again. I'd missed her when Tiffany and I divorced and I only got her in the summer after that. Georgia was only seven at that point. Summers were always tough to sort out since it was my busiest season with the business, but she was worth it. And now I had all the time in the world to get to know her again as the grown woman she was beginning to blossom into. And I'd have to buy a shotgun, you know, for any of those boyfriends she brought home to meet me. I didn't have to threaten anyone, but I could certainly be shining and cleaning it when he arrived.

Chuckling at the idea, I took one last drag, and dropped the last bit into an ashtray I kept on the deck rail. Since I was feeling a little better, I went back into the house and collapsed back into my bed before falling asleep almost immediately.

When I woke up, it was to girlish giggles and obnoxious laughter, followed by a distinct shush. That laugh was Georgia's, so it must have been Bay telling her to shut up.

The way they interacted made me laugh as I shoved my hand through my hair and unstuck my tongue from the top of my mouth. Ashes and tobacco lingered there and it wasn't pleasant. I needed coffee.

Dragging myself to the kitchen, the giggles, laughs and shushes became louder until I was witness to what the girls were laughing about.

"What the hell is that?" I asked, stopping right in the doorway as Georgia patted the strange hairdo on her head.

"Don't you love it, Daddy?" she asked, fingering the braid spiraled up her head like a fucking beehive.

Just like that, she started spinning her head and a braid right on the crown of her head spun like a helicopter blade.

A burst of laughter exploded from my mouth at the pure strangeness and exuberant youth those two were oozing.

"The f-" I started, then caught myself.

No saying fuck around Georgia and her friend.

"I know, it's weird." Georgia laughed, pointing at Bay. "She did it to me."

"When the hell did you have time to do this? It's like...nine in the morning!" I asked them, reaching around Georgia to get the carafe of coffee.

"Bay's an early riser and she woke me up. So I made her do something fun and interesting while we hung out."

"Thanks for making the coffee," I said, grabbing a mug from the drying mat near the sink.

"Bay did. I don't make good coffee, you know that."

Boy did I.

Taking a sip, I held back a moan of pleasure from the bitter stuff sliding down my throat. Dark and strong, just how I liked it.

"This. This is your new job," I told Bay, pointing to the coffee maker.

She smiled and nodded, putting a mug to her lips as she sipped her own drink.

"Hey, when did you get all buff?" Georgie asked suddenly, poking me in the pec.

I almost spewed a mouthful of coffee all over the kitchen.

"What the hell?" I asked, rubbing the little spot that hurt after she poked with her sharp fingernail.

"Last time I was over you had some serious dad bod going on," she commented, bouncing her eyebrows at me.

"I started working out." I frowned.

"You go to the gym? They let old guys like you go to the gym?" My daughter teased me with a cheeky grin.

"I'm not that old," I told her, pulling that weird braid hanging loose down the side of her head.

I bit the inside of my cheek, absolutely not going to tell her that I was hitting the gym so I could start hitting on women again. I might have experienced marriage and divorce, but I'd never been in love. After so many years, I just wanted to have that for myself. Seeing my buddies and co-workers every day talking about their wives and their kids and their white fucking picket fence. I just... I wanted more than an empty house and my overcompensating truck. I wanted a woman I could love, cherish, come home to or go on vacations with when my eye started twitching from stress. The only problem would be finding a woman my age who wanted to start a family. Family near forty? That was a tall order for any woman. But I was willing to try and find my proverbial unicorn.

"Go paint your nails or something," I said to Georgia, waving her off while I enjoyed my coffee.

She just threw up her middle finger at me as she trotted off, and I threw mine up at her back, the mug still at my mouth.

Bay just laughed into her own cup, trying to cover her smile with it.

"You got something to say?" I asked her, wondering if she had even half the sass of my daughter.

"Oh no. Just observing. I'm starting to understand where Georgia gets some of her traits from."

"Thank God she didn't get them *all* from Tiffany." I rolled my eyes before going in for a second cup of joe.

"Seriously, I always just thought she was spunky. But no, she's just channeling you."

I felt my lips lift in a half smile as I looked down into the steamy, caffeinated drink. It felt damn good to hear Bay say that Georgia had some of me in her; that our summers had actually equated to something to her while growing up. Maybe I wasn't a complete failure as a father after all.

"So what are you guys planning on doing for the last few days before school starts?" I asked, just trying to cover up the awkward silence.

19

"I'm not sure." She chuckled nervously. "I figured I'd just go along with whatever Georgie wants to do. That's usually our thing."

So I heard. Bay was the quiet artist type, as far as I could understand. And I could definitely see that in her now that we'd met.

"Swimming!" came a sudden shout from the hallway. "Let's go swimming!"

Bay looked toward the hall then at me before blanching pale as a skinless almond. Seriously.

"I-I didn't bring a swimsuit," she said weakly to her friend.

Georgia tossed a mass of strings at Bay as she went toward the back door with her own bathing suit on, taking down the funky braid around her head.

"You have five minutes!" she called at Bay.

Bay looked down at the pink and white bundle before ducking her head and settling her mug in the sink.

"You don't have to do what she says," I told her, afraid that the girl was being bullied by my own child.

"I know. It's ok," was all she said before heading toward the back of the house.

Finishing up my own drink, I rinsed the mug out at the tap, then did the same for hers, while Georgia's empty glass of orange juice was still on the countertop near the stove. I just rolled my eyes and went for that one too.

A couple minutes later Bay came from the bathroom with a towel wrapped around her body as she swiftly headed toward the back, only pausing for a second near the kitchen to scold me.

"I'll do the dishes before lunch," she said, her brows scrunched as if she was actually put out by my doing the dishes.

"Fine." I put up my palms. "No dishes."

She nodded once then turned toward the backyard.

The pool wasn't very big, mostly a glorified hot tub without the hot, but it was enough to play around in, which Georgia absolutely loved to do.

"And you don't actually get burned here," I heard Georgia telling Bay. "Not like back home. There's no sun to burn you with!"

A shrieking laugh met my ears and that made me grin. I loved my daughter's laugh.

"It's friggin' cold!" Bay groaned while testing the water, I imagined.

Laying out the cleaning rag over the kitchen faucet, I left it there and went to the back door to watch.

Bay was touching her toes into the water and reeling back like it was glacier water while Georgia laughed from inside the pool.

"C'mon! It's good for you!" Georgia called.

"Good for what?" Bay shrieked. "Catching my death?"

"It's called a Polar Bear Plunge," I added. "They do it for health all over the world."

Bay looked over her pale shoulder at me with wide eyes.

"You're on *her* side?"

Not giving a single fuck, I took a running jump and splashed into the water with a howl.

Wiping water out of my eyes, I looked up at Bay who was staring at me in horror.

I did the plunge frequently as part of my plan for fitness, to keep everything tight, so it didn't really bother me anymore like it had in the beginning.

"You're crazy!" She laughed, flicking the cold water I'd splashed onto her from her skin.

"C'mon!" Georgia groaned, grabbing Bay's ankle and yanking.

"If she doesn't want to get in, don't make her," I told Georgia, but Bay shook her head.

"I want to, but sane people don't get into cold water. I guess you're where Georgie got her crazy from, too!"

No. Georgia got her crazy from her mom.

"Then c'mon." I waved at her.

21

She touched her toes in again and squealed again, wrapping her towel around her tighter.

"Let's go!" Georgia called, yanking her ankle again.

I lifted my arms to her as if Bay were three years old, but it totally worked. Next thing I knew that towel was dropping, revealing one sexy little pink and white striped bikini. She covered her arms over her chest before shutting her eyes and leaned into the water.

I managed to catch her in my arms, and was rewarded with a shriek that left my ears ringing.

"Whoa," I said, holding her tighter until she opened her eyes, her body trembling in my arms.

"Oh my God it's so cold!" she managed through chattering teeth.

"You'll get used to it," I told her, letting go before I started to notice what it felt like to hold her.

Too late.

Georgia was right there, throwing her arms around her friend and they giggled and laughed together while I treaded water a few feet away from them.

Suddenly it started to seem weird, being in the pool with my daughter and her best friend, so I dunked my head under the frigid surface one more time, then moved over to the edge and pulled myself out, holding tight to my saggy-ass sweats as I did.

When I got out of the water, that was when the cold really hit. I felt my skin prickle with chills as I headed into the house.

"Can you bring me a towel?" Georgia called and I nodded, waving my hand at her while dripping the whole way back to my bedroom.

I changed quickly, throwing on some jeans and a t-shirt that felt a little too snug in the shoulders and chest lately, then went back out to check on the girls.

They were still playing, and there wasn't one sign of Bay dying of cold. Go figure.

Plopping two towels down by the edge, I started heading back into the house to do *something* other than stare at my daughter's best friend, until Georgia called me back over.

"We want to see who can hold their breath the longest!" she said. "You judge!"

I sighed and sat on the lounging chair before sitting and reluctantly agreeing.

"Ok. Count down and tell us who wins!"

I nodded and counted.

"Three, two, one...Go!"

Both girls gasped and dropped their heads under the surface of the water, but then Bay silently surfaced again, a grin on her face as she winked at me, putting a finger to her lips with this devilish little look on her face.

The outer corners of her eyes crinkled in mirth as she bit her lip, this seductive little move that wasn't meant to be seductive at all. She slipped back under the water not three seconds before Georgia came up, gasping for air.

"Fuck!" Georgia yelped when she saw Bay under the surface.

She came up a moment later, putting on a good show of gasping and rubbing her eyes before throwing her hands up in celebration.

"Hey," I scolded Georgia. "Don't say fuck."

"You do," she snapped with a smile on one half of her lips.

"I'm a dirty old man who can get away with it," I snipped right back, my smile mirrored back at her.

"And I'm a vibrant young woman who is free from the social restraints of her father's generation. Get used to it, Daddy-o."

"Dammit." I frowned.

Social restraints? What the hell was she talking about?

Bay laughed and folded her arms over the edge of the pool, lifting out a little as she leaned there, and oh fuck the cleavage. When my tongue started tracing my bottom lip, I sprung out of my seat and turned.

23

"Bay wins!" I called over my shoulder before practically running into the house.

I went into the laundry room to try and distract myself by folding some clean clothes, but the perfect little round globes of flesh just would not leave my brain. It was like it was somehow burned into my mind like a brand.

And it wasn't as if I hadn't seen breasts before. I'd seen probably more than my fair share in high school before I'd started dating Tiffany, and then a few here and there after the divorce, but those ones...Oh God. Those ones belonged to a teenage *girl*. Not a woman.

Biting my lip, I couldn't help but turn to look out the little window of the laundry room at the pool where the girls were getting out. And there she was in all her glory, my daughter's friend that I just barely met yesterday, all youth and curves and a wicked seduction to every inch of her skin that she didn't have the rightful ability to wield yet. The girl would be a heartbreaker in college. So would Georgia for that matter. But while I thought of Georgia dating I got furious and scared. When I pictured Bay with some little asshole skirt-chaser who wouldn't know what a clit was for if it was his fucking major, I got...*sad*. A strange fucking reaction for a girl I didn't know, and someone that I would never know as anything other than my daughter's best friend.

I rubbed my eyes, forcing my sight away from the vision outside before digging into a basket and grabbing a t-shirt.

Laundry. I knew how to do laundry.

Shoving all the rest of it out of my mind, I focused solely on getting my boxer briefs right side in before folding them in half and slapping them on the dryer, then going in for more.

Chapter 3

Blake

"Five hundred!" Georgia screeched.

She had gotten the light blue properties and put hotels on them right away. A good strategy considering I was broke with absolutely no monopolies to my name.

Bay was giggling across the table, watching me flip over all my properties to try and get enough to pay my ungrateful daughter in rainbow game money.

"I fed you, changed your poop diapers," I grumbled as I threw each hundred on the table for her to snatch up. "I paid for your clothes and your shoes and your dance lessons, soccer, and your f— damn vegetarian diet when you were six because you didn't want to eat someone's pet."

Georgia laughed and patted my shoulder. *Consoling* me.

"Tell you what dad," she said. "You can keep this."

She handed over the four ones and a single ten while stacking up her hundreds.

"How nice of you," I told her sarcastically.

I still took the sad fourteen dollars and put it with my remaining twenty-three.

Bay was just giggling and covering her mouth like if she hid her smile, I wouldn't know she was laughing at me.

On her turn she bought a bunch of houses on the pinks, one away from a hotel on each before handing me the dice.

We went around the table again, but then Bay landed on my railroads. I didn't have all four, but three was enough to put her in trouble.

She moaned and pressed her hands into her hair, flipping cards around.

"Tell you what," I told her. "Make me those brownies of yours again and we'll call it flush," I told her.

Her expression lit up.

"Really?" she asked me.

"Hell yeah! Those were so good!"

"You won't last if you don't take money, Dad," Georgia warned with amusement on her face.

"Yeah. but when I inevitably lose this game, I'll have warm, gooey brownies to look forward to while you count your fake money."

She nodded, looking impressed.

"You're sly, Dad."

"Didn't get this far in life by being stupid." I laughed, taking up the dice to roll.

Income tax.

Shit.

"Ok, I give up. Bankrupt, but I'll be well fed!"

The girls laughed and continued playing as they bought up my property between them until ultimately Bay won. She was a shrewd negotiator. Who knew?

"I'll have those brownies for you tonight, Blake!"

"Thank you!" I called, heading out to clean the pool.

Some wind had blown leaves into the water, and I intended to go on a cold swim in the morning to burn off the chocolaty calories.

"Need any help?" Georgia asked.

"Nah, that's ok. You just hang out and enjoy your time. Got any homework?"

She shrugged.

"You should probably get that done before we watch that show tonight over pizza."

"I'm not a kid, Dad. Don't tell me what to do." Rolling her eyes, she turned and went to go find her friend in the kitchen.

Where the hell did that come from? It was damn hard to try and treat her like an adult when she didn't act like it. I watched

26

Bay dedicate hours to homework and writing and math on the kitchen table while Georgia fooled around and stayed on campus most days, then she'd come home on the weekends to beg for help because she had neglected her homework and was afraid of flunking out.

Yep.

So of course I reminded her to do homework. She couldn't take care of herself, so evidently I had to keep on her ass like I did when she tried the same thing in high school.

Whoever said you stopped worrying about your kids like that when they went to college was a complete fucking liar.

Bay

The longer I was around Blake, the more I realized that all the things I loved about my best friend came from her dad. The two of them together were something else. Between the sassy comebacks and the smartass comments here and there, they were both quick to laughter and grins and they had that identical half smile. Who knew something like that was genetic?

Her dad went back to work the day after we went into the pool, and I spent some nice time hanging out and relaxing before school started, but it didn't get rid of my anxiety for it. No, that was as strong as ever.

"Bay! Do you have a dress I can borrow?" Georgia asked in a hurry, all flustered and rummaging around in her bedroom.

"I've got a couple," I told her, peeking through her doorway as she uprooted every single item of clothes she owned.

"Thank God! Show me!"

I led her quickly to my room and handed her the couple of cotton summer dresses I'd brought, and the one party dress I had gotten because Mom had insisted I had something like that with me when I went to college. Not that I would need it.

She immediately went for the sexier of the dresses and snatched it up, looking at herself in my dresser mirror.

"Thanks babe!" she told me and started heading back to her room.

"What're you doing?" I asked her, following again.

"I've got another meeting," she said with a sigh. "And someone told me to wear something sexier today."

"For a meeting?" I choked.

"Not that kind of meeting," she said, biting on her lip as she paused and looked at me.

There was something she wasn't telling me, and all the little trips she'd made out the last few days in her Dad's sports car were about this.

"I'm rushing," she said finally, looking at the floor between our feet.

"Rushing what?" I asked back, trying to understand.

"No. Like, rushing. For a sorority."

Sorority?

"What?" I shrieked.

"I know! But I just...I want to go to the parties and I want to have fun and...I really want to do this, Bay! Please, you have to understand...I knew you wouldn't want to do this with me, so I didn't tell you."

"Or your dad," I ground out.

"Dad doesn't care. Dad never really cares if I borrow his car."

But something in my gut told me he'd care about this.

"Ok," I said with a sigh. "But what happened to us, the lone rangers? You and me? I mean, you could've gone anywhere for school and you chose here because this was where I got my scholarship."

She licked her lips, nodding.

"I know, Bay. I know."

"Whatever," I said and frowned, watching her lay the dress out on the bed and move to close the door.

Stepping away, the wood door closed gently like a physical representation of the sorority thing suddenly sprouting up between us.

Grabbing my laptop and SD card, I settled myself on the couch to work on some of the pictures I took that first night when the moon was fat and low, dangling heavy in the sky.

Georgia took five more minutes to get the dress on before moving toward the door, and I just gave her a halfhearted wave that she returned before leaving and closing the door softly behind her.

It was almost dinner time and I was going to have to be the one explaining to Georgia's dad where the hell she went. Yay for me.

It wasn't even half an hour after she left that Blake stepped in the door, covered in dust and grime, his jacket wet from the summer storm that had been dumping buckets of rain outside all afternoon

He grunted by the door, leaning down to work off his muddy boots and I couldn't help but watch the slope of his back and a pretty nice butt right in view, swathed in well-worn jeans.

"Where's Georgie?" Blake asked after a minute, his boots now on the mat by the door and jacket was sliding off his shoulders.

"She went to do some...school stuff," I told him.

He lifted a dark eyebrow.

"Without you?"

"She needed to do it on her own," was all I managed to say.

I didn't want to lie to him, so I hoped he didn't ask any more questions.

"So..." he started, hanging up his jacket on a hook by the door. "She just left you here?"

I shrugged.

"I can go to my room," I offered, but he shook his head.

"Nah, don't worry about it. It's just...not like her," he said before going into the kitchen.

"I put some pot roast in the slow cooker," I called out and the sound of him moving around in the kitchen froze.

"You cook?" he asked eventually, punctuated by the sound of the lid lifting and hitting the countertop.

Putting aside my computer, I went to the kitchen as well.

"Just something simple. I'll make some gravy whenever you're ready to eat."

He looked toward me, a string of the meat in his grubby hands.

30

"Did you at least wash first?" I asked aghast, and he just grinned and poked the meat into his mouth.

With a low hum of appreciation, he slipped past me and headed toward the back rooms.

"I'll shower up and come out to help finish it up," he said before a door closed behind him.

No, I'd do it myself so he'd have a hot dinner ready when he came out.

Getting some flour and butter going in a small pot on the stove, I put in some of the juice from the roast and seasoned it before turning it off. A couple minutes later Georgia's dad, the man who was supposed to be our guardian during our first semester at WU, approached wearing sweats, a snug t-shirt with the Triforce on it, and wet hair dangling in his face. The man looked no older than thirty, but was somehow old enough to have given Georgia half her DNA.

"I went ahead and finished it up," I told him, dishing some out. "Consider it rent."

He gave that little half smile and nodded.

"You'd think this was the Ritz Carlton with how much you're doing around here to pay 'rent' Bay. You can ease up a little and let Georgie do some of the work, you know. The point is to free you up so you can do your homework without thinking about a job."

"I know. It's fine, I don't mind helping. I usually do these things at home, anyway," I told him, handing him the plate with a pool of gravy over the fingerling potatoes. "And you took a big risk taking me in, not having met me and all, and what you did really, *really* helps me out. I don't want you to change your mind and kick me out."

He just chuckled and took the plate, moving over to the couch.

"Well, I won't argue with you," he said eventually. "But don't skip on schoolwork for housework, deal?"

"Deal," I agreed, giving myself a portion before going to the couch too. I sat on the other end as he pulled up the same show he

31

was working his way through. It was all motorcycles and violence. Good thing there wasn't sex in it. There was no way I could handle anything like that with a man like Blake right next to me.

Around ten o'clock Blake said goodnight and went to his room, his phone in his hand texting Georgia for the twentieth time with no response. I just grabbed my computer and went back to my bedroom and sat on the bed, opening up the SD card again to find another picture to edit.

As I scrolled through the images, one after the other that all seemed to look pretty similar, I stopped abruptly at one that wasn't the moon or trees. On my screen was Blake, shirtless and blinking with the brightness of my flash. When I heard someone coming up behind me that night, my finger had hit the capture button accidentally when I jumped. And it had taken a beautiful, candid shot of Blake.

My bottom lip sucked between my teeth and I bit hard as my eyes greedily traced every line and detail of his body. The way his muscles bunched in surprise, and the way his pants rode so low I could see a telltale hint of the infamous and elusive adonis's belt framed between his hips. Even with his eyes closed I could picture the perfect blue that resided there, and the piercing, intelligent gaze that always took my breath away whenever he entered the room.

I really shouldn't have a crush on him, but I totally did, and I didn't even really care. Obviously nothing would ever happen and I was looking forward to meeting some guys on campus if given the chance, but for today, *tonight,* I would let myself daydream.

My eyes drifted over to the bedside table and I considered, just for a moment, using the toys hidden inside. But no. I was too close to his room, and I was totally nervous that he'd hear them buzz in the quiet of the house. So instead, I propped the laptop up on the nightstand and just stared at the picture for a while like a thirteen year old girl with a celebrity crush until I fell asleep.

"Hey! Did you tell Dad?" I heard a voice next to my face while I was sleeping.

Shrieking, I threw my arms out and whacked something as my eyes burst open.

"Dude! It's me! Did you tell Dad about the sorority?" Georgia asked, holding her nose.

A thump sounded, followed by quick footsteps.

"No," I whispered back just as another pair of thumps hit the frame of my open door, Blake and his towering figure gripping it on both sides.

"You ok?" he asked, then squinted as he saw Georgia.

"What the fuck, Georgie?" He all but growled at his daughter. "I texted you a million times last night, and now you're freaking Bay out in the middle of the night? Did you just get in?"

Georgia sighed and moved toward her dad, pressing his shoulders so she could slip by.

That was when I noticed that he wasn't in his sweats. No, he was just in a flimsy and slightly baggy pair of boxers.

"I'm fine, and I didn't mean to scare Bay. I'm going to bed, and you should too. You have work in the morning."

He sighed, wiping a hand down his face before closing my door behind him.

"The fuck is going on with you, Georgie? Seriously? You don't do this."

I could faintly hear the conversation outside the door, even though I didn't really want to.

"Daddy, please. Go to bed. We'll talk in the morning, ok?"

He just sighed again, then I heard the soft thumps of his footsteps receding again.

Well, that was interesting.

Looking at the clock it read three seventeen a.m. Where had she been for almost twelve hours?

Grabbing my phone, I read some pages in my latest raunchy romance until I was tired again, then I went back to sleep, only to wake up to the sound of Blake and Georgie yelling at each other in the kitchen.

I had to rub my eyes to get the thick crust of dust out of the corners from my lack of sleep before I tiptoed out toward the argument in my sleeping shorts and tank top.

"I'm an adult, Dad. I'm going to college now and you can't keep me from going to parties."

"It's not the parties I have an issue with, Georgia," he growled. "I have a fucking issue with you abandoning your friend, and then coming home smelling like vodka! You're underage and you fucking *drove* home. What's wrong with you?"

"I only had one shot. I wasn't drunk, for fuck's sake. Seriously! I know you weren't around much, but I'm a mature person and you don't have any say as to what I do anymore."

They both noticed me standing in the entry of the kitchen just then. Blake was dressed for work in his jeans, *Hamel Construction* shirt and boots. He worked his jaw and bit his lip before moving toward the door. A rush of air blew past me as he slipped by and out the door, only pausing for a second to get his truck keys.

"Holy cow," Georgia frowned. "Good timing, Bay. I thought he'd blow a gasket or something."

"Drinking?" I asked.

"It was only a couple shots. I was fine to drive and it was all good. I didn't kill anyone on the way home. God, don't be like him."

My jaw slackened as I stared at my friend.

Well, the body of the person who *used* to be my friend. Only problem is she wasn't *acting* like the person who was my friend. This person in front of me was someone I didn't know. She was acting like her mom.

"I thought we agreed not to drink," I whispered. "Because you didn't want to end up like your mom."

She bit her lip and sighed, plopping on one of the dining room chairs roughly.

Georgia's Mom was a stripper in Vegas where we grew up. She danced and stripped and drank every night, and came home raging drunk most of the time. She had more than one DUI and had even gotten into an accident that had led her to a couple months in prison. Luckily Georgia was in Seattle with her dad back then, but I remember the emotional wreck she was when it had all happened. Georgia had called and talked to me for hours about what a screw up her mom was sometimes and that she wanted more for her life than that.

But here she was, drinking and driving.

Georgia suddenly burst into tears and I went to her, sitting beside her while she cried, patting her back.

"I know. I don't want to be like her," she said in a broken, tear-stained voice. "I'm sorry."

"I think your dad's the one you owe an apology to," I told her.

The door burst open and I heard the low thumps of Blake's boots on the floor before he froze in the entrance of the kitchen, seeing his daughter weeping.

"Baby girl..." He sighed and came over, waving Georgia in for a hug.

"I'm sorry, Daddy," she sobbed into his shoulder. "I should have answered and I'm sorry I went out without telling you and I'm sorry I drove after I drank and..."

He shushed her and held her tight to his chest, sinking his fingers into the mop of dark hair on her head.

His gaze met mine over her shoulder and I understood the turmoil wreaking havoc in his eyes. He almost looked in pain while he held his daughter in his arms, and my heart broke just a little for him. What could it be like for him to see his daughter falling into the same rut her mother had? Only problem is you can't divorce a kid. How was he going to handle it?

"I gotta get to work. But when I get back, I'm bringing Chinese and we'll watch Matrix and we'll talk about it, ok?" he said, grasping her head between two big hands and looked into her eyes with pleading in his.

"Ok," Georgia agreed and he nodded, then kissed her on the forehead.

He went back toward the door, grabbing his coat on his way out the second time.

It didn't look like it would storm, but the week I'd spent in the Pacific Northwest had taught me one thing. The weather was unpredictable, so you had to plan for everything.

Georgia and I hung out on the couch, painting nails and talking about the party she went to all morning, then we went for another swim when it got warm enough. I'd never get used to the cold water, but it was worth it to see my friend smiling. We didn't talk about the drinking anymore because I figured that was probably her dad's job, not mine. So instead, we just had fun.

Chapter 4

Blake

With the semester well underway, I saw a whole lot less of the girls. Bay was always doing homework in her room or chores late at night, and Georgia was...somewhere. She didn't come home a lot, and when she did, it was usually to sleep. Meanwhile my Mustang was out of the picture so I was down to either using my work pickup or my motorcycle. Not that I went out much, anyway.

The little moments that I saw Georgia and the meals I had with Bay were pretty much the highlights of my days, which, for a thirty-five year old man, was pretty sad. I mean, sure, catching hints of cleavage from my young tennant and watching those mile-long legs in little shorts every morning was nice and all, I found myself nursing blue balls a lot more than I wanted to admit.

With Georgia gone and Bay in her room, I took out my phone and finally pulled up an app for 'attractive people who want to meet attractive people'. It seemed pretty shady, but I was also pretty damn desperate.

Swigging my beer one more time, I pressed the "SIGN UP" button, just to exit the app again.

No, I wasn't that desperate.

Yet.

Bay

School was rough. The first day wasn't so bad, but after that, the homework started rolling in. You'd think that with a degree in art like mine, I'd have a pretty easy time when it came to homework. But math was a nightmare and English wanted a five page paper by the end of next week. And I didn't even want to get started on freaking Biology. Evidently, word around campus was that I got the one teacher that almost nobody passed the first time. Wonderful. My first semester and I was probably going to fail a class.

My anxiety was through the roof and I couldn't figure out how to just relax for a little bit. The little crush I had for Blake wasn't going away, so even hanging out around the house was causing me nerves. And to top it all off, Georgia was almost never around. She'd found some friends in her sorority that she hung out with on campus so she didn't come home at all except to sleep.

Late at night on Friday, I finally gave in to temptation and opened my little side table drawer. Blake was in bed a couple hours before so he wouldn't be awake around to hear me, and Georgia was gone. So after a sneaky little wash in the bathroom, I relaxed myself with those damnable little toys until I could finally sleep. I didn't even care that I fell asleep naked in my bed, the things still hanging out with me on the mattress. Nope, instead I just savored the cold kiss of air on my body when I woke up feeling like I was emerging from a drugged sleep.

"Daddy," Georgia called after week three of school.

"Sup?" he asked, mouth full of pizza.

Evidently Friday night was pizza night. It was kind of nice to not have to think about dinner. And to not need to clean anything up afterwards. Georgia didn't do chores, so I had to pick up the slack. While her dad was feeding me and letting me have a room, I had to do what I could to make his life easier. To make it seem like I wasn't there since he was kind enough to pay my way for a semester.

"I've been thinking about something, and I want to talk about it with you," Georgia said evenly.

It must be important, judging from the serious tone of her voice.

"Ok, shoot," Blake told her, sitting back in his seat to look at her.

"So, I want the whole experience at school," she started off saying. "I told you that before I even came out here that I want to try it all. My grades are good too, but college is about finding yourself and who you want to be for the rest of your life..."

I saw Blake roll his eyes a little before nodding.

"Well, I put some feelers out and tried a couple of sororities over the past few weeks and I was invited to join one."

He looked interested now, but in a sort of morbid, disgusted kind of way.

"Sorority?" he asked hesitantly.

"Yeah. They do all kinds of stuff to help the community and they have little functions all the time. It's a sisterhood."

Blake's eyes cut to me for just a moment before turning back to his daughter.

"What're you trying to say?" he asked her.

"Well, they offered me a room in their house. I can live on campus and it's not very expensive since it's considered school housing. I'll even get a job if I need to, but I really, really want to do this. And I hope that I have your support in this."

"My emotional support, or *financial* support?" he asked, looking surprised and taken back a little.

Hell, *I* was surprised and taken aback by the comment. I had no idea that she'd actually joined a group, or that she planned to leave me alone with her dad.

"Both if you can swing it," she said sassily, smiling at Blake.

He ran a hand down his face with a sigh.

"I thought you were going to live here," he commented sadly.

"Well, if I live on Greek row, I don't have to drive from parties or anything like that. So that's a big bonus. And think of all the networking I can do! This is big for me, Dad."

"What about Bay?" he said, asking the question *I* was dying to know the answer to.

"She can stay here." Georgia shrugged. "We'll still see each other at school and if she wants to party, she can crash in my room! How convenient is that? She doesn't like that kind of nightlife stuff though, so I think she'll be happier here. Right Bay?"

Oh? I had a say in this?

I bit back all the million things I wanted to say to her because her dad was in the room, so instead I just shrugged.

Blake just stared at Georgia for a minute, looking at her like he didn't know who the hell she was.

"You'd rather live with a bunch of strangers than with your dad and your best friend?" he asked finally, tossing his paper plate with a half-eaten slice of pizza on it onto the coffee table.

"They're not strangers, Dad. I know them pretty well!"

Blake just sat there, staring at the pizza for a minute until Georgia threw in the kicker.

"I already talked to Mom. She's fine with it and I'm going. I just wanted you to support me, too."

And that was it. Talk of her Mom set Blake's face all hard as stone as he got up.

"Fine. I'll drive you in the truck tonight. Get your shit together and put my keys on the hook. You're not taking my car with you."

Georgia's mouth popped open in shock for a moment, but she seemed to understand that she just got what she wanted, so she made a run for her bedroom.

I followed her back and sucked in a little breath of surprise when I saw her bags packed already.

How long had she planned on leaving without even telling me?

"What the hell Georgie?" I cried.

"We'll still see each other all the time!" she said with a grin on her face. "And the guys in the frat nextdoor are *soooo* hot. Like seriously smoking. I'll introduce you when you visit me!"

Visit her? We were supposed to be in on this college thing *together*.

"I thought..." I started, but she interrupted.

"I hope you're happy for me, too. I couldn't bear you being mad at me."

I breathed out long and hard through my nose.

"Not mad," I finally said. "But this leaves me in a weird spot. You know that."

"Dad's fine," she said with a shrug. "You hang out with him more than I do, anyway. And you're kind of perfect together; all homebodies and old souls."

My jaw slacked at that.

"Besides. You only moved in because you couldn't afford another place. Just consider him a roommate. He loves your food and how you take care of the place."

I didn't think that I could get any more shocked by the words coming out of my friend's mouth.

"Have fun, then," I ground out, turning to leave.

"Baaaaay!" She whined and groaned, but I ignored her as I shut myself away in my little bedroom.

Not even half an hour later I heard Blake and Georgia bringing her things out, but after that it was quiet for some time. Meanwhile, I just stared at the door, my stomach sick with anxiety and frustration and hurt and uncertainty. Would Georgia's dad kick me out now that she wasn't even living there anymore? Maybe he wanted his bachelor pad back...

A knock on my door jolted me out of my thoughts.

"You decent?" I heard as the door cracked open.

I sat up with a weak, "yeah," and Blake pushed it open, leaning against the doorframe.

"She's gone," he said. "But I just wanted you to know that whether she's here or not, this is your home too while you need it. I'm not finicky like my daughter and I don't want or need you out of here. Ok?"

I blew out a relieved breath as I nodded.

"Ok. I just wanted you to know that. I'm sorry she did this to you, Bay. Hope you don't feel uncomfortable staying here now. Georgie pulled a real bitch move tonight."

I shrugged and he echoed it with a lift of his own shoulders.

"Alright. Goodnight, then."

As he closed the door, I let out a squeaky "Thank you, Blake," which made him pause.

"Pizza tomorrow?" he asked with the door half closed.

"Sounds good to me," I told him and the door shut the rest of the way.

Well, at least he wasn't kicking me out. But man, now I was living with my friend's dad *without* said friend. How weird does that get? Didn't matter. I was in Seattle to go to school, and honestly, I had a pretty nice setup going. Even if I only had until the end of the semester, Dad would have a job by then and things could go back to the way we planned and I could get a shared dorm on campus. Until then, I would just need to put up with a bit of awkwardness.

I let out a little chuckle as I thought about it. Yeah, a dead sexy older man as a housemate, my own room, and meals that I got to cook but not pay for. I definitely had it pretty good.

Chapter 5

Blake

"You heading out?" Marty asked as I found my water bottle.

"Yeah. Gotta get home for dinner."

"Home for dinner, huh? Your little girl cooks?"

I huffed.

"No. Georgia doesn't cook. She doesn't live with me either, as of last week," I told him.

Marty and I had been tight for a long time. We caught beers after work sometimes and I'd had holidays with him and his family for the past several years. They had kind of adopted me when I'd shown up in the area with a snotty nose and a gleam in my eyes for success after my marriage had failed. He'd been there with me when it was just a couple of us guys, and he'd continued to be there when our three man band turned into a fully functioning restoration and construction business.

"Who the hell is cooking your food then?" Marty lifted an eyebrow at me in curiosity.

"Her friend. The girl's housing dropped at the last second and she needed a place to stay to start the semester."

"But Georgia's not around?" he asked, the other brow rising to join the other.

"Nope. Just me and her friend in the house."

A devilish grin spread across his face.

"So, you've got a pretty young thing *in your house*, playing homemaker and makin' you food and doing your chores? Am I hearing your correctly?"

"Who said she was pretty?" I huffed again.

"Is she?" He blinked at me, waiting for an answer that I had no intention of giving.

"Ahah! So she's better than pretty! Must be smokin'!"

"Shut the fuck up, Marty," I growled at him, heading toward my truck outside.

The home we were working on was being built from the ground up, and we had just finished off the wiring and were ready to hand it over to the drywall people.

"Holy fuck, how hot is this girl?" he chirped, hopping to keep up with my long-legged stride.

At a stout five foot ten, Marty wasn't in danger of winning any basketball dunking contests, but he was tough and wide nonetheless. He just looked like a shrimp compared to my six foot two frame.

"If you don't stop talking about how hot my daughter's friend is, I'm going to report your ass," I told him, opening the passenger door to toss my water bottle in before dropping my tools in the foot space.

"I gotta meet her." He was practically panting by that point.

"She's barely legal, Marty," I said in a rough, deep voice. "Doesn't matter how hot she is. She's off limits."

He frowned and sighed.

"We still doing the BBQ this weekend?" he asked finally. "Gail is looking forward to your burgers."

"Of course. It's tradition. Be at my place by four though, for God's sake, or we'll miss the kickoff again."

He laughed and nodded.

"Yeah, yeah. Gotcha. See you."

I lifted a hand to wave at my friend before going around the truck and pulling myself in, plopping into the wide cab.

The drive home wasn't too bad, considering the heavy traffic I normally dealt with. But I'd heard Bay talking to herself about what she needed to make lasagna before I left and I was really fucking excited for some Italian. No more frozen shit for me; the girl knew how to cook.

44

I didn't even have to get into the house before I smelled it. The juicy tomato, sausage and cheese scent was seeping through the cracks of the door as I was unlocking it.

"Hey," Bay called from the couch.

She was on her computer again, her camera on the coffee table in front of her as was typical. The girl didn't go anywhere without her camera.

"Smells amazing in here," I said while peeling off my boots, one line of laces at a time.

"Thanks! It's my mom's recipe. I hope you like it."

For this food-loving glutton, there was about a zero percent chance that I *wouldn't*.

"Go on and shower and I'll make the salad," she told me, putting the laptop down on the table, giving me a view of a mallard swimming on water.

"Ok," I nodded, thinking about what a nice shot it was before heading toward my bathroom.

Peeling out of my work-dusted clothes, I spent a minute at the sink washing the grease and dirt off my calloused hands before stripping and getting into the shower. It felt nice after the long day I had, and I was pretty damn tired of smelling like wood dust and metal.

When I got out, I shoved my hands through my hair, watching it plop back in my face again rebelliously. I needed a haircut, but finding some time to put aside for it just seemed like too much Goddamn work. So I'd just dealt with the wildness of it. But if I wanted to take a selfie for my hookup site, well, then I'd need a cut.

Pulling on some sweats and a Black Sabbath t-shirt, I dressed before meeting Bay in the kitchen.

"I still can't believe how fast guys can shower," she said, shaking her head while she was still prepping the salad.

"Tell me what you need and I'll help," I told her, grabbing a knife from the block on the countertop.

She plopped a tomato in front of me and I got to cubing it up.

45

"Do you cook?" she asked me while scooping out half of an avocado.

"I try," I said with a chuckle. "I'm better at grilling."

"I haven't had grilling for so long," she hummed, dumping her veg into the bowl and pushing it over for me to dump my tomato in.

"I'm having a couple friends over Sunday for the NFL kickoff game, and we're having some burgers and steaks if you want to join us."

"Oh. I don't want to..."

"You're not imposing, Bay. You live here. You can join or not. It's up to you."

She pulled in her lower lip, worrying it in the cutest way possible while her eyebrows scrunched together.

"If it's a guy's day then..."

"Marty is bringing his wife. And another buddy of mine is bringing his wife and kids. It's not a guy thing. It's a friend thing."

Her face suddenly lit up.

"I think that would make me your friend, if you're inviting me," she said with amusement all over her face.

"Or you *live* here," I said slowly. "Besides, who's going to make the sides if you don't join us?"

She rolled her eyes and handed me the salad bowl.

"Wow, thanks, Blake. Makes me feel so welcome."

I plopped it down on the table and sat down while watching her moving around like she'd been in my kitchen forever.

"Here you go," she said, handing me a plate with a giant piece of lasagna on it.

Fuck yes.

I was going to have to do about two thousand pushups if I ate it all, but what the hell? I was going to enjoy my live-in chef while I had her.

Enjoy *having* one, I meant. Not enjoy the chef...

Shit.

"Thanks." I croaked a little, trying to push those raunchy thoughts out of my head as Bay sat across from me and grabbed a big serving of salad with a pair of wooden spoons to put on her plate.

We ate in silence for a few minutes, each moment getting more awkward than the next.

"Uh," she said finally, breaking the silence hesitantly. "Thanks for the invite though. I have homework, but I can join you guys for dinner if you don't mind."

Well hot damn. She was going to come. Marty would get to meet her, after all.

"Cool," I nodded. "And this dinner is…"

She looked up, meeting my eyes with her light gray ones. They were so beautiful and unique. I hadn't ever seen eyes quite like hers.

"Thanks," she grinned at me, taking the compliment I hadn't quite gotten out of my mouth. "I'll tell Mom you like it."

Just don't tell your mom that the dick you live with gets a chubby every time you enter the room.

Biting down hard on my tongue, I cut off all other thoughts and words and just focused on eating.

"You need any help?" I heard Bay call from the sliding glass door to the backyard.

I was pulling up some weeds in the pathetic little garden area near my tiny wooden deck.

"Just having a blast over here," I called back, wiping at my forehead.

I'd put on a thin white shirt and some shorts to try and combat the heat, but toward the end of summer Washington always got unbearably hot with the humidity and a heat wave that rolled in from the south.

Bay came out in shorts herself, though hers were a lot shorter than mine, and her tank top kept riding down in the front. That was honestly why I had to get out of the house. Bay was driving me

47

nuts, and I had to do double workouts on the weekend to get through two full days with her.

She smiled, kneeling down beside me on the long grass as she put her hand out for one of my gloves.

Dammit... I was already nursing blue balls and now it was going to get worse.

I slapped one of the gloves into her hand and put some space between us, going over to the far side of the little shrubbery patch that passed as a garden in my mind.

She dug in, grunting with each pull as she yanked on the roots of dandelions and spiky weeds.

We had it cleared out pretty quickly, but we were still both sweaty messes by the end, wiping our foreheads with arms as we sat back on our feet.

"Now what?" she asked, tossing my glove back at me.

I shrugged.

"Gotta clean the pool," I told her. "You can go inside and sit under a fan."

"It's too nice out here to go into a dark house," she said, shaking her head. "This is nothing compared to a Vegas summer."

Now that was true.

"But Vegas isn't humid like this," I told her. "I lived there my whole life. I know. This is worse. It just doesn't last as long."

She grinned and nodded, then tilted her head at me.

"You grew up in Vegas?"

I nodded. "Yep. Born and raised. Georgia was born there, too."

Bay bit her lip again and watched me, her hand over her eyes to block out the sun.

"Why did you move here then?" she asked eventually, her voice soft.

Fuck, I guess we were getting personal now.

"I got divorced," I said simply.

"But with Georgia there..." she started, but I watched the courage sap right out of her with the burning of my focus on her.

"Sorry. I don't mean to pry. It's just strange to me. You and Georgia seem so close and everything..."

I pulled off my glove and stood, watching her mirror my action.

"I moved because Tiffany is a psycho bitch. She threatened to take away all my custody rights when we divorced unless I moved out of the state. I got to have Georgia in the summer when she did her biggest parties and whoring around, which was most convenient for her."

I sighed and rubbed my temple.

"I don't...Georgia loves her mom. I know that. I'm not going to get in the middle of that, and I would hope that Tiffany had the same courtesy. But I'm happy here. This move and that divorce was the best thing I ever did."

She was chewing her lip again, and I just wanted to pull on it to make her stop abusing such a pretty little thing.

"Didn't you love her?" she asked weakly, her eyebrows up.

I lifted mine too, and she suddenly blushed scarlet before covering her mouth.

"I'm so sorry! Sorry! I shouldn't have asked that... It's none of my business!"

I stood there, watching her turn beet red as I considered the question. And despite knowing what the smart thing to do was, I answered her anyway.

"I married Tiffany because we were stupid teens and got pregnant at sixteen years old. It was never about love, and to be honest, we could hardly stand each other in the light of day. We tried to work it out for Georgia, but eventually it just got to be...too much."

Rubbing at my forehead, I shrugged.

"It's not your business, Bay, but I'll tell you one thing right here. I love Georgie more than anything in the world. But seriously, don't be stupid. Use a fucking condom."

Her red cheeks deepened in color at the mention of a condom, and I just turned away from her and gathered up the pulled weeds littering the grass

She dipped and gathered the ones she'd pulled, delicately grabbing the spikey ones before following me around the yard to the gate and the trash can outside of it. I held up the lid and she tossed hers in, not even meeting my eyes. Maybe I took it a little too far...

"Bay, I'm sorry if I..."

"No," she said suddenly, cutting me off. "I asked."

I shrugged.

"Well, that's true. But I didn't have to..."

"You told the truth." She shrugged back at me, finally looking at my face. "Honestly, I always wondered how you could have been married to a stripper, but I think I always assumed she didn't start that until after the divorce. But Tiffany is...she's an interesting person."

I rolled my eyes and nodded in agreement.

"No, she's always stripped and prostituted," I told her. "And maybe that's too much information for you. God... you're like, barely eighteen. You shouldn't have to know about the shit in this world yet."

It was her turn to lift an eyebrow.

"I'm nineteen," she said. "And I've seen a lot of the shit this world has to offer already. I just choose not to dwell in it and let it run my life."

Well fuck. Is that what she thought I was doing?

"Good for you." I nodded at her. "And when you deal with some real grownup stuff, you come back in ten years and tell me all about it."

Clenching her jaw, she stomped away.

"Bay," I groaned again, calling her name like I was some kind of teen in a fight with his girlfriend.

"You know, just because you've been burned in the past by a woman doesn't mean we're all like that," she said with vehemence in her voice. "And for your information, age doesn't tell you how old someone is. It's about maturity. And I can tell you right now that compared to your ex-wife, I'm pretty much ancient. So your lectures of condoms and bullshit and 'the world is so bad' just doesn't do it for me. This world isn't bad, and there are so many things out there for all kinds of people. Just because you decided not to want anything to do with it doesn't make me stupid or naïve."

I just stood there, my ass chewed to shredded pieces by this nineteen year old girl who just laid into me better than my ex ever did. And fuck it if she wasn't right.

"What does do it for you, then?" I found myself asking, suddenly choking up on the words as her eyes narrowed.

Please don't take it like that...Please don't take it like that...Please don't—

I didn't even have time to finish my rambling thoughts because the little wildcat pushed me into the pool.

Water filled my mouth and nose in my surprise, and I burst to the surface of the water with a gasp.

"Oh my God!" she was shrieking, her hand over her mouth as she approached the edge and looked at me in horror of what she'd just done. "I didn't even think! I don't know what got into—"

Yeah, I shut her up by launching out of the pool with one arm enough to grasp her around the hips and drag her in after me.

Wailing and shrieking, she hit the cold water with a big splash, flailing until she surfaced.

"What the hell?" she gasped out.

"You started it," I told her, heading toward the ladder out of the pool.

"No you don't!" she growled, her hand slipping into the waistband at the back of my shorts before pulling as hard as she could, making me splash back into the water.

I barked a laugh as I grabbed her again, boosting her by the ass out of the pool so that I could get out myself. Obviously she had a wild streak that wouldn't allow me to disrespect her by leaving the pool first.

"Oh my God!" She coughed some water up as she knelt on her hands and knees on the brick surrounding the pool.

Her tank top was weighed down and her bra was showing in front, giving me a damn good view all the way down to her bellybutton.

I just gritted my teeth and pulled myself out of the water with a growl and headed into the house with a stomp in my step.

Who did that girl think she was? She was a baby in the world of adulting and she knew nothing. She couldn't even afford to go to college properly and relied on a fucking stranger for support. I figured that disqualified her from having an opinion, even if she was right.

"Just so you know," I threw the words over my shoulder with a bite. "It's rude to push people into the pool."

"It's also rude to pull people in, asshole!" she called back.

I caught a glimpse of her stomping toward the house herself, bra still hanging out of her tank and breasts jiggling with each heavy footstep.

Fuck *me*.

Retreating, I ran away from a teenaged girl like a fucking pussy.

Chapter 6

Bay

On Sunday everyone started showing up around four for dinner. I was in the kitchen making potato salad when they began to arrive. The ladies of the group joined me and immediately asked me a million questions, the first of which being 'where is Georgia?' followed by, 'you live here alone with Blake?'

Yes, I lived with someone else's dad. Yes, I enjoyed watching him walk around the house in tight t-shirts and wet hair immensely. Yes, I made him food and cleaned his house in exchange for room and board. No, we weren't sleeping together.

One woman had actually asked me that. She blinked at me when she found out that Georgia had moved out, and she just looked me up and down in my football jersey, jeans and ponytail before asking me if I was sleeping with him. Every eye in the kitchen glued to me with horror reflected in them, but nobody bothered to come to my rescue. Instead, I just shrugged and said no.

She believed me, but she wasn't sold that something wasn't happening. You could see it in her face and the way she looked from me to Blake and back and forth, over and over again for the long, *long* hour of dinner until the game started.

Blake just ignored me the whole time, buddying up with his friends while the women congregated over the food, and drank an assortment of beer and wine that everyone had brought.

Luckily nobody was watching it, so I was able to snatch a couple and retreat back to my room while they were all busy. Nobody even noticed me leaving the room except Blake. His eyes followed me out of the room until I entered the hall where it cut him off. But then I heard his voice call and shout with the other guys as I closed my bedroom door behind me. Popping the top of my beer, I laid back in bed and drank until I started feeling tipsy. I sent Georgia a text about the 'awesome' party her dad was throwing then rolled over and went to sleep.

I woke up when it was dark outside. The house was quiet and I wasn't sure how long everyone had been gone, but the clock read eleven in the evening. A text was waiting for me on my phone.

Georgia: *I'm sure the old geezer party was a blast. If you want a real party drive over here. The frat guys are chugging from kegs! Seriously, come meet some and get laid, baby girl!*

I could only imagine the state of drunkenness she was in at that point, so instead of answering her text, I just sent back a nice one.

Me: *Stay safe, Georgie.*

Ten minutes and three games of Tetris on my phone later, she still hadn't written. She was probably passed out somewhere or with some guy. It was my biggest complaint for Georgia. She was way too boy-crazy.

My thoughts drifted back to that lady from the party, thinking me and Blake were having sex. She didn't even seem bothered that he was old enough to be my dad. Nope, she just saw an attractive-ish girl and assumed that I was paying my way with my vag.

Vegas or not, I had standards and rules and I didn't sleep with anyone who I didn't think a relationship was a viable next step. Which meant that I didn't sleep with very many people. One, to be exact. My ex-boyfriend who had gotten my virginity was someone I thought I might be with forever. Until he suddenly decided to go to New York and become a Broadway star. Oh, he told me he realized he was gay, too. That was a total boost to my self-esteem.

So my experience was pretty limited to a few encounters with my boyfriend who secretly didn't like girls, and I couldn't help but wonder if, you know, in a deep, dark, secretive world, what it

54

would be like to be with someone like Blake. Older, experienced and confident and just...not caring about much of anything anymore. Would he be a good lover? Or would he be lazy?

All those muscles and those eyes and the plump shape of his lips told me that he was probably a wildman in the sack. Not that I'd ever know.

Pulling down my laptop, I looked around at the clock again and saw that it was closer to eleven-thirty. Blake was probably asleep, and I really just... I needed it. After the argument and pool attack from the day before, and that burning gaze when I left the party this afternoon, *I needed it.*

Grabbing my little buddies from my drawer, I snuck to the bathroom to wash them off before going back to my room, locking my door and opening my laptop. The picture of Blake in the moonlight was hidden pretty well in my stash of thousands of pictures, but I knew exactly where it was. Pulling it up, I swallowed thick and hard as my eyes drifted down the hair-peppered chest and sculpted abs. Beautiful and devastatingly handsome.

Pushing my little dildo's power button on, it started buzzing in my hand, but it wasn't too loud. No way could it wake someone up at such a late hour. I pressed it against my belly and let the vibrations sink into me as I dragged it down and pressed it to the lips between my thighs. Sinking it in, I gasped in a breath when it went in with ease. Oh God...

Opening my eyes, I saw that picture again and little twinges of pleasure kept burning down my spine and through my belly as I joined the first toy with the little black bullet wand. The two together had me panting, breathing hard and jerking my hips back and forth until I finally came with a groan I tried to smother by biting my lip. Tossing the toys onto the bed after turning off the power, I laid there and panted for a moment until I heard a creak outside the door. Another creak, and then silence.

Was someone outside my door?

I lay silent for another few minutes, just listening to the sound of silence until I decided that it was just the old house.

Sometimes wooden floors creaked as they settled. I knew that much.

Rolling over, I tossed the toys onto the floor and threw a t-shirt on top of them until I woke up in the morning, and tried to go back to sleep. Luckily my relaxed hormones took over and made me drift off again with anticipation of school in the morning still rattling around in the background.

Blake

The guys didn't leave me alone the entire time. They kept asking me if I was 'tapping that', referencing my young roommate. I kept telling them to fuck off, but they couldn't keep their eyes off her young, perfect skin, perky breasts and round, spankable ass. Or maybe it was just me that couldn't keep my motherfucking eyes to myself.

When Marty and Gail headed for the door, the last to leave for the night, she put a hand on my shoulder and stopped me.

"Krissy asked her if you were sleeping together," she said in a soft voice. "I hope she's ok..."

"See? It's not just us!" Marty cut in. "Everyone could feel the sexual tension emanating from you two."

"There's no fucking sexual tension, Marty." I growled at him.

I wasn't sure if I was more mad at him, or Krissy Vanderhooth for asking a teenager if she was sleeping with me.

"I keep telling you, college girls like to explore, amigo. Take advantage of it while you got it. Don't let Tiffany fuck you up forever."

"Martin Farron! Don't you dare talk about Bay like that! Do I need to remind you that *you* have two college girls at the moment? Would you want them dating a man seventeen years older than her?"

"Sixteen," I said weakly but Gail just shook her head and grabbed Marty by the ear, leading him back to the car.

Marty just laughed and gave me a thumbs up behind his wife's back before appeasing her.

"Not our girls, Mamma. Our girls wouldn't do that. They know better."

"And are you saying that Bay doesn't?" she shouted back at him before they got in the car and the conversation was cut off from my ears.

With the house quiet and the sun going down, I cleaned up the kitchen a bit, then went to bed. Work came early in the morning, and I planned on going out to dinner with Georgia near the school afterwards, so I needed some rest. Not that I'd get any with all the comments and encouragement thrown my way to chase Bay.

Crawling under my sheets, I sighed at the cool refreshment of the cotton sheets against my skin before falling asleep, only to wake up a couple of hours later to a faint buzzing sound. It almost sounded like someone was buzzing their hair, and for half a second, I thought that maybe someone broke in and was cutting their hair in my house.

Obviously that was ridiculous, and my sleep-addled brain thought that might actually be a plausible scenario, but no, it was far more explicit than that.

I tiptoed out of my room to surprise the intruder when I heard the buzz get louder, coming from Bay's room.

I paused outside her door and listened.

Was *she* shaving her head?

A faint whimper met my ears and my lips popped open as it all hit me.

Not a buzzer. Sex toys. She was using those pink and black toys in there.

Biting on my lip, I heard her whimper again as the bed squeaked followed by a muffled moan.

My heart was hammering and I was already standing at attention in my boxers.

Holy fuck the girl was masturbating in my house, in the room next to mine.

More whines and my hand dipped down into my boxers, gripping my hard-on with an iron grip, squeezing the base.

She gasped and the bed squeaked a little more, and suddenly my hand was moving, eyes closing as I worked myself right there in the hallway, listening to her.

Her breathing picked up, those soft pants turning into moans as the bed squeaked one more time. She was coming, and I knew it.

Clamping my mouth closed and clenching my throat into silence, I came into my palm, cum sticking to my fingers as she gasped in breaths, those buzzing toys turning off with her completion.

And fuck, I was still standing in front of her door, cum dripping down my thigh and my hand still in my underwear.

I took one step and the house's original wood floors betrayed me, then another step and a second betrayal until I was back on the carpeted floor of my bedroom. Freezing there, I listened as she was completely silent for a good few minutes before I dared to go into my bathroom and wash off, using a little more force than necessary on my hands until all traces were gone and there was nothing left but the gross feeling of shame lingering on my skin.

Nineteen...

Fuck, if only she was twenty, or twenty-five. Not a fucking *teenager*.

Disgusted at myself, I grabbed my water bottle and went back into the hallway, needing to work off my thoughts until I was exhausted to the point of passing out. That was the only way I was going to get any sleep.

Heading into the garage, I hid myself away and punished every last muscle on my body until I felt like dying. And only then, in my penance, did I allow myself to go to sleep. It was three in the morning and I'd be up in just a couple of hours to go to work, but it didn't matter. I deserved it.

Bay's room was still silent when I dragged myself to my room again, so I collapsed onto my bed and closed my eyes, blocking out the rest of the world for just a little while where I could forget what a despicable human being I was.

Chapter 7

Bay

I didn't see him for a few days. Blake would just get dinner out and stay at work most nights, or one night he went to see Georgia. It almost felt like he was avoiding me, and that hurt.

Not that it should. He was a grown man and I was a college student. I was supposed to be spending my time focusing on grades and he was supposed to work and live his life like I wasn't there. That was how it was supposed to be. But it wasn't like that, and I couldn't stand it now that he had shut me out. I hadn't looked at that picture of him taken that first night again. I was too self-conscious. It was like he could read what I'd done on my skin, or maybe he sensed that I kind of liked him *'like that'*.

Either way, I needed out of that house so I finally took Georgia up on her invitation to see her new place. After my last class finished, I walked through the campus until I found my car. Throwing my books into the side seat, I checked my phone and saw a text from Mom.

Mom: *How's it going? Your dad and I miss you so much!*

Grinning, I typed out a reply.

Me: *Miss you guys too. It's fine. Getting on with classes.*

I hadn't yet told them anything about how irritating I found my classes or bothered to mention how idiotic I thought taking calculus and English was when I had an art degree, but there was no getting around it.

Mom: *Are you loving living with Georgie or are you sick of each other yet?*

Uh, so, I hadn't told her about Georgia getting a room elsewhere. Yet.

Me: *It's fine. Blake is nice and Georgie is Georgie.*

Starting the car, I drove to Greek row where my best friend had decided to move, leaving me behind. Going up to the door, I knocked while calling Georgia.

A blonde opened the door, looking me up and down before seeming confused.

"Looking for Georgie," I told her.

She continued to stare.

"Tall, dark hair. She just joined."

"You mean Gigi?" She lifted a brow at me like I was an idiot. Gigi?

"Bay!" Georgia called out at me as she came down the stairs all serene and delicate. She waved me up the stairs, calling out to the blonde, "Thanks Jess!"

I followed her, trying to understand the place that surrounded me. It was an old house but well-kept, and I didn't see many girls around.

"You're just in time to get ready for the party," Georgia said excitedly.

"Gigi?" I said instead, and she grinned.

"That's the name I go by now that I'm in college. Georgie just seems so...fifth grader."

Gigi sounded a little too stripper to me, but I kept the thought to myself.

She threw open her closet and started pulling out dresses.

"I'm not here to go to a party. I'm here to hang out with my best friend who's been neglecting me. I miss you, Georgie."

She frowned.

"Please, *please* call me Gigi, Bay. I beg you! I don't want them to think it's ok to call me that."

I ground my molars together, but nodded. Because that's what good friends do.

Just going along, I let her do whatever she wanted, layering me with a tiny dress, gallons of makeup and tall heels that her mom would have approved of.

"So, there's this guy, Barrett. He's so fucking hot, and he's single. I think you're really going to like him, and I'm kind of doing his best friend, so I think you've got awesome chances."

"Who is he?" I asked her, watching her curl up the ends of her hair to give them a timeless beachy wave.

"Barrett something."

"No, I mean, what does he do? What's his major? Is he a good person?"

She just lifted an eyebrow.

"Does it matter?" She smirked. "I think the more important questions are, 'how long is he?', 'body fat percentage?' and 'does he work out once or twice a day?'"

Wow, when did she get so superficial and shallow?

"I really don't even care about those things." I shook my head. "I'd rather measure a man by his morality and intelligence and not what he has in his pants."

"Right. I forgot that you get off on smart conversations and use mental arousal as foreplay."

I bit my lip in anger at the snarky comment.

Choosing not to say anything else, I just watched her finish, then followed her down the stairs.

Why was I doing this, anyway? Why should I go with her to a party with people I wouldn't like and do something I didn't enjoy? Was I so eager to please my friend who was acting like a total bitch?

The house was suddenly bustling with girls in party dresses and thick makeup, stalking around in sky-high heels assessing and judging each other.

"Nice hair, Gigi," one of the girls said, then looked at me with narrowed eyes. "Who's this?"

I looked back at her, eyeing her from strawberry blond head to Prada-wrapped toes.

"This is my friend Bay," she told the girl, and I could feel the nerves radiating from her, which was strange.

Georgia never got nervous, and she never introduced me to people as anything less than her sister from another mister.

"Charmed," the girl said with a bit of a snobby tone. "Tabby Thompson."

"How do you do?" I asked her with a similar stuck-up tone that she certainly didn't like.

Just like that she turned and left us near the door.

"Oh my God!" Georgia whispered harshly into my ear. "She's the head of the sorority Bay! Don't piss her off or she'll ban you from the house!"

As much as I wanted to swear and stalk off, I just shrugged a little and motioned toward the door.

"I don't want to stand here doing nothing. Let's go or I'm going home."

Georgia did curse, but quickly found a few other girls to go with us down a few houses to where an old 70's craftsman was rocking hard with music and partying.

Drunk people were already stumbling around and the sun had barely gone down.

"Here," Georgia said, handing me a beer in a plastic cup.

I took it and held it, but refused to drink.

"Jay!" Georgia said after a minute, going up to some guy with a messy man-bun and a douche smirk on his face.

And Jay? How awkward was that? It was basically *my* name!

They immediately started macking on each other, his hand moving down and gripping her butt hard through her dress. I just turned a little and looked around at the place that I hopefully wouldn't be at long.

"Hey sexy," I heard behind me, jumping a little when I found some dude had sidled up, practically touching me.

"Uh, pardon. Do I know you?"

"Not yet." He grinned at me, eyes dragging from my head and down, then slowly back up.

I felt dirty from the invasion of his eyes.

"Geor-Gigi!" I called and she pulled her eyes away from her new little boyfriend to call out a hello to the idiot in front of me.

"Barrett! You found Bay!"

"You're Bay?" he asked, eyes brightening up at the information.

"I am. And you're in my personal space."

He just laughed.

"Gigi's been telling me all about you. I have to say, my expectations have been met tenfold."

Oh, well, how nice for him.

I tried to bite back the sass. I really did. But as Blake had found out the hard way when he ended up in the pool, sometimes it just slipped and I pushed without thinking first.

"That makes one of us." I snorted. "I'd like you to back up."

He just laughed some more like I'd just made a joke and leaned in, boxing me against the wall as his head dropped towards mine, mouth going to my ear.

"Want to head upstairs and get a little better acquainted?" he murmured against my skin, and every inch of it began to crawl.

Caged in, I had to think hard before ducking away from his mouth.

"I'm going home, Gigi," I told my friend, who didn't even bother to turn around as she was heading into third base with *Jay*.

Stomping out, I made it to the front lawn before I started getting emotional. I wasn't sure if it was from the douche Barrett or from the thought sinking in that I was losing my best friend, but tears were very valiantly trying to break past my glassy eyes.

Stomping toward the Greek house, I managed to find the right one, but when I tried to go in, the door was locked. Who locked a house with so many people going in and out of it?

Looking down at Georgia's clothes I was wearing, I realized that I would have to get mine later. Sucking it up, I got into the car and went toward the house that was starting to feel more and more like home every day. Except that my best friend's dad wasn't talking to me, either.

Going in the door, I ran into him sitting on the couch in his pajama shorts and nothing else.

He looked surprised to see me, but then that surprise morphed into worry.

"You ok?" he asked, his first words to me in days.

I shook my head a little, feeling sobs working their way up my throat, bashing against it to be let out.

Blake was out of his seat instantly, his hands pressing either side of my face, cupping my cheeks like he did with Georgia when she was upset.

"What happened?" he breathed and I lost it.

Sobs tore out of my chest, terrible, aching things that kept reminding me how Georgia had changed. How she wasn't the same person anymore, and how I was losing her. Maybe I'd already lost her.

"Shit..." he murmured, pulling me into a hug, my cheek pressed against one firm pec as he held me pretty tight.

"It's Georgia," I said finally, and he loosened his grip on me enough to look me in the eyes.

"What happened? Last I heard you and Georgia were going to some party together."

I nodded, then those nods turned into shakes as I pressed my forehead against his skin again.

"She's Gigi now. She won't let me call her Georgie anymore. She's made all these new douche friends and she just...she's not our Georgie anymore." I hiccupped. "And some dude there was all..."

His entire body seized up, flexing in anger at those few words.

"Nothing happened but he was a total a-hole," I admitted.

Jaw working in anger, his eyes narrowed like he was ready to destroy something.

"You're ok?" he growled with barely restrained rage.

I nodded and stepped back. "But I'm worried about her, Blake."

Licking his lips, he dropped his hands from me, retreating back a few steps before locking his arms over his chest.

"I don't know what's happening to her, Bay. And I'm sorry that you're stuck in the middle of it. She's going through some kind of midlife crisis at eighteen years old."

"She's turning into her mom," I whispered and he closed his eyes, looking like he was in pain.

"I know," he whispered back, squeezing the bridge of his nose in frustration.

I just took a step toward my room and tried to not think about it. I had a crap ton of homework that I needed to do over the weekend and worrying about Georgia and her new alternate identity wasn't going to help me pass my tests with an A-average.

Locking myself away, I stripped out of the dress and drowned myself into my favorite oversized t-shirt before I crawled into bed, crying just a little. Eventually I was exhausted enough to fall asleep.

Chapter 8

Blake

I stood outside her door for a good three minutes before getting the balls to knock.

"Come in," she called through it.

It had been another week and absolutely nothing was getting the girl out of my brain. I kept thinking about what she was going to make for dinner, and about how nice it felt to watch shows together at night.

Things had gotten less weird since that shitshow of a party she'd tried to attend with Georgia, but evidently I wasn't the only one my daughter was avoiding or acting like an asshole toward. I felt bad, truly bad for Bay, and I wish I could make all the hurt go away, but I couldn't. Instead I watched her smile at her phone when her parents called or texted, and frown or wipe away tears when she looked at a blank screen that should have had a return text from Georgia.

"Hey," I said, opening the door. "Any chance I could get a favor from the resident photographer?"

Despite my unusual and destructive attraction to the girl, I kept living with her, and I just decided that if I was going to keep doing it, I had to find something or someone else to take my sexual frustrations out on. Because she was fucking out of the question.

"Depends on what the favor is." She smirked at me.

Fuck, I loved that smirk. It brought out this little curvy dimple on her cheek that was like a billboard sign, demanding I kiss her.

"I need you to take a profile picture for me," I told her hesitantly.

I'd just gotten a haircut a few days before and shaved recently so I didn't get a shot with a faceful of dark stubble.

Her eyes lit up.

"Sure! For Facebook or Twitter?"

"I'm uh, joining a dating site," I admitted with what must have been a rosy blush on my cheeks.

Her grin deepened into almost mischievousness.

"Which one?"

Well fuck.

"A couple of them." I lifted an eyebrow, determined not to be intimidated by a fucking little girl.

"Let's go get you a different shirt, then I'll take pictures," she said, grabbing her fancy-looking camera and shooing me out of her room.

I led her to my bedroom and felt kind of strange letting her into my sanctuary. She looked around at the masculine and minimalist design in the room before stopping at the closet next to the master bathroom.

"What's wrong with what I'm wearing?" I asked, looking down at my Zelda shirt.

I thought it would give me a fun, playful vibe.

"Unless you live in your mom's basement or want a girl to think that you're an immature hack that can't dress himself, then you have to dress the part. Like how you would on a date."

I looked down at my shirt again. It said all that?

Digging through the few hangers on the left side of the closet, separated from my work clothes on the left, she eventually chose a dark button up that I usually saved for weddings and funerals.

"Here," she said, handing it to me.

I took it and watched her ass swagger out of my bedroom.

Prying my eyes away, I stripped off my shirt and put on the other one she'd given me, feeling unusually dressed up. But she was the artist and I was the client.

She was in the living room when I emerged, rearranging a few things on the couch before pointing me to stand behind it.

68

"Now, put your hands on the back and look away like you're talking to someone. And laugh."

I lifted an eyebrow at her, but did what she asked, feeling like a moron when I grinned at the door and forced myself to chuckle.

"Nice," she said, looking through the shots. "Now, against the fireplace."

We tried a couple more quick poses before she looked up at me, biting that plump little lip of hers.

"Now, are you looking for a date, or a hookup?" she asked suddenly, her cheeks burning red at the words.

Aw hell...how could I tell her that I was mostly just desperate for a hookup now that she was living with me?

"Not that it's any of your business." I eyed her. "But I just need a profile picture for *dating* sites. Why do you ask?"

"Well, if you want something... *faster* than a date, you need to show off your assets." She squeaked the words out, her cheeks going even pinker.

"Assets?" I asked her.

"This," she circled her hand over her own chest, then pointed to me. "You have a nice body, and it'll attract girls, if that's what you want."

Sucking on my cheek, I considered it. She was right, after all, and the way her eyes were drifting down the buttons of my dress shirt I just...I just started undoing the buttons, one by one as her lips parted and her eyes dropped to follow.

Fuck...this girl liked me too. I could just feel it in my bones. The way she watched intently, the flutter of her breath quickening and her tongue dragging against her bottom lip. She wanted me and the only thing separating us was me and my fucking sense of right and wrong. Well, that and her age. But mostly her age.

"Like, all the way?" I asked, my voice huskier than I meant for it to be.

She nodded slowly, bringing her camera back up to snap a couple quick shots of me undoing the buttons.

69

"By the pool," she said breathlessly, using her chin to point me outdoors.

I obeyed, opening the back door and stepping down onto the little wood deck with bare feet.

"Roll the legs of your pants up a little," she said. "And dip your feet in the pool, then stand here."

I did as she asked, dipping my feet one by one in the pool just passed my ankles before dropping the button up off my shoulders, tossing it onto the lounge chair. "Look that way," she told me, pointing toward the fence across from her. I turned and gave her my back, not sure what else to do as I stood there.

"Now, look this way," she said, letting the camera drop to her breasts as she modeled herself to mimic how she wanted me to stand.

"We doing glamor shots or something?" I asked with an uncomfortable chuckle, pressing my hands to the waistband of my jeans and turning slightly to look back up at her at an angle.

She snapped some more, then pointed to the lounge chair.

"Lean back, get comfortable," she said, standing on the other lounge before pointing the camera down.

I curled one leg under me and bent the other before closing my eyes and turning my face toward the sun. It felt damn good.

"Really good," she said finally. "You're going to get laid, Blake. Promise you."

I choked on my reply as she grinned down at me devilishly before heading back into the house.

I just sat there a while longer, letting the semi in my pants die in the sunlight before I eventually joined her back in the living room.

Bay was on her laptop, going over the pictures when I saw her.

"Sit down," she said, patting the couch beside her.

I did and watched her go through the pictures. It looked like something out of GQ, and I was pretty impressed by the quality, if not embarrassed that I looked like I was trying way too hard.

"What the hell is this for?" I asked her, watching her scroll through some more of the pictures.

"For the other pics in your profile. You use this one as the profile picture, then add these other ones to make you look a little more...enticing."

Enticing? Did *she* find me enticing when I looked like that?

Probably not. But, I mean, a guy can hope.

"So, what sites were you looking for?" she asked after a minute, going to a browser on her laptop.

"I'm not really sure. There's that big one they talk about in the commercials."

She typed in a few letters then looked at me.

"It's like, a half hour long survey test thing to find you the perfect match," she said, motioning to the screen.

"What about that one you swipe? Isn't everyone doing that?" I asked, shrugging weakly.

"Uh, not really anymore, but you can try it. If that's the case, you're going to want to use one of those pool ones as your profile. And I'll need to find another place to sleep tonight."

Winking at me, she put out her hand and wiggled her fingers.

"Phone please!"

Handing it over, she typed away until she turned to me to start asking questions.

"So, Blake Hamel. What do you do, Mr. Hamel?"

"Construction."

"Construction what? Or do you want to stay vague?"

"Does it matter?"

She shrugged and just typed in, 'Owns construction company.'

"Dark brown hair," she murmured to herself. "Blue eyes. Heavily muscled..."

"No shit, they don't ask that, do they?" I asked, looking over my cell phone to see if that was a legitimate question.

She started laughing and shaking her head.

71

"Of course not! So, what're you looking for in a girl, Blake? Age range?"

"Between thirty and forty," I said, reminding myself that just as much as I was answering her question.

I needed an older woman and not a fucking teenager.

"Ok, body type or hair or eye color you prefer?"

"I prefer someone who's gentle and smiles a lot and likes to laugh," I said, but she just grinned at me.

"Not specific," she said as she moved on in the list.

"Animals?"

"Dogs." I nodded at her.

"Ideal vacation?"

"Camping."

She gave me this strange look of wonder, then kept writing.

"Looking for long term or short term?"

"Long term, ideally," I told her with a sigh.

Either that or a quicky in a car somewhere.

"Are you looking for your next wife?" she asked with a gentle smile.

"If I could be so lucky. I'd like to fall in love, you know?"

Smile melting, she frowned and shook her head.

"Have you ever experienced love?" she asked, practically whispering.

"I have." I nodded. "For Georgia. It was pretty much love at first sight."

She pressed her hand to her heart and sighed all dreamy-like.

"Me either," she confided. "I hope we're both lucky with that."

After a minute she handed the phone back and asked for my email before sending those pictures of myself over in an email. Taking the phone back after sending them, she downloaded then began uploading them onto my dating app profile.

"The girls are going to be flocking to you, Blake," she said eventually, handing back my phone again with my new profile on the screen.

A ding popped up and I saw that someone had already swiped right on me.

"Ohh! Put it up! I want to see her profile!" Bay said excitedly from her seat, staring at my phone screen.

I clicked onto it and a picture of an attractive woman popped up. She said she loved dogs, and that she trained them for a living, and that she lived in Tacoma with her teenage daughter.

"What do you think?" Bay asked. "Is it a match?"

I shrugged.

"I think I have to talk to her first to find that out."

"Well first you have to swipe left or right. Right means you like her too, and left means you don't."

"That's kind of insulting, isn't it?"

"It's the name of the game." She shrugged.

Swiping right on the profile, it put up a heart that said we were matched, giving me the option to send her a personal message. Which I did.

She sent one back and Bay grinned at me.

"This it?" I asked her, looking up from my third awkward message.

Another ding showed up telling me another woman had swiped right.

I did it back and then I was talking with two women.

"You're basically a pro," Bay said, winking at me before sitting up. "And you're welcome, by the way."

"Thanks." I nodded and focused on my phone.

Those were the types of women I needed to be talking to. Older women in their thirties, women with careers and an idea of what they wanted in the world. Women ready to start a family.

Bay sauntered away toward the kitchen, and my eyes followed, even with the influx of messages suddenly vibrating my phone in my hand, my eyes couldn't stop staring.

73

The fridge opened and I heard her start to chop things, veggies, probably. But the sound was just so... *domestic.* And I loved it.

The messages from both women hovered between sweet and sexy, little comments, promises of what might happen when we saw each other, and it didn't take very long before the second woman, Janet, asked to meet at a bar not too far from me.

"Got a date," I said absently, listening to the sizzle of dinner on the stove.

Looking out the window into the dimmed Sunday afternoon light, I hoped that my date would at least get my brain off Bay, and get me back into the game. I had to start somewhere, and Janet would be that start.

"You got a date?" Bay asked excitedly. "When? With who?"

"Janet." I shrugged and she beamed.

"That's awesome, Blake! What're you going to wear?"

I looked down at the shirt and jeans I was sporting, then back up at her with a raised eyebrow.

"You need new clothes," she told me, blinking at me like I was a moron.

"Why? This is how I always dress."

"And you are not going to win a girl over without putting some effort into your appearance. You need to go shopping."

"I hate shopping." I practically growled the words out.

"If you hate it so much, I can do it tomorrow after class."

Digging into my pocket, I retrieved my wallet then dragged out a credit card.

"One outfit?" I asked her and she nodded. "Try to keep it under a hundred then."

Handing the card to her, she took it gently and smiled.

"You trust me with your credit card?" she asked.

"I trust you," I agreed, wondering where the fuck I got the idea that she was worthy of my trust.

Maybe it was her smile or laugh, or maybe it was her pure, young face or the fact that my daughter loved the girl. But I trusted her, for better or worse.

"Thanks," she practically whispered the single word before slipping it in her pocket.

I bit down on my lip, turning away from her so I could refocus on my phone. I had to before I could let the little crease between her brows affect me.

Tuesday I would get together with a woman and maybe, *hopefully*, it would remind me of all the ways that Bay was still a girl.

Chapter 9

Bay

Class couldn't end fast enough. I had Blake's credit card in my pocket and I was pretty much living any girl's dream. Getting a chance to dress up the boy she liked? Yeah, that was something pretty special, and I was going to take full advantage of it, even if he wasn't dressing up for *me*.

When he'd knocked on my door asking for some pictures, I was surprised, but I also saw opportunity there waiting for me. Pictures of such a beautiful man? What an incredible model he'd been, too. And without even trying. But the moment he started unbuttoning his shirt, I almost jumped all over him and begged him to show me what it was like to be with a real man. Honestly. But of course he was relaxed about it, and he didn't think anything of it, so I tried to be calm as well. Even though my heart was beating a million miles a minute, I put on a smile and clicked away at those pictures. And after the fact, I had a nice little folder filled with pictures of him that would keep me and my toys busy for a while.

Oh, don't you even judge me. I absolutely knew it was creepy, but he'd never find out. Plus, when I eventually managed to meet a guy and actually liked him even half as much as I liked Blake, well, then I'd get rid of the pictures. That was the plan, anyway.

Walking into the mall, I turned, looking at all the little shops that provided so many opportunities. First I stopped at a skater shop to get him some jeans in the same size as the one's I'd stolen the size from when I went snooping in the laundry room. Next was a department store where I found a plain white t-shirt and a sexy-as-sin moto jacket made of denim that had some interesting ribbed texture on the sleeves. Finally, I found myself in the men's underwear department, thinking back to those baggy and worn boxers I'd seen him wear once. Sure, I realized that the woman he was going out with was the one likely to see them and absolutely not me, but I wanted him to feel confident in his skin, and if underwear gave men even half the confidence that sexy underwear gave women, then it was worth it.

I picked out a couple pairs that I thought would look amazing but also with soft and comfortable fabric. I settled, after a while, on some boxer briefs since they seemed to be all the style.

Taking my purchases back to the car, there was a grand total of five dollars left of the hundred allotted to me, and I felt pretty good with that. He had a nice, sexy and casual outfit that would get him through as many first dates as it took for him to find love. Whether I had a crush on him or not didn't bear any weight on the fact that I wanted to see him happy, and he just looked too sad most of the time. The man deserved love, even if the thought of him with someone else made me crazy with jealousy.

When I got back home, I laid out the outfit on his bed, tags taken off and all, then closed the door behind me. The room smelled like him and I felt like I was invading on something I didn't have any business enjoying. So, I took my notebook out of my backpack and my workbooks from my room before settling down to do homework until he got home.

―――――――――――◇―――――――――――

"You having dinner here or are you eating out with your date?" I called out to Blake as he took off his work boots by the door.

He told me that his date was that evening, but didn't mention anything about where they were going.

"Yeah. Date's not until eight," he said with a sigh, plopping his jacket onto the hook near the door and emptying his pockets on the little shelf right next to it.

"Ok. I made some kabobs. Just got to cook them."

"Want me to grill 'em?" he asked, stopping in the living room on his way to his bedroom.

"Sure, they'd taste better," I agreed, trying to ignore the tightening in my belly when he came into view.

His hair had little specks of white sheetrock dust in it, his knees smeared with it too and shirt peppered with the same.

"Long day?" I asked and he shrugged.

"No longer than every other day."

As he started walking away, I spotted the credit card and pile of receipts I'd put on the coffee table in front of me so I wouldn't forget to give it back.

"Oh! I have this for you," I told him, following him toward his bedroom.

He was already there, his shirt wadded up in his hands as he stared down at the outfit I got him.

"Hope it's ok." I whispered, suddenly unsure about my choices, and about what he would think of me purchasing underwear for him.

Was that going too far? Oh God...

"Thanks, looks good," he said, then turned to me and took the pile I held out.

And it was a good thing that he took it from my hands, because my brain melted into hormonal stupidity when I saw that the button and fly of his jeans were already open and gaping, peeking gray boxers at me.

"See you out there," he said after a second.

I jerked my head up, realizing that I'd been staring at the man's *junk* for way too long, then basically ran out of the room with my face lit on fire from embarrassment.

I was sitting on the couch, scrolling through Twitter on my phone to look busy, even though I was really thinking about that little sliver of hair-dusted skin I saw above his boxers band. Blake came out from his room, dressed and ready to impress.

Physically shoving my mouth closed, I had to suppress a groan of agony as he stopped in the middle of the room, putting out his arms for my inspection.

"So?" he asked, the hem of his t-shirt riding up a little with the movement and showing off the V at his hips.

"I think I work miracles," was all I managed to choke out.

He chuckled and ran his hand through his hair, glancing at the mirror across the room.

And it was a good thing that I got him those new underwear, because the jeans he had on were snug and sexy and absolutely perfect on his slim hips. Boots framed him off, though these weren't his regular work boots, but big, leather motorcycle riding boots.

"Everything fit ok?" I asked him, getting up to do a little turn around him, pretending I'm inspecting and not just plain drooling.

"Jeans are kinda tight, but I can't tell if it's supposed to be that way or not. Is that how they're wearing them these days?"

I grinned at him.

"You're not old enough to say things like that," I told him, laughing.

"I feel like it." He blew out a breath and continued to tousle his hair with his fingers nervously.

"You excited?" I asked, pulling on the collar of the denim jacket, pretending to straighten it, while I was really just getting close enough to smell his cologne.

It was orgasmic. Seriously.

Squeezing my thighs together, I stood in that same spot as he headed toward the kitchen.

"Nervous?" he echoed, looking over the kabobs I'd made right before he got home from work. "Scared, terrified, yes. Not nervous."

Licking my lips, I dragged my eyes up from his firm ass and watched him grab the plate and some tongs.

"I'll cook them," I told him all of a sudden. "Grilling will make your clothes smell like smoke."

He popped a hip and put his hand on it, narrowing his eyes on me.

"If a woman doesn't like me because I smell like life, then she can go fuck herself right off."

And just like that, he took the tray and tongs outside to the little wood patio that held a gas grill.

My heart fluttered in my chest. I wasn't quite sure why, but it did.

He set the plate down on the little table by the grill and started it up, then pulled his jacket off and hung it over a patio chair. The white shirt was thinner than I thought, and it showed just a little bit of peachy skin through the woven fabric as it stretched across his shoulders.

Only one thing could make it better.

Taking a step forward, I found myself drifting toward him until I was side by side with him.

"Thanks for making these," he said when he saw me approach.

"Of course. I like cooking, and you're easy to cook for."

"'Cause I like eating." He smiled, his grin hitting me square in the chest like a detonating bomb.

"Want me to roll these for you?" I asked in no more than a whisper.

He looked a little confused, so I just started rolling the hem of his t-shirt sleeves twice over each other.

"Have we really come full circle back to the sixties?" he asked with one eyebrow raised.

I grunted with a grin on my face.

"In some ways. It mostly just shows off your biceps. You work hard on it, so you might as well show it off."

It was true. He seemed to be getting even more muscular in the two months I'd been living with him, and I hadn't missed the late night workout sessions he had. His grunts echoed through the living room and hallway when I went to the bathroom in the middle of the night. The setup he had in the garage was pretty impressive, if a little sparse. I supposed one could do quite a lot with an elliptical and a bench seat, framed by some free and bar weight sets.

"You telling me women are suckers for biceps?" he asked with amusement.

"Most, and I'm no different," I admitted, moving to his other side to do the other sleeve.

"Good to know," he murmured, reaching around me for the kabobs.

I could swear his head was mere inches from mine, mouth so close that I didn't know what to do with myself when he moved back and started putting the sticks with steak cubes and veggies on the grill.

I backed off a little, fanning myself even though it was only seventy degrees outside.

"You use the ribeye on these?" he asked, putting the plate back down.

"Mhmm," I choked out, watching his back muscles stretching and rolling under the thin t-shirt.

"You ok with pink in the middle?"

"Mhmm," I hummed again and he turned, looking over his shoulder at me.

"You ok, Bay?"

"Mhmm."

He lifted a brow at me again, but let it go and turned back to the food on the grill.

"This'll only take me a few minutes. We having anything with it?"

"Mhmm," I said one more time, and he looked at me again, a quiet laugh bursting from his mouth.

"I'll go—"

Hurrying away from the backyard, I went to check on the peas and rice I'd put on as a side just so I could take a breath again.

We plated together, grabbing a scoop of rice each and our Asian marinated kabobs before sitting at the table to eat.

"Why are you scared?" I asked eventually, because I was incredibly curious, and my filter just disappeared around the man.

He looked up at me with a full mouth.

"Why?" he mumbled.

I nodded.

"I haven't been on a date since I was sixteen. My ex doesn't count. At least I sure hope it doesn't count, because if dates are like those, then I'm going to be forever alone."

"Dates are nice," I said eventually.

"You dating anyone?" he asked before taking a big bite.

I shook my head.

"No. Last person I dated was...Well, he came out as gay while we were dating. I'm still not sure if it was my fault or not."

He burst out laughing and little pieces of rice went flying across the table, which made me laugh too.

I threw my hand over my mouth to prevent another rice shower, and Blake was simultaneously choking, laughing, and blushing.

"Holy shit," he said eventually, taking a sip of his water. "Don't get rice in your nose. Pro tip three hundred and fifty-eight."

I laughed harder and squeezed my eyes shut as I managed to swallow, then belly laughed through my mouth.

"Oh my God!" I groaned, wiping the tears from my eyes, my hands coming away with streaks of eyeliner and mascara.

"Well, I managed to make a girl cry today," Blake said, pushing his plate away playfully. "Guess my whole night is going to go downhill from here."

I shoved it back and said between giggles, "You made a woman cry happy tears. Pretty sure that's good luck."

He smiled a devilish little smile before taking another bite.

"So, are you saying you think *you* made him go gay?" he asked me after swallowing.

"No. I don't know. Probably not."

"But it sure as hell isn't great for the self-esteem," he tried.

I nodded, pointing at him with a wink. "Bingo."

"Why haven't you dated since?" he asked me.

"Because I haven't found anyone interesting."

"Well, what're you interested in? Maybe a buddy of mine has a boy your age."

My cheeks burned red as he watched me with intent eyes.

Why was it so hard to talk about dating with this man?

"I guess...someone with a sense of humor. Someone with ambitions, and someone who's comfortable in their own skin. And someone who treats me right, you know? I don't need to be treated like a princess or anything, but opening a door or bringing me flowers every now and then would be nice."

"Are there any younger guys that do that anymore?" he asked.

"Not straight ones," I joked and he smiled again.

"I'll ask around. Marty and Gail have three girls, so they're no help."

Shrugging, I just placed another bite of savory-sweet beef in my mouth and chewed.

"I'm not desperate for a man," I told him. "So thanks, but no thanks."

He nodded slowly and poked at the remainder of his meal.

"I have to do a few things before meeting Janet," Blake said, standing. "You ok by yourself tonight?"

"You plan on being out 'til morning?" I asked, secretly hoping he wasn't.

He huffed out a single laugh before shaking his head.

"No. I'll be back before midnight most likely."

It was a warm wave of relief that surprised me the most when those words left his perfect, plump-but-not-too-plump lips.

"Want me to wait up?"

"It's a school night. So no. You go to bed and I'll see you in the morning."

"And you'll tell me all about it?" I asked him.

"Sure, if you want me to." He nodded before placing his plate in the sink and heading to the door. "Thanks for dinner, Bay."

"You're welcome!" I called as he grabbed his keys and headed back toward the garage.

Huh?

"Taking the bike out tonight," he said to my confused face.

Bike? Oh God... was that what was under that tarp in the garage?

I followed him to the door and sure enough it was one sexy beast under the tarp. It took everything in me to not beg for a ride on the thing right then.

"Don't wait up," he said to me before donning his helmet and leather jacket.

He tossed his leg over the bike and started it up with a fantastic roar.

There I was, squeezing my thighs together again.

He backed out of the garage, then hit a little button on his phone, tucked it away in one of his jacket pockets, then zoomed down the road as the garage door beeped then shut.

Automatic garage door from his phone? That was pretty cool.

Well, I was going to be alone for the next few hours at least, so I just closed the door, locked it, then went to go finish my homework. Part of me hoped that he had a good date, and the other part hoped that it was an utter disaster. I liked having my best friend's dad all to myself. Could I even say that anymore? Was she really my best friend anymore?

Taking out my phone, I sent her a text to see what she was doing before heading back to the couch. While I waited for a text back, I looked up and saw that he'd forgotten his jacket. It was the best piece of his outfit, but then again, he had that leather jacket which was just as sexy as the jean one. Before it started raining again, I went outside and brought it in. It smelled like him.

Lying down on the couch, I turned the TV on to indulge in useless, time-wasting trash while inhaling his cologne until I eventually fell asleep with no response from my supposed 'best friend'.

Chapter 10

Blake

I didn't really have anywhere to go, but I had to get out of the house. Just being that close to Bay was doing funky things to my stomach, and I couldn't even finish my food because of it. Watching her laugh so hard that she cried after I spewed rice out of my mouth and nose had just made my heart grow about three sizes too large, quite the opposite problem as the Grinch had. But hearing about her ex, then the rice thing, I was already half ready to throw the table across the room and kiss those damnable full lips, always glistening with some kind of gloss or chapstick or something. And I wanted to know what flavor it was.

God...

Twisting the throttle, I shot down the road, blowing off some steam before I was supposed to meet my date. Last thing she needed was some horny dude, lusting after the teenaged girl rooming with him while she went to college. Fuck me, I was such an asshole.

At five minutes to eight, I drove up to the bar and parked, dragging my helmet in with me before finding a place at the bar to order a beer while I waited. I needed it.

Tossing half the bottle back, I felt a hand on my shoulder and the touch made me swing my eyes over at the woman who looked mostly like the one in the picture.

"Hey," she said, eyes eating me up from head to toe. "Blake?"

"Yeah, that's me," I said awkwardly. "Janet?"

She nodded and smiled nicely before motioning to the bartender. "Can I have one of what he's having?"

A minute later she had a beer too and we were finding a booth in the corner to talk.

"I'm not going to lie, I saw your pictures and wasn't sure if you were catfishing or not," she told me, taking a ginger sip of her beer.

"Well, that would have been a shitty thing to do," I told her with a little smile. "But I'm all me."

"I only agreed to meet you because you seemed so nice over the messages. And if you were just trying to impress me, you wouldn't have said you did construction, so..."

What the hell was wrong with construction? Was that some kind of cockroach profession or something?

"What do you do?" I asked her, just trying not to show how mad her comment made me.

"I'm a real estate agent," she said with a winning smile.

Bet that smile was on her business cards.

We both sipped for a minute before noticing the helmet dropped by my side on the seat with my gloves stuffed in them.

"Helmet?" she asked, one eye raising.

"Motorcycle." I nodded.

Her eyes brightened like a Goddamn kid on Christmas morning.

"Really? What kind?"

"Harley Breakout," I told her, narrowing my eyes on her.

"Ah, nice," she nodded, as if she knew what the hell I was talking about.

A waiter came up to us and asked if we wanted to order anything.

"Mind if I order some food?" Janet asked and I shrugged, waving my hand at the server.

"Grilled chicken salad; dressing on the side."

The waiter nodded and turned to me.

"You got wings?" I asked and they nodded. "Half dozen of them, please."

"Buffalo ok?"

"Sure," I agreed and they went off.

I would need some kind of food to sop up all the alcohol I was about to ingest in order to get through this date.

"So, what do you do at your job, Blake?" Janet asked after a while of us just staring at each other, not sure what to say.

"I do everything," I told her with a shrug. "But generally my job is boss."

"Boss?" She seemed interested in that. "That's cool. You're a foreman?"

"I have my own business. We do remodels and occasionally we'll build a place from the ground up."

"A contractor then. That's nice."

Nice?

"Sure," I said, shrugging. "You staying busy? Heard the housing market's not as *nice* as it was."

"You would know." She almost huffed out the words like it was an insult.

"I would. Not as many people are needing contractors these days."

Good thing we were one of the best in the PNW at what we did.

"Why are you on a dating app?" she asked now.

It looked like the gloves were off and she was out for blood.

"Wow, getting to the meat of it, huh?" I asked her, looking down at my helmet, at the table, at my hands; anything but at her.

"I figure it's a fair question. I'll tell you first about me, if you'd like."

I didn't have time to agree. She just started talking.

"I find myself working a lot and I don't have a lot of time to date or invest in finding a partner. It's that simple for me. I use an app so I don't have to spend nights trolling bars for deadbeats."

Well fuck me.

"What about you?"

Ok, so I guess she wanted all the baggage laid out all at once.

"I'm divorced now for ten years, and I work a lot, too. My daughter is finally going to college and I figure it's time to settle

87

down and stop being a bachelor. I want to find someone to spend my life with. Who loves the simple things in life as much as I do. I haven't really dated in a decade and I didn't know where the fuck to start, so I'm starting here."

Her eyes went wide and her mouth popped open at that.

"You're a father?" she asked.

I nodded.

"And she's in college? I thought you said you were thirty-five."

"I am. And she is. We had her young."

Janet licked her lips as she fussed with a little paper napkin, her brain trying to process the information.

"I'm not going to lie," she said eventually. "I-I'm not interested in becoming a step-mom. I'm not really looking for anything serious in the first place. I'm only thirty-two and I don't want to settle down yet. Dating is as far as I'll go right now."

Shit. So we were both wasting our time.

"Thanks for telling me," I said eventually, downing the last bit of beer until I hit empty glass at the bottom.

"I still think we can have a nice date, but I guess I'll leave that to you," she added after another minute of silence.

Did I want to continue our dud of a date? I could probably use the practice, and at least the pressure was off because I knew it wasn't going anywhere.

"Sure," I agreed.

Lifting my hand to get the attention of the waiter who I asked to get me another beer.

"Want another one?" I asked her.

"No thank you." She shook her head.

So, just talking it would be.

"Did you raise your daughter?" Janet inquired after another short bout of silence.

"I got to see her during the summers. Her mom lives in a different state and so the whole every other weekend thing didn't work for us."

88

"It must have been hard to only see her a few months a year."

It was really fucking hard.

"Yeah. But I loved having her when I got her. We have a good relationship despite it."

At least, we used to. I wasn't sure where we stood since Georgia wasn't answering my texts anymore.

"What's her name?" Janet gave me an indulgent smile.

"Georgia," I said.

"That's a nice name."

I just nodded a little and breathed relief when our food arrived.

Janet dug into her salad, crunching down delicately on the leaves as if she was some kind of princess or something.

Now, don't get me wrong, but I found it really stupid when women ordered salads. Like, ok. Salads are cool and everything, but they weren't really nutritionally dense unless you specifically made it that way at home. Plus, when you eat dressing with it, well, you might as well just have a grilled chicken sandwich. Less calories, less fat, and you didn't look like someone who was obsessive over their weight. Instead she was gnawing on the leaves as if it was some kind of delicious delicacy.

Maybe I was just bitter over the millions of salads my ex had eaten when I'd known her. She was compulsive about what she ate because, in her words, *'the only thing men wanna see jiggling is my boobs.'*

Yeah. Those were the types of things she said to me in our marriage. And people wondered why I wanted out.

I ate my wings in silence, thinking just for a minute on the succulent kabobs Bay had made, and how she ate them like nobody was watching. It was charming and sexy as hell. But when I thought about her, I also reminded myself that she was nineteen, and of course she could get away with eating whatever she wanted. Maybe women my age just *liked* salads and I was really missing the memo.

"You ok over there?" Janet asked suddenly.

"Huh?" I asked and jerked my head up to look at her.

"You went into space there for a few minutes," she told me with a little smile.

"Sorry, thinking about work." I lied, giving her a little smile so she would believe it.

God forbid if anybody knew I was thinking about my daughter's friend.

"Don't apologize. I know how it is." She waved her hand and took another leafy bite.

Eating the rest of my wings, I took a couple sips of beer, but didn't finish it. I wasn't going to hang out with her at the bar when we were done eating, so I had to stay sober in order to head home afterwards.

I got the bill after that and placed a couple twenties on the little tray before standing up.

"I appreciate your time," I told Janet just then. "It's been nice to meet you, but I don't want to take any more of your time. I know I'm not what you're looking for."

She just grinned.

"Oh, you're exactly my type." She winked at me. "And I was going to ask if you were willing to take me home. I took a cab here."

Fuck...

"I just have my bike..." I started, but she shook her head.

"I don't mind. I actually like motorcycles. They're so sexy."

Ah, so it was about the bike. She just wanted a ride.

"Uh, sure. Suppose it's the least I could do," I said with a shrug and she grinned, standing.

I grabbed my helmet, took the gloves out and handed it to her as we headed out of the bar.

"Thanks," she said, holding it as I went to my bike, stacked near the entrance next to three more. "It's beautiful!"

"Thanks." I nodded, swinging my leg over while I got on my gloves.

Law was to wear a helmet, but what the hell else was I supposed to do?

She climbed on back, hips framed with mine and chest against my back as she pulled my helmet over her head, then wrapped her arms around my jacket.

I started the thing with a ragged roar and heard her giggling behind me.

After backing out, I yelled at her, "Point me in the right direction!"

She nodded, then pressed her body impossibly closer.

Idling at the exit of the parking lot, she pointed to the left, so I went left.

It wasn't too painful getting her home, but she did give me a couple shitty directions and so I missed a turn or two, but we got there eventually. Now, the thing I wasn't sure of was if she'd done it on purpose or not.

"Wow," she said, pulling off my helmet, breathing heavy.

"Not bad," I agreed and swung off, offering her a hand to get down.

She took it and held onto the helmet.

"I live alone," she said softly, stepping into me and pressing a palm against my chest. "I know we're not really in the same place when it comes to dating, but even dads need a little release here and there."

Holy hell, was I getting propositioned? On a first date?

Feeling like a fucking idiot for turning down such a golden opportunity, I shook my head.

"My kid's waiting for me to come home," I told her, lying through my teeth.

"She's an adult. She can survive a night without her daddy."

Pressing her breasts against my leather jacket, I watched as her hand slipped down and entered the belt zone.

Bay's pretty little smile flashed across my mind and I gritted my teeth. I did need a good fuck, but not like this.

Hm, maybe I really *was* getting old. Turning down sex and all.

"Thanks for tonight," I told her, taking a step back to put some space between us as I relieved her of my helmet.

Her sultry expression turned angry.

"Really? You're turning me down? A dry dad?"

Hey, hey, who said I was dry?

"It's not all about sex." I lifted one shoulder and that just pissed her off more.

"Right. Says the blue collar asshole with a divorce and college kid by thirty-five."

Oh she did *not*.

"If it weren't for blue collar assholes like *me* building the house, salespeople asskissers like *you* would have nothing to sell. You're fucking welcome. For dinner *and* the ride."

Just like that I turned and slammed the helmet back on my head, trying to ignore the faint flowery scent it now sported as I climbed back onto my bike.

Janet growled and stomped back toward her house, slamming the door with not even a single thank you.

Awesome. Best first date ever.

Chapter 11

Bay

The sound of Blake's motorcycle was what woke me up. The thing roared as he entered the garage, then shut off, leaving me in echoing silence.

Loud footsteps pounded up the two wooden stairs from the garage to the house and in walked Blake. He tossed his helmet into a kitchen chair, looking a little more than a tad pissed.

"That bad?" I asked from the couch where I'd fallen asleep after he left.

"What're you doing up?" he asked, stripping off his gloves and jacket, tossing them onto another chair.

That white shirt was still stretched across his chest. It seemed to catch the curve of every muscle as his body strained against his barely-contained anger.

"I was sleeping. You woke me up."

"Fuck... Just go to bed, Bay."

"That bad?" I asked again and he just bit his lip, standing there with his arms crossed over that wide chest.

Every nerve ending in my body was waking up while watching him, and I wanted nothing more than to kiss those lips of his. I didn't even care how old he was. He was too beautiful to say no. Maybe just a little...

"It was bad," he said, interrupting my thoughts with harsh words. "She was a total bitch and I think I give up on dating. I'll just die an old, lonely dude and hope that Georgia eventually settles down so at least I can have grandkids before I die."

I couldn't help it. I started to laugh.

His eyes narrowed on me and my grin.

"You're not going to die lonely," I told him simply. "I won't allow it."

"You won't allow it?" he asked, lifting his eyebrows in disbelief.

"My daughter's best friend won't allow me to die alone. How nice, Bay. If only you knew how fucking hard it is to date when you have a divorce and a kid and evidently some misplaced sense of chivalry that won't let you fu-"

His words cut off and he bit his lip again, looking back at the ground.

Fuck? Was he about to say fuck? Had his date thrown herself at him and he'd said no?

My heart started to pound in my chest and another piece of it broke off, falling into the box of other pieces that had set themselves aside just for him. There were too many already with his name on them.

"One bad date and you give up?" I asked, standing and taking one step toward him.

"It'd be easier," he said, closing his eyes and running a hand down his face.

"And chivalry is never a bad thing, Blake."

He scoffed and shoved that hand into his hair next, mussing it up just right after being flattened by his helmet.

One more step toward him, then another.

Those pieces marked as his inside my chest compelled me forward, and my brain was trying to play catch up as I took another step. His body froze in front of me, eyes sharp on me as I got so close only an inch of air separated us.

"What're you doing, Bay?" he asked in a breathy whisper.

My hand lifted and touched one stubble-roughened cheek. His eyes closed at the touch, then opened hooded and piercing as my fingers slid past his cheek and palmed the base of his skull.

"B—"

I wouldn't let him finish. I went onto my tip-toes and dragged his head down to meet me, pressing a kiss on his lips like I'd wanted to from the first moment I'd met him.

He gasped against my lips, then curled his body over me and slipped his hands around my ribs as he kissed me back.

It was my turn to gasp when his tongue slipped into my mouth, brushing against mine as his hands tightened their grip.

But then a rumble ground out of his chest and up his throat as he shoved me back, a look of pain written across his face.

"What the fuck, Bay?" he demanded in a hoarse voice, his body moving away from mine, but his hands still on my ribs, squeezing almost to the point of pain.

"I—I..." I stumbled over my words as my brain finally caught up to my libido, crashing into my chest like a Mac truck.

"Fuck!" he growled again and shoved me away a little more, dragging his hand across his mouth like he'd tasted something particularly bitter.

Well, he was a gentleman, sort of. And he was a gentleman who *didn't want me.*

Backing further away, I hurried to my bedroom and slammed the door closed, feeling absolutely mortified.

What was I thinking? Why did I kiss him? I liked him, yes. He was handsome, he was interesting, yes and yes. He had his life figured out and radiated confidence, sure. But I was nineteen and he was my best friend's dad. He was off limits, no matter what my heart and hormones tried to tell me. I needed to find someone *like* him, because Blake was not for me.

Ever.

Me: *You coming home anytime soon?*

Georgia: *Why? Everything ok?*

Me: *Fine. I just miss you. And it's weird being with your dad without you.*

Georgia: *Just ignore him. I miss you. Come see me.*

Me: *He misses you too.*

95

Georgia: *God! Not you too! I'm not three. I don't need my daddy around every second.*

Me: *I know, I just think it'd be nice to have you here. Maybe we can hang out this weekend and go shopping or something.*

She didn't answer my last text for a while, and I figured I'd made her mad. Again.

It'd been almost a week since that kiss. I'd avoided Blake as much as I could, but the tension in the house was almost stifling.

"Hey, Bay," I heard as I was walking out of my last class for the day.

"Mark, hey," I said back as I saw him approaching from my right.

"You doing anything tomorrow?" he asked, shouldering his bag and giving me a smile.

It was the second time he'd asked me if I was busy. The first time I had been going out with Georgia, but now...now I had no excuse.

"Uh, not really," I admitted.

"You want to go, uh, see a movie or something?"

I squeezed my eyes closed for a second and tried to think of an excuse.

But why? Why did I want an excuse? Mark was cute and nice and he was an art major, too. He was a painter instead of a photographer, but that didn't really matter. We probably had a lot in common. Mark was pretty ideal, he just wasn't Blake.

"Sure," I blurted out the moment my brain settled on Blake's name.

I needed to stop thinking about him in that way. Maybe when I did, things at the house wouldn't be so awkward anymore. If only Georgia was there...

"Really?" Mark asked, grinning.

"Yeah!" I smiled back, pausing on the sidewalk to look into his pretty yellow-gold eyes.

"Tomorrow night ok?" he asked. "Dinner and a movie maybe?"

"I'd like that," I said truthfully.

His grin turned into a little smirk before he winked.

"Awesome! Mind if I get your number? So I can get your address and we can pick a time?"

I chuckled and nodded, taking the phone he held out to me.

"Thanks, Bay. I look forward to it," he said when I handed his phone back. "Talk to you tonight, ok?"

I agreed and Mark went off, a little pep in his step as he lugged that heavy bag over his shoulder.

I just sighed and worked my way back to my car before heading home.

Blake was home when I got in, having stopped for dinner on the way so I didn't have to endure another awkward meal with my housemate.

He turned toward the door, then looked back down at his pizza before watching TV again.

"I've got a date tomorrow," I told him, hoping that maybe he'd be relieved by the fact.

His fingers tightened around his pizza and broke the crust down the middle as he asked, "With who?"

"Someone from school," I managed. "Not that it's your business."

His lips pressed together in anger as he turned away from me, dropping the strangled piece back into the cardboard box it'd come in.

Well, maybe telling him that didn't make him happy, after all. And why did *that* make *me* so happy?

Blake

A fucking date?

Good. She *should* go on a motherfucking date with an idiot little bastard her age.

With my appetite sufficiently gone, I slapped the pizza box closed and stomped into the kitchen to shove it into the fridge before calling it a night.

It wasn't late, but it was late enough that I'd be ok with my six a.m. alarm. Staring at the clock over the fireplace that read seven thirty, I sighed.

It was too early to go to bed, but I didn't want to be sitting on that couch alone. Just in the weeks she'd lived with me, Bay had become a part of my routine and it felt weird without her sitting with me, rolling her eyes at the TV. But I couldn't stop thinking about that kiss that *she* gave *me*. Why? Why the hell would she kiss me? I wanted to ask her so bad, but we weren't really on talking terms. Little interactions like her informing me of her date was all we said to each other, and that was driving me nuts, too.

Pulling out my phone, I got back on that app and decided that I'd go on another date, and if she wanted to fuck, well then, I wouldn't be stupid enough to say no three times.

Swiping right on five different women, I laid back on my bed in my boxer briefs that Bay had got for me and waited to hear back, playing a stupid, time-killing game in the process.

An hour later I heard Bay leave her room, her soft footsteps creaking against the floor as she went presumably to the kitchen, then made her way back down the hallway. I heard silence for a minute, then she was in the bathroom.

The girl went to bed around ten every night, and I figured that was one of the things I liked about her. She was an old woman in a teen's body. For some odd reason, I liked that.

A few minutes later she went back into her room and closed the door behind her. My phone buzzed with a match and I went to the messaging to chat her up just as a buzzing filtered through the wall.

Fucking *hell...*

As if I wasn't horny enough, the girl had to use her fucking toys. Memories of the sounds she made when she came was suddenly on repeat in my head and I was getting hard just thinking about it. She used them pretty regularly twice a week, and I was the unfortunate one to know. But I never went to her door to listen to her again. She deserved privacy and I wasn't going to be a perv again. Instead I channeled the sexual frustration and chatted up the woman on the app, and the next who wrote only a couple minutes later after swiping right on me, too.

Before Bay turned those toys off, I had another date lined up for the next night. At least it would keep my brain off Bay and whatever asshole guy she was going out with. And maybe I'd get my rocks off so I could fucking *think* again.

Chapter 12

Bay

Georgia: *Sorry. Got home late from my party. This weekend? Dad will be relentless.*

Me: *It's ok. I have a date today, actually.*

Georgia: *What?! With who???*

Me: *Guy in my class. He's cute and an art student too.*

Georgia: *How absolutely nerdy and perfect for you!*

Me: *Is that a compliment or an insult??*

Georgia: *Total compliment for you. Let me know how it goes. Barrett asked after you, BTW.*

Me: *Barrett the asshole? No thanks.*

Georgia: *But he's so hot! He'd be a good lay if that nerdy art student doesn't work out.*

Me: *It's not about getting laid, Georgie.*

Georgia: *We're in college, Bay. Of course it is!*

Georgia: *Now is the time to explore!*

Me: *I am. But I'm also focusing on school. I've got to keep up grades with a scholarship, you know?*

Georgia: *Like you ever had trouble keeping up with grades. You were pretty much born perfect.*

Me: *Your dad misses you. You should see him.*

She didn't answer my texts any time I mentioned her dad, and I couldn't for the life of me understand why. Georgia had always loved her dad, but for some reason she was pulling away, and my heart hurt for Blake. At least she was still answering my texts. He didn't even get that.

Putting the last finishing touches on my makeup, I paused for a moment to check my phone again and nothing. No returned texts or anything of the sort.

I heard the doorbell from my room, then hurried up to get the door before Blake had a chance.

Too late.

"Are you Bay's...brother?" I heard Mark asking as I approached the door.

"Her housemate," Blake ground out, staring Mark down like he was bubblegum attached to his shoe.

Mark blinked, then he smiled when he saw me.

"Bay! Wow, you look so pretty!"

I smiled at him and slipped out the door.

"When are you going to be home?" Blake asked as I pulled on Mark's hand.

"When I'm home," I told him, which made Blake growl as we went back to the driveway where Mark's beat up car was waiting for us.

"You have a dude roommate?" Mark asked with a laugh, opening my door for me.

"Yeah. He's actually my friend's dad. We live there with him," I said, hoping it wasn't fibbing too much to use present tense in that sentence, seeing as how Georgia didn't live with us anymore.

"That's cool. I'm not friends like that with my buddy's parents."

I shrugged and waited as he closed the door and went around the car.

"Um, I was thinking that it'd be cool to go to the glass museum, since you're not from around here, right? Didn't you say you're from Las Vegas?"

I nodded and smiled at him, putting out all thoughts of Blake from my head so I could enjoy my first official date of college.

"But if you're alright with it, I'm friggin' hungry. What do you like to eat, Bay?"

Smiling at him, I gave a little shrug.

"I'm not going to lie. I like cooking and eating, so I'm up for whatever you're craving," I told him.

Mark laughed, his eyes crinkling at the sides just like Blakes did when he smiled.

"That's so awesome! Ok, I know a hole in the wall place that makes the best burgers and shakes, if you're up for it."

"Bring it on!" I grinned at him and sat back in the seat of his old but still decent looking car.

"So, we don't get much chance to talk in class," Mark started as we pulled away just as Blake was leaving the house and climbing into his sports car.

Where was he going?

"...what do you think?" Mark continued, but I'd missed it all.

"Uh, sorry, what?" I managed, my cheeks coloring as we left my friend's dad and his car behind us.

"I was asking you if you like to paint," Mark said with a smirk on his face, like *he'd* somehow made my brain go blank and not my sexy housemate.

"Oh, well, I like painting a little. I tried it in middle school but I like photography better."

"Yeah? Your parents supportive of you going to school for art? Mine think I'm wasting my time, but I couldn't just put it aside, you know?"

"They're actually really supportive of me. I know I'm lucky. I got a scholarship to come here, so I think that maybe that helped with them being ok with my major."

"Really?" He seemed impressed. "That's really cool. I wish I could see some of your work. You don't happen to have your portfolio with you, do you?"

We both laughed at the ridiculous question, then moved on to talking about other simple things like family, friends, and our art.

"You've got to try the pumpkin pie shake," he told me when we waited in line for our dinner.

The restaurant was a little old and broken down, but it was also packed with people, which said a lot for the food. If all these people could look past the physical appearance because of how good the food was, I could overlook it, too.

I got the pie shake as suggested and he got a cupcake shake, and we ended up sharing each other's ice creams because it was *so* good. Honestly, I'd never had better shakes or burgers in my life.

"I'll owe you forever for showing me this place," I told him as we cleaned up our wrappers and napkins, stashing them in the trash on the way back to the car.

"I've been coming here since I could drive. A buddy of mine actually worked here, and he'd get me free shakes when I made it up to visit him. I fell in love and never looked back."

I just smiled at him. How incredibly adorable was that?

"So, the glass museum?" he asked, opening my car door for me.

"Let's do it!" I agreed.

We went to the museum from there and it was incredible to see all the art, reflecting the lights and glowing in front, above and underneath our feet.

I was completely enchanted by the time we walked out of the place, the night dark and damp, while my spirit soared.

"Do you come here a lot?" I asked him, hugging my jacket over my body against the cold.

"Not too often. About once a month, maybe. I like to see all the new exhibits. And it reminds me why I do this."

"Ever painted it?" I lifted a brow.

"God yes." He chuckled, looking down at his feet as he walked. "I paint everything."

His eyes drifted up to meet mine and I caught my breath a little, but not in a good way.

Had he painted me? Why did that sit so...weird?

"So you think you'll sell your art for a living?" I rushed, hoping to get off the awkward subject with literally any other topic.

103

"Oh, I don't know. Probably not. I figure it'll be something I do for fun. I'm a double major with business administration. It was my compromise with my parents."

"Wow," I hummed wide-eyed. "That sounds like a lot of work."

He grunted in acknowledgement.

"I did the worst classes my first year. I'm finally getting to the good stuff this year. That's how we ended up in the same class."

Crawling back into his car, the conversation waned for a while, and I just watched the street lights as we sped through the darkened freeway.

"I had a lot of fun tonight," Mark said as he stood with me on the porch of my temporary home.

"Me too. Thanks for asking me out," I said.

Truly, it'd been one of the best dates of my life. To be fair, there wasn't much to compare it to though.

"Do it again next Saturday?" he asked, moving his hand to hold mine between us.

"Sounds good," I agreed, though my voice wavered.

Why did his hand feel so...gross?

Leaning forward a little, I gasped in a breath of shock as I realized he was going in for a kiss.

Oh my God, I wasn't ready!

A sloppy wet kiss landed on my lips and I cringed as he pulled away, all smiles and happiness.

"Thanks for coming out with me," he said, a grin still on his lips. "I'll call you so we can set up a time for next week."

I nodded and waved, watching him roll out of the parking lot before I turned and wiped away the awful kiss.

Everything inside of me wanted to rage and scream and burst into tears at the same time. Why? Why did his touch have to be so...*bad*? Like kissing a brother or a cousin or something... Ick!

The house was still dark when I let myself in and grabbed my camera from off my dresser, then went back into the night. There was a beautiful park not more than a few blocks away, and I needed to get my mind off the amazing night with my unfortunate, friend-zoned date.

When I got to the park, the fountains were still running, but there weren't any ducks on the water since it was so late. But the moon looked amazing against the water and the trees were so beautiful in the faint light.

"Bay?" I heard beside me, that voice sending ripples of goosebumps all over my skin.

I turned and saw Blake a few yards away, leaning against the side of his Mustang.

What was he doing at the park at close to ten at night?

"What the hell are you doing out this late by yourself?" he demanded, moving away from the car to stand beside me on the sidewalk.

"I needed to think," I told him, feeling my hands sweat against the rubber grip of my camera. "Taking pictures helps me think."

"Fuck, woman... It's dangerous at night. You can't just go walking around on your own!"

"Well you're here now," I huffed, turning away from him so I could snap some pictures of the dark horizon.

Adjusting the settings, I lowered the ISO before trying the shot again.

It was a little blurry, so I changed the shutter speed again then placed the camera against the back of a park bench to help stabilize it.

"What are you out here thinking about?" Blake asked after a few minutes of silence.

"How unfair life is." I sighed, then looked over my shoulder at him for a moment before asking. "Why are you here?"

His lips pressed together and I saw him blow out a long breath in the dim light.

"Needed to think," he eventually admitted.

"About what?" I asked, working with the camera again.

"A whole lot of shit you don't need to know about."

"Because I'm too young and dumb?" I raised an eyebrow, but I doubted he saw it in the dark.

"Because I'm really hoping you never have to deal with this shit," he corrected me. "I'm hoping you eventually marry the person you stay with forever and don't find yourself back on the meat market."

"Did you have another date tonight?" I asked, looking at him again and seeing the jean jacket and the white t-shirt he was wearing.

The date clothes I'd gotten him.

"Sure did." He nodded, crossing his arms over his chest, stretching at the sleeves of his jacket until it was probably uncomfortable.

"And?"

"And, I don't want to talk about it."

Just like that he shut me out and moved over a few steps, walking away from me before coming back with a big, heaving sigh.

"You can talk to me," I told him. "I know I'm nineteen. But I understand a lot and I'm not a young, dumb, immature kid like you seem to think I am."

He chewed his lip and nodded.

"I know you're not, Bay. That's kind of the problem." He murmured the words so low I almost missed them.

Turning back to him, he was rubbing at his face and growling in irritation.

"If you won't talk to me," I told him. "Then go stand there so I can use you for the shot."

He looked up at me and I pointed.

Blake moved, facing his back against the water and staring at me as I set up the best shot. But it wasn't right.

"Like this," I said, moving toward him to adjust his shoulders a little and his angle, then grasping his chin and moving his face to a profile.

Stepping away from the heat already building in my limbs by being in his vicinity, I tried to hide behind my lens, taking some beautiful images.

"How much longer are you going to be doing this?" he asked, barely moving his mouth to keep the pose.

"Few more minutes, but move to a more comfortable pose."

Blake moved away from the water and sat on the bench, leaning his forearms against his thighs and turning to look at the moon.

"This ok?" he asked, voice low and sensual.

Those goosebumps were back, traveling through my skin until my nipples were hard and my legs were crossing, trying to relieve the sudden pressure that had built up between them.

Why couldn't Mark do that for me? Why?

Stifling a groan at the injustice of it all, I lifted my camera to take another shot.

Blake

I had no idea how long I was sitting there, letting Bay take shot after shot of me in the dark. I never even asked to see the pictures; I just wanted to make her happy. Like an idiot, I'd do just about anything to see her smiling and happy. If posing like a moron for her did that, then so be it.

"It's getting late," I said eventually.

It's not that I was tired, but the company outdoors was going to get less savory soon and I wanted Bay indoors when that happened.

"I'm done," she said, wrapping her camera around her neck before turning to me again.

She was swathed in knit and denim and peace and I just couldn't keep my fucking eyes off her.

Wrapping herself in her big, tan knit sweater, she made her way toward my car.

"Is it ok if I drive home with you?" she asked.

What the hell kind of question was that?

"Course," I said, going to the side door and throwing it open before closing it up again when she plopped down into the leather seats.

She was the second girl in my car in as many hours, but she was the only one of the two I'd take home with me.

Jenni the masseuse wanted a lay, and I had thought that was what I wanted, too. We'd ended up in my car outside the bar where we met, making out in the front seat. But then Jenni started tearing out of her clothes and I was suddenly flipping out and trying to cover her back up again. To put it nicely, she didn't take it well. She'd cussed me out then slammed the door behind her when she got out of the seat, still pulling down her skirt as she did.

Why I couldn't mindlessly fuck someone to just get my rocks off was beyond me. I was thirty-five and single. I should have been a master of that by this point in my life, but I wasn't. And the thought of meeting some complete stranger on the internet and fucking them in a car just...it didn't sit right. Especially when angelic, wavy hair and stormy eyes were all I saw when I closed my eyes. I was ruined, and I didn't know how to fix whatever was broken in me to be attracted to someone sixteen years younger than myself.

There had to be something wrong with me, right?

Chapter 13

Bay

The house was dark when we got back, just as I'd left it when I'd gotten my camera. But it didn't feel so empty and alone with Blake. His body and his presence filled the place in a way I couldn't quite explain. But it was comforting and it made me feel so...welcome, and just plain *right*.

Blake shrugged off his jacket, slinging it over the back of the couch before turning to me to ask, "How was your date with what's-his-name?"

"It was good." I shrugged. "And I have an amazing new burger and shake shop that I'll definitely be returning to."

I watched Blake work his jaw a little as he nodded.

"That's good," he mumbled, continuing with the nodding.

"I don't think...it's going to work out, though," I told him, feeling my stomach tightening up as he looked over at me, his gaze intense and focused all on me.

"Why not?" The two words rumbled so deep and gritty I was shivering again with the sound of his voice.

"Because kissing him was...it wasn't..."

You.

That's what I wanted to say, anyway. But I couldn't. I just couldn't.

"You kissed him?" he choked out, hands turning into balls at his sides.

"He kissed me," I said, taking a step toward him before taking one of the tightly fisted hands in between mine. "It was like kissing a goldfish."

He didn't smile like I thought he would. No, he just stood there staring like he wanted to kill something or someone.

His hand released a little in mine, gaze moving from the wall to mine, then down to my lips as I flipped his hand in mine, stringing my fingers through his.

"Do you want to...kiss me?" I asked him.

His eyes shot up to mine and that hand fisted again.

"You're fucking nineteen," he gritted against the silent room.

"I'm an adult," I breathed. "A woman. And I liked your kiss."

He sighed and swallowed, something suspiciously like a whine breathing out with his sigh.

"Sixteen years," he forced out, though his hand loosened in mine again.

While I hadn't once considered seducing an older man in my lifetime, I knew that I would never move on until I at least...*tried*. If he didn't want me, then fine. But it really felt like he wanted me just as much as I wanted him, and something as stupid as age shouldn't be the deciding factor in whether two people should explore something.

Now, being housemates...that was a much more logical repellent, but I ignored that too as I took his hand in mine and wrapped it around my waist, stepping in closer to him.

"I'm not an ageist," I said, smiling at him as I lifted myself on my toes, feeling his arm tightening around me until we were chest to chest.

"I'm old enough to be your fucking *dad*," he growled out, head dipping closer to me, then jerking back again, while his jaw worked in anger.

"But you're *not* my dad," I whispered, tentatively lifting a hand to his jaw, feeling the rough texture of his day-old shave.

His head jerked forward again, but he fought it, as if his body was moving without his permission, going after what it wanted without his explicit say so.

"Kiss me," I breathed, pressing harder into him until his head dropped and his mouth met mine with a silent crash of lips, teeth and tongue.

I panted a breath against his lips, then breathed in his intoxicating scent of wood and air through my nose as his other hand moved around me, taking my hips into his grip and squeezing, pulling me even closer as his body bent over mine, making me feel tiny and fragile and strong. Like I was made of tungsten, firm and tough, but ready to shatter with the slightest drop.

His lips worked like magic, tongue grazing mine greedily as we tasted each other like I'd wanted for so long. My skin burned with absolute need. Need that told me that I would burn up and incinerate to ash if he *didn't* touch me, kiss me, *feel me* like my body demanded.

"I need you," I panted against his lips, slipping my hands around his neck and palming the base of his skull. His hands dropped from my hips and gripped my thighs just below my butt, pulling me up against him and wrapping my legs around him.

My body ached, core throbbing as his heat seared through my clothes, scorching me in the best possible way. But I needed his skin, and I needed it immediately.

Blake dropped back against the couch, sitting as he shifted my legs to frame him, knees pressed into the cushions as I straddled his lap.

I might not have been the most experienced woman in the world when it came to men, but I knew what the burning meant, and I knew that I needed more.

Dropping my hands from his neck, I grasped the hem of his white t-shirt and yanked it up to his arms where it stopped.

"Bay," he groaned against my lips, pushing against my hips and thighs as if he was going to push me off his lap.

"*No*," I told him. "Don't you dare."

Hooded eyes met mine, and that's all it took for him to shuck the shirt the rest of the way and press his lips to me again, hand wrapped around my jaw as his kisses intensified from a burn to an inferno.

I gripped my own shirt in my hands, grasping handfuls of it before trying to lift it over my head, my knit sweater still holding on fast to my arms. It took him shoving the sweater off my shoulders before the shirt would pop over my head to land on the floor beside his. Our lips met immediately again, but then his lips trailed down my cheek and jaw and neck until he was devouring my throat and reaching for the bra clasp behind my back. The adorable fumble his fingers made of it made me want to laugh, but I held it back and reached behind myself, undoing it before moving my shoulders forward for the straps to drop off.

It was gone in a flash, lace cups and underwire flying across the room as his fingers met my peaked and puckered nipples.

"Fuck, you are beautiful..." He breathed the words against the skin of my neck, his lips drawing lines up before his teeth bit down on my earlobe, spiking a whimper out of my mouth as shivers spread from my ear to the hot spot between my thighs that suddenly felt so neglected.

"I need you," I told him again, dropping my hands to his pants buckle now, trying to rip it open.

"Fuck," he breathed again, lifting his hips with me on him, a true feat in and of itself before unbuckling his jeans and spreading open the fly.

Red boxer briefs popped into view before his fists wrapped into the fabric and jerked it down. He pulled until he was proudly standing erect in front of me, silk and steel and throbbing desire just inches from where I wanted him the most. His butt hit the couch again as those strong, wide hands gripped my hips, giving me a simple but powerful thrust from below. I felt him even through my jeans.

Stumbling off his lap while ripping at my pants button, I managed to shove them down while he retrieved his wallet from his pocket, then pulled out a foil packet.

Eyes meeting one another's, I paused to watch him put it on all eight thick inches of himself.

"Faster," I told him, kicking off my jeans and panties.

113

But he paused, catching his first glimpse of me naked and standing in front of him. I should have been embarrassed. I should have been worried about my small boobs and round hips, like I had the first time I'd had sex, but I didn't. Not with him looking at me like that, like I was the most beautiful goddess, and he was unworthy.

Straddling his hips again, I felt his hands slide from my hips to my ribs as I settled down, feeling his erection grazing my clit, taunting and teasing. But I was in control, and I could have him when I wanted him. Which was absolutely immediately.

My hand reached down and fingers folded around his length as he hissed in pleasure.

"I need you," I whispered into his ear again just as I met my slit with his cock, dropping onto him as we both groaned at the meeting.

"Fucking *hell*," he moaned as I hit bottom, balls to my ass as we got used to the thickness and tightness of him inside me.

His eyes lifted again, meeting mine with a fire burning hot like blue flames.

My hips shifted and I shut my eyes, feeling that scorching all the way through me as I lifted and dropped on him again, making us both grunt again. Grinding down against his hips, I felt his hands circle my waist as he shifted to thrust himself up so we met in the middle.

DING-DONG

"Dad? You awake?" came Georgia's voice through the door.

Our eyes flew open before zeroing in on the door where my best friend and Blake's daughter stood, waiting to be let in.

"Bay? Anyone up?"

"*FUCK*," Blake growled shoving me over to the side I was already tipping myself over onto.

He was pulling up his pants, condom still on and all before dipping for his shirt.

"Go get dressed," he said, shoving my shirt into my hands and bending back over for my jeans and panties.

"Damn it! Are you going to make me dig out my keys?" the voice said through the door and my eyes opened wider as I began to haul ass, looking for the bra Blake had tossed.

"*Fuck*," he ground out again, pulling his shirt back on before wiping at his lips and shoving his hand through his hair to straighten out his appearance before heading to the door.

Keys scraped the lock just as I saw the buttercup yellow of my bra hiding behind the TV. Snatching it up, I made a naked run toward my bedroom.

I heard Blake sigh heavily from his spot at the door before I disappeared into my room, frantically trying to get my clothes back on.

"Baby girl," Blake murmured, his voice rattling through the house like a deep echo.

He didn't sound like he'd just been balls deep, and I kind of admired him for that.

I, on the other hand, was shaking like a leaf.

"I missed you," I heard him say next, and while I was furious and freaked out that Georgia was around while I was trying to seduce her *dad*...I was just really happy that Blake got to see his daughter. He'd really missed her and I had thought it was so uncool and unfair that she was avoiding him.

"Heard Bay went on a date and thought I'd come around." I heard Georgia's voice through the door while I pulled on my pants, then my shirt.

I looked put together, but I was sure she would see it on me like a tattoo.

"She might still be awake," Blake told her.

Lying.

"Ok. I'll let you go to bed. See you in the morning?" Georgia's voice said as creaky footsteps headed down the hallway.

Georgia threw open my door just as I was reaching for the handle.

"I thought I heard your voice!" I said all excited.

It wasn't quite a lie. I did hear her voice.

"Surprise!" Georgia said, throwing up her hands.

She smelled like beer and weed and I figured at least that whatever strange actions Blake or I would make wouldn't mean much to her in her intoxicated state.

Blake appeared at the door, leaning on the doorframe just as our eyes met. His were still simmering and I felt it from six feet away how much he still wanted me. But nothing would happen with Georgia around.

"I'll leave you girls," he said eventually as Georgia collapsed on my bed.

"Blake," I called, following him out of the room.

"That should have never happened," he whispered so low I barely heard him.

"Yes it should have," I stated, not withering from the look in his eyes. "And I should have been able to know what it feels like when you come inside of me."

He took a sharp breath, panting again as his palm settled over the bulge in his jeans that somehow Georgia had missed.

Framing my hand over his, I slipped my fingers through his until they grazed the denim fly. "Temporary pause. You're not getting away that easily."

I watched a tremor flood down his body with my words, and it just made me even braver. Reaching up, I squeezed the bulge in my hand as the other curled around the back of his head, then I took a blazing kiss from his lips to content myself for the moment.

"Now go to bed," I told him and a smirk inched across his mouth.

He liked it when I was bossy, huh? Luckily for him, I was naturally bossy and I just was able to shove it down most of the time because most people didn't like it. Except around him. For some reason he brought out the animal in me and it was kind of thrilling.

I left him in the hallway before joining Georgia again who was looking sleepy-eyed at her phone.

"So, tell me about your date," she said to me.

"Not much to say." I shrugged at her. "He's nice, but I don't think it'll work out. He kissed me."

She blinked at me, then rolled her wrist as if to tell me to go on.

"It was bad, Georgie. Like, really bad."

Georgia laughed and closed her eyes.

"You should go out with Barrett."

With her only half aware, I wasn't about to argue about it, so I just laid on my bed beside her and pulled up the blanket like we'd done a million times during our friendship.

"Why won't you come back here?" I asked her in a whisper.

"Mom's right about Dad," she said with a yawn. "He's uptight and kills all the joy out of me."

Now, I couldn't explain why I felt outraged by the simple words. Maybe it was because I had gotten to know him and knew he was a good man with a great sense of humor, or if it was because he was just inside me less than ten minutes before, but I wanted to slap the sleepiness off her face for saying something so stupid and untrue.

"You're wrong," I whispered. "He's a good man, and he's funny and..."

I couldn't finish the sentence without giving myself away to her, so I just left the words hanging between us.

She opened one eye and looked at me, one eye and then the other.

"Do you have a crush on my dad?" she asked simply, staring into my eye with one of hers, the other closed again.

I choked on a cough, trying to buy myself some more time before I had to answer.

Georgia grinned, closing both her eyes.

"Dad would do good with someone like you. You like boring, and he could use a lay. Seriously."

Was she...? Did she...? Was Georgia suggesting that I should be with him? Have sex with him?

"Wh-wh-" I started blurting, but she waved her hand at me.

117

"Not you, silly. That'd be gross. Someone that's like, ten years older than you. But I don't blame you for having a crush. Dad's pretty hot."

I bit down hard on my lip as she shifted and shoved her butt into my stomach before sighing and going to sleep.

Not me? Someone *like* me, but not *me*. I rubbed at my eyes, smearing my eyeliner and mascara a bit before closing my eyes, trying desperately to ignore the throbbing emptiness between my legs where Blake *should* have been, whether Georgia approved or not.

I'd just have to wait for the right moment...then I would get what my body craved.

Chapter 14

Bay

I couldn't wait any longer. Honestly, I couldn't. Georgia left not even three minutes before, determined to catch a bus back to campus before her dad was up.

Blake was still asleep in his room, so when the front door closed and Georgia was off in the glowing dawn, I was tracing my footsteps back to my bedroom to take off my clothes.

Dropping them on the floor just inside the door, I paused for a second in the bathroom to use a little toothpaste on my tongue and teeth with my finger before letting myself into Blake's room.

He liked my crazy, and I was going to show him just a little bit more as his eyes opened from slumber.

Crawling onto his bed from the bottom, I slithered under the comforter and straddled his knees, making him jump awake just as my mouth found his morning-hardened cock ready for me.

A palm landed on the back of my head. A deep, guttural growl emanated from his lips when I took him as far as I could on the first thrust. Choking on his girthy length.

"The fuck?" he questioned in that gravelly voice as the blanket tore off us, exposing both our naked bodies to the early morning air.

I smiled, him still in my mouth as our eyes met.

"I thought you were a wet dream," was all he said at first, then his fingers gripped my hair and he lifted his hips, shoving his length practically down my throat.

I gagged and he chuckled, but retreated, pulling my hair gently again until I was chest to chest with him.

"Are you a dream, Bay? 'Cause you sure as hell don't seem real."

119

"Is that a compliment or an insult?" I asked, breathing a ragged little laugh as he grinned languidly at me.

"Depends on how you take it."

"I have a hard time accepting that you already forgot what it felt like to be inside me to think I'm some kind of dream."

This sexy little purr came from his throat as his fingers let go of my hair to take my face in his hand.

"I'll never forget it as long as I live," he said before sitting up to take my bottom lip so softly between his teeth.

"You're really cheesy." I smiled at him and he grinned again before laying back down, stretching and folding his arms behind his head.

"If you have a problem with that, you should probably leave now," he warned, winking at me before his eyes drifted down to my lips and down my neck and shoulders.

"Georgie left," I said, which made him jerk upright again.

"Shit," he grumbled, looking at the clock beside him on the nightstand.

"She said bye and that she'd come back next weekend for dinner or something."

He scrubbed his hands down his face with a nod, then let his eyes settle on me.

"What the hell are we doing, Bay?"

I shook my head, feeling the slightest bit awkward just straddling and laying on him while we were both naked but not actually doing anything.

"I don't know," I admitted. "But it feels..."

"It's idiotic." He shook his head and frowned, pressing a strand of hair that fell out of my top bun behind my ear.

"Why is it idiotic?"

"Because you're practically a child, Bay...For fuck's sake... you're a *teenager*, and I'll be forty soon."

"I don't think nineteen really counts as a teenager." I frowned at him, drawing back until I was sitting up again, exposing my breasts to his greedy eyes that drew there immediately. "And you're not forty. You're thirty-four."

"Thirty-five," he mumbled, lifting a hand to palm one lust-heavy breast.

"But even if I am, and even if you were, we're both adults. Right?"

His eyes barely broke away from my naked chest to meet mine.

"And if we're both adults, who's stopping us from having a little fun? You seem to like me just fine..."

"Liking isn't the problem," he told me, taking the other breast in his second hand with rough intensity.

"I don't see a problem." I hiccuped, my eyes drifting closed involuntarily with the pleasure of it. "Just make sure you wear a condom and we're good."

He gave me a choking laugh before sitting up and hooking his hand behind my head, bringing it to his for a charged kiss. And oh God...what an amazing kiss it was.

"Nobody can know," he whispered against my mouth. "Not Georgia, not your parents, not my friends or yours. Nobody."

"Deal." I nodded as his lips left mine and drifted down my chest for a moment, taking each pebbled nipple into his mouth before shoving me over into the pile of sheets and blankets on his bed.

"This is such a fucking bad idea," he murmured before opening his bedside table and drawing out another little foil package.

"Did you ache as much for me as I did for you?" I breathed, watching his hands slide the rubbery thing down his solid length.

"I took a shower and thought about your tits the whole time," he told me as he plunged into me without warning.

I grunted at the invasion, glad at least that I was really worked up already and wet for him. And wow did he feel good.

"So you'll last a little longer for me?" I teased and he just grinned at me before dropping his face to give me a searing kiss.

"I'll see what I can do," he said, then put his palm over my mouth. "But if you don't stop talking to me like that, I'm going to come way too early. You know I like it when you get all feisty."

I knew. That was why I gave that part of me to him so willingly.

"I'm glad you like it." I moaned, feeling little pulses of pleasure already building up in me as he worked in and out at a furious pace. "Just don't break your hip, old man."

He growled. Like, legitimately growled before pulling out and grabbing me on one side, rolling me over.

"Mess with the bull," he started saying, hooking my thighs and spreading them before he was in me again. "Get the fucking horns."

The first thrust was fine, but the second one had my head bumping hard against the headboard. Doggy style...I kind of liked it. Like, *a lot*.

He was hitting my G-spot with each thrust and I just groaned into it, feeling myself tighten in waves around him as I got ready to come. Blake's hands wrapped around my hips, digging into the fleshy skin as he used me like a battering ram. But then his fingers got involved, slinking around my thigh and belly and between my legs before they hit my clit.

That was all it took before I was a goner.

His pace quickened for just a moment before he was grunting too, his cock throbbing and softening inside me until we were quiet; nothing but heaving breaths.

"Holy shit," he gasped after a moment, pulling out of me and dropping back to the bed with a grunt.

I did the same, sans the 'shit' and watched him remove the soggy condom.

"You sure about this?" he asked me as he dropped it in the trash can on the other side of the bed.

"Isn't it a bit late for that?" I asked back with a grin.

He just stared at me and shook his head.

"You should still date," he told me now. "Even if we're fucking, you should still date guys your age. This won't last."

"I know. And same goes for you. You decide to do this with someone else and this stops. Until then... I get my daddy fantasy and you get your schoolgirl one."

He rubbed at his face with a painful groan.

"Daddy fantasy?" He lifted an eyebrow, rubbing at his temple.

I just laughed and shook my head.

"No. No daddy fantasy. You're just really, *really* hot, and I don't care how old you are."

"Fuck me..." he mumbled, rubbing his face again before getting up and moving toward the shower. "I gotta get shit done today. What are you doing?"

"I have some homework, and I want to work on those pictures from last night. But other than that, nothing."

"Then you're coming with me," he told me before going into his bathroom, turning on the light and fan.

Was I supposed to join him? Was I supposed to go to my own shower?

Suddenly the bravado wheezed out of me like a holey balloon and I slinked right back out of his room the same way I'd snuck in.

What in God's name had I done? What was I thinking?

Everything I'd said was true. That was for sure, but I hadn't really been thinking about how it would matter to everyone else. Georgia would kill me, and Dad would kill Blake. Or, at least he would try. Blake probably weighed two of my dad, one half of that double being pure muscle. That was why nobody could know. I wouldn't tell and neither would he. I'd even keep going on dates until I found someone worthwhile, and would just have the occasional fling with Blake until then. As raw and swollen as I felt between the legs, I still wanted it all over again.

But not right now.

I had to go and get myself ready because evidently I was going to go run some errands with him, and I was going to enjoy every freaking second.

Blake

I honestly had no fucking idea what I was doing. Seriously. Nineteen. Nineteen and sweet and fucking lush as hell... I could almost still feel her hips in my hands, her tits in my mouth and her pussy swallowing me whole.

If I had been ten years younger, I'd be jacking off in the shower to those thoughts of her. But I wasn't. I was a grown man and I *knew* better than to get involved with Bay. She was just so damnably hard to say no to. And when she decided to seduce me, crawling into my bed and taking my dick into her mouth like she owned it...Well, she pretty much won me over right then.

Finishing off my shower, I was only a little disappointed she didn't join me. The other half of me was grateful for some minutes of space to think. Not that space was great. Space meant thinking and thinking meant reminding myself just what a terrible idea all of it was.

And I still didn't care.

I'd beat myself up most of the night after being balls deep in her the first time. Not only was it a bad idea, but when Georgia started knocking on the door, I realized just *why* it was a bad idea. She was my daughter's best friend.

But evidently that didn't matter to Bay whatsoever, because she was initiating yet again by crawling into my bed and sucking me off while I was still sleeping. If it had been anybody else, I'd have gone berserk. But for her, I didn't mind. Hell, I'd take it every single day if I could get it. What guy wouldn't?

It was raining outside when I checked the weather, so I grabbed the jean jacket that Bay had gotten and coupled it with a black Mario shirt and some worn work jeans before heading out to go get my riding boots on.

I needed a few things for our current job, so I was going to take Bay as company.

The thought had me smiling. Female company at the home improvement store? I hadn't ever had it before, but I knew that Bay would not only go along, but she'd *like* it. That was the type of girl she was.

When I got to the kitchen, I made some coffee while she showered in her own bathroom, then leaned on the counter and waited. Unlike my ex, Bay was in and out, heading toward the living room with her hair still in wet strings and fresh-faced with not a lick of makeup to smudge the pretty pink flush on her skin.

"Sorry, I'm hurrying," she told me as she propped herself against a wall and slipped some socks on her feet.

"You're fine," I told her, watching intently as she pulled on tennis shoes to go with the yoga pants and tank top she was wearing.

"Ok! Ready!" she said cheerily, throwing up her hands with a grin as if she was five years old.

Georgia used to do that. Hell, she *still* did that last time I checked. Maybe Bay got it from her.

"Coffee?" I asked, pouring her a cup.

She took it with a smile. After pouring in some creamer, she sipped gingerly.

"Mmm... Breakfast? Or is this breakfast?"

"I'll buy you breakfast when we're done," I told her, moving toward the door to grab my truck keys.

She hurried and gulped her drink before following me out.

"So, what do we need to get?" she asked as she climbed up into my truck.

It smelled like metal and wood and stale, lingering fast food in the cab. I should probably get it detailed...

"Just getting some things for the project. The kitchen and bathrooms need some fixtures and hardware."

Bay picked up my bright orange hard hat and stared at it.

"My dad does construction," she said after a minute, staring at the thing. "His hat is white."

"What does he do?" I asked, reaching over to grab her seatbelt and click it in around her hips since she seemed to have forgotten all about it.

"He's an electrician."

She was still staring at the hard hat in her hands, tears spilling down her cheeks.

"Hey, why are you crying?" I asked her, wiping up the drops.

"Oh, sorry. I just miss my parents. I haven't ever been away from them this long, you know?"

I nodded.

Of course I knew what that was like. I moved out of my house when I was sixteen years old. Homeless and staying on a friend's couch, I started working construction full time. No college. No high school diploma. I'd worked my way up in the field until I soaked up what knowledge I could get. My training was on-the-job, and it taught me everything I needed to know. I missed my parents so much back then, especially when I had a new baby and a girlfriend/baby mama I didn't get along with, but they'd disowned me for knocking up a girl, so I went about my own life without them.

"I know how you feel," I told her. "But you're a dozen hours away. You get to see them again whenever you want. You going home for fall break?"

She smiled and nodded, wiping up her cheeks. "Yep. Me and Georgia are supposed to go back for Thanksgiving."

God, she's so young...

"That's good," I agreed, even though that meant that *I* was going to be alone for the holiday. That was nothing new though.

"What are you going to be doing?" she asked. "If Georgia's going to be with Tiffany..."

I shuddered at the name, and Bay laughed at me.

"I'll be here." I shrugged.

It was quiet for a minute as we got onto the I-5.

"You should come back," she told me after some time of just listening to the engine humming in the background.

127

"Come back where?" I grunted. "Vegas?"

"Yeah, I mean, if anything you can have dinner with my family. I'm sure you wouldn't want to go with Georgia."

I let out a loud laugh and Bay grinned.

"Nope, rather not see the ex, thanks," I told her, sending a sideways glance her way to emphasize just how sarcastic I was being.

"Don't want to spend your holiday with Tiffany?" She winked at me and I was caught between wanting to scoff and grin at the girl.

"Yeah. Pretty sure they save that kind of torture for terrorists and the like. I'd take waterboarding any day over Thanksgiving with Georgie's mom."

"That bad, huh?"

"You've got no fucking clue," I mumbled, rolling my eyes. "I'm sure she's been nice to you and everything, so I'll reserve my comments."

"I'd like to know what it was like for you," she said in a soft voice, her hand coming down to settle on my thigh.

Somehow the touch shocked me. I was balls deep in her literally *hours* ago, but her hand on my thigh in the car was somehow so much more intimate.

"I really don't think you do," I said, shaking my head as I took my exit on the freeway. "Besides, I don't want to ruin anything with you guys. My issues with her are just that. They're *mine.* And it's all in the past, so let's let it stay buried there."

"But it's obviously not in the past if you still feel so strongly about it."

"It's in the past. Believe me. Besides, you're the one who brought up Thanksgiving in Vegas."

"Because I want you to come home with me."

My throat swelled instantly, because those words she said were followed up with a silent 'to meet my parents'.

"I'm sure they'd like to meet you. They took a chance on sending me to your house and everything, and it'll make them feel better if they get to know you."

Well, that made sense. I would feel the same.

"I don't know. It just sounds like it'd be a whole fuckload of awkward. Especially after last night..."

"And this morning," she added, grinning. "You just can't tell them that Georgie moved out. They don't exactly know about that yet."

"The hell, Bay?" I asked, pulling into a parking spot at the home improvement store. "Why didn't you tell them?"

"Because then I'd have to admit that I'm living alone with a virile man who I'm attracted to, who they don't know."

"Virile?" I lifted an eyebrow and she winked before opening her door and sliding out with the clink of her seatbelt clip hitting the metal of the car chassis.

"I could think of a few other adjectives if you'd like." She giggled, just her shoulders and head showed above the bed of my truck as we both walked around it.

"What the hell happened to you, Bay? You went from this little shy butterfly to a fucking killer bee."

"I like to think of myself more as a praying mantis," she said, considering her thoughts as she leaned her perky little ass against the back bumper of my truck. "Generally pretty harmless and nice to have around, but I have a snap and a bite when I need to."

Yeah, I could agree with that.

"Besides. I thought you didn't mind it when I was feisty."

I grinned and nodded.

"You won't hear me complaining," I said simply.

"Good."

Just like that, with the simple word, she swung forward and planted a kiss on my lips. In the middle of the parking lot. Where anyone could see us.

And yet I still couldn't say no.

Accepting her kiss eagerly, I drew what I could from her lips before she backed away with this sexy little come-hither look that threatened to tent my pants, biting her lip with a grin and looking at me through her surprisingly dark lashes.

"You're going to be the death of me," I told her, pressing my hand into the small of her back to get her walking so I didn't stare at her beautiful face any longer.

Didn't stop me from dropping my hand a little and squeezing that perky ass in one of my calloused hands.

She shrieked and giggled, then bumped me with her hip before accepting a decent distance between us as we went through the front door.

"So, what do you need?"

Now, that was a fucking loaded question.

Chapter 15

Bay

"What do I need?" he asked with a chuckle. "A little more of those yoga pants while you pick Cheerios up off the floor."

I burst out laughing, meeting his smile with one of my own.

"But while we're here, I need those fixtures and hardware for the bathrooms."

"Right, I already forgot."

"I tend to do that to women," he said with a sigh, as if it was a fact he was resigned to.

"Are you flirting with me, Blake?"

"You started it," he countered.

"I don't mind. I think it's cute, actually."

"Cute that an old guy like me can still flirt?" he asked, lifting one dark brow.

"Cute that you like me enough to bother flirting," I corrected him.

"Every woman is worth flirting with."

"Do you flirt with all of us, then?" I lifted an eyebrow right back at him.

"Just the ones I like." He winked before grinning then shoved his cart forward down the aisle.

"So, I need twenty-eight pulls and sixteen knobs. Help a brother out, huh?"

We stood there, staring at the wall of cabinet knobs and pulls for a couple seconds before I started pointing to some.

"Is it a modern house or more traditional? Country?"

"Modern. Steel, tile, white kitchen and bathrooms."

"So you want something to match it then. I'm guessing brushed steel instead of chrome."

He nodded, looking impressed.

"We could go the bar route, and that's pretty contemporary, but it might not be edgy enough if the entire place is super modern." I hummed as I looked at the choices. "Any curvature or industrial influences?"

"You secretly a designer or something?" he asked with a chuckle.

"It might be a talent and an interest of mine. Besides, as a photographer, you have to look at the whole picture with both still life and with live models. One thing doesn't fit, and the whole picture looks wrong."

He nodded thoughtfully before saying, "It's all pretty hard edges, but there's some small things, like the tub is rounded upstairs similar to an old clawfoot but more modern. And there's an arch in the entry."

"What about this?" I asked, pointing to a knob that had what looked like metal wire as the handle. "Too industrial?"

"Yeah, probably."

"This?"

I was pointing to something that just looked like a bent piece of metal that would act as the pull.

He hummed again, picking one out of the little receptacle and turned it around in his hands.

"Good choice," he told me. Then dug back in for some more.

"Are you building the home?" I asked him.

Dumb question.

"Yep. Me and my guys."

"Shouldn't the buyers be the one picking out this stuff?" I asked.

"The people buying the home can't be bothered," he said with a shrug, dumping the things into the cart. "They're out of state most of the time, so we talk over the phone and email, and I get samples of what they like here and there so I keep to their personal style. But creativity is up to me, which is pretty fucking scary because I'm not very creative with this type of shit."

"That's why you have me," I pinched his cheek and pulled a matching knob. "How many of these?"

"Sixteen," he said, rubbing his rough cheek with a silly grin.

I got what we needed and put those in the cart as well so we could move on.

Fixtures were next, so we strolled that way.

"So you're an art major, right?" Blake asked as we walked.

"Right." I nodded.

"How did you get a scholarship for art?"

"It wasn't easy," I admitted. "I entered a contest and after a few months of it all, I made it. The finals came and I got it. The competition was really tough, but somehow I managed."

"I've seen what you did with me, and I can tell you that you've got talent. I've never taken a good picture. No joke."

"Oh give me a break," I scoffed at him.

"I'm not even joking. My buddies used to make fun of me in Vegas because I *cannot* take good pictures. It's always double chins or blinking or something. They just always turn out bad."

Was that why I never saw pictures of him even though I'd been friends with Georgia so long?

"I have to see this. Do you understand that? I have to see this strange curse you're saying you have."

"Shit..." He shook his head, chuckling.

When we arrived at the faucets, we chose an industrial looking sprayer for the kitchen that the owner had requested, and for the bathroom sinks we got some that looked like literal pipes coming out of the wall. Shower and tub fixtures were similar, same as the other hooks and bars and toilet paper holders.

"Think that's it," Blake said as he rifled through the cart again. "If it's not, I'll be back tomorrow."

"You almost done with the house then?" I asked as we got in line at the register. "If you're putting the final touches on, you must be almost done."

"Getting close." He nodded. "Finishing up floors too, and gotta get the countertops in when they eventually get here. Our

133

supplier is normally pretty good, but getting them on the phone on this project has been a bitch."

Side eyeing me, he paused.

"What?" I asked.

"You don't want to hear all this. Sorry."

The apology actually made me mad.

"Don't apologize for talking about yourself and your life. Ever."

A little smile tipped his lips before his hand found mine, giving it a quick little squeeze.

We went through line without any more talking, then loaded everything into the truck before Blake asked me what I wanted for breakfast.

"Uh...food?" was my awesome answer.

"Food?" he asked back.

"I like all kinds of places and things. Take your pick."

He checked his phone before nodding.

"Ok, get in. We're going to get pancakes the size of your face."

Face-sized pancakes? I could get on board with that.

"Deal!" I called as I opened the passenger door.

He grabbed the door from me, helped me into the lifted cab, then closed it behind me when I was settled inside like it was no big deal.

What a gentleman.

The little diner was tucked in some grungy little strip mall, but inside it was busy. Servers bustled around, dropping massive plates in front of people with pancakes or waffles and all kinds of other breakfast things on them.

"Hey honey," an older woman said to Blake before blinking, surprised to see me. "This ain't my little Georgie pie."

"Nope. This is Bay," was all he said.

"Well honey, I think this is a record day! Blake ain't never come in here with someone other than our little Georgie pie!

Always sits right there all lonesome in the corner that nobody else wants."

"You got a problem with doing your job and getting me some menus and a table, Donna?"

She just laughed at Blake and his playful grin before waving us after her.

"Here you go honey. You can enjoy your breakfast with your sweet little thing in peace. I'll be back soon with your OJ. What do you want to drink, sugar?"

The question was aimed at me, so I just went with the flow, trying not to show my embarrassment of being called Blake's 'sweet little thing'.

"Orange juice sounds good to me," I told her and she nodded before wandering off.

Blake looked at me with this expression of amusement mixed with annoyance and embarrassment. It was obvious that she knew him well enough to know his name, so he must have been a regular.

"Donna is a..." he started, but then shook his head and ran his hands through his hair.

"A character?" I asked, eyebrow raising.

He just nodded, chuckling a little and rubbing his hands down his face.

"Ok, here you go. And coffee."

We both took the mugs she offered, and set them between us with the orange juice on the tray.

"Know what you want?"

"Uh..." I mumbled, quickly opening the menu to see what they had.

"Give us a minute, won't you?" Blake asked her and she just nodded before strolling away to fill more coffee cups.

"What's good here?" I asked him.

"Other than the pancakes?" he asked. "They make good sandwiches and you can't go wrong with bacon, sausage, eggs and hashbrowns."

"Oh my God...am I a linebacker or something?" I asked, laughing while he looked at me expectantly.

"Hell no. You'd get cut immediately. You're too scrawny."

"Scrawny?" I asked, trying to look offended.

"For a linebacker? Yeah. You'd need at least another hundred pounds."

We both laughed at the ridiculousness of the conversation.

"You're welcome that I am *not* a linebacker," I told him, narrowing my eyes on him with a flirty smirk.

"Yeah, I guess that would make things harder, huh?" he said, smirking right back.

"I thought things were plenty hard this morning." I bit my lip in anticipation of what he'd say to my innuendo.

"Fuck, Bay," he murmured, pressing his finger over his lips to shush me. "You trying to kill me?"

I just laughed as he wiggled in his seat, his hand dropping between his thighs to shift things around.

"Ya ready?" Donna asked, approaching our table again.

"You ready, Bay?" Blake asked me.

"I am." I nodded, feeling a flash of naughty fill me to the brim. "Blake said those pancakes are the best, so I'll get one of those with some over-easy eggs, hash browns, and sausage. Lots of sausage. Biggest sausage you have."

Blake snorted while drinking his orange juice, groaning when the acidic drink hit his nose.

Donna looked at me like I was nuts, then made a note on her paper before asking Blake if he wanted his normal.

He nodded, reaching for a napkin for his orange juice-dripping nose. I laughed, watching him as he tried to get rid of the burn of laughing up the drink.

"What the *hell* was that?" he asked, wiggling his nose to regain normal functioning again.

"What? I like sausage. Is that a crime?"

He gave me this sexy look of knowing, like he was well aware of what I was alluding to.

"You're trying to get me in trouble. I get it," he said, pushing aside his wrinkled napkin.

"Define trouble?" I asked and he just smirked again, shaking his head at me.

When Donna got back, she placed two plates in front of Blake. One with a massive pancake on it, the other with eggs, hashbrowns and a mixture of sausage and bacon. The man was going to eat like a linebacker for the both of us.

Next was my pancake, also bigger than my head, then the rest of my breakfast. And right there on the plate rolling around were two big sausages, either bratwurst or Italian.

"Cook said that's the biggest one we had," Donna told me, still eyeing me like I might be a psycho.

Hell, maybe I was.

Blake was laughing again, those belly laughs that made my stomach flutter and my skin prickle.

Walking away, I heard Donna mumble about giant sausages, which made Blake and I burst into laughter again.

"You going to actually eat those?" Blake asked when he calmed enough to talk.

"Uh, probably not," I said, shaking my head. "I don't usually let sausage that big past my throat."

His eyes sparkled in humor as he shook his head again, digging into his pancake.

I did the same, generously scooping the melty whipped cream mountain from the center into my mouth.

"Oh my God... What's better than a mouthful of cream, right?" I mumbled around the whipped cream.

"Oh God..." he murmured to himself, covering his face with one hand, head shaking again.

I just laughed, feeling naughty and brilliant and funny. That smile on his face was everything. Who cared if I had to make a fool of myself to get it?

Conversation mostly stopped as we ate. While the food was good, it was just nice to be with him, make him smile and laugh.

When Donna came back, we were done with the pancakes and most of the rest of the food, minus the big ol' sausages. She put her hands on her hips, looked at the sausages, then at me, then back and forth with a look telling me that I'd annoyed the hell out of her by not eating the specially made meat.

"I was too full," I told her, fluttering my eyelashes as nicely as I could to pull off the innocent kid look.

Blake grunted and held out some cash for her.

"Thanks Donna," he told her.

"Did you like everything else?" she asked us.

"It was so good, I even licked the rim," I told her and Blake's eyes popped open in shock, then he was smothering a laugh again.

"You know, we don't mind plate lickers here," she said, sounding pleased. "It's a compliment to the chef!"

"That it is!" I agreed, trying to hide my satisfied grin.

"You two have a nice day," she told us as she started to walk away. "And say hello to your little peach for me!"

"Will do," Blake called after her, then turned to me and shook his head again, like he couldn't believe I'd said that, and in front of Donna no less.

"Any more errands?" I asked him as I stood, stretching with a full belly.

"Nope. Ready to go home," he said, shoving his hands in his pockets as we headed out of the diner.

We got to the car and I sat back, luxuriating in the fat leather seats of his truck as we headed out of the parking lot.

It was silent in the car, and I felt it build up with tension the closer we got to home. Getting out of the car, I followed him, a few steps behind as he unlocked and opened the door, waving me in.

"Guess you should probably get to that homework, huh?" Blake said, suddenly just standing there awkward and adorable. "Thanks for going out with me today. Getting that kind of shit isn't usually so... provocative."

I hummed in agreement, taking a step toward him.

He watched me with his sharp gaze as I got closer, his breathing picking up just like mine.

"What're you doing, Bay?" he asked in a soft, low voice.

"Whatever I want to do," I whispered back, feeling my bravado from the diner disappearing as uncertainty eased back in.

Did he still want me? Was it too soon? I wanted him so much and I wanted to try so many things but...

His hand reached out, cupped my skull and dragged my head closer before he was kissing me again.

I gasped against his lips, but opened up for his tongue as it touched mine tentatively.

"I've been hard since you started talking about that fucking sausage," he breathed against my lips. "Do you have any idea what that does to a man?"

"I've never been with a *man* besides you," I breathed back. "So no. What does it do?"

His other hand slid off my cheek and down my shoulder and arm until my palm was cupped in his. He took my wrist, pressing it firmly to his crotch and he was hard, his jeans barely holding back his erection.

I moaned into his mouth as my fingers curled around him, drawing a moan from his own throat.

My fingers left his crotch to grip the button of his jeans right above. He helped a little, flicking it open before grabbing my cheeks with both hands, concentrating on our kiss. That's not what I had in mind, though.

"I want to try..." My voice choked as I went to my knees in front of him.

"What're you—"

I cut him off by unzipping, then pulling his jeans down. His fingers dug into the hair at the top of my head, tangling in the pale waves.

"I want to try this," I managed, pressing my hand against the warm bulge in his boxer briefs.

139

He was wearing the new ones I got him. I wasn't sure why I loved it so much, but I did.

"You never—?" He started to question me, but then I was yanking down the black underwear, leaving him bobbing and hot and needy right in front of my face.

But something else caught my eye, too.

"What is this?" I asked, lifting my hand to his right hip where a picture of a small peach was tattooed into his skin.

"Tell you later," was his response.

I could live with that.

"You never done this before?" he asked me, his voice sounding strained as he stayed so very still.

"No. Except this morning," I admitted, wrapping my hand around his velvety length. "Doesn't seem too hard though."

I dipped my head and took him down to where my fist wrapped around him, and he let out a strangled little groan. It was *empowering*.

Earlier in the morning, I'd had him in my mouth, but I was so concerned about seduction that I hadn't stopped to feel it, to taste him. He tasted a little salty and strange, but I didn't really mind it. The musky scent around him breathed into my lungs like a drug as I wrapped my tongue around him next, exploring every ridge and vein.

"*Fuck!*" He groaned, jaw clenched as I took my sweet time getting acquainted with his cock.

I moved my head a little, taking him in and out of my lips until his hand tightened on my hair, stopping me.

"Grip it hard, right here," he managed to say, wrapping his hand around mine and applying sturdy pressure until I felt like I might hurt him, we were squeezing so hard. "And move your hand."

He dragged my hand back, then thrust it forward again until we were basically punching him in the pelvis. Blake grunted, but it didn't sound like he was displeased with the motion, so I did it again, his hand still guiding mine.

"Is this ok?" I asked, my mouth still around him.

"It's good, babe." He grunted. "Keep moving your tongue."

So I did.

After a few more strokes he dropped his hand from mine and slid it into my hair with the other, pulling so hard it hurt a little, but I didn't want him to stop. I felt gentle little pulls on my hair, urging my head forward, further and further until I was letting my hand go to take him further, gagging myself again.

"Don't hurt yourself," he murmured, his voice now stuck somewhere between painful torture and blissed-out relaxation.

I just smiled and paused to circle the ring of his head with my tongue, which made him moan all over again. My hand joined in movement again and between it and my mouth, I managed to find some sort of rhythm so I could put my other hand into action too. Curious, I pressed the back of my fingers against his scrotum, pressing gently over the coarse hair there. His grip tightened in my hair again and his eyes opened just a little to watch.

"Not too hard," he told me, letting go of my hair with one hand to stroke my cheek. "Soft, firm pressure. Play with 'em but don't pull too hard."

Pull? Play?

Cupping him in my palm, I felt the pair of balls I knew were there, but had never had the chance to really touch before. It was incredible and alien at the same time.

"Mhmm..." he hummed in confirmation that I was doing ok.

Not a minute later between my hand gripping him, the other playing with his balls, and my mouth thrusting around his shaft, he warned me with a rough voice, "I'm gonna come, babe."

Good. I wanted it all.

He tried to pull my head back, but I wouldn't let him. I tore his hand from my hair and gripped it in mine as he growled his release. Cock bobbing in my mouth, throbbing in waves, I felt his salty cum hit the back of my tongue. While not necessarily pleasant, it wasn't bad either. I could get used to it if that was how amazing it felt to watch him come completely apart under my ministration.

"Fucking hell," he gasped, finally breathing after the roar that escaped his lips.

Mouthful of salty cum, I wasn't sure what to do with it. Swallow? Spit? Would it offend him if I spit it out?

"Your turn," he rumbled at me.

Gulp.

Well, I guess swallowing it is.

"My turn?" I squeaked and the grin that splayed his lips was nothing short of predacious.

He helped me up, hands gripping my hips as he maneuvered me through the kitchen and around until I was ass-first against the dining room table.

"Relax," he said, slipping his fingers into my yoga pants and pulling them down, inch by stretchy inch.

All of a sudden I could hardly breathe as his fingers got my feet out of my shoes and the leg holes of my pants, then it was just my tank top and my panties left to cover me up.

"Ok?" he asked for confirmation, and I just nodded like an idiot.

His hands wrapped around my thighs just under my butt and he lifted me up, holding us chest to chest for a moment. My arms curled around him instantly, my mouth finding his as he settled me down on the edge of the table, giving me a few good kisses before releasing me and pulling off his pants the rest of the way.

Oh, ok. This I could handle. On the table though? Whatever. I just wanted him inside me.

His boxers were back over his softened erection, and it still looked pretty flaccid to me. How was this going to work?

But then, with his pants and boots off, nothing but those cute little underwear on his hips, he knelt again while dragging off my panties in the process. That left me and my bare ass on the table.

Keeping my eyes connected to him, he kissed the inside of my thigh as the panties came off my last ankle and dropped to the floor.

Oh my God... Nope, he was doing what I thought he was doing.

He dragged me further down the table and lifted one knee over his shoulder, and then the other before his mouth was right there, hot breath drifting across my clit.

That same sort of strangled noise was coming out of *my* mouth now as his lips kissed me *down there*.

OhGodohGodohGod...

My back weakened as he kept tasting me, and I had to brace myself with one hand in his hair and the other gripping the edge of the table to keep from collapsing completely.

God it felt so good...

"Feet on my shoulders," he murmured against my crotch.

Feet. Shoulders. Got it.

I managed, and it opened me up spread eagle as my palms hit the tabletop behind me, propping me up as he started really digging in. The hot, thrumming pressure was starting to build up, and I let only little noises fall past my lips for him so he knew how much I loved it. Then he paused for just a moment. Then—OH GOD!

His fingers joined the party and his lips and tongue focused in on my clit just as his other hand reached up and pulled on the neck of my tank. One breast broke loose and he had it in his grasp within a moment, my nipple trapped in strong fingers that were pinching the hell out of it. It felt like fireworks were bursting inside my head at the same time some fiery inferno was lit inside my belly. It was so good that it *hurt*, and then I was coming around his fingers.

Blake moaned with me the moment I started to throb around him, and the vibrations of it kept the orgasm flowing, something harsh and brilliant and blinding as I panted his name over and over until the best was over and the gentler waves settled in around me.

"Wow..." I breathed and he softened the pressure, looking up at me. "I've been missing out on *that* all this time?"

He grinned, chuckling as he gave me a final lick before moving his head out from between my legs again. His lips met mine with gentle fervor, and I accepted a kiss that tasted like...well me, I assumed. And it was pretty good, all mixed up on his tongue.

Strong hands circled me, gripping my thighs again so he could pull me against himself while lifting me and moving me toward the bedrooms.

When we got to his bed, he lowered me so softly onto the mattress that it felt more like a cloud than a stack of springs, foam and fabric. Reaching over I pulled the hip of his boxer briefs and they came down a little; just enough to expose his hardened length again.

Now that was a fast recovery.

His mouth was back on me, leaving me only for a second to reach into his bedside drawer to get out a condom. It took talent to kiss me and roll the thing on at the same time, but maybe that was a perk of doing an older man. There were quite a few perks, it would seem.

His cock was at my entrance in moments, and with his tongue still in my mouth, I pulled his hips until he was inside me, filling me almost to bursting.

"Fuck me," I breathed between kisses.

So he did.

He hiked up one of my knees in his hands, planted his on either side of my hips, and thrust into me so hard the entire bed jostled, hitting the wall with a bang and a squeak. It was pure heaven.

My lips couldn't keep up anymore, so his mouth descended to my neck as he continued, abusing my swollen pussy until I was coming again, the orgasm rolling off my already oversensitized clit as it ground against him with each drive of his hips.

I yelled this time, unable to hold it back two times in one afternoon, and it seemed to make him go mad. All of a sudden he was out of sync, his rhythm shot as he went from urgency to desperation, then his shout of ecstasy followed on the tail end of mine as he thrust one, two more times then went still.

We panted, breathing heavy and shallow as we tried to catch our breath again.

How? *HOW* did Tiffany let this man go? For the sex alone, my *GOD*.

My hand lifted and planted on his cheek as his chest heaved above me.

"You can do that anytime," I told him, and he just grinned and laughed breathlessly at me.

"Ditto," was all he said back, which made me laugh too.

College boys were going to seem like infants after this man. How was I supposed to deal with that? By seducing my best friend's dad, I might have just fucked myself forever.

But it felt so *good*.

Chapter 16

Bay

"So, the peach," I said quietly, my cheek planted on Blake's chest as we laid there, sweaty, but finally with our wind back.

He pressed his hand to his face and groaned.

"I know it's cheesy as hell. It didn't seem cheesy at the time," he told me, pulling the sheets higher over his hips.

"What is it?" I asked yet again in little more than a whisper.

"When Georgia was born," he said in his own quiet voice, "I got this. 'Cause she's my little Georgia peach."

I bit my lip so I wouldn't laugh.

Drawing the sheet down again, I got another eyeful of the golf ball-sized tattoo there and just grinned.

"You are such a cheesy little romantic," I told him. "You know how much I love that?"

"Hopefully more than every other woman who's laughed at it."

"I'm not every other woman, Blake."

He sobered and looked up at me, his back flat on the bed while I leaned over him on my elbow.

"I know," he agreed, pressing my hair behind my ear.

"To be honest, I'm not sure how I missed this little gem the first time."

"We were a little busy," he said, a half smile curving his lips up.

My head dropped to his chest again and I pressed my hand against his firm belly, feeling every ridge of his abs beneath my fingers.

"Thank you," I whispered against his skin.

"For what?" he asked, seeming confused.

"For being patient and talking to me, and explaining stuff. For not making fun of *me* because I'm a nineteen year old that doesn't know much about sex."

He heaved a sigh before stroking his fingers through my hair.

"Well, if that statement doesn't make me feel old..."

I just smiled.

"How was it though? For reals. I want to know the truth. Am I bad at it?"

He just shook his head and chuckled.

"No babe. You're a born natural. Don't you remember how fast you got me off?"

"Really?" I asked with a grin.

"Mhmm," he hummed.

"Sure that wasn't just your old man libido getting the best of you?"

"You little brat!" he called out with a laugh as I lunged away from him on the bed.

It was hopeless though; he caught me around the ribs instantly and pressed me down into the mattress before administering a soft, seductive kiss to my mouth.

"Try any boy your age and you'll be able to see what a ridiculous question that was," he whispered against my lips.

My lips parted in anticipation of another kiss, but it didn't come. Instead he threw his legs over the side of the bed and pulled on his underwear again.

"Where are you going?"

"Need a smoke. Be back in ten."

He grabbed a couple things out of some clothes on the floor, then headed toward the door without looking back.

Blake needed some time, so I'd give it to him. To be honest, *I* needed some time to process what had just happened between us, too. Yeah, a little space would be good. But not too much.

147

Blake

Fucking *hell...* That girl was destroying my mind. The moment she got on her knees in front of me, bye bye brain. It just flew out the fucking window along with all my common sense. Her plump lips, innocent eyes, soft breasts, sweet cunt...fuck... *All of her*, basically. Every last hair on her head called to me like a siren. I was weak toward her, and I wasn't entirely sure it was a bad thing.

But nineteen... Yeah, that was a bad thing.

I stuck my cigarette in my mouth and lit it quickly to calm my nerves. Not that my nerves were shot or anything after two fucking *amazing* orgasms, but I needed to create some space, because I was feeling some things towards her that I shouldn't be.

Bay had her whole life ahead of her. She was smart, talented, sweet with a streak of bold that would get her as far as she wanted to go in her career. And yet, all I could think of when I was savoring her taste on my lips was that I could do it forever. Hers could honestly be the last cunt I ever saw or tasted or filled and I'd be ok with that.

That was the problem.

The bitter smoke of my cigarette filled my lungs like a welcome, suffocating hug. It took the flavor of her out of my mouth, but with each lungful I was able to calm my blood and think a little more logically. Think about how old she was, about where she was in life as opposed to where I was; about how the world would look on something like what we had started together.

Nobody would care how we got along. Nobody would care that we had the same kind of humor or that where her talents ended, mine began. Nobody would give a single shit that we fit together like two pieces of a puzzle because I was born in a different decade and already had a kid her age. I would be looked on as a pervert, not a man who was falling in complete lust with a girl who should have been off limits.

No, that wasn't right. Falling in lust was what we'd done in bed when I was inside her. When I looked into her eyes, that wasn't lust. It was something indiscernible to me that made no sense, and I couldn't put my finger on just what it was. Which scared the ever living shit out of me. Because if I didn't know what it was, then it wasn't lust. And if it wasn't lust, it had to be love. How that was possible, I couldn't explain. Still didn't change the facts, though.

Drawing another lungful of smoke, I closed my eyes and leaned on the railing, feeling a drop of water falling on my back. Then another, and another.

Soon it was sprinkling, but I still stood there.

She'd seen my tattoo and didn't laugh. She called me a romantic. She looked at me like I was a god. She was smart mouthed, headstrong, but soft and gentle when she needed to be. The girl was a conundrum and I wanted to unravel every last contradiction living inside of her. But that would take years, and I had months, at most. Weeks, more likely, since her parents would no doubt tell her to return home when they found out she was fucking her friend's dad. I would kill my friend if they'd gone after Georgia. No doubt. And yet there I was. That was exactly the situation I found myself in.

"You ok?" I heard that soft voice weave its velvet tendrils around me and I sank into it instantly, even though I knew I shouldn't.

"Yeah, just needed…"

"Some space?" she asked, perceptive as ever.

"Yeah," I agreed, nodding hesitantly.

"Want me to go back in?" she asked in nothing but a whisper.

I just shook my head and took another draw.

"I should, but I don't," I admitted.

A soft hand touched my back as she approached, her hair already laying in sheets of shiny gold as it continued to get even wetter by the second in the weather.

"You shouldn't be in the rain," I told her, looking up into her eyes just then, and the words choked off in my throat.

Her skin glowed and her eyes shone bright and blue and happy as she stared back at me with a little smile on her face.

"Neither should you."

"I'm used to it."

"You're basically naked."

"So are you."

She grinned and pulled her tank top up a little, splitting a line of pale flesh between the hem and where her panties began.

"Do you regret me?"

What the hell kind of question was that?

"Regret you?" I asked with a scoff.

"Today, I mean. Do you regret being with me?"

I turned to her and saw the vulnerable expression she wore, full of uncertainty and worry. And it made her the strongest woman I ever knew.

"No, I don't regret you, Bay. Tiffany, maybe, but not you."

She gave a weak smile but didn't look reassured.

"I don't want to pressure you or anything..."

I couldn't help it. I laughed.

"What the hell are you laughing about?" she demanded, freeing some of that spit and fire that I loved so much.

"I'm laughing," I huffed out, trying to stop my laughing even though her words were so ridiculously stupid. "Because you honestly think that you pressured me into doing anything with you. I'm not a soft-headed idiot, Bay. I fucked you because I really, *really* wanted to."

She sighed and leaned on the rail beside me.

"Ok. So if that's the case, why are you out here sulking?"

Rolling my eyes, I gave myself a moment to think of the right words. "Because now the whole dating thing is paltry compared to this. And somehow I'm going to have to go back to it when you're ready to move on."

She bit her lip, wiping some rain from her face.

"Ready to move on?" she asked quietly. "Who says I'll be ready to move on?"

"You'll get tired of me eventually," I whispered right back.

"I don't see how that's possible. Just for the sex alone you're quite the catch."

I huffed a laugh again before tossing my cigarette stub into the little bucket of sand I kept on the tiny porch.

"Glad there's one reason to keep me around." My fingers already itched for another smoke.

"Then there's the funny side," she mused out loud, turning so her back was against the railing, elbow propped behind her. "I mean, you trying to be funny is really freaking funny!"

I eyed her with a frown and she grinned, but still didn't look at me.

"And there's the quiet side that just radiates warmth and safety without even having to say a word. Not to mention the manly, sexy side that is half asshole and half confidence."

I couldn't help another smile.

Did she really feel that way about me?

"Then there's the fatherly side of you that worries over all the little things and the big things. The side that cares if I'm out late at night. The protective side, I guess."

I moved toward her and lifted my hand to her cheek.

"What about the part that really loves your cooking?" I asked, our noses practically touching.

"Every man has that part. That's not particularly special."

The quirk of her eyebrow had me grinning. Mostly because she wasn't wrong about that.

"Fair enough," I murmured, pressing my lips to hers for a kiss.

Well, I kissed her until she pushed me away, sputtering.

"You taste like ashes!" she said, gagging.

Well, that's a real self-esteem booster, watching someone gag after kissing them.

"I *was* just smoking," I told her, pulling away.

"I'll tell you what," she said, sticking her tongue out in distaste. "Next time you have the urge to smoke, come kiss me instead."

"I'll be kissing you all hours of the day and night, babe." I smirked.

Bay just smirked back and gave me this challenging look. Daring me.

"Fine. Just brush your teeth first."

"As you wish," I said, pushing off the railing to go do just that.

"Do you really regret her?" Bay asked suddenly, following me as I headed toward my bedroom.

"Who?"

"Tiffany. Your ex-wife."

Oh fuck it all... so we were having *that* conversation.

"Yes and no," was all I managed to get out.

"No because of Georgia?" she inquired, sticking her nose where it didn't belong.

"And because I wouldn't be where I am now if I hadn't dealt with all her bullshit. And yes because she's a fucking nightmare. Always has been, always will be. There's a Goddamn reason she's still single."

"But you're still single."

I paused in my bathroom doorway and turned back to her.

"Yeah, thanks for pointing that out for me," I said sarcastically before grabbing my toothbrush.

At least with the thing in my mouth she wasn't expecting an answer. Yet.

A ding sounded from somewhere in the house and we both turned to it. Another ding, then it started ringing.

Judging by the ringtone, it wasn't my phone.

"Who is that?" Bay asked, leaving me alone in the bathroom to finish brushing while she went to find her phone.

"Hi Mom!" I heard her say, answering the phone. "No, sorry. I didn't hear any of your texts. I've been...busy."

Busy fucking a guy who was too old for her. But of course she didn't tell that to her mom.

"Oh, yeah! No, I was just talking about that with Blake. I'm excited to come home! I miss you guys a lot!"

Sounded like she was talking Thanksgiving plans. The holiday was less than a month away, and I honestly wasn't so excited to be alone.

After spitting out my toothpaste, I sent a text to Georgia.

Me: *What're you planning on doing for Thxgvg?*

To my surprise, she answered pretty quickly as I went toward Bay in the living room.

Georgia: *What is that supposed to be?*

Me: *Thanksgiving.*

Georgia: *You don't shorten Thanksgiving. And I'm going home.*

Me: *Spending the holiday with your mom?*

"She is? I love Aunt Julia!" Bay yipped as she talked to her mom.

Turning her eyes to me, a devilish look crossed her face as she folded one arm around her waist and turned away from me.

"Speaking of guests for Thanksgiving, I was wondering how you'd feel if Blake came. Georgia is going to Tiffany's and he'll be here alone. I thought it might be nice to invite him after all he's done to help me."

I groaned quietly and the sound made a big ol' smile bloom across her lips as she winked at me.

"Not cool," I rumbled at her as my phone vibrated in my hand.

Georgia: *Yes. You're going to your buddy's house like usual, right?*

Me: *Not sure. We'll see.*

153

"I'll let him know! Thanks Mom! I figured you'd like to meet him, so it would be nice to introduce you guys. He's a really good man, and he's nice and funny..."

Bay paused, then laughed.

"Sure, sure Mom. Ok, I'll see you in a few weeks! Love you!"

When she hung up the phone, Bay turned to me with her fists on her hips.

"There! Perfect! You're coming to Thanksgiving. All three of us will ride down together."

"Three of us?"

"You, me and Georgia."

I wouldn't begrudge a chance to be with my daughter again, even if it was bound to be awkward.

"And who said I want to go to Thanksgiving?" I demanded, taking a step toward her.

"You didn't have to. I know what you want."

"Oh, do you?" I hummed, body so close I was brushing against hers.

My lips turned in toward her cheek and I pressed a simple, gentle kiss there as she stood straight, letting me do what I wanted.

"You're not as hard to figure out as you think you are, Blake Hamel."

"Then what am I thinking about right now?" I asked her, letting my lips brush the line of her jaw and up to her ear.

She gave a breathy chuckle and pressed her palms against my chest, raking her nails against my skin.

"You're thinking about my talent for cooking," she murmured with a grin. "'Cause you're hungry."

Damn it.

I was.

"Then what're you waiting for?" I asked, moving back even though I was also craving her skin.

"Give me a few and I'll make sandwiches."

Watching her full ass wiggle toward the kitchen, I couldn't help the smile that broke over my face.

How did I get so lucky that a girl like that would want to be with someone like me?

The good feeling dimmed, however, when I also remembered that she only wanted me for the moment. Another guy would roam into her life eventually. He'd have better potential, a younger, stronger body and goals outside of sending his kid to college and saving for retirement.

I was sure Bay wouldn't want kids like I did. At least, not yet, and if I didn't have them ASAP, then it would never happen for me, anyway.

Turning away from her, I headed back to my room to get my clothes back on.

A week, maybe two; it wouldn't last too long. And I gave myself permission to enjoy it as I figured out how the fuck I was supposed to find love on an app. Signing up for the twenty thousand question matchmaking system seemed like my last option after the failed attempts by the shitty dates I'd been on.

But for now, I would get my clothes on, get a show started on the TV, then cuddle and eat with Bay on the couch and just take in every last morsel of her that she was willing to give.

Chapter 17

Bay

I only felt a little bad about forcing Blake to go to Thanksgiving dinner with my family. But only a *little*. There was no way I'd let him spend the holiday alone.

We didn't bring it up again though, and I just let it go. As fall break approached, we'd deal with it again, but I had several weeks until then where I would get to know Blake and his body on a much more intimate level.

It felt like something was blooming inside me, and it was really hard to explain exactly what that thing was. But every time our skin touched, or every time he looked into my eyes...I just felt *right*. Almost like we'd been touching and living together our whole lives and that we would continue to do so forever. But would we? Would he want someone like me forever?

I knew that Blake was looking for love. I knew he wanted something more than what he had. But was I enough? Could I be what he was looking for?

That awful need for reassurance leached through every limb as we watched a few episodes of Blake's show, and I found myself moving closer into his side, relishing the feeling of his arm wrapping around my back as I rested my cheek against his hard chest.

It wasn't even ten in the evening when Blake was yawning and sitting up.

"I'm falling asleep, so I'm going to bed," he told me, scooching his butt off the couch and stretching as he stood.

"Ok," I agreed, trying to hide my disappointment.

Hours. So many hours until I would see him again.

"Night," he told me, smiling at me over his shoulder before heading toward his room.

Without anything else to do, I grabbed my laptop and worked on some homework, then let myself indulge in some editing on my favorite picture of Blake before seeing that it was almost midnight. And I had an early class in the morning.

Groaning, I did my own little stretch to ease my kinked neck and back before heading toward my bedroom. I paused in front of my door, looking over to see Blake's door cracked open instead of firmly shut and felt my heart race again.

Was that an invitation?

Probably not. It didn't stop me though. I undressed in my bedroom again and snuck into his room, letting my eyes adjust to the cool glow of the moon as it came in little stripes through the slats covering the window.

I lifted the blanket and wiggled my body in, not entirely sure what to do next. Was I trying to start something? Or did I just want to sleep with my skin against his skin?

Not entirely sure, I just laid there on my back for a minute before Blake turned over and moved his arm around me with a happy sigh.

His eyes cracked open and he looked at me.

"What're you doing here, Bay?" he asked with a low, raspy voice.

"I missed you," I whispered back.

He just smiled and tightened his arm around me before letting his palm draw a long line down and back up until he found my bare shoulder.

His hand dropped a little, following the planes of my breasts and belly down until he brushed his fingers over the mound between my legs.

"Mmm..." he moaned in his sleep, dragging that hand back up before gripping one breast and kneading it.

And of course it felt so good. So freaking good.

I closed my eyes to enjoy the feeling as he slowly woke up, fingers becoming more deft and explorative as his eyes opened to look at me again.

"Wanna try top?" he asked in that gravelly voice.

I didn't bother answering. I just crawled on top of him instead.

Reaching over to the side drawer, I got out a condom and held it up to his face.

"Put it on," he whispered, gripping my thighs with his strong hands.

My hands shook as I managed to get the package open, then I moved onto his legs so I could get the rubber ring around him. But it wouldn't go on.

"Upside down," he told me before turning it around and leaving it just around the tip for me to finish.

I drew my hand down his length, unrolling the condom onto him until he was covered and lubed.

"Get on, Bay," he rasped at me, his hips flexing under me with his eyes closed.

So I did. I straddled his lap, gripping him until I sank down, filling myself with his warmth as we both moaned at the connection.

It seemed pretty simple, and my body told me what to do as I wiggled my hips, drawing him in and out until his fingers clutching my legs began to get painfully tight.

"That hurts," I whispered to him, prying up his fingers.

Little white dots appeared on my skin in the reflecting moonlight when he moved his hands, replacing them instead on my hips where he helped me move as he lifted his hips to meet mine.

"I need you to go faster, babe," he said breathlessly.

I sat back instead, pressing my hands onto his thighs behind me as I arched my back to give my body a little more support as I increased in speed. His hand grazed up my belly and clutched a breast, squeezing and pulling on the nipple as pangs of sharp pleasure spiked through me with each movement of our hips.

"You're so fucking beautiful," he breathed just before he groaned and lifted his hips even more until my knees left the bed and I fell forward onto his chest.

He was panting while I used him to grind out the last few strokes I needed to hit my pleasure, sinking into the comfortable warmth its throbbing brought me.

It wasn't the wild fucking like before, but a gentle reminder of lovers, one to another that they were meant to be. Except we weren't lovers, and we weren't meant to be.

Yet.

Not unless I made it so.

I fell over to the bed breathless as he removed the condom and dropped it in the trash beside him. Turning to his side, he pulled me to him all sweaty and out of breath under the blanket. He was warm and comfortable and I never ever wanted to leave his embrace so long as I lived.

"Night, babe," he murmured against the top of my head, the tone of his voice filled with exhaustion.

I waited until his breathing evened out before turning and pressing my back to him, enjoying the feeling of his hands pulling me into his chest in his sleep before embracing the quiet breaths of another person in the room with me. Sharing a bed with me.

"I think I could easily love you," I whispered to the almost silent room.

No answers followed my comment, so I just closed my eyes and fell asleep.

Blake

My alarm went off just as it always did, but instead of rolling over, I squeezed the hot little body in my arms.

Wait.

What?

I cracked an eye open and immediately recognized the blond hair filling my vision.

Bay. Bay was in my bed and the thought brought a big fucking grin to my face. I'd almost forgotten how nice it was to wake up to a warm body next to me. But this wasn't any warm body. This was *Bay's* body. This body was attached to the eyes that sank peace into my weary brain and to the mind that shared my humor, my playfulness and my serious side.

Before, when people would talk about that 'other half' I used to scoff and roll my eyes, but now I was beginning to understand. If there was someone out there who would be that other half, it was Bay.

What a cruel joke we'd been born so far apart. But if we hadn't, we likely never would have even met.

My alarm woke Bay up, and she turned in my arms, meeting my eyes with a grin.

"Morning," she hummed in an adorable sleepy voice I could easily become addicted to.

"Morning," I said back, sitting up.

I was a little sticky between the thighs and it brought me back to our midnight romp. She must have dripped all over me when she rode me. And fuck if that didn't get me going hard again.

"Work," I said, moving toward the side of the bed but her soft hand gripping my bicep stopped me.

She leaned forward, not even caring that the sheets and blankets dropped, leaving her bare in front of me, she kissed me hard.

"I'll get breakfast," she promised before moving toward the side of the bed too.

She got up and headed out of the room with her sexy ass swaying, as if she had no self-conscious bones in her body.

How does a guy say no to that?

The sight put a wider smile on my face as I dressed in my stained up work clothes. A few minutes later I moved toward the kitchen and saw Bay fussing with some eggs in a pan, stirring them around in her typical night shorts and tank top, her hair thrown into a messy bun on top of her head that was so fucking hot.

I rolled my eyes at myself as I put a couple slices of bread into the toaster then leaned against the counter while she finished the eggs, putting them on a plate with one solitary piece of bacon.

I looked at the lonely little piece of meat for a moment, then turned my gaze back up at her.

"I burned the other one. Sorry."

With a simple shrug, she grabbed the toast that popped and placed it on my plate before pointing me to the table.

"Eat up before it gets cold."

I just gave her my standard half smile and leaned in to kiss her on the cheek.

"Thanks," I told her, then took my plate and sat at the table.

She made her way over with my fork and a fresh cup of coffee before going back to the stove to make her own breakfast.

A guy could get used to so much attention.

"When's your first class?" I asked.

I hadn't bothered asking before because it was none of my business, but now I was curious and I figured we'd crossed so many boundaries by now, she wouldn't mind.

"First class today is eight-thirty," she said, yawning.

It was only just past six.

"Then get your ass back to bed," I told her, waving her back toward her bedroom.

"I can wait until you leave." She yawned again.

"I'm a big boy. I can get myself to work just fine. Go."

She smiled at me and stood, leaning down to give me a kiss right on the lips.

I had to suck in a breath because the action felt familiar and wonderful. As if we'd been doing it forever. It'd been years since I'd gotten a goodbye kiss when I went to work. Honest to God *years*.

"Fine. But I'm going back to sleep in your bed," she told me, her lips brushing against mine as she spoke, a sexy little smirk tipping them up at the ends.

"Go," I told her again, half afraid I was going to sit her on the table and have my way with her all over again if she stayed there, looking at me like that.

She went, and I slapped her ass as she did, which made her give this adorable little giggle as she strode away.

I finished my breakfast in a hurry and went out the door, grabbing my jacket on the way so I could head to the construction site.

Marty had been staring at me all day with a smirk on his face. And every time I asked what was up his ass, he just shook his head like he knew all my dirty little secrets. I wasn't going to get anything out of him at the site, so I told him he was going with me to lunch.

In the car he just turned to me and gave me this shit-eating grin.

"I knew it," was all he said before breaking down into some evil laugh that I'd never heard from him before.

For a forty-three year old guy, you wouldn't think he'd be so interested in my sex life.

"What the hell are you talking about?" I asked, flicking the blinker up as I waited to take a left.

"You did it. I'm so proud of you. You're glowing like a new mother, man."

"New mother?" I sputtered, trying to digest the strange comparison.

"So, what's it like? I haven't been with anyone but my wife in twenty-three years. I gotta know!"

I gave him a glare that made his smile break a little.

"Hey, you know I love Gail with all my heart and I wouldn't change one Goddamn thing."

"I know," I agreed. "And if I told her, she'd skin your sorry ass and leave it to hang on your clothes line."

He looked properly chastised.

"And it's none of your fucking business who or what I'm fucking."

"Well, there *are* laws against beastiality..."

"Oh my God..." I groaned, turning into a McDonald's drive-thru.

He just chuckled and settled on simply patting my shoulder.

"Well, if you don't want to talk about it, that's fine. But I want to tell you that I've got your back no matter what. And I'm glad she's making you happy. I haven't seen you like this since you arrived and after the divorce finalized."

Yeah, that day felt pretty awesome, too.

"To be honest, you look like you're in love."

"Love?" I scoffed, feeling my heart start to palpitate at having such a deep-rooted fear brought so directly to the surface. "With a nineteen year old?"

"Love transcends everything, Blake. Gail's parents were more than eighteen years apart when they married."

"Eighteen years?"

"Mhmm. She remarried to an older man when her husband passed at twenty-one years old. Gail was still a baby."

"Sure, but even still, that means that her mom was a woman. She had been married. She'd had a baby and made choices already for how she wanted her life. That's not how it is with me and Bay..."

Shit. Guess I'll just lay my guilt for the world to see.

No. Just for my best friend to see.

"Doesn't matter. Besides, you're making all these decisions for the girl. Did you ever once stop and ask her what *she* wants? Doesn't Bay get a chance to decide if she is interested in you long term? Maybe she just wants a fling. That's something you need to know, Blake. Especially if your heart's getting involved."

I sighed and sliced my fingers through my hair, shoving it back away from my face.

"Let's talk about something else."

Marty nodded in agreement and looked out the window.

"You watch the game last—"

"How would you feel if Marley or Katy got involved with a guy almost twice their age?" I asked abruptly, interrupting his question.

He just smiled.

"I'd want to kill the guy," he said, and I just frowned as we got one car closer to the ordering box. "But then I'd demand to meet him, and if he was like you, I wouldn't have a problem. My girls could do a lot worse than a guy like you."

My chest grew warm at the incredible compliment.

"Wow... Thanks, man."

He just nodded and patted my shoulder again before motioning at me to roll my window down.

After ordering we sat in the car and ate in silence before heading back to the site.

Marty was one hell of a man. A truly good father, husband and example of what I wanted to be and what I wanted to have in my life. And if even *he* thought that somehow it could work out, then just maybe it was possible. But like he said, I would have to talk to Bay first and see what it was she was looking for. If I was just a cheap fuck, then what was I going to do?

I'd keep being there for her, that's what. One hundred percent at her disposal.

Because I needed that girl.

Like a fucking idiot.

164

Chapter 18

Bay

Walking into class after the amazing and mind-warping weekend I had with Blake felt a little like walking into another universe. Saturday night I was out with Mark, and there he was, staring at me from his seat like I was the queen of Sheba coming into class.

My mind flashed back to the burgers and shakes, to the glass museum, and to that awful fishy kiss he gave me afterwards. After what I'd had with Blake it all just seemed so...*juvenile*. Maybe that was pretentious of me. Maybe I had just been utterly spoiled by hot sex and powerful orgasms that I knew no boy like Mark could give me. But either way, that spoiling had happened and now I couldn't look at my classmate without feeling dread for the idiotic promise I'd made to him about a second date.

"Come sit over here!" Mark called to me as I was about to sit on a desk near the back.

Groaning internally, I moved toward him and sat my butt in the seat beside him, which made him beam in his adorable boyish way.

"I've been thinking about you all weekend," he told me in little more than a whisper.

"Alright class!" our professor called from the front of class, saving me from having to answer him that I hadn't once thought of him from the moment Blake was inside me.

The teacher went on about shadows and light, our subject for the week, and I tried to pay attention. She was incredibly smart, after all, but I couldn't keep my mind off Blake and Mark and what Blake would think if I had to go on another date with Mark on Saturday.

When we were let out for the day, Mark followed me out like a puppy, at my heels as I tried to hurry so I didn't have to talk.

"I've been thinking about what to do this weekend," Mark said, shouldering his heavy bag. "What do you think about seeing the Space Needle?"

The idea intrigued me. I could get so many great shots from the top of it...

"That actually sounds really cool," I admitted.

"Great! You ok with a lunch date this time? It might take some time in the city, so we could get lunch first and look around at the historical sites, that sort of thing. I'm sure you'd get awesome shots, too. So bring your camera!"

I gave him a smile and nodded. "Ok, I'll do that."

He waved, leaving me at my car before heading to his own.

I sat inside my beat up old Camery and frowned. What would Blake think of me going on a date with someone else? Would he still think it was ok?

There was only one way to know. And if he didn't like it, well then, I guess I had to cancel because I wasn't about to lose Blake.

I did the only thing I knew to butter Blake up for our upcoming uncomfortable talk.

I made food.

He walked into the house with a smile on his face and turned to me while he hung up his coat.

"Smells amazing," were his first words. "Are we Italian?"

I smiled and nodded, watching him bend to take off his boots before placing them on the mat next to the door.

"Go shower up and it'll be ready," I told him.

"Sure. Thanks Bay."

He left and did as I asked, and I pressed my hand over my belly to calm my nerves. I wasn't ready to have this conversation. I wasn't ready to ask him if there was actually anything between us other than sex. Was I just something young to pass the time while

166

he waited to find his real prize? Or was I actually someone he could give a real chance to?

Oh God...I'm going to throw up...

Trying to busy myself, I pulled the loaf of French bread I'd bought for dinner out of the oven and placed it on a cutting board to slice.

That's right. I'd gone to the store and spent some of my precious funds on the meal because I wanted something special and Blake didn't give me the credit card for groceries until Wednesday.

When he emerged, his hair was wet and hanging in his face and he was pulling on his t-shirt.

"Where'd this come from?" he asked, looking around the kitchen quizzically.

"I stopped by the store on the way home..."

"What?" he asked, eyebrows drawing together. "But you didn't have my card to go shopping."

"I know, but..."

"Hold on," he said, putting his finger up and leaving me standing in the kitchen with my mouth open to speak.

Well then.

He came back with a credit card in his hand.

"Here. Get whatever you need from the store. I don't want you spending your own money to feed me. Ok? As long as you're living here, keep it."

Words escaped me, but my mouth was still hanging open, in shock, this time.

"What?" he asked, sticking the card in the cleavage of my tank top before turning to the bread.

I grinned, picking the card out again, watching him put the French bread on a plate.

"This looks delicious," he murmured, looking in the pan of sauce.

"Go sit and I'll plate it," I told him.

He obeyed, taking the bread with him to the table.

The chicken parmesan I'd made was still in the oven, so the cheese would be perfectly melty. I got that out and stacked it on top of some spaghetti dredged in sauce before putting it on the table.

"Holy shit, what's the occasion?" he asked, looking at the feast before us.

While he dug in, I sat quietly watching him eat. I wasn't sure how he'd react and that had me nervous as hell.

"I don't like it when you're quiet, Bay," he said eventually. "Quiet, smart girls means I either did something stupid or you have bad news."

I couldn't help my laugh, which made his lips part in a grin.

"Seriously though. What's up?"

I licked my lips and just dove in.

"Before my last date ended with Mark we agreed to go out again this weekend," I blurted. "I want to know what you think about—"

"You should go," he interrupted.

Shoving his fork aside, he looked into my eyes and gave a shrug.

"We know this isn't...permanent. You should be exploring your options. We talked about this already."

He stood from the table and I could sense his anxiety rolling off him like tear gas.

"If you're not ok with it, I won't go," I told him, turning to follow him as he headed out of the kitchen.

"Go, Bay. Go and have fun and fuck whatever you want. I won't hold you back from your future."

He didn't look back and it broke my heart a little. His plate remained mostly full, just a few bites taken from the crispy breaded chicken before he'd abandoned it with what I assumed was a loss of appetite.

My chest twinged with regret, because I could feel right then that I'd just lost a part of him. He'd given me so much over the past weekend and suddenly he'd stolen one of those pieces back.

The place in my chest where I kept those pieces felt empty and I didn't like the feeling. Not one bit.

Blake kept himself busy at his weights and at the pool, cleaning it in the twilight of the setting sun, and I watched through the window like a total creeper. Until my phone buzzed, anyway.

Georgia: *Hey girl. Want to come hang out this weekend? I want a sleepover!*

Me: *Got a date Saturday.*

Georgia: *So, come Friday night.*

I thought about it for a minute, and after seeing the distance Blake had put between us after our little talk, some real space actually sounded pretty nice.

Me: *Ok. But no parties. Just you and me and chocolate. I'll rent some raunchy romance.*

Georgia: *That sounds awesome! You have a deal. Come over after school.*

Me: *See you then!*

Blake brushed past me on his way toward the sink to wash his hands.

"I'm calling it early," he said. "It's been a long day."

"Ok," I agreed, not sure what that meant.

The sweat on his brow told me that maybe he really was tired, but I also had seen him do much more than work out and do some yard work and not be so exhausted he had to go to bed early.

Blake gave me an awkward wave as he went to his room.

Now what?

His door clicked shut.

We were in for one strange week, weren't we?

"I swear, Georgie. Sometimes your dad is a little psycho."

Georgia laughed heartily, pressing her hand against her chest as she did so.

"I know. You saw him when I came home drunk. He goes a little nuts sometimes. Why? Did you get drunk? What'd he do?"

How could I explain to her how the last week had been? How could I tell my best friend that her dad and I had been together, but then I was going on a date with another guy that her dad *said* was just fine, but now he wouldn't even look at me or talk to me unless he had something important to say about where he'd be or what he was doing that affected me.

I finally settled on, "he's just so...hot and cold."

She nodded.

"I know. He's always been like that. Dad does this weird octopus thing where he just sucks up into himself when he's uncomfortable or stressed."

The little sucky noise she made while describing the octopus thing made me laugh, but her words rang true.

"So he's stressed?" I asked.

"Or uncomfortable. I'm sure with me leaving there have been plenty of moments where he gets all weird living with a virtual stranger. But he's fine. Dad's always fine."

But we weren't strangers.

And he wasn't always fine.

"He misses you," I said eventually and she rolled her eyes.

"I couldn't live there anymore, Bay. He's so controlling and..."

"What do you mean, 'controlling'?" I asked. "He only wanted to know where you'd be and when to expect you home."

"Like a boyfriend," she said, wrinkling up her nose. "I'm an adult now. I shouldn't have to answer to anyone."

"No. He's acting like a dad. My dad did the same before I came out here. If I still lived at home, he'd ask those same questions. And that's not being unreasonable, Georgie. Blake cares about you. He wants to know about you and that you're safe."

She just shrugged again.

"That's also why I haven't told him about Jay."

"What, that you're still dating him?" I asked. "Didn't you promise?"

"Yeah, well..." She fussed with her chipping nail polish for a moment before her eyes brightened up. "Oh yeah! I forgot to show you this!"

She pulled out her phone and took a moment scrolling through it before handing it to me.

"That was us at his family's barbecue. It was pretty cool, and they're all really chill."

I looked up at her in shock.

"You met his family and haven't even told Blake you're dating him?"

She shrugged again.

"If I didn't know better, I'd think you were on his side," she said with a snotty tinge to her voice. "You're my best friend. You're supposed to be happy for me."

But I also cared for Blake, and he deserved better than how she was treating him.

"You should tell him," I whispered before adding, "But it looks like you had fun. I'm glad you all got along."

She shrugged one last time before throwing a grocery bag at me and holding her hand out.

"I got the chocolate, you brought a movie, right?"

I dug through my bag before handing over a classic. *The Notebook.*

"I thought you said it'd be raunchy?"

"I couldn't find anything raunchy!" I laughed. "The movie store had this. And it's Ryan Gosling, after all."

"Yeah, ok. You have a point. But dammit! If I cry, I'm blaming you!"

It was a blame I was happy to take.

We cuddled together on the bed, snuggled down in the sheets while we munched on chocolate and swooned for such a romantic story. No tears were shed, but it was nice for it to feel like it used to between us. No boys, no drama. Just her and me and our friendship. Maybe it was salvageable after all. I sure hoped we

171

were on the path to healing the rift between us, because I needed
my best friend.

Blake

I was so fucking tense all week. Two seconds away from blurting out all my feelings and hopes and dreams every single time I looked at Bay. I had to live in that same house while trying to convince her and myself that she should date that little asshole from her school. Of course I didn't want her dating him. I wanted her to date *me*.

But I had to do this. I had to let her go. If she ever did choose me, it had to be of her own volition. She had to *choose* me, and all that came with that.

The only person I could confide in was Marty, and he just looked at me with sympathy before butting in with a hopeful, 'maybe the date will be so bad she won't want to see him anymore.'

I could hope. But the likelihood of that happening was...slim.

Bay spent Friday night with Georgia at her place near the school so I just paced every moment I was home and not busy at work. I didn't see hide nor hair of her Saturday either, and that just made it way fucking worse. I sat, I tapped my fingers, and I wore a hole through my carpets going from one side of the living room to the other. I was also so weak from working out so hard that I eventually had to just sit and eat something. Even protein shakes needed to give way to real food.

If Bay got a boyfriend, she'd likely move out. Maybe she'd move in with Georgia and I'd...

I'd lose her forever.

The thought closed my throat like some strange form of mental anaphylactic shock. I couldn't breathe and I couldn't even think straight at the thought of her leaving me. But it was what I had to do, right? I couldn't hold a girl like her back...*right?*

I missed her already, and I missed the feeling of her skin and the taste of her lips. I missed her smile and her eyes and the sass she gave me. I missed every thoughtful little thing she did, and even just her presence around the house. She made me feel peaceful. She made me feel like my house was a home. For once in my life I felt...*love*.

For the first time in my fucked up life, *I was in love.*

The word love tasted bitter on my lips because the woman I loved was out with another man. She was holding *his* hand, kissing *his* lips. Maybe even letting him fuck her, for all I knew. Not like I'd done that since she'd told me about the date. No, I hid like a pussy since then, lingering in the shadows where I could still be around her since I couldn't be *with* her.

Not anymore.

When she got home she needed to know how I felt. She needed to know that my heart was in the game now, and she had to choose. If she didn't want me long term, then I had to cut ties before I got any more invested. It'd been hard leaving Tiffany, despite all the things she did to me. And as I imagined trying to say goodbye to Bay, my heart just started bleeding all over my ribs. I knew she would likely tell me to take a hike, but at least there was still some semblance of pride in me that would at least pretend to go on if she broke my heart. In a week, a month, a whole year...there would be nothing left to try and put back together. Bay had already taken over my heart and my mind like an invasive species of ivy, wrapping her tendrils around me and choking off anything that didn't breathe for her.

One way or another, I needed answers, and I'd stay up as late as I needed in order to get them.

Chapter 19

Bay

"Tonight's been a blast," Mark said as he drove me home.

I smiled back the best I could.

The entire date had felt so strange and awkward to me. I couldn't stop thinking about Blake and how my going out with Mark had felt like bitter betrayal. I needed to get home and tell him that I didn't want to date other people. Where that would leave us, I didn't know, but I had to tell him, because I was pretty sure I was falling in love with the guy. Which also made me feel like crap while on my date because Mark was investing himself in me, thinking that things were going somewhere. He had to know, too.

"So uh, next weekend?"

I sat there in silence and he glanced at me while we drove.

"I'll take that as a resounding no." He chuckled, but his face was mirthless.

"I'm sorry, Mark. Going out with you has been really fun, but I...I don't see us going anywhere. I don't want to be one of those girls who—"

"Friendzone?" he asked, lifting an eyebrow. "Nah. I figured this was going to happen. You've been off all night."

"I'm really sorry..." The words were paltry, but nonetheless true.

"Yeah, well, better sooner than later. I'd hate to find out after buying a ring, right?"

The ring comment just had me squirming even more in my seat, counting down the seconds until we got back to the house.

When he pulled up to the curb, he didn't get out to open my door like he had before.

"It was fun," he told me, giving me a little half smile.

"You're awesome," I told him. "I did have a lot of fun. Any chance you want a friend that's a girl instead of a girlfriend?"

He chuckled again and shrugged.

"There's no such thing as too many friends. See you in class, Bay."

"See you," I agreed and opened the door, throwing back a thank you into the car and meeting his eyes.

He was hurt. I could tell. But he was too much of a gentleman to tell me so.

Why wasn't I attracted to him? He was cute, but he... he wasn't Blake.

I ambled up the pathway toward the door with my keys in my hand, and before the door was even unlocked he was gone, his car only dim tail lights in the distance.

Well, maybe friends was a little too much to ask for.

The house was mostly dark when I went in, but a single lamp glowed in the living room, spreading the massive shadow of a large man sitting in the chair beside it.

"What're you still doing up, Blake?" I asked as I got in.

It was only eleven at night, but he was normally in bed sometime between nine and ten.

"How was your date?" he asked, voice clipped like he was upset or on edge.

"It was...ok, I guess."

"Ok?" The single word growled out of his lips, half like a question, and half like an accusation. "What kind of little asshole gives a girl like you an 'ok' date?"

His body slowly unfolded out of the chair, his shadow growing exponentially as he eclipsed the room in mostly darkness, only one side of him lit in the orange glow of the light.

"What are you doing up?" I asked again.

Things had been so weird between us, and I didn't know what to think, but he was talking to me, so I wasn't sure if I really cared why he was up, so much that he *was* up. Maybe because he missed me. Maybe because he was jealous.

God I hoped it was one of those things.

Or both.

He took one step forward, then another until he was only a couple feet away from me. Close, but not close enough.

"We need to talk," was all he said as his brilliant eyes pierced mine through the shadowed room.

"Then talk."

He worked his jaw a little, ran his tongue over his teeth and stared down at his feet as he contemplated his words. Likely choosing each one carefully, because that was just the kind of man he was.

"I don't want you going on dates, Bay," he said eventually. "Not with anyone but me."

One eyebrow lifted as I stared at him, still eyeing his toes on the carpeted floor.

"I don't want you with anybody else. I thought I could handle it but I...I'm selfish. I want you all for myself."

My heart picked up its pace with the simple words. I didn't want to be anywhere but with him, either. And him saying so was just...It was exactly what I wanted him to say.

"I want you for myself because..."

He paused and looked up at me. His shoulders were slumped and he looked so lost and...*vulnerable*. He looked scared about what he was going to say. And that made my chest throb with the rapid pulse of my heart.

Thuh-thump.

Thuh-thump.

"I don't know what the hell happened. This was supposed to be simple lust. Sex, kink, fantasies... I don't know when my heart got involved but I...I can't share you because I—"

I wasn't sure what he said, or rather, what he *would* have said if I'd have given him the chance. My body sprung forward and

I was wrapped around him, pressing my lips against his and coaxing a demanding kiss from his beautiful, honest lips.

His arms curled around my waist, pressing my body against his as he accepted my kiss; accepted *me*. Strong hands cupped my ass and I was rising, chest grinding against his as he lifted me into his arms. His mouth left mine and drew kisses and bites down my neck, making my breath stutter and my head fall back as he worshiped my skin, holding me aloft like some kind of goddess worth exalting.

And then he was on his knees.

Dropping us both with a gentle jarring, he held me against him while he took the brunt of it. Lips met mine again as fingers pressed under the hem of my tank top, lifting it inch by inch until it was off my body, my arms lifted above my head so it wouldn't obstruct us any longer. I needed him against my skin, and clothes did nothing but hinder that. Those strong, rough fingers were back to my waist as he lowered me to the ground slowly until my body hit the carpet.

My back arched as one cup of my bra was peeled back. His hot mouth was on my pebbled nipple instantly while his other hand skimmed up my arm until our hands were locked together, finger's tangled in each other as I writhed underneath him.

"Blake," I breathed, feeling like I might just explode from the intensity swelling inside me. "I need you..."

He bit gently on my nipple and I moaned, the sound ricocheting in the quiet room, only punctuated by the stilting sound of our heavy breathing mingling together.

"I love the sounds you make," he whispered against my skin, drifting hot breath against my breast.

"Are you going to make me beg?"

"A little begging never hurt anyone," he said, giving a breathy little chuckle before letting his mouth embrace my other breast.

"Please, please, please, *please*," I mumbled, over and over as I wriggled against the pleasure his lips were bringing me. But I needed those lips elsewhere and I needed him naked and inside me.

He chuckled again until I felt sure fingers unlatch my shorts and tug them down my legs.

I bit back the string of '*yeses*' that wanted to burst from my mouth as he pulled my panties next, baring me to the cool air of the room. The drifting chill against my wet, bare core caused a tremor to bolt up my spine just as I felt the coarse hair of his chin against my thigh.

I gasped in a breath the moment his mouth touched me. His talented tongue flicked up my seam but avoided the one place I needed him. My fingers dug through his hair, holding the locks like reins as my hands begged for him to give me what I needed.

He gave in, circling my clit with his tongue before pulling it into his mouth while two fingers pressed into me simultaneously.

I wailed, eyes closing at the feelings that shot through me, pleasure and pain and desire and need relentlessly sweeping every nerve until I was burning up from the inside out.

His name tumbled from my lips as I fell back into consciousness, my eyes drifting open again as he moved above me, his chest brushing my breasts and his mouth taking control of mine since he'd conquered everywhere else on me already.

"If you won't give it to me..." I breathed against his lips. "Then I'm going to take it."

His sharp inhale told me everything I needed to know.

Biting his bottom lip to the point of pain, I pushed on his chest until he was tumbling over, rolling onto his back.

"Glad you know your place," I told him, dragging his shirt up that amazing chest, baring it to my eyes.

His pants were next, simply a buckle, zip, and a tug away from everything I wanted and needed in that moment.

As my lips descended down on him, just as he'd done to me, he groaned, his cock hard and hot in my mouth as he writhed, hips dancing and back twisting, arching just at the touch. Hands dug into my hair, pulling on my long blond strands as I pumped my mouth down and up and down, making him groan like he was freaking dying. It was one of the single most amazing moments of my life, watching how I affected such a strong, unbreakable man.

I didn't stay there for long. While I loved the feeling of him in my mouth, I needed him to fill me up elsewhere because I was aching and empty and yearning for him.

My body moved up until I was straddling his hips again, then I unhooked my bra, the last thing separating us from hot skin against skin. With a single grind, we both gripped each other, me his chest and him my thighs as I took him in slowly, no guidance needed, until he was inside me, filling me to bursting in more ways than one.

He dug his fingers into my hips, begging me to move, so I obeyed.

My eyes closed again as I moved so slowly, grinding more than rocking. Evidently it wasn't enough for him. He sat up, legs crossed as I sat back onto his thighs. Our lips met in consuming heat as his hands pulled me closer onto him, then up and down at the pace he wanted as my legs wrapped around his waist. I was happy with the help since my body was limp already with my first release, but I could feel a second orgasm burning through me like a shooting star.

He snarled and bucked just as my mind exited my body again in waves of bliss, but they crashed back together as my back hit the ground, warm cum landing flat on my chest as he reached his release above me.

Our panting mingled, warm breath clashing as we sat there recovering.

"I'm sorry," were his first words to me.

Words I couldn't possibly understand.

"I forgot the condom and... I pulled out."

I pressed my hand to my face as I realized just why he was apologizing. But it was me who should be apologizing.

"I shouldn't have..."

He didn't give me a chance to say anything else. His lips stopped me from uttering my apology.

Our kiss was so much more languid than the burning heat of the first. Satisfied and lazy now, our tongues stroked slowly, sated in their greedy lust for now.

"Come to bed with me," he whispered against my lips.

"I only want to be in your bed, Blake," I breathed back, but the words meant so much more than their literal interpretation.

There was no other man for me, and I knew that instinctively like I knew how to breathe, eat or drink. He was one of those vital parts of me now that I knew I would die without. Even if my body survived, without him, my soul would wither away and die.

He lifted me in his arms and held me to his chest as I was carried to his bed. After putting me down on top of his sheets, he went to the bathroom and came back with a warm cloth that he wiped my belly and chest with. His sticky seed came off, but the heady remnants of him didn't leave me. That feeling would stay with me every moment for the rest of my life. I never wanted to forget a single second.

"I need you, Bay," he said, echoing my words back to me. "Not just your body. I need your mind and your humor, your eyes, and your sassy mouth."

I dragged my fingers through his hair and pulled him close for a single kiss.

"I need you too. Just don't let me go."

He looked into my eyes, as if not sure if I meant it literally or not. As if he wanted to be sure I understood him.

But I did. I understood it all, and it overwhelmed me while bursting forth hope in my belly like I'd never experienced before.

I was his and he was mine. We'd figure the rest out later, but for now, that was all I wanted to focus on.

Chapter 20

Blake

I didn't really sleep. I couldn't. Not with Bay in my arms. Honestly, I didn't want to sleep and risk the night having been a dream. Having her with me, tucked up naked against my side was everything I ever wanted, and I was afraid to lose it. Wasn't that just the fucked up truth; the moment you gain something worth having, you're consumed in jealousy that someone or something might take it from you? That was me. And that was why I didn't want to sleep.

My fingers stroked strands of her hair that lay sprawled against her pillow as she slept peacefully. She looked calm and content, and I wished I could keep her that way the rest of her life. I wished she would stay there in my bed, sleeping beside me every night for the rest of *my* life.

But she'd at least said she wanted me too. She wanted to try things, just the two of us, for now. I wasn't sure what that meant when we went to Vegas for Thanksgiving, or what she was going to tell her parents, but I would just have to be alright with being her dirty little secret.

And me, well, I needed to figure out just how much I was willing to potentially give up to be with her.

Everything. I'm willing to give up everything.

The sigh that left my lungs carried with it every last ounce of reserve.

Everything. Even Georgia? Even my little Georgia peach? How would she feel about it? As cool as she was about just about everything in life, I had a feeling that this was something she would adamantly oppose. It was just another one of the million things Bay and I needed to discuss. Our relationship came with so many ifs and whys and maybes, and it almost felt unfair. Who cared if we were a few years apart? Who fucking cared? I didn't, and she didn't. Weren't our opinions the only ones that mattered?

Pressing my face into her hair, I closed my eyes and eventually fell asleep. I gave in to my tiredness with resolute decisions twirling through my brain. It would all be ok, one way or the other. We'd face what we had to, and we'd face it together.

Me: *Miss you baby girl.*

That text had been sitting in my pile of 'sent's for almost a week now. And only the next weekend did she finally send a message back.

Georgia: *I need a new dress.*

Right. Clothes, money, parties. That's all she wanted. I was just a paycheck. And you'd think that the much younger woman I was dating would be the one looking for a sugar daddy. Nope. That'd be my daughter.

Me: *I'm not giving you any more money than I already have.*

Georgia: *It's really important, Daddy.*

Fuck...she always got me when she said daddy. The girl had me twisted around her little finger since she was a baby, and while I thought it'd be different when she was older, it really wasn't. I was still a sucker for her every whim. Damn it!

Me: *Make you a deal. Come for dinner. I want to see you, and I'll give you some money before you leave.*

Yep. I was officially down to bribing my daughter to see me.

There was a long pause, but she eventually wrote me back.

Georgia: *Ok. Bay cooking?*

Me: *Always.*

Georgia: *Be there at 6.*

"Bay," I called, moving toward the kitchen where Bay was fixing lunch.

"What's up?" she asked, turning her face up to me with puckered lips.

I smiled for just a moment before leaning down and pressing a kiss to her mouth that left me even hungrier than I'd been five minutes before.

"Georgia's coming for dinner," I murmured.

She withdrew, her eyes surprised but only for a moment.

"Dinner? Georgie? How did you manage that miracle, oh great one?"

I kissed her sassy lips with a grin.

"Just had to offer her the one thing she couldn't refuse."

"Love? A homemade dinner?"

"Money," I said, my smile melting just a little, the same as hers.

"Money?" she asked, looking confused again.

"How else am I supposed to get her here? She won't see me. She doesn't want anything to do with me. But she's my *daughter*."

"You can't fix everything by handing out money, Blake. Money is not going to heal the relationship between you."

"Then what will?" I asked, slicing my fingers through my hair. "I don't even know what went *wrong*."

"Nothing really went wrong, Blake. Georgia's going through some...stuff. She's trying to find herself and she's trying to learn how to be an adult. When she realizes that independence is a state of mind, not a state of being, she'll come back. Until then, I guess you have to decide if you want to be around while she self-destructs."

I just stared at her.

"How old are you again?" I asked her with my mouth hanging open just a little bit.

She grinned.

"What can I say? I've got an old soul."

"Yeah, I can see that," I agreed, a little smile turning up the side of my mouth.

She paused in her assembly of sandwiches to just smile at me.

"I love that little smile. You know Georgie has your smile?"

I knew. And I loved it.

"Yeah." I nodded simply before taking another step toward her.

She just leaned against the counter as I stepped into her, pressing my chest and hips to hers as I looked down into her eyes.

"You're beautiful, you know that?"

"You've only told me about a million times today," she said with a grin, lifting onto her toes to try and steal a kiss.

I pulled my head back just enough to say in a whisper, "Not just physically. Every part of you is beautiful, Bay. Pretty is subjective and fading. The parts of you that are beautiful will never fade unless you let them. That's the kind of woman you are."

Her lips parted in surprise as she looked into my eyes.

"Wow, you're a romantic. Who would have thought behind all that brooding and leather and tough guy you're secretly a squishy little teddy bear?"

I chuckled and dropped my head to shut her up with a kiss.

"Thanks. I tell you your beauty is timeless and you tell me I'm squishy. Great compliment B."

She grinned and pressed her fingers through my hair, lowering my head again for another kiss.

"It is a compliment. Most men are squishy on the outside and hard on the inside. You're the opposite. Soft in all the ways I need, and hard when it counts."

Speaking of hard...

I pressed into her, letting her feel that 'hard' she was talking about and she laughed, pressing back.

"You know, I look forward to weekends with you. We're in bed more often than we're out of it."

"Got a problem with that?" I asked, moving my hands down from her waist to her hips.

"Nope. If I ever do, I'll let you know."

Slipping my fingers down until they were digging into her fleshy ass, I hiked her up into my arms and started toward the bedroom, leaving lunch waiting on the counter.

"Sounds awfully permanent, that statement," I told her. "You intend to stay with me until you get bored of me in bed?"

"Got a problem with that?" she echoed back to me.

No. Not one fucking tiny little problem with that.

Bay

We eventually peeled away from each other and went to eat the lunch I'd prepared over an hour ago. That was somewhat of a problem for us; putting everything on the back burner when we were together. Metaphorically and rather literally. But the weekends were absolutely the best. Even when I had to do homework, Blake would sit beside me and fool around on his phone quietly while we sat on the couch, a thick book in my hand as I tried to keep up with the chapters in my biology class.

"What do you want for dinner?" I asked while I sat there on the couch, my book in hand while he scrolled through his emails, my feet in his lap.

"I don't know," he said with a shrug. "Everything you make is delicious, babe."

The easy way he called me babe or sexy just...it made my heart and stomach flutter every time he said it.

"Even a chop salad?" I asked, wondering if I could get a reaction from him.

He paused, then slowly gave me a sexy little look that spoke of mischief.

"Depends. What kind of meat will this salad be packing?"

"Oh, no, it'll be vegan," I told him, eyebrows up in feigned innocence.

The man didn't know how to eat without meat. It was one of his funny little quirks.

"Vegan?" He raised an eyebrow. "Well, I suppose we could go to a steakhouse for dinner instead..."

I burst out laughing as he grinned his signature half smile, taking my feet in his hands before rubbing them, starting at the center of my arch.

A groan erupted from my mouth and he hummed in satisfaction.

"Keep making those sounds and we're going right back into that room, Bay. Homework and dinner be damned."

I grinned and closed my eyes just to enjoy it.

All I had to do was plop my feet in his lap and I'd get at least a five minute rub. Maybe more if he was distracted with a TV show or if I'd had a particularly hard day.

"Alright, well..." I grunted when he hit a particularly sore spot near my heel. "I can put chicken or steak in it. We have both. Plus boiled eggs and bacon."

"Can I just have the steak, sans the salad?"

"Don't you want to live into your sixties?" I countered. "Or are you already planning your funeral, you old man?"

His hands paused on my feet and I peeked an eye open to see his expression to my tease.

"Old. Man." The words exited his mouth stilted in disbelief.

I giggled and hid my head under the thick biology book just as he took his hands from my feet.

"Old. Man?" he said again, then I felt fingers dig into the waistband of my yoga pants and *yank*.

I moved down the couch a little with the aggressive tug, but they flew off my legs in one smooth pull.

"*This* old man is going to teach you a lesson, you little brat," he growled, taking my hands and pulling me up, making my book fly onto the ground.

Somehow I ended up sprawled across his lap with his hand slamming down on my butt with a vengeance.

I shrieked, wiggling to get off his lap, but he got three good smacks in before I plopped onto the ground, half laughing, half sobbing from the incredibly sharp spanks he got in.

"I thought you liked me!" I wailed with a grin.

"I do. And because of that I thought I'd teach you a little lesson not to call me an old man again."

I sprawled on my back, the carpet plush and warm under my body. It felt good.

He followed me to the ground and settled between my sprawled legs before dragging my underwear down next, slow and sexy until I was writhing in anticipation.

"You learned your lesson?" he asked, his voice a deep rumble.

"I learned," I agreed, feeling his fingers drag up the skin of my legs, making little tingles shoot up my body.

"Good girl," he whispered.

The spanking had been worth it the moment his mouth touched the insides of my thighs. His lips brushed my skin until he was right there between my legs, leaving gentle, languid kisses along my slit. My hands brushed into his hair and I held him there as he moved, shoulders spreading my thighs further apart as he added his hands to the mix.

"How can I ever settle for someone else?" I breathed.

My eyes were shut in the pleasure pain that came when he sucked on my clit for just a moment before teasing me again with his tongue.

I wasn't sure if he heard me, but just then he sped up and I was coming around him in moments, panting and whining and choking off the screams that swelled my throat.

"Don't," he eventually said when his head lifted.

His lips and the shadow of hair across his chin glistened, and his eyes reflected that overwhelming feeling of rightness that I felt every time we were together.

He'd heard me.

And he told me *not* to settle for someone else.

What did that mean?

A light clip on the door echoed through the silent room, breaking us out of our private little cocoon.

His eyes flicked to the door, then back to me before he crawled forward and pressed a kiss to my lips. Standing, he made his way to the door while I pulled on my underwear and pants.

"Girl Scout Cookies?" he asked whoever was on the other side of the door. "Heck yes!"

189

Hearing him say heck instead of hell just made me grin. The man had a soft spot for kids that I saw for the first time at the barbeque. He always would crouch down to talk to his friend's kids and cleaned up his language to fit a PG Disney movie.

Watching him interact with the kids at the door made my heart swell. I could see just what kind of a father he was, and I momentarily wondered what kind of person Georgia would have been if she'd spent more time with Blake instead of Tiffany. Maybe she wouldn't be going through an identity crisis if she had.

Thirty bucks and a handful of cookie boxes later, Blake was struggling to close the door and trying not to drop any of his precious cargo.

"Hungry?" I asked, approaching him with a grin.

He bounced his eyebrows and stacked the boxes on the counter. He was sorting through the loot when I took his head between my hands and stole a demanding kiss from his lips.

"Fuck me... If I'd have known all it took was some cookies..." he started, but I cut him off again with another kiss.

When I eventually pulled away, he looked at me with curious eyes.

"Do you want kids?" I asked him. "Other than Georgia, I mean. You're so good with them."

He gave a sort of fake smile before turning back to the boxes.

"I do like kids. But I'm not sure if I'll get the chance to have more. I'd like to be able to raise one, but the women I've tried dating aren't interested in kids this late in life."

"Since when is thirty-five late in life?" I demanded.

He just shrugged and opened a box before shoving one of the cookies into his mouth.

He closed his eyes to savor the taste, then offered the box to me.

"Georgia's going to steal half of these boxes," he said, mouth full of the treat.

"I know. I never knew she got her affinity for these things from you."

He winked and ate another before commenting. "We got a shitload of these every summer and we'd work through them together before she went home."

Hearing him call her mother's house Georgia's home was heartbreaking for some reason. As if the place he made for her was only a vacation spot, and not her home, as well.

"I want kids too," I murmured eventually. "I want the whole family experience."

He looked up at me, pausing in his eating.

"What about your career as a photographer?"

I shrugged.

"I can do that on the weekends or evenings. I want to be the kind of mom that stays home. Like my mom did."

He gave a little smile, then dropped his eyes and bit his lip.

Blake turned away and stacked the boxes in the pantry, giving us some space that we really needed.

"So, steak house or salad?" I asked eventually just to get us off the subject.

"I'll have the Goddamn salad," he growled from the pantry, several cookies in his hand. "I'll just eat these first to fill me up beforehand."

I laughed and watched him smirk as he sat on the couch again, picking up the remote while he was at it.

Chapter 21

Blake

Georgia showed up right on time, which I was rather surprised about, to be honest. She had a bad habit of being late.

"Hi Dad," she said, hugging me halfheartedly before going to Bay and giving her a real embrace.

It felt a little like a punch in the gut. Dad instead of Daddy. What the hell did I do to piss her off so badly?

"So, you dating anyone?" I asked, watching Bay's eyes widen and turn to her friend in expectation.

"Not really," Georgia said with a shrug before seating herself at the table where our *salad* was already laid out and waiting, dressing in a bottle on the side.

The look on Bay's face betrayed her. Georgia was hiding something and Bay knew it.

She purposefully turned away from me and fussed with plates and forks while I sat beside my daughter.

"Nobody?" I asked, which earned me an irritated look.

"Seriously. Can we talk about something else?"

The severed feeling of losing a limb? Yeah, parents feel that too, when their children do this kind of shit.

"Sure. How's school going?"

Georgia huffed and turned to me, her arms folded across her chest.

"School is fine. Are you done trying to invade my life now?"

"Whoa! I'm just trying to ask how you are, Georgie. Asking how your life is going. I haven't seen you in close to a month."

A growl emanated from her throat as she stared me down.

"You know, Dad. This is why I liked living with Mom. She doesn't care what I do and trusts me to actually be an adult. I'm not a child. You don't have to treat me like one. I have my own life that doesn't involve you."

My jaw dropped at the same time I heard a murmured but harsh "Georgia!" from Bay behind me.

"So I'm not allowed to ask you about your life? What the hell else am I supposed to talk to you about?" I demanded.

"Why do you think I don't come over here?" she asked back, lifting an eyebrow for effect.

"What the hell is wrong with you?" Bay whispered over my shoulder. "He's your dad! He only cares about you!"

"So you're taking his side?" Georgia frowned. "Great. Guess you never minded having your parents micromanage your life. Dad just fit right into that role, huh? Is he your dad too now?"

I looked over my shoulder at Bay and watched her blink a few times in shock before a tear dripped down her cheek.

And that was it.

"Get the hell out of my house," I breathed.

"Excuse me?" It was Georgie's turn to blink in shock.

"You were invited to come share a meal and to have an evening with your dad and your best friend. How fucking *dare* you talk to her like that? You're more like your mom than I ever gave you credit for. You inject poison in your relationships to protect yourself, but where is that going to leave you? Huh, Georgia? It'll leave you alone, drunk, fucking for money just like *her* because nobody can stand to be with her for longer than it takes to get off. I know that it may seem glamorous, the kind of freedom she has, but she's not really free. Tiffany is a prisoner to her own self-pity, her own depreciation, and her need for approval from everyone she meets. You're better than that, Georgia. *I* raised you better than that."

"You didn't fucking raise me at all," Georgia cried, tears streaming down her face.

"And whose fault is that, again?" I demanded. "Your mom threatened me. She threatened to take you away from me, Georgia, unless I left Vegas. I came *here* because I love you. You want to blame someone for me being gone? Blame her. I'm not going to pretend anymore that she was ever any kind of good mom. Tiffany is a selfish bitch who deserves what life will eventually throw at her. And it will kill me if I see you going down that same path of destruction that she did..."

I choked on the last words, my throat closing up with tears as I stared at my daughter, little rivulets of tears flowing down her cheeks.

"I love you, Georgia... I love you more than anything..."

Georgia stood up, grabbing her coat as she headed toward the door.

My eyes caught on the boxes of cookies on the counter and the envelope of cash I'd made for her, and I grabbed them both, following her to the door.

I grabbed her arm and she tore it away from me, just as her eyes caught on what was in my hand.

She took the envelope quickly, but her eyes lingered on the boxes of cookies and what they meant between us. They encapsulated so many summer nights we'd spent eating them and watching movies, playing games, or swimming in the pool.

"I moved here, Georgia, so that we could have a fresh start, and that you could have another home away from her to go to if you needed it. Your mom was selfish with you, and we got the shit end of the deal...but it was worth it. It was worth every single night that I got to tuck you into bed. Worth every time I fucked up your hair while trying to braid it for the pool. Every single time I had to say goodbye and it tore my heart to shreds...it was worth it. *You're* worth it. You're so much better than *this*."

Shoving the boxes back at me, she pocketed the envelope and left, getting into some red sedan that I didn't recognize before leaving me behind.

Pain that I didn't know was possible seared through my chest, cutting deep like an abrasion straight to my heart. It bled and throbbed and ached like she'd opened my chest and taken the organ with her.

A soft hand slid into mine, squeezing it tight as Bay eased up to me by the door. Tears were falling down her cheeks too, and that was when I realized that no, Georgia hadn't taken my heart with her. Not completely. Because Bay was there, and she owned it, too.

Her arms circled me and I felt calm seep through my bones, radiating right through the pain until I was a swirl of love and hate, sadness and happiness, calm and anxiety. That was what I had become. Two parts of my heart battled it out in my chest, but only one echoed love back to me, so I clung to it.

My head sank to her shoulder and my chest heaved in a breath of her, lingering like a rose garden in my lungs. Thorns and all.

"It'll get better," she whispered into my ear as tears slipped past my eyes, tickling my nose. "It has to. It'll get better."

I just nodded into her, pulling her close and hugging her until I could breathe again.

Bay

I was realizing that maybe convincing Georgia to drive down to Vegas with Blake and Me was probably a bad idea the moment she and her boyfriend Jay showed up at the house. Of course, they didn't knock. No, Georgia texted me to tell me that they'd arrived and to unlock my car. To *her* surprise, I was bringing my boyfriend, too. Her dad.

"Uh, what the hell, Bay?" Georgia asked when she spotted her dad behind me, carrying out two bags, one of them his.

"Blake is coming too!" I said in the happiest voice I could muster.

Even if it was bound to end in disaster, I was going to at least try to make it a good experience.

"Really?" Georgia asked, lifting an eyebrow at me. "Let me guess. We're supposed to heal the wounds and sing 'ninety-nine bottles of pop on the wall'?"

"Hey, that's not a bad idea!" I said, but Blake paused beside me when he saw his daughter, then the guy she was standing next to.

"So this is your boyfriend?" he asked, looking at Georgia.

"Not that it's any of your business, but yeah. This is Jay. Looks like we're all going to get acquainted a whole hell of a lot more than we want to."

Jay shifted his weight from one foot to the other.

"That's your dad, Gigi?" he asked Georgia.

"Yeah, but don't worry. Just ignore him; it'll be fine. We're staying with my mom, so once we arrive it'll be just like we planned."

Jay looked Blake up and down, then did the same to me before turning back to Georgia, content to ignore us from then on.

"Fuck me..." Blake murmured under his breath as he moved past all of us and shoved our bags into the trunk of his Mustang.

It would be a tight squeeze, but we could do it.

Once Georgia and Jay were tucked into the back, I climbed into the passenger seat and waited for Blake to lock up and join us.

"Isn't this your car, Gigi?" Jay asked as we were pulling out.

A flush covered her face as she met Blake's eyes in the rearview mirror.

"Uh, it was, for a few weeks. I borrowed it from Dad."

Jay humphed and leaned back, looking a little miserable as he tried to get comfortable for the seventeen hour trip.

Maybe disaster was too nice of a word for what we were in for.

"I can't. I literally can't. Pull over!" Georgia called after just ten hours in the car. "I can't fucking handle it anymore! We need a hotel right fucking now!"

It wasn't what one would imagine. Georgia wasn't demanding a hotel room because she missed her boyfriend. No. It was because the two men in the car kept clipping comments at each other, neither saying anything *too* argumentative, but the tension in the car was growing thicker by the second, and it wasn't the good kind that ended in sex.

Blake pushed his foot down on the gas pedal and took the next exit up just five miles down the freeway. It was some podunk town, but it had a Super 8 and that was good enough.

When we parked, I was shoved forward as Jay and Georgia tried to get out through my seat, so I stumbled from the car and let them out.

"We leave tomorrow at eight sharp," Blake growled out. "Georgia, you're bunking with Bay."

Georgia paused and turned around. Slowly.

"Excuse me?" she said, blinking at her father. "I'll be staying with my boyfriend. If you're too cheap to get Bay her own room, then I guess you two can share since you're so Goddamn chummy lately. Enjoy the asshole, Bay."

197

Georgia stomped off with Jay on her heels, a wicked grin on his face as he went.

Blake surged forward but I pressed my hand against his chest, murmuring for him to stop.

"It's not worth it, Blake. She's trying to provoke us. Both of them are. Let's just get a room and...take a break from this."

He closed his eyes with a sigh and shoved his hand through his hair before nodding.

"Ok," he said. "You want a room for yourself? I don't mind paying if you—"

I didn't let him finish. I pressed my hand against his mouth and smiled.

"I'm not stupid. I'll take any chance to slip into your bed as I can get. This week is going to be torturous, pretending that nothing's going on between us. It already *has* been torture."

He finally gave a little smile before looking after where Georgia and Jay disappeared into the lobby.

"I wouldn't be able to do this without you," he whispered. "Thank you."

I nodded, watching the door too for just a moment to ensure that nobody was watching so I could safely get on my tip toes and kiss the man.

He breathed out a long, weary sigh, but that half smile was still there.

"Let's go get a room. I'm exhausted," Blake said, squeezing my hand before letting it go.

I followed him into the lobby where Jay was just finishing up at the counter, paying for their room for the night.

They ignored us as we traded places with them, getting our room for the night.

"We only have doubles left," the lady at the counter said, blinking at Blake.

"Doubles? You're that full?" he asked back in disbelief.

"You and your girlfriend can still share a double," the woman said.

Blake flicked his tongue over his bottom lip and turned to me the same moment she said 'girlfriend' before handing her his card.

It sort of felt like one of those 'shut up and take my money' kind of moments.

So, with a keycard to a room with two double beds, we headed up the outdoor concrete stairs.

"Not too bad," Blake said as he looked around the room, doing an initial investigation.

"It'll do," I agreed. "And it gets us out of that toxic atmosphere for a dozen hours, so I'll take it."

He rolled his eyes while nodding, agreeing with my sentiment.

"What do you want for dinner?" he asked. "I'll go pick it up before we get comfortable."

"I'll eat whatever you get," I told him.

"Ok. Pizza it is," he said, leaning toward me to steal another kiss. "Half combo, half disgusting."

I laughed as he grinned, then let himself out the door.

"Lock up!" he called before shutting the door behind him.

I did, flipping the deadbolt before getting into the shower.

My phone rang just as I was getting out, so I ran to it just in time for the screen to darken.

Three missed calls from Blake.

I called him back immediately and he answered with a chuckle and a sigh.

"I'm outside," he said.

"Oh God...I'm so sorry," I told him, still talking as I went to unlock the door.

There he was, standing with our bags and a large pizza in his hands outside the door.

"I've only been out here a couple minutes," he said before pausing and perusing my towel-clad body.

"Still...I should've waited for the shower until you were back."

"Not a big deal, babe," he hummed, sliding the bags in with his booted foot before dropping the pizza on the little table in the corner of the room.

With the door closed and our hands empty, he took a long moment to just give me a simple, savoring kiss.

"You bring condoms?" I asked him with a smile as he kissed down my neck next.

"Why the hell would I?" he questioned with a laugh. "I was bringing my kid's friend to her parents house for the holiday. When would I ever be able to use them?"

"I don't know, but I don't believe in looking gift horses in the mouth."

He laughed again before letting me go so he could get the pizza.

"What do you say we try and figure out this TV, and we'll watch something while we eat?" he asked, picking up the remote control.

I agreed, stooping to get some of my clothes from my bag that I put on right in front of him.

He was biting his lip and the inside of his cheek while he watched, but he didn't stop what he was doing to attack me and rain kisses on me like I'd silently hoped.

Blake and I struggled so much with the TV that we eventually gave it up in favor of my laptop and Wi-Fi, where we watched another episode of his show while we cuddled and ate. We fell asleep halfway through our third episode of the night.

My phone rang just past seven in the morning and I answered it groggily.

"Hey Bay. You have a tampon I can use? I started early."

Well, ok.

"Uh, yeah Georgie. I've got some in my backpack. I always keep some in there."

"Cool, thanks. What room?"

I gave her our room number before hanging up and digging through my backpack. She was knocking on the door a moment later.

Blake stretched and turned onto his belly at the sound, but didn't wake.

"Here you go," I told Georgia when I answered the door.

She took it, then paused as she looked over my shoulder.

There was a sharp moment as she stared at her shirtless dad still in bed when my foggy mind recognized that not only were we sharing a room, but the second bed had our bags laid out on it, clothes scattered over the untouched bedding.

She stared at her dad for a minute, and I just prayed and hoped that she didn't notice the unused second bed as I let myself out of the room and closed the door behind me.

Good thing she didn't see that Blake was still naked from the night before, curled up in the sheets we'd shared.

"So..." Georgia drawled.

"So, will they get along better today?" I asked, positive that my only chance of getting her mind off what she saw was by completely changing the subject.

"Who, Jay and Dad?" she asked. "Not likely. Jay doesn't like him."

I just sighed and rubbed my forehead.

"Why? Plus, we have like, seven hours left in this trip. Then we have the trip *back*. We have to make it somehow, and Jay poking at a wild beast is not going to help matters."

"Wild beast?" was the only part Georgia heard.

I rolled my eyes and frowned just as the door opened to Blake, shirtless and ruffled and squinting in the early morning light.

"What the hell are you two doing out here?" he asked in his deep, scratchy morning voice.

At least he'd slipped on some sweats before opening the door.

"Georgie needed to borrow something," I told him. "Go back to bed."

"Nah. We're all awake now. Let's just head out. We'll do a drive-thru for breakfast."

He closed the door most of the way, leaving it ajar for me luckily since I hadn't thought to take my keycard with me.

Georgia stared at where her dad disappeared, then she leveled that inquisitive look on me.

"You two are actually pretty cozy together, aren't you?" she asked in almost disbelief.

"We get along well, Georgie. You know that."

She just shook her head, then turned on her heels and went to her own room which just happened to be three doors down.

At least we hadn't shared a wall, or else the secret would be out. No doubt she would have heard every moan through the wall as we made do without a condom and got creative with our fingers and mouths in the middle of the night.

I slipped back into the room and frowned. That look on Georgia's face...I didn't like it. She was figuring it out, and it was only a matter of time.

My eyes lifted to Blakes as he sat on the end of the bed, his hands twined as he leaned forward, elbows on his knees.

"She figure it out?" he asked slowly.

"I don't think so," I said just as carefully. "But it's a matter of time now. She...I think she saw the other bed. She'll know that we shared one once she gets to thinking about it."

"Fuck..." he breathed, rubbing his face with his palms before shoving his fingers through his dark hair.

But was it such a bad thing? If she knew, and if my parents knew, then we could be together for real. We wouldn't have to hide anymore.

Unless he *wanted* to hide me...

I had to shove the thoughts away because they were leaching toxic uncertainty into the good thing we had going on between us.

"So, Vegas today," I said instead. "You'll get to meet my parents."

He nodded, standing and pulling down his sweats so he could change.

I watched every cord of muscle and every twitch of his arms and shoulders as he pulled on some underwear, pants and a t-shirt.

"Yep," he said eventually.

"How do you feel about that?" I managed through the tremor of nervousness in my voice.

It was so big, bringing him home...

"I'm excited to meet the people who raised you," he said, looking me in the eyes. "But I'm nervous too. I feel like your dad's going to see it written all over my skin and my lips that I've been all over every part of you."

I smiled a real grin while I shook my head.

"Dad's not that observant. Besides, he trusts me in my decisions with boys."

"But I'm not a boy, Bay," he said.Bay

Somehow those words hit extra hard right in my belly. They couldn't have been any more true. He was a man, and I loved it. I just hoped my parents loved him as much as I did.

Chapter 22

Blake

"We leave Friday afternoon," I told Georgia as she and her boyfriend crawled out of my car in front of her mom's trashy house.

The front door of my ex's house opened and Tiffany stepped out dressed in her usual, which was not nearly enough.

Her daisy dukes and low cut tank top were more fitting for a girl in her early twenties, but she pulled it off anyway, tying the outfit together with one of her many pairs of stripper heels.

Tiffany stood there for a minute, looking at the car and her daughter, then her eyes drifted up to where I stood just outside my driver side door. A grin spread over her face and those stripper heels started clicking down the sidewalk.

"Blake?" she asked as if she was happy to see me.

I just stared at her.

"Oh my God! It is you! Wow, you look good!"

I saw Bay's hands fist in her lap as she watched my ex come down the sidewalk, ignoring our child so she could say 'hi' to me instead.

Georgia watched with shock written across her face.

"Wish I could say the same," I said back and Tiffany reeled back like she'd been slapped.

"Wow. Guess you didn't change much, huh? Always the abusive one."

I let out a bark of laughter before shutting my door, hoping to shut out the conversation from Bay in the process. But Georgia? She needed to hear it.

"Me? Abusive? Is that what you've been telling yourself all this time? Georgia is eighteen now and you hold nothing over my head anymore. I can say whatever the hell I want, *be* wherever the hell I want, and you can't do a fucking thing about it anymore."

I turned to Georgia again who had blanched at the interaction.

"I'll see you in a few days, baby girl. I'd love to get breakfast on Thursday if you're up for it. Let me know if you are."

Just like that I opened the door again and dropped into the driver's seat where I slid my seatbelt on. Tiffany was going red with anger, and it was a beautiful sight. I'd bided my time for so long, and I finally had a chance to say all the things I'd been too scared to do all those years. Now there was nothing she could take away from me, and that felt fucking amazing.

"Who's that?" came Tiffany's muffled words through the window, her long fake fingernail pointing Bay's way.

"It's just Bay, Mom. He's taking her to her family's house."

Tiffany stomped back into the house, leaving Georgia with no greeting and only with an expression of sadness on her face as I put the car into drive.

I wanted to get out of the car and hug her. I wanted to save her from her mother, but I couldn't. Georgia needed to experience the train wreck that was her mother, and I couldn't keep protecting her from it. She was an adult now, and she needed to see the bad and the ugly of it before she ended up in the same place as her mom.

"My house is just down a couple blocks," Bay said as I pulled forward and away from my ex.

"Sorry about her," I murmured while stopping at the stop sign at the end of the street.

"Don't you apologize for her. She doesn't reflect on you, Blake. What she does only makes *her* look bad."

I grinned and nodded, renewed with gratitude that Tiffany wasn't my problem anymore. Those years together had been a living nightmare.

"I'm just right here..." Bay said, pointing to the street her folks lived on just as I passed it.

"We'll head there in a minute," I told her before pulling into a parking lot a few blocks away. It was a gas station, but it would give us enough privacy to do what I needed to do.

Bay was looking at me like I was crazy, but I just threw the car in park and slid my seat back as far as it would go before putting my hand out to her. She took it, still looking confused as I pulled, edging her toward me until she was sitting straddle in my lap, her back against the steering wheel.

"What are you doing?" she asked with a little laugh.

"I'm about to go days without touching you. So sue me if I want to say a temporary goodbye."

She grinned but accepted the kiss I drew from her lips.

"It's going to be hard having you there but not able to touch you," she whispered against my mouth. "Think they'll let us share a room without getting any ideas?"

I laughed quietly with a slow shake of my head.

"No way. That's why this is necessary."

I just curled my arms around her and pulled her to my chest for a few minutes before taking one last kiss, helping her back into her seat.

I fixed mine before taking a deep breath, then we went back toward her parent's house.

We parked outside and I got our bags as Bay hurried up to the door and let herself in.

"I'm home!" I heard her shout, which made a grin spread across my face.

I loved hearing her so excited. I also loved how much she adored her parents.

With her bag in hand, I made my way to the front door to greet the people who had accepted me into their home for a family holiday, and whose daughter I was incidentally fucking.

"Blake!" An older woman smiled brightly at me, opening her arms toward me before taking me in a big hug.

She looked a little like her daughter, and I could definitely see where Bay got her coloring and the heart-melting smile.

"Hi," I said stupidly, accepting the hug as best I could while still holding Bay's bag.

"Now, now Judith," a man said, approaching who I now knew was Judith before putting out his hand and curling his arm around who I assumed was his wife and Bay's mom.

"Frank," he said to me with a smile, though his eyes narrowed a little as he looked me over.

"Blake," I said with a shrug. "But I guess you already know that. It's nice to meet you Frank, and you as well, Judith."

They both continued to smile at me while checking me out in a way I hadn't expected.

"You don't look a day over twenty-five," Judith said with a hand on her cheek. "Are you sure you brought the right man with you honey?"

The question was aimed at Bay who stood by with a grin.

"Positive Mom. You'll see soon enough. Georgia is just like him."

I just shrugged and gave my little half smile.

What the hell else was I supposed to do?

"If I'd have known he was so attractive, I'd never have let you live there!" I just choked on my spit as Bay's mom said it so loudly that others peeked around the corner, kids included.

"Who's attractive?" a voice very similar to Judith's echoed in the room.

"Aunt Julie!" Bay hollered and the two women hugged.

"Well ain't you a sight for sore eyes!" the woman, Julie, said to Bay.

"It's been over a year. You know that's too long," Bay told her, then pointed to me. "This is Georgie's Dad, Blake! He's who mom's having a heart attack over."

Julie's eyes lighted on me and a grin spread over her face.

"Well, I've got to say your mom's right! You aren't old enough to have a baby Bay's age, sweetheart. Now, are you her secret boyfriend or somethin'?"

My eyes widened and Bay's did the same as Julie gave me a hug next.

"Oh, I'm just kiddin', honey. Welcome to a Jenkins family holiday! We nominate you as an honorary member of the family for the duration of your stay!"

Shit, now what was I supposed to say to *that*? I found myself incredibly speechless at the warmth and acceptance Bay's family offered me; a stranger. If only they knew...

"We can't even tell you how grateful we are to you for taking in our little girl," Judith said, her voice serious this time. "You've been a blessing while poor Frank struggled to find a job. Thank the heavens he's found one! Anyway, we're so glad you decided to come join us for Thanksgiving. Isn't that right, Frank?"

Frank nodded and gently moved his wife before waving me into the room.

"Now, Georgia is with Tiffany, right?" Judith asked her daughter.

"Right. I asked her to come but she brought her boyfriend and wants him to meet her."

"Well, it's her loss. She won't get a home cooked meal like she would here, that's for sure!" Judith declared, then she put her hand over her lips and turned to me. "Oh, honey. No offense."

I just laughed.

"Tiffany never could cook."

She gave one simple nod and moved on.

"Bay!" young voices called before tackling Bay to the ground.

She was surrounded by three young kids, two boys and a little girl who all crawled over her, excited to see her.

"Ok! Ok!" Bay laughed, shoving them off her. "I'm calling uncle!"

They moved, ending their tickles before hugging her one after the other.

"I missed you guys," she told them, pressing a kiss on the top of the little girl's head.

My throat swelled at the sight, her eyes sparkling as she talked to the child.

"How're you doing, baby Marmy?"

The girl shrugged, sitting on Bay's lap.

"I'm good. School stinks."

Bay just smiled, pressing her wild, white-blond hair out of the girl's face before lifting her little chin.

"I know school can be hard sometimes, Marm. But you know why you go to school."

"I know! But I want a boyfriend like Lucy!"

"Lucy? You're seven years old! Why does Lucy have a boyfriend?"

"She said they even kissed," the girl whispered loudly.

"I'll tell you what," Bay said, leaning in close to whisper into Marmy's ear.

A couple seconds later they both looked at me. Just like that, the little girl was standing and moving my way.

"Mister Blake," the girl said in a sweet voice. "Will you kiss me?"

I lifted an eyebrow, looking over at Bay who was still sitting on the floor, winking at me. Dropping to my haunches, I met the girl's eyes.

"Your friend has a boyfriend?" I asked her.

"Yeah! And I want a kiss too! Will you kiss me?"

I just chuckled and took her chin in my hand, turning her head a little so I could plant a kiss on her cheek.

"Yay!" the girl shrieked in my ear, making it ring a little. "I got a kiss from the handsomest man in the world!"

Marmy ran away to join her brothers to go play with a grin on her face as my eyes turned to Bay again.

She was still grinning, that sparkle in her eyes making my stomach all wibbly wobbly with butterflies.

Bay stood and moved over to me, speaking just low enough that nobody else would hear. "Hope you don't mind, but she's going to go around calling you her boyfriend."

I just shrugged.

"She'll find someone better than me eventually. I'll be ok when she breaks up with me."

Bay smiled, beaming her sweetness my way and I had to fist my hands not to take her in them and give her a kiss next.

"C'mon. Meet my uncle Rick."

I followed, my hand fluttering for just a moment to the small of her back because I just couldn't keep my hands off her.

Chapter 23

Bay

Uncle Rick was sitting at the table with a bowl, shucking peas into a bowl.

"Well now! There's my baby girl! C'mon and give yer old uncle a hug!"

I did, throwing my arms around my adorable uncle.

"You don't have to fake that accent," I told him, taking some of the peas and throwing them in my mouth. "You might live in Texas, but you're a Nevadan through and through!"

He just chuckled and grinned at me.

"You know, sometimes I wonder if you got your dad in you at all. All I see is your mom's sassy mouth."

"You like a sassy mouth, don't you complain!" Aunt Julie called from the sink where she was shucking corn.

"Did you guys bring your whole farm with you?" I asked with a laugh.

"We just brought some of the goods," she said, patting the counter next to her. "You come and make those idle hands useful. You too, Blake!"

I felt Blake's hard, hot body behind me as he moved through the crowd of adults and kids with me to get to Aunt Juile. How I wished I could just announce our relationship to my whole family right then... But I wasn't ready for that, and neither was Blake.

Aunt Julie gave me and Blake a quick tutorial about how to properly de-husk and strip the silk from the corn cobs before leaving us to work and joining her husband at the table with the peas.

"They own a farm in Texas," I told Blake. "And every time we get together they bring a trailer full of produce from their farm."

"How do they get it past state lines?" he asked in a hushed tone.

"They use a U-haul. Nobody stops a moving trailer."

He chuckled and nodded.

"You have an amazing family, Bay. You're lucky."

I was.

"Now, Blake! Tell us about yourself!" Mom said, moving toward us.

Blake just kind of shrugged.

"Honestly not a lot to tell, Judith. I own a little construction company in Seattle and we stay busy enough."

"You're from the area, right? You don't have family near-abouts?"

"No." He shook his head firmly.

Mom looked like she wanted to ask, but she tucked it back and moved on to other subjects.

"Well, we're glad you're here. There's always room at our table."

"I appreciate that," Blake said with a smile toward her. "You've all been so hospitable and welcoming."

That made Mom flush with satisfaction.

While she moved on and talked to Uncle Rick, I looked around the room and, seeing that everyone was busy, I hip-checked Blake and smiled at him the moment he turned to me. We shared a private little moment right there in my family's kitchen and it felt so good; so *right*.

I had to tear my eyes away from him so we wouldn't look conspicuous, and they landed right on my aunt, whose eyes were flickering between us with a devilish grin on her face.

Oh God... That look.

She knows.

⁂

"Well, I should probably head out for the night," Blake said eventually, his hand over his flat belly after having eaten so much.

My aunt and uncle knew how to barbeque something fierce, and he'd taken advantage of their good Texas cooking.

"Where are you staying?" Mom asked.

"Oh, there's a hotel just down the road—" Blake started, but Mom cut him off.

"Nonsense!" she said. "There's room here. You can take the guest room. Rick and Julie are staying at a rental house nearby so it's just us here. You'll stay with us until you go home!"

There wasn't much room for arguments, so Blake had no choice but to agree.

"Good, now with that decided, let's have dessert! Can you get it, Bay?"

I agreed and went to the kitchen for our poke cake.

"Bay Marie Jenkins," Aunt Julie said in a whisper when she joined me in the kitchen. "You and I need to have a little talk just as soon as we're done handing out dessert."

A cold chill rushed through my limbs as my hands suddenly began to shake.

She knew.

We gave dessert out and Aunt Julie led me to the back porch where we sat on the dining set out there just next to the grill.

"Are you and that man doin' somethin'?" she asked straight up, a serious look on her face as she questioned me.

I gulped.

"I see how you two look at each other, and you're always finding reasons to touch and—"

"Yes!" I yipped out, then flopped my hand over my mouth in shock.

That devilish grin was back on her lips with my admission.

"You've got good taste in that one there," she said, then her face went to something more serious. "What are you two up to? Are you sleeping with him?"

I bit my lip and looked away, and that was as much confirmation as she needed.

"Oh, baby girl," she said with a sigh.

213

"I know..." I sighed, sinking my teeth into my lip again until it was painful. "We didn't mean to, it just..."

"You two have some sort of spark. That's for sure. I could feel it the moment you two walked into that house."

"What do you mean?" I asked her, finally meeting her eyes again.

She looked at me with the gentlest expression and I sighed at the sight.

"First you tell me how you feel about it all."

I just shrugged.

"It wasn't supposed to happen but we...there's just something that we can't deny, you know? We meant for it to be temporary, until one of us found something else...but I don't want something else. I just want him."

"You in love, honey?" she asked, taking my hand firmly in hers.

Was I?

If I was completely honest with myself...

"Yeah, I think I am."

She sighed, and I wasn't sure if it was disappointment or not, but she looked a little sad.

"He's got a girl your age, honey. He's a lot older than you."

"Sixteen years," I agreed.

"Well, that's not too bad," she said slowly, turning up my face to meet her eyes. "This is a tough one, because that man loves you too, honey."

My eyes widened in shock.

"What?" I demanded. "Why do you think so?"

She just smiled again.

"You can't see the way that man looks at you? Like you're the little baby Jesus himself. He worships you just with his eyes, honey. Ain't getting any clearer than that."

I squeezed my eyes closed, trying to push my tears back, but they slipped out anyway.

"Oh, honey," Aunt Julie murmured as she wiped the tears away. "You really do love him, huh?"

I nodded and just breathed. All I could do was breathe.

"Well then, I guess we'd best get your daddy on the same page."

"Dad will be so mad," I whispered. "He'll never forgive either of us."

"Now, that's a bit dramatic," she chastised. "Your daddy is open minded enough, and he only wants what's best for his little girl. If you really love him, then your daddy will come around one way or the other. I promise you that. Might take some time, but he will."

"And what if he doesn't?" I squeaked.

It was my biggest fear. Mom would understand eventually, and I knew that. But Dad? Dad was a little more classic in his dreams for me. There's no way he ever imagined me with my best friend's dad.

"Even if he didn't, honey, your mama would and even if *she* didn't, then you gotta do you. You gotta do what's best for you, no matter what. If it's real love, then it's worth taking a risk for."

"Are you really encouraging me?" I asked her in disbelief.

"I want you to be happy, honey. And I ain't seen you more happy than you've been tonight. The way you smile at that man, that's true happiness."

I couldn't remember ever being so happy as I'd been the past few weeks with Blake.

"What do I do?" I finally asked her. "Should I just scream it out for everyone to hear?"

"No. You don't say a damn thing until you're absolutely sure that he's the one you want. After that, you start dropping hints that you've started dating a man and he's a bit older than you. A man with a career. It'll prepare them for when you do drop that bomb."

That actually sounded...smart.

"You're a real schemer, aren't you?" I gave a little laugh, looking at my aunt in a new light.

"Damn tootin'. Now, you get back in there. Think you can manage to share a house and keep your hands to yourselves?"

"We're both adults. I'm pretty sure we can manage that," I told her with a teary laugh.

"Good. Now git."

She waved me away and I left, taking my dessert into the living room where Blake and my parents were talking. Uncle Rick was at the door with Marmy in his arms, already asleep.

"You seen your aunt?" he asked me when I went in.

"I'm right here you old man," Aunt Julie said, getting her purse.

They said goodbye and gave everyone hugs before going out the door.

"I should probably get my bag," Blake said, getting up too.

He left the room, leaving me to stare at my parents with guilt swirling around in my guts from my secret.

"He's certainly a fun person," Mom said to me, tilting her head toward where Blake disappeared out the door.

"He is. I've had a lot of fun staying with him."

"And Georgia?" she asked.

I bit my lip, not sure what amount of truth they were ready for.

"Georgia actually...she moved out recently. She wanted to stay at the house her sorority has."

Dad's eyebrows raised.

"You mean you've been living *alone* with a man in his house?" he asked. "I don't think I like that."

"I'm going to school. It honestly doesn't make any difference one way or the other whether she's there or not. Blake's been a very generous host and I'm glad I've had all these experiences. It's way better than a little shared dorm with strangers. We get along really well."

Dad looked unsure, but Mom seemed like she agreed with me, which surprised me.

"So, uh," Blake said, coming in through the door with his suitcase.

"Let me show you back," Mom said, motioning toward the hallway.

He smiled at her and nodded.

"Bay," Dad said, almost growling my name like he did when I was in trouble.

"What?" I asked innocently.

"If something was going on...if you ever feel threatened or..."

"I never will, Dad," I told him in a hushed voice. "Blake's a good man."

"But if you ever do..."

"I'll tell you. And I have keys and a car and gas money in my account. I'll come home. I promise, Dad. I'm safe with him."

He finally gave in, giving a simple nod before leaning back in his recliner with his beer in hand.

The work boots at the front door reminded me of all the nights I'd watched Blake pull his off, and the mornings when he'd put them on while I made breakfast. It made my heart flutter a little, but I had to put it out of my head because it wasn't the time or place to get horny for him. We had to make it through Thanksgiving and another night, plus the drive home with Georgia and her boyfriend before we would be able to even kiss again.

"Tell me about your classes," Dad said after another sip of his beer. "Is it what you hoped?"

"College is everything I hoped for," I gushed with a grin. "I love learning from all the art teachers. I've learned a lot about light and shadow this semester, and I've been trying it out in Washington. The sunsets are just beautiful."

"I bet," Dad said with a soft smile.

It was the same smile he got on his face every time I got to talking about the things I was passionate about. He loved listening to me and asking questions about what was going on with me. We actually had a pretty good relationship, although I wished I had more time with him. He was always working growing up.

217

Mom and Blake joined us again and settled into the couch while I sat on the floor and listened to the adults talking.

"Bay told me you're an electrician," Blake said eventually.

"For about thirty-five years." Dad nodded.

"Thirty-five years?" Blake asked with a smile. "You must have the patience of Mother Teresa."

Dad barked out a laugh.

"Gotta do what you gotta do," he said with a shrug. "How long have you had your company?"

"Coming up on ten years, actually. And I owe it to my guys."

"If only all bosses felt that way." Dad chuckled.

Blake nodded in agreement.

I yawned just then, and everybody stopped to notice.

"You should go to bed, Bay," Mom said. "I'm sure it was a long trip."

I just nodded and stood.

"I actually think I'll turn in too, if you don't mind," Blake said, standing.

"Of course not. Let me know if you need anything," Mom told him before settling back on the couch as Dad reached for the remote.

I led the way down the hallway and Blake followed behind me, but left space between us until we got to first my room, then his.

"Night," he whispered at me, grasping the handle to his door, right next to mine.

I looked back and heard the TV go on before lifting onto my toes to press a soft and quick kiss on his lips.

"Night," I told him, grinning before slipping into my room.

His door closed a second later and I just stood there, knowing that he was only one wall away, and yet it felt like a million miles because my parents were out there and I wouldn't see him all night, despite being so close.

I tried to go to sleep, but I stayed awake all the way until I heard the TV flick off and the footsteps of my parents going down the hall and to their bedroom. The door shut and I let out a long breath.

Getting out of bed, I tiptoed out of my room and shut my door silently before turning the handle of Blake's door. He didn't lock it, so it opened easily.

I slipped in and shut his door behind me just as Blake sat up, looking all ruffled and sleepy, his hair in his face and his chest bare under the sheets.

"Bay?" he asked, but I shushed him.

Crawling into bed with him, I pressed a kiss to his lips that he accepted quickly, taking charge of it and drawing all the contrasting and overwhelming emotions from the day out of me.

I pressed my fingertips against his chest and he stopped kissing me, licking his lips as he looked into my eyes.

"Aunt Julie knows," I whispered. "She... I don't know how she knows, but she does. I admitted it when she confronted me."

The hunger and sex dropped from his face as worry set in.

He cursed and plopped back onto the pillow.

"But she supports us. I even got to ask her advice. She was really helpful, actually."

He looked at me, his hand shoved into his hair as we silently spoke a thousand words through our eyes.

Blake sighed and his hand moved from his hair to brush through mine, taking a moment to finger my blond waves before meeting my eyes again.

"How do you want to handle that?" he asked. "Seems we're worse at this whole pretending thing than we realized. Pretty sure Georgia is suspicious, too."

"I...don't know. I guess that all depends on what we want."

Neither of us wanted to answer that unasked question. We weren't ready for *that* talk. A couple weeks ago, all we were to each other was someone we liked to have sex with, but after seeing him break down, after seeing the extent of which he loved...somehow I fell in love with him. And the idea of tearing out his ambitions for our relationship killed me, because I knew that I wasn't what he would want. I was young and that was probably exciting after not dating for so long, but eventually he'd want someone his age, and that thought made my stomach ache and tears threaten my eyes.

"What's wrong?" he asked, his brows pulling together as he looked into each of my eyes, searching for something.

I just shook my head.

"Let's just take it a day at a time," I whispered and he nodded in agreement before pulling my head to rest on his shoulder.

We lay there for a while, and I found my eyes growing heavy now that his smell was in my nose. Already, I couldn't sleep without him at my side.

"You should probably go back to your room before you fall asleep," he said eventually, always looking out for me.

I knew I should, but I didn't want to.

"I know," I said, getting up slowly.

He sat up too, the blankets and sheets dropping to the waistband of his sweats.

"Couple more days and I get you all to myself," he told me, gently stroking my cheek with his thumb. "But I want you to enjoy this time with your folks. I know you've missed them. I'll be around, but you spend the day with them tomorrow, ok?"

Once again, my heart swelled with love for the man.

"I'll try, but no promise. I never can get my mind off you."

He smiled that cocky little half smile before kissing me one more time as he pushed me out of his bed.

"See you in the morning, Bay."

Before I spit out any more sentimental thoughts or words, I just waved and slipped back into my room and to my bed.

It was missing something though.

Him.

Chapter 24

Bay

Everyone was up early for Thanksgiving, and I found myself in the kitchen with Mom and Aunt Julie making an over-the-top feast. I peeked into the living room once in a while and saw the guys all watching a game on the TV, and once I even saw Marmy sitting in Blake's lap, her hands on his cheeks while she talked to him. The answering smile on his face melted my heart and I had a hard time breaking away from the sight.

Aunt Julie joined me after a minute of my staring and I heard her hum at the sight.

"He seems like a good man," she said in almost a whisper.

I just nodded before taking the tray of butter crackers topped with cream cheese and olives.

"Why don't you go take those to the boys and you take a little break. I'd like some time to talk to your mom."

Time alone to talk? It sounded suspicious, but I missed Blake and ached to just get closer, so I went quickly into the living room.

"Hungry?" I asked the men.

Each one looked at me with lit up eyes, happy to see some food.

After making my way to Dad and Uncle Rick with the snack, I moved over to Blake, whose eyes I caught immediately when I got closer. He reached over and grabbed a cracker just as his other hand slipped beneath the tray and traced the outline of my fingers gripping it. I shifted the tray to my other hand immediately to take his hand and he gave mine a gentle squeeze. He met my eyes with a contented smile before turning away so he wouldn't attract attention.

But I wanted attention. I wanted *his* attention. And I wanted the world to know.

"Bay!" Mom called with the edge of a bite to her voice.

I placed the tray down on the coffee table and headed toward the kitchen before I started to sweat or bite a hole through my tongue to silence myself. One or the other.

When I got to Mom and Aunt Julie, Mom was waiting for me with her hands on her hips and a scowl on her face.

"Bay Marie Jenkins, you have some explaining to do, girl."

Oh shit.

My eyes flicked over to Aunt Julie and she looked ashamed, but also a little amused.

"Sorry honey. I tried easing her into the whole Blake thing and she guessed."

My eyes widened in horror as they shifted back over to Mom.

"In your room. Now."

I followed her back toward my bedroom, a million words and thoughts swirling around my head like a hurricane.

"Really?" was the first thing Mom said when my bedroom door closed us away from everyone else.

My jaw just dropped and flopped wordlessly.

"We sent you up there and that man... I can't believe he'd take advantage of you like that! We trusted him, that he'd treat you like a daughter!"

I gulped and held up a hand.

"He has, Mom—"

"Oh, he sleeps with his daughter too?" she asked, her face going a little red.

"Will you let me talk?" I asked her, raising my eyebrows. "Or do you just want to chastise me for falling in love with someone other than who you anticipated?"

It was her turn for her mouth to pop open in shock.

"Mom, Blake is...He's a kindred spirit. We didn't...*plan* this. In fact, we both dated other people but we just kept...finding each other. I know that his age isn't ideal, but he's not that old, either.

222

You've seen him. He's only got sixteen years on me. He has a career, and he knows what he wants in his life."

"He also has a divorce under his belt. And a daughter who just happens to be your best friend."

I licked my lips, trying to buy myself a moment to think.

"I know. I'm well aware."

"Is it..." Mom paused for a second and put her hands over her face like she was overwhelmed before taking a deep breath and digging right into the heart of it. "Is this about sex?"

I choked.

"It's not about sex," I squeaked.

"Oh, so if you just took that out of the equation, then you'd still want to be with a thirty-five year old divorcee?"

"That's really unfair," I told her with a stern expression. "But yes. Even if there was no sex, it doesn't change the fact that he makes me feel good and comfortable and welcome and loved and cherished."

Mom sighed and plopped onto my bed, leaning her elbows against her knees.

"So, tell me these wonderful things then, Bay, because I'm kind of freaking out here. You should be dating boys in college, not men who have their own kid in college."

I sat beside her and took her soft hand into mine. She'd done the same to me so many times, the last time of which was when I'd left for Washington to go live with a stranger and my best friend.

"What is good about Blake?" I asked quietly. "He's a man who knows what he wants and goes for it."

"Even a nineteen year old girl," she growled.

"He wanted a future for himself and for Georgie, and he did what it took to make it happen. He has a successful business, and he has really nice friends. After going through that with Georgia's mom, he has surrounded himself with good people and positivity. He's a strong man, Mom. He lasted being with Tiffany for years before eventually getting that divorce. And he stayed in that

223

abusive relationship because of her. He sacrificed because he felt it was best for Georgie."

Mom met my eyes and listened quietly, her hand clasping mine back.

"Blake is simple. He finds happiness and joy in small things like having dinner together. We'll cook together sometimes and those are some of the best nights we've had together."

"How long has Georgia been moved out?" she asked in a whisper.

"For a few weeks," I admitted. "But Blake and I...we only started..." Oh God...What was the name for what we were doing? "*seeing* each other...about a month ago."

"And what, is this a fling, then? Is this some kind of phase that you'll outgrow, or are you seeing a future with him?"

"I love him. Of course I see a future with him."

"And what about when he doesn't want kids because he already *raised* one?"

"He wants a family," I told her. "I know what his hopes and dreams are, and we want the same things in life, Mom. He wants to start a family, and that's why he hasn't had success in dating women his age."

"That's nonsense..."

"You can say what you want, but you don't know what it's been like for him. He missed out on most of Georgia's childhood, and he wants a chance to actually raise kids. Not just having them for the summer like a day camp."

"You're sounding like you want to marry this man," Mom said, her eyebrows squeezing together in concern. "Oh my God...have you talked about that?"

I just smiled and shook my head.

"No," I said firmly. "We never talked about permanence or marriage or even a real relationship. I haven't even told him I love him."

Mom's face softened and she took me into her arms as I felt tears slipping down my cheeks.

"Oh baby," she whispered, squeezing me tight.

She knew about my last boyfriend. My *only* real boyfriend. And she knew how broken he had left me.

"Who knows? Maybe I'll tell him that I love him and that'll scare him off and this will be a whole conversation for nothing. That's why I haven't said anything yet."

Mom pressed my hair behind my ear and looked into my eyes.

"You need to know something that important, Bay. If you love him that much, then you need to know."

I nodded.

"And don't you dare hide this from me anymore. We'll hide it from your father, because if he finds out while Blake is here, he'll try and beat the man up."

We shared a commiserating look, because we both knew that Blake could take him on, easy. But Dad loved me, and he'd do it for my honor, as misguided as it was.

"I kind of knew," Mom hummed, stroking away my tears. "I could see it in your eyes, and he was looking at you in a way no man looks at his daughter's friend."

"That's what Aunt Julie said."

"Well, if you think you're being inconspicuous, you're wrong. I hadn't guessed before because I thought for sure you knew better than that."

I gave a little chuckle, still weary of her reaction.

We sat in silence for a minute before I managed to gather the gumption to ask, "so, do you approve or are you starkly against this?"

Mom lifted her eyes to the ceiling and breathed in long and slow before blowing it out.

"Do I approve? No. I still think it's really immoral for a thirty-five year old man to make moves on a nineteen year old girl, but I do understand *why*. So for now, I'll withhold judgment. Like you said, we very well could be having a pointless conversation.

But before break is over, you have that conversation, is that clear? If you just drag this out, I will *really* become upset."

I just nodded.

"I'll talk to him this weekend when we get home."

Mom just shook her head and sighed for the millionth time.

"Ok. I still just can't believe it."

"What's so hard to believe?" I asked. "Grandma and Grandpa were twelve years apart in age. What's another couple of years?"

She gave me a little smirk.

"You know, I'm thinking you should have gone to college for debate instead of photography."

I just chuckled and stood with her, exiting the room behind her before joining Aunt Julie again.

"Are you convinced?" she asked Mom.

"Convinced that she's in love? Yes. Convinced that she's probably making a mistake? Also yes."

"Oh, come now! Look at that man! You think she's missing out on anything by him having a few extra years on him? She won't even have to deal with the whole insecure college age boys like we had to. She gets to skip right to the good stuff!"

"Oh heaven help us all!" Mom moaned. "That's the last thing I want to be thinking about, Julie! Don't talk like that about Bay!"

Aunt Julie laughed and leaned into me.

"So, is he a tiger?"

"Huh?" I asked, confused.

"You know. All those muscles; experience in the sack. The best?"

My eyes widened to saucers again and I choked.

"Bay?" I heard behind me, his voice breathing like velvet against my ears.

We all turned to him and his hands were tucked into his pockets, eyes darting across each of our faces.

He knew.

How was everyone figuring it all out? For the love of God! Can a girl get a break?

Mom crossed her arms over her chest and Blake breathed a long sigh before taking a step forward.

"Judith...I—"

Mom cut him off.

"I've talked to Bay plenty about it. And I'm not ready to talk any more, to be perfectly honest. I don't like the secrets and the hiding. That's not how my Bay usually acts."

"That's my fault," he tried, but I interrupted him next.

"It's *our* fault," I piped in. "We chose this together."

Our fingers met and his strong grip was reassuring.

"No, Bay. I'm the grown up here. This is on me," he said, but I just stared daggers at him while Mom nodded.

"That's right," she said in a harsh whisper. "What kind of man takes advantage of a teenage girl?"

Blake just squeezed his eyes closed and nodded slowly, pinching the bridge of his nose with his fingers.

"I know how this looks, Judith. Believe me I do. If this was someone with Georgie, I'd...I'd lose my shit."

Mom nodded again, looking satisfied.

"Damn tootin'," Aunt Julie said, folding her arms across her chest to echo Mom's stance.

"But that doesn't change anything," Blake said next. "I know how it looks, and I tore myself apart about it, too. Still do, to be honest. This isn't what I'd been planning on, and we haven't made commitments or anything... But..."

Blake's hand closed tighter on mine as he looked back at me and met my eyes.

"I know the consequences of this. I know how the rest of the world would look on a relationship like ours. That's the only reason we kept it a secret. Not because we're ashamed, but because I didn't want this to somehow backlash on Bay, and I didn't want it to affect her relationship with Georgie, either."

"Because it's temporary."

"We haven't decided what it is, yet," he said firmly, showing just a little of that steel spine I knew he had. "And I'm not about to

227

pressure Bay into deciding what she wants right now. It's her decision, not mine. When she's ready to walk away or..."

He ran his tongue over his teeth as he looked away like he was collecting his thoughts again.

"What she decides, I'll go with."

"And if she wants to marry you?" Mom asked with raised eyebrows.

His head jerked up and he looked at me surprised.

I just stared like I had no idea what Mom was talking about.

He took a minute, turned back to my mom, then said the words I hadn't ever expected from his lips.

"If Bay wanted to marry me, then that'd make me the damn luckiest man in the world. But even I know that she deserves better than me."

Mom's eyes narrowed as she looked him over, probably gauging Blake's honesty.

Just then, she turned to me and nodded firmly.

"I approve."

That quick the conversation was over and the two older women got back to hacking away at sweet potatoes.

Blake's eyes were on me, his expression filled with a million unspoken words.

"Come with me," I told him, pulling his hand until we were out the sliding glass door and in the backyard in the still stifling eighty-five degree heat.

"I'm sorry, Bay. That's not how I—"

I cut him off with my kiss. I just couldn't keep my hands and lips to myself. Not after that confession.

"Did you mean it?" I asked against his lips as my back hit the scratchy stucco on the side of the house.

"Every fucking word," he said, though he still looked unsure.

I kissed him again, then took his cheeks in my hands and looked him in the eyes.

"I love you, Blake."

He gave a little huff of disbelief, emotions playing across his face like a movie.

Surprise was prominent, but there was also relief there before he kissed me again, a savage, biting kiss that told me just how much the words affected him.

"I love you too, Bay," he breathed, lips trailing to my neck where he tucked his cheek and just paused, holding me.

I tightened my arms around his neck and stood there, absorbing the feeling those words brought as they washed over me, over and over again.

He loved me.

"Really?" I finally asked.

"Really." He grinned, shaking his head. "I've got no idea why you would love me, but yeah. I'd be a blind idiot not to fall in love with someone like you, Bay."

Pressing one long, hopeful kiss to his lips, I hugged him again for a few minutes until a window slid open above us.

"You know, the men are going to get suspicious if you keep hanging out there," Aunt Julie said in a laughing tone.

Blake grinned and nodded before pulling me back toward the house, fingering his hair back into place where I'd run my own hand through it backwards during our kiss.

He went toward the living room to plop back on the couch with Dad and Uncle Rick and the kids and I joined Mom in the kitchen with a giant grin spread over my face that I just couldn't squash.

"Well, judging by the look on your face, the feeling was mutual," Mom said with a twinkle in her eyes.

"He loves me too," I breathed a hopeful whisper.

Aunt Julie clapped happily and hugged me before pointing me to the oven.

"You get that out, would you?" she asked, winking at me with a grin.

Yeah, I was pretty happy. At least if she was smiling too, I wouldn't look completely insane walking around with my face-splitting grin.

Chapter 25

Blake

She loved me.

She honestly loved me.

Why? How? Did it matter? Because she *did*. Well, she loved as well as a nineteen year old girl could, anyway. My brain kept telling me that she didn't know the difference between love and lust, and while it might be true, my heart told me that it was worth the risk. Even if she had fallen in lust with me, I still had a chance to win her heart.

Her words couldn't have made me any happier than I was when I sat down on that couch and pretended to watch the game with a grin on my face. I probably looked like a psycho, but I really didn't even give a shit at that point. Nope. It was all about Bay and, well, it kind of all turned out.

Well, except we hadn't told her dad yet. There was that. But her mom had somehow found out, or maybe Bay just told her. I should have been mad that she'd spilled our secret *again*, but part of me was glad she did. Keeping her from the people I loved was slowly killing me. I'd been honest with her mom about why we'd kept it a secret, too. It was for her, but it was also for Georgia. Georgia wouldn't take it well, but then again, she wasn't taking anything well recently. It was Bay's decision who she wanted to tell and how much.

But for now, I had what I needed. Her declaration of love was all I wanted. If only I could show her just how much I loved her. Words seemed paltry compared to the passion I had inside me when it came to her. Not just sex, while there was that too, but in my mind, my heart, my limbs; everything functioned for her. My lonely existence was now filled with purpose, and I wished she knew just how much she meant to me.

I had time to tell her; to show her. I repeated that to myself over and over every time my fingers itched to take her in my arms again.

Sitting there and watching the game got to be too much, so I played with the kids, wrestling with the boys on the living room floor while trying not to get my eye poked out in order to distract myself. Meanwhile Bay would come out periodically with some new snack and we'd meet eyes and I would flood with warmth everywhere. Even just the look on her face, the love in her eyes, was enough.

Dinner was really nice. I hadn't felt so comfortable at a Thanksgiving dinner —besides with Marty and his family— in years. Even still, I almost felt like I'd been intruding on their holiday. But now that Judith and Julia knew, and with Bay beside me, it felt like home.

"We're glad you were able to join us," Frank said, lifting his beer to me.

"You've been more than hospitable, and this has been the best Thanksgiving I've had..." *Ever.* "In a long time."

Frank smiled with satisfaction, grinning at his wife.

"And this food is the best, as always, babe."

Judith grinned back at her husband.

"Bay and Julia helped too, you know."

"I know. I'll thank them later."

The table erupted with laughter and I just smiled.

This.

This was the kind of family I'd always ached for. Love, acceptance, and humor. No wonder Bay had turned out to be such an angel.

I met her eyes with her across the table and she bit her lip, smiling back at me.

The words 'I love you' wanted to burst out of my mouth, but I waited. We had to wait. There was still Georgia to consider, and Bay's dad. We had to figure it out amongst ourselves before blurting everything out for the world to hear.

When everyone was done with eating, the cameras came out.

"Ok! Time to capture the post-turkey bloat!" Julie screamed which made everyone cheer.

What the actual hell?

Each kid lined up first, poking out their distended bellies before taking a nice, normal picture afterwards. The other men were next, then *me*.

"Uh...I don't take good pictures or..."

"Oh, nonsense! Come on. Time's a-wasting and we're all going to be passed out soon. Let's get to it!"

I pushed out my belly the same as the others, lifting my eyebrow as Julie took a picture of my profile, then she demanded a nice picture.

"You get in there too, Bay," she said with a wink. "You can show Georgia what she missed out on!"

Bay slipped under my arm quickly, easing into my side and for the first time since the camera came out, a real smile burst across my face.

"There it is!" she said, snapping a picture on Bay's camera. "Now one of you, Bay!"

Bay did an exaggerated pregnant belly look, holding it like a precious baby, and my throat went dry at the imagery. I wanted her pregnant. I wanted her pregnant with *my* baby, not a food baby.

Holy hell... I was getting way ahead of myself.

Next were the older women who did a Charlie's Angels pose with finger guns before they went to join their husbands in the living room, leaving the dishes for later.

Bay flipped through the pictures for a couple minutes, then burst into laughter.

"Oh my God! You weren't joking!" she snorted, pointing to the little screen on the camera.

Looking down was me, and it was a terrible shot.

"I wasn't joking. You're the only one who's ever managed to get good shots of me."

She lifted the camera and snapped a shot of my smirk. Looking at the shot again, it was like wool spun to gold. How did she manage it? It was fucking magic!

"I don't know. I guess I have a special talent of making people look their best."

"You'd make a fortune with kids and pregnant ladies," I told her. "They're always struggling to look their best."

She just grinned.

"Are you kidding? I would love that! The problem is getting people to actually pay me to take their pictures."

Business? I knew business.

"So you're saying you'd get into photographing people like that if you had customer acquisition?"

"Of course. That's my dream."

"Then why are you going to college for an art degree?" I asked.

"Because that's what my scholarship was for, first of all, and I've heard everywhere that it doesn't matter what your degree is in, just that you have one. Also, I've been learning quite a bit from my art classes. We've talked a lot about light and shadow in this first semester and it's incredible listening to a professional explain the mechanical side of art like that."

I bit my cheek before I said something stupid, like commenting on how beautiful she looked when she talked about the things she's passionate about, or how hot it made me for her.

"Sounds to me like I need to help you get a business plan together."

Her eyes lit up in interested awe.

"You'd do that?"

I just shook my head, staring down at her.

"Of course I would," I breathed. "I love you."

Her cheeks flushed pink and she smiled up at me, lifting onto her toes a little before catching herself. She turned to her family, half of which was watching us with private little grins on their matronly faces. Good thing her dad and uncle were too busy watching TV.

"Bay!" her mom called to her. "Come sit! I want to hear all about school."

I watched her go, shoving my hands into my pockets so I wouldn't reach for her.

The kids were playing Legos on the floor, so I went to them and dropped to my ass before clicking some pieces together.

"What're you guys making?" I asked while assembling some kind of awkward spaceship.

"I'm making an airplane," Nate, the eldest boy said with a grin, showing me his boxy plane.

"I'm building a plane too!" the younger boy said, holding up this giant square monstrosity that looked more like a house than an airplane.

"Awesome!" I said, fist bumping the boys before turning to Marmy who was clicking some random pieces together.

"What're you making, kiddo?" I asked her, and she grinned before holding up a tire pressed onto a long green piece.

"It's a *flower*!" she yelped, holding it up by its 'stem'.

She reminded me of Georgia a little when she was that age. Cute and unassuming, trusting and curious about what was going on around her.

What had happened?

A pang of sadness shot through my chest, but I pushed it down so I could concentrate on the kids in front of me, not the shadow of the one I used to have.

Half an hour later I looked back up and saw Bay watching us with this incredible look on her face, tears glistening in her eyes and cheeks flushed. Judith was watching her daughter and I saw

235

matching tears well in her eyes too as Bay watched on, meeting my eyes from across the room.

She really did love me.

How could I have questioned it?

It hit me like a punch square in the chest, but she did. Bay loved an asshole like me. I was the luckiest man in the world.

Chapter 26

Bay

Saying goodbye was hard.

Of course I was glad to get back to Washington and regain normalcy, but at the same time, it felt so strange that home didn't feel like *home* anymore. Blake's house was my home. With him.

He'd said his goodbyes first, thanking Mom and Dad for letting him invade our holiday. My parents just waved off his thanks and gave him hugs, inviting him for Christmas.

Mom gave me the biggest hug, telling me to be a good girl and to be happy in a whisper right into my ear. The words brought tears to my eyes all over again. Something about finding out the man of my dreams loved me back had left me pretty weepy. I was just glad Dad didn't seem to notice.

Our bags were in the car, so after another round of hugs, I got into the car beside Blake and we took off for Tiffany's house.

Now, I didn't know what I'd been expecting when we showed up, but clothes on the lawn and suitcases strewn over the grass was definitely not it.

Jay was standing there, his arms wrapped around his head as Georgia was snatching the clothes up one by one, screaming at Tiffany who stood on the porch, pointing at her with a smoking cigarette between her fingers.

"You Goddamn tramp!" I heard through the window when the car shut off.

Blake was out of the car in a flash, stomping up the steps to the house, his hand outstretched with an accusing finger as he growled at his ex-wife.

Georgia was crying and I found myself jumping out and hurrying to her to take her in my arms.

"Don't you ever fucking call our daughter a tramp!" Blake bit out. "Despite having *you* as a mom, she's turned into a beautiful, intelligent, scrappy young woman, and I will not have you poisoning her one fucking second longer!"

"Oh, shut up!" Tiffany shrieked, chest bumping him back a step with her fake boobs. "She's my daughter, not yours. You have no idea what it's like to be a real parent. All you are is a sperm donor!"

My jaw dropped as I watched Blake's chest rise and fall with massive, angry breaths.

"Georgie," he called, staring at Tiffany. "Did she hurt you?"

Georgia just cried harder in her arms before her boyfriend came to the rescue.

"She slapped her," Jay said with a scowl, his hands and arms still folded around his head like he didn't know what to do. "Twice."

Blake's jaw worked and his hands fisted at his sides. Tiffany watched too, and a wicked smile spread across her face.

"Aw, are you mad, baby?" she asked in a sickeningly sweet voice.

Then it happened. I didn't see it coming, and I didn't think Blake did either because he just stood there and took it while Tiffany's hand lifted and landed with a resounding slap on his cheek.

His head jerked to the side, skin blooming into an angry red as she wound back and did it again.

On the third slap he caught her wrist in one of his hands before saying something low and serious, which had Tiffany blanching. She turned instantly and stomped back into her house before slamming the door so loud, I was sure my parents could hear it several blocks away.

Blake just stood there for a minute, getting his anger under control with some more heaving breaths before he made his way slowly over to me and Georgia.

He met my eyes for just a moment before taking his daughter from me, enveloping her in his strong arms where she started to sob.

With Georgia taken care of, I went about picking up the clothes that were still all over the grass.

Jay joined me, tossing them into the open suitcases.

"What happened?" I asked him in a low voice.

"No fucking idea. She just flipped."

I'd seen that happen once or twice before, but I'd never seen Tiffany actually hurt Georgia.

Blake had her face in his hands, his forehead against hers as he asked her things quietly and she just nodded, tears streaming down her cheeks as she cried.

The pain evident in the eyes of the man I loved was incredible, and I felt it in my gut, making me nauseous and confused.

"No joke. We were just talking then her mom took a phone call. All of a sudden she started calling Gigi a whore and a slut and all that, and she started throwing our stuff outside, telling us to get out."

"A phone call?" I asked.

He just nodded.

"Gigi tried to talk to her, but that's when her mom just started slapping her, just like she did a minute ago. That bitch is *crazy*!"

Jay was shaking his head as he zipped up one of the bags before bringing it to the Mustang.

A minute later Blake was bringing Georgia toward the car and she got into the back seat with Jay while Blake moved to help me pick up the last couple pieces of clothes.

"Are you ok?" I asked in a whisper, touching his cheek.

He shook his head, but stayed silent.

At least he was being honest. He would tell me when he was ready.

We got Georgia's bag together and put it in the back of the car before peeling away from that house and that awful woman. Blake was a tense mess for miles on the road, but city after city, he started to relax, little by little until eventually he took my hand in my lap.

Georgia was asleep on Jay's shoulder and he was watching something on his phone, so it was safe.

Dipping my head down, I pressed a kiss to his hand before sitting back and closing my eyes. Evidently while we were having a great holiday, it was World War III at Tiffany's home. Poor Georgia...

We got home in one straight shot. No hotel, no stopping except to eat and pee, and it was past dark when we pulled up to the safe little blue house nestled away in what I now considered home.

Jay didn't say much the whole drive, and Georgia drifted in and out of sleep, not saying much either. It'd been a really, *really* long day.

"You guys ok getting back to campus?" Blake asked as he helped Jay move their bags to Jay's car.

Georgia nodded, slipping into the front seat, leaving Jay to deal with us.

After shutting the trunk with their bags stowed away, he approached where Blake and I stood cautiously before looking up at his girlfriend's dad.

"Thanks, for what you did today. I had no fucking idea what to do and Gigi was just breaking down and..."

"She's my daughter," was all Blake said. "I'd do anything for her."

Jay's eyes shifted from him to me and back.

"So, does she know?"

Blake's eyebrow went up,

"Know what?"

"About you two."

240

Blake's curious expression turned almost threatening.

"What the hell are you talking about?"

It was Jay's turn to lift an eyebrow.

"You won't see me judging. But she won't forgive you if you hide it from her."

"Get out of here, Jay," Blake said with an exasperated sigh and he did.

Jay got into his car and he drove away, leaving me and Blake on the small front lawn.

"I think we're really bad at this," I said simply.

Blake huffed out a little chuckle before taking my hand and leading me into the house, opening the front door with his key.

"Yeah, after the week we've had, I'd agree. Georgie needs to be told. Soon."

I could agree with that.

"Do you want me to tell her?" I asked him.

"No. I will. I'm her dad, she should hear it from me."

My stomach fluttered.

After that, the only person left to tell was my dad. And he would probably be the toughest nut to crack, right behind Georgia.

"What happens if she..."

I couldn't even get the words out. They stuck in my throat like dry bread.

"Then Georgia will have to find a way to accept it," he said. "I love her, but I cannot make decisions about my happiness based on what she wants."

"Are you saying that I make you happy, Blake?"

He turned to me, pressing his palms to my cheeks as he stared into my eyes.

"That's a stupid question from such a smart girl."

"A stupid question that you still haven't answered."

He just gave a tired smile and nodded.

"Of course you make me happy." After a short pause, he motioned toward the bedroom. "Shower and sleep?"

That sounded like heaven.

"So, where do you see yourself five years from now?" I asked in a whisper as we laid in bed, cuddling at almost eleven in the evening.

We were both tired, but I couldn't get my brain to shut off in order to actually sleep.

Blake sighed and wiggled closer to me, his bare chest against my back, searing me with his incredible heat.

"Five years?" he asked in a low grumble, his voice already boasting that rough, sleepy quality I loved so much. "In five years I hope to be married and starting a family."

"Really?" I asked, finding myself turning to him to look into his deep blue eyes. "You want to start a family from scratch?"

Blake breathed out a long sigh before meeting my eyes with acute intensity.

"That's exactly what I want. With the right woman."

My breath caught in my throat as I stared into his eyes; into his *soul*.

"You said before," I whispered. "You said that you always wanted to fall in love. That you'd never experienced love before. And you told me that you love me."

A funny expression shifted over his face for a second before it turned a little sad.

"I did say that, and it's true," he said in a low voice, deep and soft. "And now I finally know what it feels like."

My lips popped open in shock and he shifted onto his elbow, leaning over me.

"But I hope you know that me saying that isn't meant to put pressure on you. If you chose to love me today, tomorrow, or twenty years from now, I'll forever be grateful that I have found love. I am capable of it. And I know more than ever that it is what I want. I know—I know that I'm not what you were hoping for. I get it. You're young and you're carefree right now. You're going to college and you're exploring the world. And I'm part of that. I get that, too. So yes, I love you. Yes, if I had the opportunity, I would marry you and we'd have the cutest little family and I don't think I could ever be anything but happy ever again. But that's *my* dream. And my dream isn't your dream. With me, you're trading *way* down. I know that Bay. I know that all too well."

His words sparked both empathy and anger in my lungs. Trading down? He wasn't a trade down at *all*. Blake was everything I didn't know I wanted. He was strong, sweet, hard working, content, funny and easy-going with a wicked streak of mischief that I adored. Did his age really take away from that? Did it even matter?

"You'll have to explain to me just how you are me 'trading down'," I asked. "Because I can't think of one way."

He lifted an eyebrow.

"Uh, how about what's glaringly obvious. I'm a lot older than you. That's a huge fucking trade down."

"How so? As I see it, it's like I'm getting the perfected model. I don't have to deal with the drunk frat boys or the twenty-five year old midlife crisis of not knowing what they want to do with the rest of their lives. I don't have to worry about whether you'd change your mind and prefer to be single. I don't have to worry about what kind of dad you'll be, because I already know. And hey, I don't even have to worry about you divorcing me to get the younger model, because I'm it."

He burst into quiet laughter, his face brimming with a grin.

"That's one hell of a way to look at it," he said with a shake of his head. "And I guess some of those things are true. But what about this? When you turn twenty-five, Bay, I'll have just turned forty. Or what about this? You turn thirty-five and I'll be *fifty*. Holy shit, I don't even want to think about fifty right now, but it is what it is. That would be our life if you actually wanted to stay with me."

"Do men lose their sex drives when they get older?" I asked, completely avoiding the subject.

For now.

"No. But they lose their ability to get it up."

"But there's a pill for that."

"Y-yeah, I guess."

"Well, there you go!" I said with a smile. "My only problem would be you losing your drive for me eventually with your *advanced* years. So, what if we sign a contract that you'll make sure we kept those pills around until you're well into your seventies? That should cover us. I'm sure I'll be a grouchy old ninny by the time you're seventy-something."

He gave a disbelieving laugh.

"As for the rest of that stuff, I don't see how any of that changes whether you're five months older than me or fifty years. You're not suddenly going to change who you are the moment you turn fifty. And to be honest, I don't have that many grand ambitions. In my life, the one thing I am looking forward to the most is being a mom. I want to stay home with the kids and I really want to be a *mom*. I'll do my photography on the side, and even bring in some money if I can manage to make a business out of it. But I never really wanted to be a working woman. That's not what gives me joy. I have the opportunity to change the world one life at a time, and I can't think of another calling in life more incredible than that."

My eyes glanced back up to his so I could gauge what he thought of my traditional ambitions, and I wasn't expecting the moisture gathered there, or the tear that slipped from his eye and down the bridge of his nose before dropping warm and wet onto my cheek.

As his eyes misted, his head dropped, searing a soft kiss on my lips as another tear fell onto my face. His emotions got the best of me and I started crying too, silently letting salty trails stripe my face as I accepted his simple kiss. And that kiss? It was the most intimate thing I'd ever experienced in my life. It was a kiss filled to the brim with love.

"The only problem," I said in a whisper when his lips separated from mine. "Is that I need to find a man who has those ambitions too. I only ever wanted a simple life, and a happy life. If you can give that to me, then where is the problem?"

He just shook his head, staring into my eyes again.

"How are you real?" he asked the cheesiest line ever.

But it didn't feel cheesy. His voice was so full of heartbreak and hope that my heart began to bleed for him.

"What do you love about me?" I asked him.

He coughed out a laugh before he answered with a small smile on his face.

"I love your face and your body. Of course I do. But that's not what made me love you. What I fell in love with is your mind, your smiles, your sticky sweetness that always seems to balm me somehow. I fell in love with your cooking, let's be honest, and I fell in love with your sassy mouth that manages to put me in my place without tearing me down. You know just how to work me in every single way while simultaneously taking me for who I am and making me better. You're talented but you're not self-absorbed. You're so strong in both mind and heart that you're willing to open the doors to the likes of *me* and still manage to love me anyway. Do you know how incredible that is?"

"Well, it did start out as a physical thing," I whispered, trying to wipe at my leaky eyes.

"Sure. But physical lust isn't love," he said, wiping at the tears for me. "I've experienced lust plenty, but this is so much more than that. For me, it always has been. I never would have taken the chance on you if it was just for sex. I turned down several women just since you started living here, because they weren't *you*. They couldn't even hold a candle."

"Stop being all sentimental," I laugh/sobbed. "If I keep crying like this I'm going to dry out like a worm on the sidewalk!"

He laughed with me and we just stayed like that, him hovering over me and me laying contentedly cocooned in him.

"I love that you love my cooking," I hiccupped. "And I love that you're so content with the smallest things. I love that you have ambitions, but you don't put everything aside in order to achieve them. I love how good of a dad you've been to Georgie. She might have only been around for a couple months a year, but she talked about you all the time. The times you spent having pizza and how you've teased her forever about pineapple on pizza. You know she doesn't even really like Hawaiin pizza anymore? She gets it because it reminds her of you. I know she's going through this weird...stage maybe? But no matter what, you've been there for her. What an incredible trait in a man.

"I love how you're not afraid to take calculated risks like jumping into freezing cold water, and how you somehow make me take risks too that I never would have on my own. You make me a better person too, because you draw me out of my shell. The only people in my life I can really be myself with are my family, Georgia, and you. And I'm glad you like my sass, because that's not going anywhere anytime soon."

He didn't respond with words. No, he let his hands and his mouth say everything his words didn't. Blake was so gentle with me. His kisses and touches were nothing but acute adoration radiating from him each time his tongue stroked mine or his fingertips brushed over every inch of my skin.

"I love you," he whispered as his fingers drew down my hip, dragging my cotton panties with them.

"Love you more," I breathed as his teeth nipped my throat.

My tank came off next, leaving me nude and writhing on the sheets beneath me as his mouth dropped to my breast, nibbling on the marbled tip between his lips.

"As much as I love how much you can worship my body, I need you inside me right now," I told him, feeling the ache between my thighs intensify with each scrape of his teeth against my nipple.

"Whatever you want, love," he said, smiling as he moved over me again, his mouth dropping to me as I wrapped my legs around his hips.

One of his hands gripped my thigh around his waist as we ground together, sweet torture of being so close but not close enough.

"You're still wearing your boxers," I reminded with a little gasp as he pressed his hips into mine, searing me through his clothes.

"You have a problem with that?"

"Blake!" I barked and he laughed, then shimmied out of his boxers in seconds.

Then he was inside me with a pair of echoing grunts from each of us.

He paused like that, pressing a kiss to my lips to give me a moment to adjust to him before he started moving. My eyes drifted closed and my hand curled around his neck, holding onto him in the gentle sway of the bed underneath us.

I could live like that forever, in his arms, his body all around me.

"Oh fuck," I heard him murmur before he started moving away from me.

"What?" I asked.

"Condom," he said simply.

"Just...it's ok," I breathed. "I want to have your baby, Blake."

He smiled wanly and kissed me one more time before going to the drawer and getting a condom anyway.

"You want my baby? Then marry me first," was his answer.

Marry?

"Is that a proposal?" I asked, gasping against the feel of him slamming into me again, a little less gentle and a little more needy.

He paused at that, buried inside me.

"Proposal?" He hummed the words as if to himself. "If it was, what would you say?"

"I'd ask you when we would tell Dad and Georgia so we could start planning the wedding."

He stayed frozen for a moment, until I jerked my hips, which made him start moving again.

We didn't mention it again, simply drifting into the bliss of each other until we were sweaty and so exhausted, panting and boneless on the bed beside each other.

"Are you serious?" he asked me after getting rid of the condom.

I looked his way and smiled.

"Of course I am. I want to marry you, Blake."

He bit his lip a little before laying back and staring at the ceiling where a fan turned slowly over us.

"You're nineteen. And you're ready to get married?"

"I'll be twenty in three weeks. And yes. I know what I want, Blake. And you're it."

He met my eyes again with this sort of shell-shocked expression on his face. Like he couldn't believe the words coming out of my mouth. After our conversation and making love afterwards, he was shocked that I actually, truly wanted him forever.

Blake didn't comment on that, and I swallowed down my insecurity because I knew it was a lot for him to take in.

We'd started out as nothing to each other but someone we heard about through a person we both knew and loved. Then we became almost friends, and that turned into dangerous attraction that buckled into hot sex. But now we were so much more. I hadn't planned it, and I knew he didn't either. I never once in my life thought that I would fall for an older man with some gray beginning to thread through the hair on his temples. I never once considered starting a family with a man who already had raised a child. I never once thought that I would fall for my best friend's dad. But I did. And there was no going back from that. I'd fallen for him every single day of the months we'd lived together, and my heart both broke and stitched back together as we leaned on each other to get through the hardships with Georgia.

But would Georgia ever forgive me? I loved her with my whole heart, but I loved her dad, too.

No matter what she said, nothing could take me away from Blake. Not even Georgia. I just had to hope really hard that she could understand.

Chapter 27

Blake

I wasn't sure exactly how to get my head on straight again. At work I was a bumbling mess, my brain still back in bed with Bay, her lips telling me words that I just couldn't seem to understand.

'*I know what I want, Blake. And you're it.*'

"What's up with you?" Marty asked, flinging his arm around my shoulders before leading me out of the construction zone and to the small lot of trucks parked out front.

"What do you mean?" I asked, looking to see if anyone else was around.

I needed to talk to the man. I didn't have anyone else I could talk it out with other than Bay, and honestly, I couldn't think straight with her in my vicinity. Marty had always been there for me, and I knew he wouldn't lead me wrong, even if it wasn't what I wanted to hear.

"Is it about the girl?" he asked, lifting an eyebrow.

I nodded and looked around again before taking a step closer to him, whispering.

"I love her, Marty. I'm a fucking idiot and I love her."

He frowned.

"And? You tell *her* this?"

I worked my jaw for a second as I slowly nodded.

"Over Thanksgiving. It just kind of came out."

"Ok. What did she say?"

"She said she loves me too."

Marty's eyebrow raised as he met my eyes.

"I don't see where the problem is, you lucky bastard."

"Because how the hell do I know if she actually loves me? I've been there, I know the difference, but she's so young...she's too young to know what she wants in her life, right? I can't marry her at twenty years old... I can't—"

"Whoa, slow down. Marry?"

I nodded.

"She said she wants to marry me."

Marty just stared in shock at me, shaking his head.

"Well, seems like she's done all the hard work for you, you idiot. I still don't see the problem."

"She's fucking *nineteen*," I growled.

"*And*?"

"*And*, she's a kid. I'm a man. I-I-I can't take advantage of—"

"Oh shut it for one minute." Marty waved his hand around to stop me. "If you love this girl, then she's got to be something special."

"She is..."

"Right. And if she's so Goddamn special for *you* to fall in love with her —*Mr. Bitter*— then she obviously isn't some idiotic teenager who falls in love every two seconds with her crush of the week."

"Well...no, but—"

"No buts! Think logically for a second here, Blake. A girl like her would only say it if she meant it. I've met her, and I like her. Hell, even Gail likes her! And that's saying a lot. That girl has an old soul, and that just seems to have worked in your favor. Don't look a gift horse in the mouth. Accept the miracle for what it is, and don't you dare analyze someone else's proclamations of love. It's not up to you to decide if she *means* it or not. Trust yourself, and trust her. If you can't trust her, then you definitely shouldn't be marrying her."

My chest felt extra tight as the truth in his words hit me over and over again like a semi truck.

"Now, if you love her, and she loves you, then there's no reason you can't get married. But I do suggest you cool it for a little bit. You haven't known each other long enough to talk marriage. Not really. But if that's something you'll consider in the near future, you definitely need to stop hiding her from everyone. You got that? You can't love her and be ashamed of her at the same time."

"I'm not ashamed," I admitted. "I just don't want to share her."

He grunted at that, crossing his arms over his chest.

"Good. Now, get your head back into the game. You can discuss this with your sweet little thing later. Right now you need to be the boss, not a teenager, stupid in love. Got it?"

I blew out a breath and nodded.

"Right. Thanks Marty."

"Mhmm. Now, the moment Gail finds out about this, because she will the moment I get home, she's going to want to meet that girl for real. Dinner Friday night?"

I smiled and nodded.

"I'll ask Bay, but I'm sure it's ok."

"Good. We'll plan on it and if that changes, let me know."

I nodded again and he walked away, giving me a minute to clear my head so I could do my job.

He had a point.

If we could get through all the hell that no doubt would follow us through the next couple months after telling her dad and Georgia, then we could get through anything. And if we got through it intact, then I was going to marry that girl, no more questions asked.

A grin spread across my face as I settled on the decision. It bloomed hope in my belly that I hadn't felt in a long, long time.

———————◇———————

"Hey," I greeted Bay the same as I had for so many weeks.

But it was different now. Suddenly I could see that moment happening for the rest of my life instead of a passing dream that I had to hoard in my heart until it was gone.

She kissed me with a grin as her greeting before going back to the kitchen where she was making something that smelled like tomatoes and spices and rice.

"I never asked, but I made curry. You like curry?"

I shrugged.

"Can't recall ever having it, to be honest," I told her, plopping my boots on the mat by the door.

"Ok, well, we're traveling to India today. I even got naan bread!"

The excitement on her face drew me in like a moth to a flame.

"Sounds delicious," I told her, pressing a kiss into the curve of her neck. "You busy Friday night?"

She looked over her shoulder at me while shaking her head.

"Marty asked us over. They want to meet you for real."

She paused and met my eyes.

"They know?"

I nodded.

"Marty figured it out, too. Love isn't a look I usually wear. He saw it a mile away."

She grinned contentedly before stirring whatever was in the pan again.

"I'd like to get to know them better. They seemed nice when I met them at the barbeque. And they're important to you."

"He's like a brother to me," I told her, slipping my hands around her waist as she slowly swayed her hips to the soft music coming from her phone. "A much older brother."

"In that case, I better get to know them well then."

The certainty and permanence in her words hit me all over again.

I wasn't sure exactly what it was about her being so sure about me that made me want to flee like a wild deer, but it sat so strange on my chest that someone actually *wanted* me. She *chose* me.

Just like that, it hit like lightning in my brain as it suddenly made sense.

Nobody had ever *chosen* me before. Not my parents, not Tiffany, not Georgia. Nobody ever picked to be with me, they were just...*stuck* with me.

And I was so fucking scared that Bay eventually wouldn't want me, either.

My hands fell away from her hips as I backed up, needing some space because my lungs suddenly weren't working anymore.

"I'm going to go take a shower," I told her in a choked voice.

She watched me leave with concern in her eyes, but she didn't follow. I was grateful for that, at least.

In the shower I turned the water to scalding as I stood there, rivulets drawing lines down each limb as my brain worked in overtime.

As hard as it had been with Tiffany, I had made it through because I never loved her. But with Bay? Would I survive if she changed her mind?

Little did she know that I wasn't worried one bit about me changing my mind about her. No, I was worried about her changing her mind about me. Bay was the angel and I was the mortal. She could have the world, and yet she was with me, in my kitchen, kissing me when I got back from work.

But I could be what she wanted. I knew I could. I could give her everything I had, mind, heart and soul. I was hers, utterly and completely. She just needed to know that.

And so did everyone else.

Chapter 28

Bay

He was acting so weird.

Like, ever since we got home from Vegas, he'd been acting strange, but while we were eating, he didn't say anything, and he was inside his own head, and I didn't know how to reach out to him.

We had a bowl of ice cream each while sitting in front of the TV, watching a new show because we'd run out of episodes from all the biker shows, and I just kept looking at him. But he wouldn't look at me. His eyes stayed fastened on the screen, blank, as if he wasn't even watching.

"Blake?" I asked after some time, watching the sun go down and the moon rise, large and bright in the sky.

"Yeah?" he asked back, almost startled by the sound of his name.

"Are you ok?"

He gave a little smile and nodded.

"Yeah. I'm good. You ok? You've been quiet."

I was quiet?

"Uh, I've only been quiet because you've been staring at the wall or the TV or at your plate since you got out of the shower."

He frowned.

"Sorry, babe... I've got a lot on my mind."

I watched his fingers twitching on the fabric of his sweats, like he was missing something from them.

"Something's going on, Blake."

"I, uh— I need a smoke."

He stood abruptly and went to his room before emerging again a minute later with his cigarettes and a lighter.

What was going on with him?

I battled with myself on whether I should join him or not, but something in my heart just told me to give him space. He was going through a lot, just like I was, and I needed to be ok with that. I would expect him to understand if I needed a little time, so that was what I'd give him.

And by *time*, I really meant like, ten minutes.

He didn't even take that long, luckily. He came back inside after having leaned on the porch railing, drawing on that cigarette until it was nothing but cinders.

"So, I know I'm acting weird, and that's because I don't really know what to think right now," he said when he stepped back in the door. "I'm not going to lie. I kind of feel like someone is offering me my dream on a silver platter, and instead of taking it like I should, my bitter, fucked up brain is telling me that I shouldn't even think about reaching for it because it's just going to be torn away the moment I get a taste of happiness."

My mouth opened in shock for a moment, then it flopped closed with a pop.

"You think I'm going to leave you," I managed.

"I don't think you're going to leave me, Bay. But I'm scared as all hell that you will." He blew out a breath and shook his head angrily. "Everyone in my life has left me, Bay. Everyone. Even Georgia left me... Eventually you get to thinking that you're not worth sticking around for."

I just frowned.

"I get it, Blake," I told him. "I mean, I don't know what *that* kind of rejection feels like but I get it... My family has been there for me, and it's always been that way, but Georgia didn't leave you. She's going through some weird crisis, and she'll be back. I *know* she will. You have to give her time. And secondly, that's not fair to me at all."

The change in my approach had him looking into my eyes with a startled expression.

"It's not fair to tell me that I'm going to leave. Because I'm not. And I'm not ok with you even considering something like that. I love you. You know how many people in my life I've said that to besides my family?"

"No," he whispered.

"One. Georgia. Well, and you. It's kind of an exclusive club."

His lip tucked under his teeth in a bite that had me mentally waving my hand in front of my face.

My boyfriend's hot. Give me a break!

"I hear you," he said, eventually. "Just give me some time, ok? I'm not going anywhere, and I'll try and trust you that you aren't either."

That would just have to be good enough for me.

"Ok. Now, go brush your teeth because you're not getting a goodnight kiss with cigarette on your breath."

He gave me a little smile and nodded, moving toward his bedroom.

I followed, stopping for just a minute to observe my things strewn about his room. I'd been careful before about keeping my things in my own room, but after getting back from Thanksgiving, I gave up and just kept my stuff with Blake's. My toothbrush sat beside his, my makeup littered his counter, my shampoo was sharing a shelf with his in the master shower. And the place of honor on his dresser top beside the TV was my camera case, sitting untouched since we'd returned from our trip.

After brushing his teeth, Blake moved toward the bed, shedding his shirt in one swift move and dropping his sweats by the foot of the mattress. Crawling under the sheets in just his boxers, I found my fingers digging into my camera case, taking the thing out and adjusting it to the dark.

Blake sprawled across the mattress with a sigh, eyes closing with his hands tucked under his head.

Beautiful.

Sure, men weren't supposed to be considered beautiful so much as handsome or hot or whatever, but each and every curve of his body spoke just as plainly as a woman's.

The blinds were partially open, drawing stark white lines of moonlight across the bed where he lay, and they followed the hills and valleys along his form, painting his face into the exact mold of perfection. Chiseled, strong, but still soft and attainable. He was an artist's wet dream, and *I had him.*

He was mine.

257

"You coming to bed?" he asked, his gravel voice floating through the room toward me.

"Not yet," I told him, watching for another moment before I lifted the camera and took a shot.

He recognized the sound of the shutter whooshing and opened his eyes, watching me back.

"What're you doing, baby?" he asked as I took another shot.

"I can't let this moment go without capturing it," I whispered, clicking the capture button again.

My feet dragged me closer to him, and I dropped to my knees to get his face in profile where the light hit him the best, streaking against his lips in stark contrast, black and white against his tan skin.

Two whooshes of my shutter had him opening his eyes again, watching me.

Intimacy was definitely something mental. I understood that. But there was something about that moment when he let me in, let me capture him at his most vulnerable, mostly naked in bed... It had my heart beating faster, pounding against my chest and making my fingers jitter to touch him.

So, one hand still with the camera, finger on the trigger, I lifted the other and barely touched the tips of my fingers to the base of his belly, dragging them over his taut skin, just grazing the band of his boxers.

His stomach dipped at the touch, eyes fluttering closed as his back arched into the sensation.

I caught the ragged breath he released, my camera working overtime to get every single movement of his lips and bend of his neck as he pressed further into the pillow under him, chin raising in pleasure.

My throat got thick and my body trembled as stuttered breaths left my lips too. He was like electricity. Igniting my blood, as if it was gasoline someone had struck a match to. Hot, burning, I melted into him. Not pausing in their gentle exploration, my fingers tucked just under the band of his boxers.

A soft moan breathed from him as I began to pull the elastic, it curved over his hip, tempting me with a sliver of muscle and skin.

He lifted his hips from the mattress and together we pulled them down until all that was covering him was the strategically placed sheets, pulled over one leg but dipping dangerously low.

Artist that I was, I took the placement for what it was, but I also knew I could make it better. I arranged the sheet just under his Adonis V and cupped it around his most intimate parts before exposing one solid thigh to the harsh moonlight coming in through the slatted window.

His arms hadn't moved, but his eyes were open again as he watched me take picture after picture until I was satisfied. But then again, I never really was satisfied.

I wasn't sure how much time had gone by, but when I felt like I had enough pictures in each angle of him, I whispered just loud enough for him to hear, "turn over."

Blake watched me for another moment, his hair dipping into his eyes as he peered through at me, and then he did as I asked, shifting and rolling until he was on his belly.

Again with my inability to breathe.

The shadows curved around him again as he propped himself up on his elbows, looking over at me as I stared at his bare back, ass and thighs.

No, women's figures weren't the most beautiful. They definitely had competition with Blake.

Dropping to my knees again, I took a couple shots from his side, then I moved toward his head. His eyes met mine as I reached out and thrust my fingers into his wild hair, nudging his head into the right position.

With his head dipped and his upper body angled high, the dramatic dip of his back stood out in the striped light. A few more shots later, I couldn't help my hand, lifting to touch him again. This time my hand drew down the bow of his back, causing tremors to flood down each vertebrae of his spine.

"Bay..." he rumbled in the sexiest, most controlled growl I'd ever heard him use. "Come here."

I knew I'd pushed him to his limits, and honestly, I'd pushed myself past my own. I was so ready for him, camera and pictures be damned at that point.

I put the camera down on his bedside table then pulled up the edge of my t-shirt, easing it over my head as he turned again, leaning against his elbows still as the sheets slipped completely off the bed and onto the floor.

My clothes couldn't get off fast enough as I watched him watching me. Fire stared back at me, and I saw that barely restrained passion snapping like sparks behind his eyes.

Desperation wasn't a strong enough word for how much I needed him. Mind, body, heart and soul. This man would be mine. Every last part of him would belong to me. He just didn't know it yet.

Dragging down my panties last, I began to move, crawling over him and settling straddle on his hips as our mouths clashed in greedy lips, teeth and tongue. His hand curled around my head, digging into my hair and pulling me closer until it almost hurt, and then his hips bucked beneath me.

My gasp encouraged him, and his hands dropped to my hips and thighs, digging his fingers into my flesh as he ground into me again, making us both moan.

"This is mine," I told him in a whisper. "This is my choice."

His eyes met mine just as I sank down on him, skin to skin. Blake's face tightened in a mixture of tortured pleasure, a hummed moan breathing over my lips as his eyes squeezed shut.

"You don't know what it's like, Bay," he breathed as I rode him.

Coherent mind was long gone by that point. All I wanted was harder, faster, hotter.

"If you got pregnant and you had to be with me because of it..."

I pressed my hand over his lips, grinding hard before giving him my simple finality.

"I wouldn't marry you just because I got pregnant, Blake," I whispered. "And it's too late anyway. Whether you want it or not, I'm going to marry you. Do you understand that? You're mine. Every single part of you, you're *mine*."

His jaw clenched, eyes still shut as he suddenly bucked me up like a freaking wild horse.

"Fuck..." he ground out, knawing on the word in an angry breath as his hands gripped me tighter, urging me to move just like I wanted.

Harder. Faster. Hotter.

A whimper breathed unbidden from my lips as pleasure skyrocketed. I could move just as much as I wanted, just the way I wanted and I did. God...

His fingers bit into my flesh as he growled, finishing inside me just as I reached my tipping point, heat suffusing through my belly and breasts, I came. He was cursing again, his head digging into the pillow as my nails made little angry crescents in his shoulders until the intensity passed, settling me into weightless afterglow.

I sat there, still on him as he was still in me, us both panting and sweating and holding tightly onto each other. Then his eyes met mine, and I could immediately see that something had changed; shifted. Determination stared back at me instead of confused uncertainty.

Yes, he was mine.

Chapter 29

Blake

I was going to ask her to marry me.

I wasn't sure when, or how, but I was.

After that night with her, I could see it in her eyes. She meant it. She meant every single thing she said, and she was right. I was hers. I'd been hers the moment she blushed over those stupid fucking sex toys. I was hers the moment I tasted her cooking. I was hers again and again and again each and every time I kissed her. The woman owned my fucking *soul*. I didn't even know that was possible.

So I was planning. She deserved something incredible, but before all that, I had to find a time and a way to tell Georgia that I was going to marry her friend.

"Blake!" Bay called from the bedroom door. "Dinner! Hurry your turtle butt up! Food's getting cold!"

I grinned.

"Coming!" I called, pulling on fresh boxer briefs that Bay had just bought me, because evidently she liked the tighter stuff better than my old threadbare, baggy ones.

And hell, whatever made her happy, I'd do.

Heading out to the dining room in just some oversized sweatpants, I threaded my fingers through my damp hair and pulled out a chair just as there was a knock on the door.

What the hell?

Bay met my eyes with equal surprise, but I just shrugged it off and went to the door. What were the chances that the cookie campers were back? I could use some more mint chocolate ones. Bay liked those ones best, frozen in the freezer like a monster.

I grinned again at my own thoughts and pulled the door open to a tearstained face staring back at me.

"Georgie?" I practically gasped, already stretching my arms out to her.

She fell into my embrace and started sobbing, dropping a bag down by our feet as she did.

Bay moved forward and peeked around the door at the sound of her friend's name.

"Georgia? Are you ok?" she asked, her eyes wide in shock.

Georgia just shook her head against my chest, leaving little slick spots of tears against my skin and hers.

"They...those girls... I can't do it anymore, Daddy..."

I didn't care that my stomach was growling. I just needed to hold my baby girl.

"Come inside," Bay said to us both, being the voice of reason as always.

I did as she said, keeping my arms around Georgia as we shimmied further into the house while Bay closed the door.

"What happened?" Bay asked, and that had Georgia turning away from me, wiping at her tears enough to answer her friend's question.

"They...they..."

She paused, then looked back over at me, fresh tears brimming in her eyes.

"Daddy...I'm...I'm going to have a baby."

Air left my lungs as a thousand pounds of pressure hit me all at once.

Baby? A fucking *baby*?

"It's Jay's. He doesn't know yet. I told one of the girls and she just...she told everyone! They've been writing horrible things on the mirrors and spreading rumors and they even cut up my clothes..."

What else could I do?

I hugged her again.

"It's ok, baby girl," I whispered to her.

I knew that feeling. I knew it so fucking well. I found out I was going to be a dad at sixteen years old, for hell's sake. At least Georgia had graduated from high school, and she still had a future in front of her. Baby or no baby, she had me. She had her father, which was something I never had.

I looked over Georgia's shoulder toward Bay, who had this serene expression that I just couldn't understand. How could she be so calm?

"Georgie," Bay whispered, turning Georgia's attention to her. "Remember what we talked about forever ago?"

Georgia suddenly gave a teary laugh.

"Of course I do."

"We promised that if one of us ever got pregnant like that, God forbid, that we'd just marry each other and have affairs like a grown up."

I snorted a strangled laugh which had both girls turning toward me with grins on their faces.

"You saying you're going to marry me?" Georgia asked, accepting Bay's hand when she folded hers over my daughter's.

"No. But I promise you right here, right now. I will be there for you. You'll hate me with how much I'm going to love that baby. 'Cause they'll love me more."

Georgia gave a teary laugh and nodded, hugging her friend.

"There are options," I whispered. "Have you thought about the options?"

Georgia shook her head vehemently.

"I'm keeping it. I don't even care if Jay doesn't want it. What if you and Mom had gotten rid of me? I wouldn't even exist."

My heart bled and wept for her. I knew the excruciating decision of deciding to keep a baby at the worst time. But we had, and I couldn't say that I ever made a better decision in my life. Besides the fact that Tiffany had used the baby to manipulate me to do what she wanted, she had agreed to keep our child, too. And at least I had her to thank for that.

"It's your decision, Georgie," I told her, taking her hand in mine. "I'll support you no matter what you decide to do. You two can stay here and you can finish your degree and we'll figure it out. The baby can have the spare room and..."

"But Bay is in the spare room." Georgia frowned. "I won't let you kick her out for this."

Oh shit... I forgot about that. Bay had been in my room for so long now, I'd forgotten that she was supposed to have her own space away from me.

"Right. That's not what I meant..."

Hell...how was I supposed to tell her now, with all of this weighing on her? Georgia was going through enough without adding my shit on her shoulders, too.

"We'll figure it out, one way or the other." Bay nodded firmly, meeting my eyes with a resolute expression.

She was right. We would.

Eventually.

"When are you going to tell Jay?" I asked.

"I don't know... I'll text him and tell him where I am."

"You don't need to do it tonight. Let's get you settled in and we can talk about it later. Bay just made dinner."

For once, Georgia seemed to take stock of the situation surrounding her. She saw Bay in her tight yoga pants and tank top, and me in just my sweats and her eyebrows knitted together.

"Where's your shirt?" she asked with a frown.

"I just got out of the shower," I admitted.

The truth.

"Well, go get dressed. Bay doesn't want to see all that."

I met Bay's eyes over Georgia's shoulder and she grinned conspiratorially.

She did. She totally wanted to see 'all that'. But she wouldn't get a chance for a while, it seemed.

"I'll just go...put on a shirt."

The girls whispered together and I saw Bay put her hand over Georgia's belly before they both broke into tears together.

They needed that, so I just left the room and gave them a few minutes to themselves as I slowly found a shirt, then pressed my back against the wall to let it all soak in.

Baby.

My baby was having a baby.

I was going to be a grandfather at thirty-fucking-six years old.

Oh fuck...Tiffany would have a heyday when she found out. I had to talk to Georgia about that, too.

Moving out of my room and toward the girls again, I heard their conversation for a moment and stopped, just listening.

"What do you think Jay is going to say?" I heard Bay say, asking the tough questions.

God, I loved that woman.

"I don't know." Georgia sighed. "I think he'll be a little freaked out, but I don't think he'll leave me in the dust. We're probably over, though. We've been rocky ever since we got back from Vegas. He hasn't been talking a lot."

"Well, I guess we'll see if I need to castrate him in his sleep," Bay said, sounding almost bored. "Did you tell your mom?"

Georgia snorted.

"No! After what she did last week, I don't think I want to tell her at all until I have to. Maybe a few years after the baby is here."

Bay chuckled and in their silence, I made myself known.

"Let's eat," Bay told us both. "My food is hopelessly cold, so it's a good thing we're having salad."

Of course.

A smirk drifted across my lips and Bay noticed, sending me her own little grin as she led Georgia to the table.

Dinner was awkward. It was so strange to not be able to hold Bay's hand or look her in the eyes while I talked to her, or even just make little flirty remarks that had become our norm. I was absolutely struggling for things to say that wouldn't give us away prematurely, and Georgia was in her own head the whole time, just picking at the chicken and lettuce half-heartedly.

266

"Tomorrow," Bay said finally. "You have to tell Jay tomorrow. Ok? For better or worse, he has to know. Sooner than later."

I agreed with that. The sooner he knew the sooner he could plan for it, like I had.

"Ok," Georgia said with a sigh, then pushed her plate away. "Sorry, but I have to lay down. I don't feel so good."

Getting up too, I followed her to her bedroom with her bag and helped her get settled in before closing the door behind me as I left the room.

"She ok?" Bay asked, still sitting at the table, not eating.

"I fucking hope not," I breathed. "A baby? At eighteen? I raised her so she knew *not* to follow in our footsteps..."

Bay shrugged.

"Doesn't really matter now. We just find out how we can help her and give her what she needs to get through it. And really, *really* hope that Jay will back her up."

"If he doesn't..." I growled, but Bay gave me a look that had me shutting up.

"Jay isn't that old, either, Blake. He'll make stupid mistakes in his life, just like all of us do. Not every boy was raised to be a man like you. You know that."

Her words were flattering, but also disheartening. I hoped Jay was a man like me.

"I didn't hate him," I admitted. "You know, when we weren't at each other's throats, he was ok."

"I think if you'd have had conversations without the enclosed space of your Mustang, it probably would have gone better. And he was fine on the way home. He even thanked you for handling Tiffany."

"Yeah, well Tiffany needs a special sort of hand to put her back in her place. He had no chance."

I could still taste the bitter words I'd whispered to her over that awful situation. It took a threat of calling the cops on her for drugs I had correctly guessed she had hidden in her house. I might

267

have added just a little on how an addict prostitute like her would do in prison. Either way, it worked.

"Well, you handled it like a champ."

I just shrugged and poked at the salad before pushing mine away too.

After dinner we had a hard time settling down, so we took advantage of the fact that Georgia was in her room to move Bay's things out of my bedroom.

"We have to tell her," Bay told me. "She'll find out and she'll be even more hurt."

"Yeah, but right now she's got enough on her plate," I said. "I don't want to overwhelm her."

Bay frowned but nodded.

"I get it. I don't know. I guess we'll play it by ear."

"Yeah," I agreed, then paused before going to Bay and pulling her into my arms.

"How are you doing?" she whispered.

I just shook my head and released all my stress as her sweet calm sank into me.

"It'll be ok, Blake. I know it will."

And I believed her.

Chapter 30

Bay

I missed classes with Georgia the next day. Blake went to work since he was up against deadlines again, so I promised to take care of her and he just smiled his thanks when he left, long before Georgia was even up.

I convinced her to send our address to Jay and tell him she needed to talk to him while we made dinner, and it was a little more than an hour later that there was raucous knocking on the door.

We both knew who it was. Unfortunately, Blake answered the door.

Jay was there, his beanie on his head like usual, but his face was full of worry as he spotted Georgia.

"Fucking hell, woman!" he practically yelled. "The girls said you left and never came back! I've been looking for you all fucking night and day!"

The dark circles under his usually bright eyes spoke the truth of his words, and I could see the guilt on Georgia's face.

Blake just stood there with his fists clenched as Jay pushed past him to embrace Georgia.

"Seriously, what the hell is wrong with you?" I heard Jay murmuring as he held her.

"I'm pregnant," Georgia hiccupped, then squeezed her eyes shut as if expecting a blow or something.

Jay's grip on her loosened as he stared at her with shock fresh over his face.

"You're kidding," he breathed.

She just shook her head in jerky little motions before adding, "Thirteen weeks."

Basically since we arrived. Wow...

Jay shoved his hand through his hair, his beanie dropping to the ground behind him as he soaked in her words.

"A baby?" he asked, and finally Georgia looked up at him, almost annoyed.

"No. A puppy."

I stifled a laugh, but I was the only one. The other three in the room were all dead serious.

"A baby," Jay said more firmly, circling his arms around his head before crouching on his haunches, making himself into a little ball of stress.

"I don't expect anything from you," Georgia said finally. "I'm keeping it, and if you don't want to be part of our lives, then—"

"What the fuck?" Jay practically yelled, shooting to his feet again. "Give me a fucking second, ok? I just found out I'm about to be a *dad*. I need to let this process. That doesn't mean I don't want the baby or you."

So, did he?

"Well, you're not saying anything..." Georgia shrugged, her bravado back now that the words were off her shoulders.

Jay just shook his head, staring at Georgia for a minute before he sprang forward, taking her into his arms and kissing the hell out of her.

Well, I hadn't expected that.

Jay had always seemed the perfect little partying frat boy. I hadn't expected him to be so...*accepting*.

"So, what? We get married? You want to get married, Gigi?"

Georgia choked as she got her breath back.

"Married?" She almost laughed. "Who says we have to get married?"

He gave a weak shrug and a sad smile.

"I don't know! I've never done this before!"

"I fucking hope not," Blake finally spoke up, his voice hard as he watched the scene unfold.

It was like Jay and Georgia had forgotten our presence, because with Blake's words, they both turned to him, and then me.

"Little privacy?" Jay asked us.

"No. Privacy was what got you in this position," Blake said with a frown.

"Dad. We've had sex. A lot. And that's not about to change. You need to give us a few minutes...please?"

At the word please, Blake's frown deepened, but he did as she asked. He grabbed my hand and led me outside. It was a little blustery with a few rogue raindrops, but it gave each of us some privacy.

"Well, that went well," I told him.

Blake just frowned more and worked his jaw.

"Don't you even be mad, Blake. You've literally been in his exact spot. You don't get to be angry for something you've done yourself."

"You don't think I know that?" he snapped, then sighed and lifted my hand to his mouth to kiss. "Sorry..."

I could understand his volatile feelings. It was all a lot, and Blake felt things so deeply.

"Blake," I whispered. "Come here."

He met my eyes and obeyed, taking a few steps forward until my back was pressed into the side of the house, completely out of sight from Georgia and Jay. I pulled his head down to meet mine, and I kissed him long and hard until he loosened up. Then the door rattled, opening.

We jerked apart, both wiping our lips as Jay peeked out the door, giving us a look like he knew exactly what we were doing.

"Hypocrite," I heard him chuckle under his breath before motioning us back into the house.

Blake met my eyes across the deck and took an enormous breath before following Jay in.

I took another minute to gather myself, checking in the kitchen window to make sure I didn't have the ring-around-the-lips from kissing a man with stubble on his cheeks before making my way back into the house.

"No, he's not moving in," Blake said sternly. "We've got six months before the baby is even here. And Georgie, you have me and Bay here to support you. You two want to get married, then fine. Do that and we'll talk about him living here, but if not, then we can work it out *after* the baby is born. One thing at a time. There's enough shit going on that we don't need to add to."

"Like what?" Georgia asked, her eyes flicking between me and Blake.

I watched Blake run his tongue over his teeth, probably trying to think of what to say.

"It's...we'll talk about it later. Right now this is about you. We're focusing on you."

Georgia frowned and looked over at Jay who was staring at the ceiling, lips clamped shut.

"Fine. Nobody wants to talk*? Fine*. But I'm done with this. I'm hungry, so let's eat. Can Jay at least stay for dinner? Or is that asking too much?"

Blake growled in his chest for a moment before giving a harsh nod of approval.

The two of them headed toward the kitchen, and I followed, trying to give Blake a minute to get himself together. The poor guy was pretty hard in the pants, and that probably didn't really help his mood either. Good thing he was wearing his sweats that hid it pretty well.

We were bad at it, but we could put the focus on Georgia long enough to figure out how we could tell her.

There was no way we could keep it a secret any longer. Blake and I were sitting at an awful level of blue balls with each stolen kiss with the short moments we managed to sneak away. Georgia had been staying home, and while I still went to classes, we didn't have time alone. Blake's mood became progressively worse, and to add the crap cherry on top of our bad situation, Jay was hanging out every evening, which meant that Georgia was out in the living room with him, leaving no semblance of privacy to be stolen.

I couldn't even sneak into Blake's room at night because the floor squeaked and the walls were thin. Georgia would hear and know immediately.

So we just stayed away, close but so far. We had to cancel our dinner with his friends because how would we explain that? *'Oh, I'm going with your dad to his friend's house for no reason. Just hanging out.'*

Yeah...no. No way in hell.

So I usually sat on the couch and Blake sat on the recliner while Jay and Georgia cuddled on the floor as we watched movies and shows after dinner. Well, until Blake kicked Jay out at about ten.

Two weeks. It went on for two torturous weeks.

"Get the hell out of my house," Blake had said to Jay in the living room one night.

Jay understood Blake's grouchy moods by that point and just did what was asked, and usually left Georgia with a searing kiss that just rubbed salt in our metaphorical wounds.

I wanted to kiss Blake like that. I wanted to hold him and talk to him and ask how he was handling it all... Instead I just sat there and frowned.

I was doing a lot of that lately.

"I'm going to bed," I announced, trying not to meet Blake's eyes as he watched me go, a look of frustration on his face.

His hand sliced through his hair and he sighed into his palm as I left him. I couldn't watch him suffer like that a second longer or else I might just fold myself into his lap and sink into him right in front of his daughter.

We had to tell her...

"Wait for me," Georgia called as she gave Jay one last kiss goodnight, closing the door behind him.

Wait for her?

Georgia followed me to my room and crawled into bed with me, sharing it like we used to when we were little. We did that sometimes even as adults, but we hadn't done it much since she'd gone crazy and left, joining her sorority.

It was actually kind of nice to have her back like that.

The lights were off, and we could hear Blake flicking off all the lights in the house before his footsteps echoed with creaks through the house as he went to his bedroom. His door shut with a thud, leaving the air around us silent.

"So," Georgia whispered. "We haven't talked since I got back."

"What do you mean?" I asked with a nervous laugh. "We talk all the time."

"About me. Not about you. I want to know about you. But before I do, I owe you an apology."

I turned to her and her eyes glittered with tears.

"I'm really sorry, Bay. I shouldn't have ditched you here... I don't know what I was trying to do. I just wanted to be accepted and loved, you know? Mom convinced me that I had to join a sorority if I was going to survive socially, and I believed her. I freaking believed her. Why? I don't know. I feel really stupid, because they only liked me so long as they could use me. They weren't real friends. You are. You're the only real friend I ever had. I love you, sis."

I choked on tears over the confession.

"It's ok, Georgie... It's—"

"No, it's not. I treated you and Dad like shit. And you know how I know you guys really love me? Because you loved me despite it all. You loved me anyway, and you were there for me, even though I was a total bitch."

I couldn't really disagree, so I just hugged her, instead.

We cuddled, our arms around each other in the darkened silence for a few minutes before she whispered, "What's going on between you and Dad?"

My eyes shut tight and I pulled in a silent gasp.

She knew.

"I want to know the truth, Bay. No more lies, no more half truths."

At least in the dark, it was easier to tell her the dirty truth.

But it wasn't dirty. Not really. I just hoped she would see it that way.

"We... We're together," I whispered eventually, and Georgia tensed in my arms.

"Together?" she asked, her voice tight.

"We love each other, Georgie."

There was a long string of quiet before she spoke again.

"Do you love each other? Like, for reals?"

"It started kind of strange," I admitted. "You know how hot your dad is."

She gave a huff of a laugh as I went on.

"I kind of...fell in lust with him. He drew me in, and after you left, it was just him and me at night and we just...we happened. He tried to stop it, but I wouldn't let him."

"And?"

"And, after we got together, we spent more time, and fell in love instead of lust. Your dad is an amazing man."

Georgia blew out a long breath.

"What the hell, Bay?" she said eventually. "You're having sex with my *dad*? That's so gross!"

I just laughed quietly, still feeling flutters of nervousness in my belly.

"And when I told you that he needs someone *like* you, I didn't mean he needed *you*. For fuck's sake... What's wrong with you? He's my dad!"

I wasn't sure what to say to that. He was her dad, and my being with him probably felt like a sort of betrayal for her.

"Who the hell am I to judge..." she said after another minute, her tense body finally relaxing again. "I'm the one who's eighteen and pregnant. At least Dad's not stupid enough to do that twice in one lifetime."

275

I harrumphed at that.

He might not be stupid enough, but maybe I was.

We laid there another couple minutes before Georgia sighed.

"You know, you and I are kind of soul mates. If I was a dude, we'd totally hook up." We giggled at that before she went on. "And Dad's like me. I get what he sees in you."

That almost sounded like...dare I say...*approval*?

"I love him with my whole heart, Georgie. I want to marry him."

"Marry?" She coughed, choking on the single word. "You mean like...*step-mom*?"

I grimaced.

"I'd never be your step-mom, Georgie! Ew!"

"If you married Dad you would be! I mean seriously! Have you guys thought this through? Have you considered how gross this is for me?"

Sobering, I nodded.

"We've talked about it extensively, actually," I whispered. "And of course we thought about you. That's why we didn't tell you yet."

"Why didn't you tell me?" she demanded. "Seriously, I deserved to know that you guys have been...*fucking*."

She shuddered at the word.

"It's so much more than that, Georgia..."

"I...I need a while," she said eventually, sliding out of my bed.

"We were going to tell you that week," I blurted out. "But then you showed up and with the baby and everything...we didn't want to add on the stress or anything..."

"So that's why Dad's been the royal-ass grouch," she said, enlightenment in her voice. "'Cause you guys haven't been boning because of me."

I couldn't deny it.

"You should have told me, Bay."

I could hear the hurt in her voice.

"You weren't exactly acting like our Georgie," I admitted. "How was I supposed to tell you that I'd fallen in love with your dad? You already wouldn't really even talk to me."

She was quiet for a minute, then climbed the rest of the way out of bed before slipping out of the room without another word.

Well, now that the damage was done, I got out of bed too and made my way to Blake's room.

He jumped when the door opened, sitting stark upright in bed.

"Georgie?" he asked, rubbing at his eyes.

"It's me," I whispered.

"Bay...you can't be in here," he breathed in a tortured tone.

"I can now. Georgia knows."

He was silent as I slipped under his sheets and wrapped myself around him.

God it felt so good after so many days of staying away.

He breathed a massive sigh of relief when our skin touched.

"How?" he asked eventually.

"She asked. Straight up asked. You know how she is."

He sighed again and nodded before pressing a kiss into my hair.

"I missed you," he breathed, squeezing me tighter.

"Missed you more," I told him.

"Don't think that's possible."

It was a little too soon to let Georgia hear just how much we loved each other, so I restrained myself from crawling on top of him and riding him until we were both writhing in pleasure.

"How mad is she?"

"I think it'll be ok," I said, kissing his pec before closing my eyes. "I told her I'm going to marry you."

He chuckled and the warm, deep sound soothed my soul.

"Good," was all he said before we went silent, wrapped in each other.

Chapter 31

Blake

The next morning was fucking awkward. We all sat at the table staring at each other, having breakfast. Why wasn't it a work day? Why couldn't I have been out of the house at six like I always was? Georgia wouldn't look at either of us as we ate, and there was nothing but metallic clinks on plates.

And then breakfast was over. That's when the real hell began.

"Dad I'd like to talk to you," Georgia suddenly said, still seated at her chair as Bay picked up her plate as well as mine.

We met eyes for a second, both a little bit scared before I had to buck it up.

"Sure, baby girl."

Bay started to sit, but Georgia shot her narrowed eyes and said, "Just dad."

Ohhhh-kay.

Bay squeezed my hand for just a moment before leaving the room, making herself scarce.

Suddenly, it was my turn for Georgia's interrogation.

"So," she said with a frown on her pretty face. "You're fucking my best friend."

Ok, starting out right at the heart of the matter.

"It's a hell of a lot more than fucking."

"How so? Please explain this to me. How in the *world* did this even happen? I mean, you're my dad, for hell's sake!"

"That's not fair, Georgie," I started, but she just shook her head. "I have finally found happiness and you, out of all people should be on my side about this. You love her just as much as I do."

278

"Love? You know how pervy that sounds? You love your daughter's best friend."

She wasn't wrong.

"So, what? It wouldn't be weird if she wasn't your friend? If I would have just found a twenty year old on my own, then it would have been fine?"

"She's not twenty yet,"

"Five days, Georgie. Five days and she is."

"Don't you hear yourself?"

I lifted an eyebrow.

"I don't need your approval, kiddo. I'm a grown up, and so are you. I had hoped that when I was able to tell you, that you'd support me the way that I will always support you. I wanted to wait until you had things a little more in hand, but you've always been astute, and I've found recently that we really suck at pretending."

She blew out a breath and leaned back in her chair.

"Really? You're telling me that it's Bay? She's who you're finally going to settle down with? Bay is going to be my step-mom?"

Oh shit, I hadn't thought about that.

I just gave a nervous chuckle and rubbed at my eyes.

"I mean, I get it. Bay is so freaking awesome. And she's loyal and smart and the most loving and forgiving person I've ever met. I don't blame you, Dad. I just wonder what the hell you're thinking sometimes. And I can't believe you hid this from me."

I just nodded.

"I know. I was wrong to hide it. We just weren't sure if it was some fling at first and then when we finally realized that it was so much more than that, shit happened. You weren't around and we were just trying to cope with this ourselves."

She frowned, twining her fingers over her belly like all pregnant women do.

Holy hell, my baby was pregnant... I still couldn't believe it.

279

"Besides," I said eventually, shoving my fingers through my hair. "I'm not the only one hiding their relationship. You promised me that I'd get to meet any guy you dated."

Georgia nodded slowly, picking at the paint on her fingernails as she murmured, "I'm sorry, Dad. Mom just...she said so many things. She warned me you'd be suffocating and overbearing and I guess that just skewed my brain. She called every week, you know? She just went on and on about you and all the things you ever did wrong. I didn't really believe her, but it was easier to just do what I thought I wanted. Mom said I needed to be in a sorority, so I got into a sorority. And that was the worst. I thought they were my friends, but they were just predators, waiting to pounce the moment you show weakness."

How could I explain the type of woman her mother was? Georgia loved her mom, and I didn't want to ruin that, even with the truth.

"I was wrong. I shouldn't have left, and I shouldn't have treated you like that. Either of you. Jay helped me see that."

Well, maybe he wasn't so bad after all.

"He's still asking me to marry him every night when he leaves. I'm starting to think that maybe I want to."

"Do you love him?" I asked her, feeling a strange sort of nervousness for her.

"How the hell should I know? I've never loved anyone before."

"Yeah, well it's new for me too," I admitted. "But you know I always loved you. You've always been my little peach."

She snorted, but I could see the tears glistening in her eyes.

"And I realized that I loved Bay because she suddenly meant as much to me as you do. The thought of *not* being with her makes me sick, and when I'm at work all day, I can't stop thinking about her smile or craving her hugs."

Georgia wrinkled her nose, but she smiled, too.

"That's so gross Dad!"

"Yeah, well you better get used to it," I told her. "Given a little more time, I'm going to ask her to marry me. And if she says yes, then you're going to be staring at that for the rest of my life."

Her face softened.

"Oh, she'll say yes," Georgia hummed, nodding as she picked a string from the hem of her shirt. "She's head over heels for you. And Bay doesn't love easily. Not like that. Not fully and unhindered."

"What do you mean?"

"Bay doesn't show her real face to everyone," she said. "She hides behind a good girl façade that people just accept. If she shows that sassy side to you, then she trusts you. But to earn her love? That's kind of a big deal."

My chest swelled with the knowledge.

"So, I guess that's it? I don't have a say in this?"

"Not really." I shrugged, giving her a little helpless smile. "But we'll try and ease you into it, ok?"

"Yeah. Let's start by drawing the line of no sex in the house. At least while I'm here. I don't want to know what sounds my best friend makes while my Dad is..."

Georgia gagged, not finishing her statement.

"That's fair," I agreed. "Same goes for you."

"Swear," she said, putting out her pinky like we always did when we made a promise.

It had started years ago when she was a little girl. When I'd packed up my car and had to say goodbye to my baby girl for the first time, I told her '*I'll be back, baby. Promise you.*' She looked confused and hurt and on the verge of tears, but she took my hand in a pinky promise. '*Swear?*' she asked in her high pitched, childish voice. '*Swear,*' I'd whispered back before hugging her. It was the first time in my life that I had cried from sadness.

"Swear." I curled my pinky around hers and looked her in the eyes. "We ok?"

She just rolled her eyes and said, "I'm sure you are. This will take time for me to...wrap my head around."

"I get that. And I'm here to talk, and so is Bay."

"No, I think I'm pretty much talked out. Now I just need some bleach for my brain."

Just like that, my daughter stood and made her way toward the door.

"Where are you going?" I asked, standing too.

"Jay will be here soon to pick me up. I'm going on a walk to clear my head until he gets here."

She huddled in a jacket and a beanie, slipping into her short boots before leaving the house.

"Everything ok?" Bay asked, suddenly appearing from behind the dividing wall between the kitchen and the living room.

"Yeah, it's ok."

"I heard all that," she admitted, a touch of pink blushing her cheeks.

"Good. I'd hate to have to repeat it all," I told her, winking.

Hope and happiness blossomed in my chest and I couldn't help the grin that spread over my mouth. For the first time, maybe in my whole life, everything felt like it would turn out alright.

"So...we have the house to ourselves..." Bay hummed, taking another step closer to me.

"That's true," I agreed, pulling her into my arms.

I'd missed the hell out of her and she'd been in front of me the whole time. But now she was mine. All mine, and the only thing I wanted to do was show her just how much I loved her.

She had the same idea, evidently, because she pulled me back toward my bedroom, dropping her clothes in the process.

Yeah, life was pretty damn good.

Bay

"Dad?" I shrieked the moment the door swung open, Dad stumbling through the door with a closed fist, heading toward Blake.

It made contact right on his jaw, and Blake stumbled back, flinging his hand up to take cover from the assault Dad was raining on him.

"Dad!" I yelled again, hurrying between the two so Dad wouldn't hit him again.

"No," Blake growled, holding his hand out to me just as Dad got him again, on the cheek bone this time.

"*DAD!*" I shouted, moving behind him next to halt his arm.

"Bay!" Blake yelled at me, worry etching his eyes.

Worry, but not for him. For me.

"Get out of the way! You're gonna get hurt!" he called just as Dad started panting, leaning his hands on his thighs as he took a short break.

"I can't believe you!" I snapped at Dad, taking a moment to push Blake away from this beast that had taken over my father's body.

"Mom told me," Dad snarled, pointing at Blake. "I *trusted* you! I fucking trusted you with my daughter! And you lied to all of our faces!"

Blake licked the blood off his lip, but he didn't say anything in defense of himself.

"What do you mean Mom told you?" I demanded. "Told you what?"

"That you're sleeping with this...asshole!"

Blake sighed and leaned against the wall, wiping up the blood that had started dripping from his nose.

"Really? And this is what you do? Seriously, Dad! You hurt him!"

283

"I deserve it," Blake said, a half smile on his face as he shook his head in disbelief. "I would do the same, except a hell of a lot harder."

Dad huffed and growled again. "Give me a minute and I'll wipe that smug smile off your face!"

"You will not! Did Mom tell you all of it?" I asked. I couldn't believe that he would do this if he knew I loved Blake.

"She told me enough. Said you were in some kind of 'relationship'. I grabbed my keys and started driving."

"You drove all the way here?" I was shocked.

Dumbfounded, really. But I wasn't surprised. Dad would do anything for me, even beat up someone he thought was a threat.

"I love him, Dad. I love him and I'm going to marry him."

Dad's eyes widened as he stood again, his wind back.

"The hell you will! You're coming home with me, *now*!"

Dad's phone started ringing, and when he didn't answer it, mine started going.

I saw Mom's face flash at me on the screen.

"Mom?" I asked so many questions in the one word.

"Sweetie, your dad's on the warpath. I thought he'd come to his senses, turn around and come home, but he's not answering me and he's been on the road long enough to maybe be in town. I wanted to warn you so you don't answer the door while he's acting insane."

Too little too late.

"Yeah, I could have used the call like, five minutes ago," I told her, and Mom growled.

"Frank!" she yelled, so I put my phone on speaker. "Dammit you stupid man! You better not have hurt that poor man! Or maybe he punched your lights out and I should be thanking him. Hope he knocked some sense into you, too!"

Blake laughed a little, still wiping at his mouth and nose.

"No, Dad drew blood," I assured, glaring at Dad.

"Dammit Frank!" Mom yelled. "Way to welcome your future son-in-law!"

284

"Hell no!" Dad hollered into the phone that I was holding out toward him. "My baby girl ain't marrying some asshole pervert who likes to seduce kids!"

Blake's smile melted away, turning into a grimace.

"First of all, our daughter is not a child. She's a grown woman who just turned twenty, if you remember. And secondly, she gets to choose whoever she wants to marry, to be with, and to sleep with."

Dad scowled, looking away from me.

Well, it was official. We hadn't gotten a chance to tell anyone important to us. We'd put it off too long and they'd all found out some other way. The hurt on Dad's face showed me just how much it had upset him to learn about it from Mom.

"I love him, Dad," I added in a softer voice.

Dad just stood there, shoulders drooped as he shook his head and stared at the floor.

"Frank Jenkins, you listen to me. You talk to your daughter and you listen. Then when you're done hearing her out, you talk to that boy. What you didn't wait to hear before you went storming off, was that I think Blake is a good man, and I approve."

He looked like he was in a new state of shock.

"Approve?" he croaked.

"I do. Now, stop being a dumbass and you sit down, have some calming tea, and you get to know him."

I could see him still fighting it, and then there was this moment when he exhaled and all the fight left him.

"Yes dear," he said finally and Mom hung up the phone, dropping the call.

Dad turned to me and asked softly, "You got any calming tea?"

I nodded and pointed him to a chair where he sat, pulling at his hair with his hands.

Getting some water on to boil, I dug through the freezer and grabbed a couple bags of peas.

I stomped over to Blake and put the bags to his face a little more forcefully than was really necessary.

"Ow!" he yipped when the bag hit his bruising cheek.

"Why the hell did you just let him punch you?" I demanded. "Seriously! Look at you! You could have at least dodged!"

He was smiling again at that.

"I told you baby, I deserve it," was all he said, settling the cold bags to his face where he was starting to blacken with bruises.

"Damn right," Dad said again, leaning back in the chair before looking around the living room.

I saw a stray pair of pants in the hallway where I *might* have gotten a little frisky earlier since Georgia was staying the night with Jay, but after the way Dad had acted, I refused to be embarrassed.

Oh, and I forgot to mention. It was also three in the morning.

After Dad had his tea in his hands, he just sipped it and stared at us, my tough dad looking a little helpless now that his anger and bravado had worn out.

"So, what do you want to know?" I asked him. "I already told you everything you need to know. Obviously you have questions."

"Well, you can start with just how many years there are, again."

I sighed, glancing at my boyfriend/unofficial fiancé and the pea bags on his face before starting the story from scratch. Well, I might have left out all the sex. There was a lot of it. The story felt a little choppy without those moments, as it was in those times that we seemed to open up the most, physical intimacy leading to emotional intimacy and all that.

Dad was quiet through it all. He stared at me, glancing once or twice at Blake who looked absolutely ridiculous with his bruises and the red patches from where the cold peas had irritated his skin.

"So, that's it?" Dad asked eventually. "There's no convincing you otherwise?"

I went to him, kneeling beside the chair he'd sunk down into.

286

"I know I've always been your little girl," I told him in almost a whisper. "And I know you love me so much. I love you too, Dad, but eventually you knew I'd grow up. That I'd move out and take care of myself. That I'd eventually marry someone who I'd want to give that role to as a protector and provider; someone else who loves me."

Tears glistened in his eyes as he stared into mine.

"But no matter what, you're always going to be my dad. No man can ever take that away from you, and I will *always* need my dad."

He put his arms around me, hugging me there while Blake watched on, silently observing.

"So I'm stuck with this asshole?" Dad asked me.

I just let out a little laugh and nodded.

"Yep."

He let out a sigh of resignation before turning his gaze to Blake, holding it from across the room.

"I'm not sorry," Dad said, and Blake dipped his head in acceptance of the non-apology.

"Neither am I," Blake threw back.

Now, if two men on Earth could be more alike, I didn't know them. They shared so many things like their world view, their priorities and their profession, but Dad had always been one of those straight-tempered people. At least he had, until he'd shown up at our door in the middle of the night swinging his fists, anyway.

We heard a beeping from the back of the house, indicating that it was now time for Blake to wake up and get ready for work.

He rubbed at his eyes, wincing at the black eye he was sporting, then stood.

"I do wish that we could have had this conversation sooner," Blake said as he stretched a little. "I'm not going to make excuses. We're all adults and we messed up. I know that. We were...surprised by this between us and we weren't really sure *how* to tell the people we love. And that's on us. But I can make this

287

promise, whether it means anything or not to you. But I promise to take care of Bay. She will always have love and support, and if life goes to hell, I will give her the shirt off my back. We all know how unpredictable life can be, but I work hard, and I refuse to fail, especially when it comes to my family. And Bay is my family. Her and Georgia."

"Dad, why don't you come get some rest," I said, interrupting them both.

Blake didn't give himself much time to get ready in the morning, and he was already ticking away the minutes trying to win Dad over. Not that I could complain about that, but he was the boss and he needed to be at his jobsite.

"I'll show him to the room and you go get dressed. I'll make you breakfast."

Blake took my hand and squeezed it instead of kissing me with his split lip before heading toward his bedroom.

Dad stood too and followed me to the guest room, AKA my old bedroom. We'd officially moved into the same room since we were all on the same page, and even though Georgia gave us flack for it, we didn't mind. And that meant that the guest room had fresh sheets ready for Dad to lay his head and rest off the strange anger hangover he was dazed with. Or maybe it was just exhaustion.

After he was settled, I went to the kitchen to put together a quick breakfast burrito for Blake to take with him.

Coming out in his work clothes, I could see the tiredness in his eyes.

"The guys are going to give me so much shit," he told me, leaning in to give me a tender and gentle kiss on my cheek that made him wince.

"Well, I guess that lip is my revenge," I said, giving him the stink eye. "I can't believe you just let him punch you."

"You have no idea how guys work." he said, smiling then twinging when it stretched his scabbed lip. "Your dad needed to do it. We'd never be able to get past this if he didn't. Now we can start over. Hopefully."

Men... Barbarians, more like.

"Whatever. Just try and take it easy, ok? I don't like you going to work with so little sleep."

"I'll be just fine. I've gone to work with worse."

"Worse?" I demanded, eyes going wide as saucers.

He chuckled, kissed my lips softly, then headed toward the door.

"Love you, Bay."

"Love you too, you stupid man."

He laughed again and slipped out the door, holding his warm burrito in his hand as he went.

Chapter 32

Blake

"Ohh!" Marty sang as I got out of my truck, running a little late.

The guys were already gathered around, sipping coffee from their thermoses and Marty was grinning like an asshole.

"Her dad?" he guessed correctly, of course.

"Who else?" I countered, which made Marty laugh harder.

By that point, the other guys had noticed and were murmuring and laughing.

"Yeah, yeah. I know. Get a good eyefull, then get your asses to work!" I called at them, holding out my arms in a challenge.

They did, then most of the guys got to work immediately.

"So, I take it *that* didn't go over too well." Marty was still chuckling and trying to smother his grin.

"Showed up in the middle of the night," I told him, sipping on the coffee I'd stopped to get since I didn't have time to make some before leaving. "Came into the house fists blazing, but it turned out alright."

"Sometimes a guy just needs to draw blood, then the beast inside is satisfied."

"I sure hope so." I grunted. "It upset Bay more than both of us men combined."

"Of course it did. That girl is as tender hearted as they come. She'll make a great mom. You see her with Martinaz's kids? A natural born caretaker."

I had seen her back then at the barbecue. I saw her and it drew me towards her even more.

"So now what? Daddy give his blessing?"

290

"Not really, but he's sleeping in my guest room. I guess that says something."

Yawning, I tried not to re-split my lip with the stretch while Marty looked on with sympathy in his eyes.

"And when are you going to tell Georgia?"

"The girl already knows. Figured it out over the weekend."

"Hell's bells... So you're all out of the closet, so to speak?" he asked.

"Pretty sure that's not what that phrase means, but yeah. Everyone who needs to know does."

"Good." Marty nodded and patted my shoulder. "Now, I have to talk to you about the plumbers. Those little asscracks tore up the original floors."

"Who the hell gave them permission to do that?" I demanded. "Those floors are early 1900's originals!"

Rubbing at my forehead, I just sighed. A working man's job is never done.

Bay

"You sure you don't want to stay a while longer?" I asked Dad.

I'd gotten home from school to find him sitting on the couch with one of Blake's beers in his hand.

"Nope. I've been waiting for you. I have to go home. Your mom is ready to tear off my balls and feed 'em to the cat."

Gagging, I tried to expunge that sentence from my brain.

"I'll have dinner ready in a couple hours, and that would give you time to have some conversation with Blake."

"You know, to be honest I don't know if I want to have a conversation with him right now," Dad said with a sigh. "I'll give him a chance because I love you Bay, but right now I need some time. And maybe your mother can make some sense of this to me, because I'm pretty lost as to how this is all happening."

"It's...complicated," I admitted.

"Yeah, and I don't do complicated. You know that. But if you say he's a good man and he's treating you good, then I'll just have to believe you. I don't trust him, but I trust *you*. And if something *does* happen, I'll do a hell of a lot more than punch him next time."

I laughed through my teary eyes and nodded.

"I know, Daddy. And thank you. I know you did this because you're worried about me."

He sighed and nodded before standing.

"Guess I shouldn't finish this," he said, handing me the beer. "Throw that out for me, would you?"

I agreed and hugged Dad so tight, he made a grunt when I squeezed.

"You're getting stronger." He smiled down at me then kissed my forehead. "You coming for Christmas in a couple weeks?"

"Of course," I said. "But Blake is coming with me, and maybe Georgia if she's not going to her boyfriend's house."

He frowned, but nodded anyway.

"Alright. I'll see if I can get to the point of looking at that man's face without wanting to punch his lights out by then."

"You'd better," I warned with a grin, and he just rolled his eyes at me before heading to the door.

"You're going to have to accept him at some point, Dad," I told him, opening the door as he put on his tennis shoes. "Or else you can't come to the wedding."

"Let's just put a pin in the wedding talk for now, can we?" he asked in a pleading tone. "I'm not ready to see my baby married off yet."

So it wasn't all about Blake. It was about me growing up, too.

"Love you Dad."

"Love you, honey."

Just as Dad moved onto the steps outside, Blake's truck slowly rolled into the driveway.

"You've got good timing," I called to him as he slid out of the truck. "And you're also home early."

"Yeah, well my face hurt, so I thought I'd take off an hour early. Marty has it covered," he said, moving toward us and stopping just at the bottom of the steps. "You're leaving already, Frank?"

Dad scowled.

"Gotta get home. Judith is waiting for me, but I had to wait to say goodbye to Bay before I left."

"You're welcome to stay the night and head out in the morning so you don't have to drive in the dark," Blake offered.

"Nah, I'd feel better going home. I got plenty of rest, and I'll be fine."

"You sure?" It was my turn to be overprotective.

"I'll be fine," Dad said, giving me another hug before moving around Blake to go to his car parked on the street.

I waved and watched him go, then turned my attention to Blake.

"You look terrible," I told him.

"Feel like shit," he agreed, giving me a little smile.

"You're an idiot."

"I know."

"I love you."

"Love you more."

"Prove it," I whispered and his grin turned into a smirk as he marched up the steps and lifted me in his arms.

Guess it was only his face that was bruised, because his strength wasn't lacking.

"Challenge accepted," he murmured into my ear before biting down gently.

I needed to challenge him more often, if that was my reward.

"Georgia!" I called after dropping my backpack by the door.

"What?" she yelled back across the house.

"Get your big pregnant butt out here!"

That did it.

I heard her footsteps slap the floor as she came to confront me. Grinning at her, my face made her drop her comeback and she just smiled back.

"Do you have plans tonight?" I asked.

"Yeah. Jay was going to come over and—"

"Not anymore!" I said cheerfully. "Tonight is girl night. No boys allowed."

Her eyes lit up in pleased surprise.

"Chocolate?" she asked.

"Got it."

"Cheesy chips?"

"Yep."

"Movie with a hot guy in it and maybe just a little hanky panky?"

"Affirmative." I nodded and patted my backpack. "And your dad is paying for pizza."

Georgia's face flared up in wicked pleasure.

"You've got a deal! I'll go call Jay and tell him to go fuck himself tonight."

I laughed and listened as she pulled up her phone and did exactly that.

"Get the nail polish!" I called after her as she went toward her room while laughing at whatever Jay said in response.

While she was busy, I pulled all our snacks and treats out of my backpack and plopped them onto the coffee table in the living room. The movie was plugged in, Channing Tatum shirtless on the screen and smirking in the most glorious way. Georgia only took a few minutes before she came over to me with a handful of nail polishes, and some remover with cotton pads.

"Alright, let's do this!" she said, putting it all on the table alongside our snacks. "Pizza before or after nails?"

"After," I told her, noticing that it wasn't even five o'clock yet.

"Roger," she agreed, then proceeded to weigh the color choices and their pros and cons. "You don't think this hurts the baby, do you?" she asked in a whisper, sniffing the toxic stuff.

"I don't think so. Aunt Julie wore nail polish while she was pregnant."

Georgia gave me a wan smile as she started removing the old chipped purple polish on her fingernails.

"I'm so lost on this," she said eventually, focusing carefully on her nails. "Normally girls go to their moms about this kind of stuff, and I haven't even told mine yet."

"You've got me," I told her with a little smile. "Although, I'm not sure what help I'll be. But you have Mom and I can ask Aunt Julie anything, too. They'll be there for you too, Georgie."

Georgia smiled at me, her eyes misting.

"God, I can't stop crying over the stupidest shit!" she cried, wiping at her face and smearing her mascara and eyeliner a little.

"Yeah, that's not going to get better anytime soon," I admitted and she just groaned.

We were most of the way through our fingernails drying when the doorknob rattled and Blake entered the house, unlacing his boots at the door.

"Hey girls," he said, looking over at us with a smile. "What're you up to?"

"Having girl night," I told him, winking.

"Girls night?" He looked surprised, but also happy. "That mean good ol' dad can't join in?"

"EW!" Georgia and I both shrieked at the same time.

"Don't you dare say that again!" I howled, gagging. "You're *not* my dad!"

He belly laughed at that before moving over to us.

"Fine. I'll get lost. Marty wanted to grab a beer tonight, anyway. I'll just get some wings or something."

"Good," I told him, leaning my head up to accept a kiss he bent down to give me.

Georgia gagged again at the sight but I savored it. His lips tasted like sawdust and he smelled like metal and sheetrock and just a hint of his skin. Maybe that wasn't an attractive scent, but to me, I loved it.

"Can I at least shower?" he asked and I nodded, stealing another kiss before showing him my nails.

"What do you think?" I asked.

"Sexy." He bounced his eyebrows and nipped at my ear lobe.

"Disgusting! Go away Dad!"

Blake chuckled low in his throat and pressed a kiss to my neck before standing and making his way to his—*our* bedroom.

"Just *gag*," Georgia grimaced at me. "I will never, ever get used to you kissing my dad. Hell, I don't think I'll ever get used to dad kissing anyone!"

I just laughed.

"Like, no joke. In my head, Dad has been a celibate monk. He never talked about women, never dated when I was around, never had women around or anything...I don't know how you managed to nail him down."

She heard the innuendo in her own words and gagged again, putting her hand out to stop me from making a 'that's what she said' joke.

"Not saying anything," I told her, winking over and over again while she mimicked throwing up.

"Oh, God. I need to stop that or I'll actually throw up," she said after a minute, holding her belly as she laughed.

"You're a psycho," I told her, laughing myself.

"That's what I like to hear! My girls laughing!" came Blake's voice echoing down the hall.

"Go away Dad!" Georgia hollered.

"I'm going, I'm going," he said with a grin on his face. "Meeting Marty and a couple other guys at a bar across town. You two good?"

"We're grown ups who can take care of ourselves, thank you very much," I told him with a wink. "Oh, except you're buying dinner."

He rolled his eyes, but was still grinning.

"Of course I am. I'll let you two *broke* ladies take care of yourself all on your own with my credit card while I go get buzzed. Too bad you're not adult enough to do that!"

"Asshole!" Georgia called, choking on a laugh while she threw a couch pillow at Blake.

He snickered, dodging the pillow before grabbing his keys and leather jacket.

"Taking the bike?" I asked him.

"Yeah." He nodded.

"Be safe, ok?" I told him, knowing the roads were a little slick with the light sprinkle that had been falling all day.

"I'll be fine," he told me, crouching to give me one more kiss and to whisper, "love you."

I said it back, then pushed him away before I could beg him to stay.

Georgia and I needed that time together, even if it came at the expense of my time with Blake.

"Bye!" he called, heading toward the garage door and disappearing inside.

"You guys are so sappy it's gross," Georgia told me, but her face wasn't laughing or gagging.

No, her expression was soft and sweet.

"I know," I agreed. "But I love it."

"I know. You're weird like that. See, Jay knows I like it hard and fast and almost mean."

I just laughed.

"Who said I don't like those things too?" My eyebrows bounced at her, taking a note from Blake's book.

Georgia's face transformed, this time looking like she just might actually throw up for real.

"Ok, we're done. I've reached my max overload of disgusting for the night. No more talk of Dad or Jay. The only man allowed in this room for the rest of the night is Channing and his chiseled jaw, sexy ass and boyish smile."

"You've got a deal!" I called, taking a chip from the bag and shoving it in my mouth before I made another comment about just how hard and fast Blake could move between the sheets.

Chapter 33

Blake

"Finally got out from under the old lady's thumb?" Marty asked, winking at me.

I just rolled my eyes at him as I tucked my helmet under my arm, going through the dinging door of the shop in front of us.

We were going to get beers, of course, but I asked him to make one pitstop with me beforehand.

"How can I help you?" asked a woman who was moving out from behind the glass counters.

"This man is going to propose!" Marty told her, putting his arm around my shoulders, making my leather jacket creak.

"Aw! That's so great! Lucky lady!"

I just grinned like a lovesick idiot. Basically because that's exactly what I was.

"Can you tell me a little about her? Or do you know what she would like?"

Marty was out of smartassed remarks and finally just shut up and stared at me.

It had been many years since he'd done this, so he was pretty much useless other than as moral support.

"Uh, not really sure exactly what she would want, but I'm looking for something that's minimal and classic. That's what she would appreciate."

The woman nodded, then stretched out her hand, offering her name. "I'm Kenzy. I'll go ahead and pull a few things and we can look at them. Sound good?" I nodded and followed her into the room.

Marty sat next to me at the glass counter as we went over rings, ranging from the classic solitaire diamond to some more extravagant pieces that were beautiful, but also pretty gaudy.

"Is there a price range you're looking to stay in?" she asked after I'd said no to several rings.

"Not really. I just want to find the right one."

She just nodded and went to get a few more.

"No budget?" Marty asked with a raised eyebrow. "Since when do you not have a budget for everything?"

"Oh, I still have a budget for everything," I told him, leaving out the little fact that I had a budget for everything in my life *except* Bay.

There was no amount of money that could put a price on her happiness. He would lose his shit if he knew I'd given Bay free rein over the grocery budget.

"Ok, well how about these? They're classic and beautiful, but they're functional too."

I sighed and stared hard at the tray of rings she put in front of me. Pointing at a few, she started rattling off numbers as I glanced over each ring.

And then I saw it.

"This," I interrupted her hardcore, but she didn't seem to mind.

"Oh, that's beautiful," she said. "That right there is a 1.1 carat, lab created emerald cut diamond. It's set in a 24K gold band, and it has very unique eagle claw prongs on top and on the sides."

I saw it all, not that it mattered much to me. It just looked stunning.

"That's the one," I told her. "What's the damage on this?"

She just checked the tag and said simply, "Three thousand, six hundred."

My eyes about rolled into the back of my head at the price, but damn, it was an engagement ring!

"Ok," I choked the words out and Marty just patted me on the back with empathy.

"Just tell her not to lose it, huh?" Marty winked at me, which made me chuckle.

"Yeah, pretty sure she'll try not to, anyway."

The woman asked the next question in the process, that I hadn't once thought of.

"What size are you looking for?"

Ah shit...

"Uh, I actually don't know," I said, feeling butterflies erupt in my belly.

Was I really doing this? Was I really going to get married again?

I hadn't done this with Tiffany, opting for a simple silver band that she never wore, since it was all we could afford at the time. Actually, we couldn't even afford *that*, but I'd made it a priority, because a woman deserved to have a wedding ring.

"You know what? I'll just take the ring now and I'll come back if it doesn't fit, alright?"

"Ok, so I'll get this wrapped up for you. How would you like to pay? Would you like to look at our payment plans?"

"No, just put it on this," I told her, handing my credit card to her.

I'd have to move some money out of my savings to pay my card back off, but every penny was worth it.

"Great!" she said, looking way too happy while I was dropping three and a half grand.

After going over the final numbers, edging just *over* the thirty-six hundred mark, I had a fancy-ass ring hidden in my jacket pocket and a dry thirst in the back of my throat for something a little stronger than a beer.

Good thing the girls were busy for a while, because I intended to drink in celebration, play some pool, and bathe in buffalo sauce and ranch with some wings to go with it.

Bay

"Bay!" Blake called when he got home from work.

"Yeah babe?" I hollered back from the kitchen, tasting the simple pet name on my lips.

And it tasted good.

"Babe?" he asked, entering the kitchen with a smile on his face. "I like it."

"That's good, because I decided that it's your new name."

"You won't hear me complaining," he said, wrapping his arms around my waist and nuzzling the curve of my neck where it met my shoulder.

"You need something?" I asked, inhaling the smell of his work all over him.

"I need *you* to go change," he whispered into my ear, sending chills down my spine that settled just at the crux of my thighs. "I'm taking you out."

"Really?" I asked, all kinds of excited already by the idea of an actual date.

"Hell yes. It's about time I take you out like a proper lady. I've hidden you away to myself long enough."

I couldn't even get out of my mouth just how much his words meant. Before we'd been a secret, hiding our relationship from the world in fear of judgment. This was his way of throwing caution to the wind to parade me proudly on his arm. And that was pretty damn exciting.

"I can be ready in half an hour," I told him, thinking of all the things I needed to do.

"Ok. I gotta shower, but I'll wait however long it takes. I'll clean this up, too."

Date and no chores? He was seriously spoiling me.

"I could get used to this," I told him with a wink.

"You'd better," he said. "You're not earning your keep anymore. We're a fifty-fifty team now."

Now that sounded like a dream.

I hurried to our bedroom and picked out a dress to wear before taking off my mascara and sitting at the vanity in the bathroom to put on a little more makeup. Luckily I'd shaved that morning when I was considering wearing a skirt to school, but the chilly temperatures had kept me from attempting it. For Blake though? I would freeze my butt off just to be able to wear something other than stretchy pants and tank tops under a hoodie.

Blake came into the bathroom about twenty minutes later and got into the shower, which distracted me, of course. Sexy, naked man in the room? Uh yeah, serious distraction. But by the time he got out and pulled some jeans on, I was basically ready to go. So, I just watched him.

He noticed me watching and stared back into my eyes as he slowly pulled a white t-shirt over his head.

Wait... it was *the* white t-shirt that I'd picked out for him months ago. And those were the hot, tight jeans that I'd gotten as well. When he slipped his arms into the denim jacket that went with the outfit, I was mentally fanning myself to cool my jets. I was already running hot for the man, and that certainly wasn't helping.

"Ready?" he asked, pulling out some socks from his dresser before moving toward me.

I had lipstick clutched in my hand, ready to put it on, but I just nodded. The lipstick could wait.

Blake leaned down and pressed a kiss right onto my mouth; that split lip was a thing of the past, as were the bruises from Dad's visit.

I accepted his kiss eagerly, and we practically stumbled as I leaned into the vanity, him following as his hands gripped the counter on both sides of me.

"If we don't get out of here now, we won't at all," he murmured against my lips.

As tempting as that sounded, I really wanted my first date with the man I loved.

"Let's go," I told him, giving his lips a little lick before slipping under his arm to stand.

He groaned good naturedly but smiled, following me out of the room.

"Also, I got you these," he said as we got to the living room.

I turned back to him and he handed me a black leather jacket and a motorcycle helmet.

"Ever rode on the back of a Harley?" he asked.

That was all he had to say for me to shriek and jump in my booties.

Snatching up the coat, I slipped the thing over my arms and grinned up at him.

"You better be taking me on your bike, or I'll throw a tantrum."

"Good thing we're taking the bike, then," he said with a chuckle of his own.

I threw the lipstick on the coffee table, knowing it would do nothing but smudge under the helmet and followed Blake to the garage.

"So, you don't need to lean into the turns," Blake said as he opened the garage door, letting a cool draft into the room that flooded immediately up my skirt.

"You going to be ok in the dress?" he asked, pausing for a second to look at my bare legs.

"I think I'll put some tights on, if you don't mind waiting."

"Of course, baby," he told me, leaning against the bike and crossing his arms over his chest as he waited.

And oh boy did that man look sexy with tight jeans, a leather jacket and arms crossed, leaning against that motorcycle.

I took a mental image of that while itching for my camera, then hurried to go put on some thick tights. It went with the black, halter top style bodycon dress that I was wearing.

Blake was in the exact same spot when I got back, and he perused my body with his eyes the moment I appeared through the garage door.

"Wow," he said, the word popping out of his mouth as he shook his head. "You're way out of my league. You know that, right?"

I just laughed.

The man was blind. He was definitely the hotter one of the two of us.

"I'll take the compliment, even if you're delusional," I told him, pressing my hand against his chest as I approached him.

He helped me onto the back of the bike and then slid on himself, positioning my bootie-covered feet over the foot pegs before roaring the bike to life.

"Make sure that helmet is on right," he told me over the loud, idling engine.

I did, adjusting the chin strap a couple times until it felt right. He put on his helmet next, his head disappearing in the thing.

Blake kicked and nudged a few things before we were moving. My arms tightened around his waist and I pressed my helmeted head into his back as we backed out of the garage.

Within a few moments, we were slowly heading down the street, the wind rushing around my legs and hands, both getting cold in the chilly night air.

Blake moved with the bike like it was a second skin, and I just held on tight, trusting him completely.

We pulled up eventually to a restaurant in town, a place that was fancier than I was ready to eat at.

"Really?" I asked, looking down at my simple dress. "You didn't tell me you were bringing me here!"

He just grinned, his helmet coming off his head and leaving his hair a complete and utter mess. A mess that had me practically drooling with want.

Pushing a hand through his hair to straighten it again, he shrugged.

"You look incredible. And nobody cares what you're wearing. I wanted to take you somewhere nice."

"You already won me over, you know," I told him. "You don't have to take me somewhere fancy to convince me to like you."

"Yes I do," he said, his face sobering a little. "You deserve this."

And again, the man was melting my heart.

He slid off the bike and helped me down, keeping my hand in his as we went into the restaurant.

"Two?" the host asked us with a smile.

"Yeah," Blake said. "I have a reservation for six-thirty. Name's Hamel."

We were about fifteen minutes early

"Yes! I'll go check on your table. Meanwhile, please relax here in the lobby."

The 'lobby' was really just a few nice chairs lining the room, but we took a seat, our jackets squeaking together in the best and most embarrassing sound ever.

"I love the jacket," I told him, peeling out of it.

"I'm glad. I had to make sure you had at least some protection while we went. I assumed you'd be ok to ride tonight."

"You know how many times I've wanted to beg you for a ride?" I asked.

He smiled.

Feeling my naughty side slip out of the neat little box I kept it in most of the time, I let it loose and whispered, "Not that I usually like protection when I go for a ride."

His eyes flared hot as he met mine, desire blackening their usual dark blue.

"Careful," he whispered back, leaning toward my ear before tracing his tongue up the shell of it. "Or you might just get your wish."

306

A shiver spilled down my spine again as he leaned back, slipping his hand over my thigh and leaving it there as we waited.

My naughty self was speechless, so I just sat silently until the host came back and showed us to our table. We sat across from each other and I looked up at the man that, honestly, I couldn't quite believe I'd managed to wrangle. Sometimes I struggled to understand what he saw in me, other than my youth. But even that wasn't necessarily something that would be considered a good thing. I was career-less and broke, naïve in a lot of ways, but that didn't seem to matter to him. He loved me anyway, despite it all.

"Have you ever been here?" I asked him.

"Once," he said, nodding. "Had their steak and it was fucking *amazing*."

I glanced at the small menu and decided on the same. Steak sounded good.

We both ordered that and Blake asked for water for each of us.

"You can drink," I told him with a grin. "I don't mind."

"Not 'til you can, too," he told me. "But on your twenty-first birthday, we're going crazy. I'm going to get you *sooo* drunk."

"Ew," I laughed. "I don't want to get drunk."

"You're such a weird woman," he said, grinning and shaking his head. "What twenty-one year old doesn't want to get drunk on their birthday?"

"One who doesn't see the point in getting drunk?"

"Like I said..." he drawled before looking up at the waiter who brought our drinks.

We both sipped water as we waited for our meals.

It was a little awkward, us sitting there over dinner, and it felt more like a first date than I would have liked, but it would only get better from there. We had many more dates to look forward to in the future, so I didn't put a lot of pressure on myself to think of something witty to say. Blake would love me even if I were silent all throughout the meal. That reassurance was pretty amazing. He'd still love me anyway.

Eventually we got to talking about his work and the job and the timeline they were aiming for. They were halfway through this job, and the timeline hadn't gotten too tight yet.

"What are you planning for Christmas?" Blake asked eventually after we'd exhausted all other routes of conversation.

"I was planning on going home," I said, realizing that those plans were something we should discuss. "But I mean, we can decide what we do together."

He just shrugged.

"I'm sure your parents would want you home for the holiday, and honestly, I could use some brownie points where they're concerned."

I chuckled.

"Just give it time, babe."

He smiled at the pet name again before tucking the last bite of his steak into his mouth.

After paying, Blake and I headed back to the bike, hand in hand.

"Blake," I said finally as we got to his motorcycle. "I need to know..."

"What's up?" he asked, squeezing my hand.

"I uh...I wanted to ask you. We never really talked about it after that one night, but I want to ask you what you expect of me."

"What do you mean?" he asked, looking almost confused.

"I mean, after we get married. I'd like to finish college and everything, but we talked about kids and how I'd like to stay home with them. You never said how you felt about that."

Blake licked his lips, then sighed.

"I didn't say anything about it because I don't really see a problem."

"You don't mind if I don't work?"

"What I want from you," he said, taking my chin in his hand, looking into my eyes, "is for you to be happy. If working makes you happy, or pursuing photography, then I'll support that. If staying home and raising kids makes you happy, then I support that too. I

308

make enough for us to be comfortable, and I like to save just in case there are lean months. We'll be ok whether you decide to work or not. I want you to pursue your passion, whatever that may be."

I just smiled.

"You're kind of incredible," I told him.

"No, I'm just finally in a place in my life where I can actually offer that," he said with a sad chuckle. "What I have is yours."

His hand went into the pocket of his jacket and I thought for just half a moment that maybe he would propose. But then his hand came back out empty and he was helping me onto the bike again.

"Want to go ride by the water?" he asked, handing me my helmet.

"I'd love that," I agreed.

We drove off again, me plastered to his back in the cold night as we caught glimpses of Lake Washington. Eventually we passed over two bridges, heading toward Seattle. Halfway through the ride, we stopped at a little park just by the water. Blake cut the engine and all we could hear was the soft rush of tiny waves hitting the pebbled beach.

"This is incredible," I said, setting my helmet down by our feet.

"Nice spot, huh?" he asked, doing the same with his helmet.

We were in a little turnoff tucked behind some trees and blocked from the street, facing the large expanse of water.

"This is one of my favorite rides," he told me, looking out over the lake.

"The view is awesome," I agreed.

"C'mere," he said as he turned, catching my waist in his arms and pulling me against his chest.

I awkwardly wrapped my legs around his waist as he moved me onto his lap, chest to chest with him as my back bit into the cold handlebars.

"That's better," he told me, eyes dropping to my lips as his thumb traced the bow-shaped lines.

I wanted nothing more than to feel his lips on mine, and I hardly thought about the fact that anyone could come upon us. Well, only a little bit.

"You know," he whispered, his fingers brushing across my lower back until he had a handful of my butt in each hand. "Ever since I got this thing, I've wanted to take the woman I loved on this ride."

"But you didn't know me," I whispered back, my breath hitching as his lips teased mine, just brushing faintly against me but not giving up any kisses.

"No, but I was preparing for you. I just didn't know it was *you* yet."

Our breath mingled, foggy in the night air before he finally leaned in a little more and gave me what I was craving.

"Want to know something else?" he panted, pulling me closer, the bulge in his pants already pressing into me as I rocked on his lap.

"What?" I breathed.

"I always wanted to fuck on this bike, too."

Welp, there goes any semblance of self control.

The simple words had me grinding on him in a frenzy, and he gripped me harder, firmer, surer as he rocked against me, too. Our lips grappled, tongues dancing as we tried to ease the burning desire with our mouths alone, but it wasn't enough. It was never enough.

A faint zip sounded in the air, accompanied by our panting breaths as he unzipped my jacket, then slipped one hand inside, cupping a breast with the same eagerness as his other hand gripped my ass, squeezing and kneading as if that, too, might ease the pressure of our carnal need.

"Mind if I make your wish come true?" I asked, desperate to feel him inside me.

He didn't even answer, he just worked his hands under the hem of my dress, moving it up a little before he started pulling on the waistband of my tights.

"Fuck..." he murmured, leaving my lips so he could pay attention to what his hands were doing.

The only way those tights were coming off was if I got off his lap and pulled them off in public, which I most definitely wasn't going to do.

"Rip 'em," I told him, biting his bottom lip. "I don't care. Break them."

He didn't need me to tell him twice. His strong fingers curled into the stretchy black material and I could hear the sound of it tearing between my thighs, ripping a huge hole. And damn if that didn't get me even hotter.

Within moments my thong, carefully chosen to not leave an underwear line in my dress, was pushed over, the string hooked in his fingers as he nudged my thighs further apart.

"You sure?" He asked, panting with his arousal.

Fingers pressed against my core, dipping in just as I let out a yelping 'yes'.

His hand left me again, though the other one was still holding back my thong as he unbuckled his jeans and worked them open. I wasn't sure how he managed the angle, but it only took seconds before his arms were around me again and I was riding him, his length inside me and stretching almost uncomfortably. I could feel the string of my thong pulling between us, and after a few movements it settled across my clit, scraping and pressing and moving until I was gasping for air against the pleasure of it.

Soft grunts left Blake's chest with each movement, but we tried to be quiet, hushing each moan into little vibrations in our throats, only loud enough for us to hear.

Grinding down on him, I watched his eyes close as I got ever closer to my peak, that thong still digging into me in the best way, almost like fingers begging me to come.

311

I whimpered, my head digging into his neck as I finally reached my climax, searing, beautiful waves of heat bursting inside me

He grunted out a moan and dug his teeth gently into my bared shoulder as he followed me to his peak, pulsing and throbbing as he thrust once, twice more inside me.

We just sat there for another minute, recovering as the weightless glow of orgasmic bliss settled over us.

"Was it everything you hoped for?" I asked finally.

He just laughed against my neck, head still tucked into its curve.

"Better," he answered before sitting straight, kissing me deep and long.

"We just did it in public."

"Also on my list of places to fuck," he said.

"There's a list?" I demanded good-naturedly.

"About ten feet long," he joked.

I just shook my head, finally feeling the tremors in my limbs give way as I gained my strength back.

"You're incredible," he whispered.

"I know," I told him with a smile that he returned.

"Ready to go home?"

Oh yeah, I was ready. I wanted a repeat performance, hopefully on a nice, warm bed.

I straightened out my underwear and dress before crawling back into my spot on the bike while Blake started it again with a roar.

When we got home, I got that repeat performance.

Chapter 34

Bay

I stood in the bathroom with shaking hands, staring at the little thing that completely changed my life forever.

So this is what Georgia felt like.

Well, maybe not quite.

"You ok in there?" I heard Blake ask through the bathroom door.

We were supposed to head to Seattle soon, but as soon as I realized that I'd missed my period, I had to check.

"Uh, kind of?" I choked.

The door clicked open and Blake popped his head in, looking a little worried.

"You feeling ok?"

Well, I had been feeling a little queasy in the mornings lately, but nothing I couldn't blame on nerves.

Christmas had been ok, but there was still some unease between Dad and Blake. No punching or bloodshed, but no bonding, either. It was New Year's Eve and Blake had planned the whole evening out, including dinner at the Space Needle, which we were coming close to missing the longer I spent in the bathroom, staring at the two blue lines in front of me.

Blake's eyes moved from my teary face to the little plastic stick in my hand. He paled for a minute, then looked back up at me.

"I'm pregnant," I whispered, gulping.

We'd talked about it. We knew we'd had sex a few times without a condom. *We knew.* It still didn't ease the sting of surprise.

"You-you're sure?" he asked, coming into the bathroom to stare at the blue lines with me.

Positive.

I was pregnant.

Two lines, not one.

Pregnant.

After a moment of blinking blankly at the pregnancy test, he looked up into my eyes, and what stared back at me was fear.

"Are you ok?" he whispered. "Is this ok?"

"What do you mean?" I asked back.

"I mean...is this ok? You want a baby?"

"Of course I want a baby," I said, eyebrows drawing together in confusion. "Do you?"

"Fuck, of course I do," he assured me. "But you're only twenty..."

I stopped him from saying anything else stupid by kissing him.

"This is all I ever wanted," I breathed. "A baby. A family. I'd just hoped I would be married first, then kids after that."

He gave a choked laugh.

"Yeah, sometimes that doesn't work out the way we think it will."

I bit my lip for a minute before asking, "You sure?"

A grin spread over his face as his strong arms wrapped around me.

"You have no idea how happy I am, Bay."

My fear rushed out in one long sigh and excitement flooded through my bones.

A baby!

"Wow," Blake sighed, kissing me again. "Should we take another test? Just to be sure?"

"I'm pretty sure there's no such thing as false positives," I told him with a laugh.

"Hot damn...A baby."

"You know what that means?" I asked.

"What?"

"It means I'm not getting drunk on my twenty-first birthday."

"Damn it," he mumbled with a grin on his face. "Fine. I'll allow it. But once you're able to, I'm getting you drunk. I want to see what kind of drunk you are."

"Fine. but it'll be a while."

His grin widened as he spoke the most amazing words. "That's ok. We have the rest of forever."

Fireworks were bursting all around us after the countdown. The New Year was here and we celebrated with one long kiss.

Blake moved, and then suddenly his lips were leaving mine and I wanted to whine in protest. But the complaint was lost on my tongue as he dropped to one knee in front of me.

"Bay," he said, almost shouting over the crowd of people celebrating around us. "Baby or not, I need you."

The little velvet box in his hand opened to the most beautiful engagement ring.

"I don't deserve you, but I'm going to ask anyway. Will you marry me?"

His hand shook as he offered the ring to me, and again, I wished I had my camera. It was a moment I wanted to keep with me forever.

"Of course," I breathed.

He burst to his feet and kissed me again before fitting the ring over my finger.

"How cliché." I laughed and his eyes twinkled with happy amusement. "It's a perfect fit."

Epilogue

Blake

"What the ever-living *hell*!" Georgia shrieked, hands pressing over her belly that wasn't quite showing yet. "You're having a baby? Really, Dad? You're supposed to know better!"

Bay laughed and hugged her friend. "Yep. We get to do this together, peach."

Georgia glared at her, still hating the nickname.

On New Year's Eve, after we got back, Bay was fingering the little peach on my hip as we laid naked in bed together; my favorite place. She mused out loud that she liked the name peach, and ever since had started calling Georgia by my endearing name for my daughter.

"First of all, you don't get to call me that. Only Dad does. Secondly, you do realize that my *sibling* is going to be the same age as their *niece or nephew*."

Oh my God... Why did she have to word things in the worst way?

"Doesn't matter who I had a baby with, Georgie," I told her with a laugh. "That was going to happen anyway."

Georgia whined again, but then she couldn't help her smile as she hugged Bay, then me, then all of us together.

"You guys suck."

"I know," Bay and I answered together, then met eyes and grinned.

"I kind of hate you."

"That's ok." We did the whole weird twin answer again.

When we all let go, Georgie took Bay's hand and looked at her with wide eyes.

"We're having babies!"

The girls jumped around and shrieked together, and I just laughed, looking on as the friends bonded over the incredible fact that they would have babies together.

"Jay is going to lose his shit!" she said.

Finally, she paused and turned to me.

"So, when's the wedding?"

Yeah, the whole engagement news had gotten a little lost under the 'we're having a baby' news.

"Whenever Bay wants," I said, turning to my fiancée.

Georgia looked at her friend and said in a straight-ass face, "Double wedding."

Bay's eyes went wide as she answered in just as serious of a voice.

"Hell. Yes."

I rolled my eyes to heaven and prayed for lightning to just take me.

A double wedding with my daughter, her baby daddy and her best friend? Sounded like a nightmare to me. But it didn't matter. The wedding was about Bay, and if that's what she wanted, then so be it.

We'd just talked to her parents over the phone earlier in the morning and they'd both been surprised, but receptive. Maybe getting her pregnant *before* the wedding wasn't ideal, but we announced our engagement before mentioning the baby, which helped to settle the water a little.

I had hope that Frank and I would get along eventually. We were too alike *not* to. And on top of that, we both loved Bay and just wanted her to be happy. He would come around, whether it took weeks or months or years, I would win him over.

"Alright. Spring wedding. We better get planning!" Georgia said all excited. "You're paying, right Dad?"

I groaned out loud at the thought of how much it'd cost to put on a double wedding.

"Of course he is," Bay answered for me with a smirk on her beautiful face. "Only the best for his girls."

I eyed them, pointing my finger at each of them.

"Cheap wedding and I'll pay for the honeymoon. Keep that in mind."

"And what if I want a destination wedding in the Florida Keys?" Bay asked, her attitude coming out full force.

I just grinned and winked. "Guess you better get to saving then, huh?"

Georgia pulled Bay aside and whispered in her ear for a moment before both women came back and began to barter.

"Ok. Destination wedding. Minimal guests. And you pay for all of it."

"Deal," I agreed.

Georgia made me a pinky promise, and I did, which made Bay giggle uncontrollably.

Yeah, well, I was a dad just as much as I was a man, and soon I would add husband to that list. And I couldn't think of anything better than that.

Bay

My baby bump was only beginning to show, but Blake liked to lay next to me and stroke it anyway.

"I'm excited to meet him," he whispered as we laid sprawled on the beach with a hundred other sunbathers.

It was our honeymoon, and even still, Georgia and Jay were laying not too far away, enjoying their own vacation.

Our dual wedding was only two days before, and everyone had gone home except for us. To be honest, there hadn't been many people to attend the wedding. Mostly my family and a few people from Jay's side also joined us, along with Marty and his wife, Gail. But they only stayed in town for a couple days preceding the wedding. Mom and Dad had stayed the longest, taking a nice vacation before the wedding as we prepared for it, but now they were gone and it was just me, Blake, Georgia and her new husband, Jay.

What a mess it all was. A blessed, beautiful mess.

"Dad!" Georgia called, rubbing her belly that was only slightly bigger than my own.

Blake closed his eyes and groaned quietly.

"Who the fuck takes their *kid* on their honeymoon?" he questioned himself as he got up to go to her.

"Might I remind you," I called after him. "This was *your* idea."

"Remind me not to have any ideas in the future," he called back to me, grinning.

I watched him go to Georgia, my eyes tracing every line, dip and curve of his body in those sexy swim shorts. He was so incredibly handsome.

When he came back to me, I bit my lip, watching the way his pecs flexed with each step, his abs peeking at me while he dropped back down to the sand beside me.

"I have an idea," he told me, stroking his hand through my hair, slightly ratted with salt water and sand.

"Uh oh!" I laughed.

He did too, but reached around me for my camera.

"It's my turn," he told me, pulling off the lens cap before putting it to his eye, aiming and taking a picture with the soft sound of the shutter whooshing.

"No!" I laughed, hiding my face.

"Hey! I've modeled enough for you. I get to do this for you. I want pictures of our baby getting fat in your stomach!"

"Wow, you have a way with words," I teased.

"Please?" he begged.

Damn. Why did he have to ask so nicely?

I dropped my arms and just let him take the pictures. Because, let's be honest. What girl didn't want all that attention from the man she loved?

A smile broke across my face as he took picture after picture, moving around me and having me sit up or stand so he could get a shot of my tiny little baby bump.

"There's my boy!" he said.

"You never know. It could be a girl!" I laughed.

He looked up at me with wide, horrified eyes.

"Do you really want another Georgie?"

I met his horror with my own.

"I heard that!" came Georgia's answer to the question.

We both burst into laughter before Blake leaned forward and kissed me.

"I'm rooting for a boy, but you know, I'll like a girl too. Even if she's like her sister."

"You're such a strange man," I chuckled, stealing another kiss.

"I know. But I love you."

"Yeah, yeah. Love you too," I droned, winking at him.

Blake went back to taking pictures and I dropped back to the sand, basking in the sun and the warmth of my husband's love.

Sure, it wasn't how I always thought it would happen, but I was so happy that I didn't really care. I'd found my happily ever after in my best friend's dad, and I wasn't even slightly ashamed.

And that's what it all came down to at the end of the day. Where I started and stopped, where I laughed and cried and dreamed and hoped—

HIM.

END

Get a free *BONUS CHAPTER* about Blake and Bay's HEA now!

It doesn't have to end here!
Keep reading for a sneak peek of the next book in the series, Teach Me, plus a special first two chapters of BoyFrenemy.

If you enjoyed this book, please leave a **review** and **subscribe** to my mailing list for first dibs on deals and freebies!

Teach Me

Sophisticated Seduction Series

By L. L. Ash

ISBN: 9798371828033

Image by Tverdokhlib

Cover art by L. L. Ash

Chapter 1

-Mia-

Writing was my life.

And I'm not joking about that. If I couldn't write, I would be absolutely useless to society. Some people take antidepressants, or do yoga or hike, or eat really good chocolate ice cream. For me, I write. It's my therapy, if you will.

So, to say that my creative writing class was my favorite my first year of college was a bit of an understatement. I mean, I'd taken it every year since I started college. When I became knowledgeable enough to become the class's TA, oh my God, it was like a dream come true.

Sure, being a teaching assistant was mostly just correcting tests, reading papers and doing the grunt work that my professor didn't have time to do, but I didn't care. I was going to be learning from some of the best, and my writing was going to benefit. Hell, maybe I'd even try to publish!

Now, the big obstacle ahead of me was *getting* the job.

I stood outside my professor's office door, waiting for time to tick by because I was ten minutes early.

"Goddamnit!" I heard from behind the office door and my eyes widened.

Professor Harlo was new, replacing my recently retired professor. A spike of worry shot through me, wondering if the man had a temper.

The door swung open and there Professor Harlo was, over six feet tall, in slacks and a white shirt, deft fingers ripping off his tie.

"Oh, shit," he whispered, jumping a little when he saw me there outside his door. "You here for the TA job?"

I nodded dumbly, my head bobbing up and down while he dabbed at his shirt. The big brown coffee stain on the front of his shirt finally grabbed my attention.

"Are you ok?" I finally bumbled, grabbing the tissue out of his hand so I could vigorously rub at the stain. "Did it burn you?"

Professor Harlo raised an eyebrow at me and watched me make a bloody fool of myself while I *cleaned off* my professor.

Oh God...

I finally blinked, realizing what I was doing, and shoved the napkin back at him.

"Sorry, I don't know what I was..."

"Know how to get this out?" he asked, pointing to the spot and interrupting my apology.

I nodded.

"Good," he said, waving me into his office as he wandered back in himself.

Those fingers, long and dexterous, started unbuttoning his shirt, starting from the neck down. I watched slack-jawed while he didn't even bother glancing at me.

"Consider this a trial run," he said finally, sliding his shirt off his arms before he bunched it against his bare chest.

Uh, yes, *bare chest*. And what a chest it was! His skin was pale, but there were muscles there that many academic men never bothered to develop. A dusting of freckles sprinkled across his pecs, and a dusting of dark hair trailed down into the band of his slacks.

"Hey," he called, making the 'I'm watching you' motion with his fingers and eyes. "Get this all cleaned up and you've got the job."

I blinked, clearing my mind as he shoved the shirt at me and pulled on an old man cardigan that fit him so well. The horn rimmed glasses on his face accentuating his dark, carmel colored eyes.

"What's your name, by the way?" he asked once he was dressed again.

I drew my eyes away from the little triangle of chest and neck I was staring at and looked him in the face.

"Mia," I stammered. "Mia Miller."

"That's fun enunciation," he said with a grunt. "Ok, Miss Mia Miller. I want that back by tomorrow. Can you handle it?"

I lifted my eyebrows and nodded.

"Good," was all he said before grabbing his leather briefcase bag and moving past me through the door, locking it on the way out. "By lunch tomorrow!"

I watched him saunter off after locking his office door behind us, and felt like my entire world had just imploded in that tiny room.

Once he was gone though, it was easier to breathe, and when I got some oxygen into my brain, I was able to finally convince myself of how idiotic my little instant crush was. Not only was my professor likely 'over the hill' and in his forties, but he was going to be my *boss*. Because yeah, I was getting the darn job, and no amount of coffee stained shirts were going to get in my way.

Shutting off the blood flow to my little love button, I stuffed the shirt into my backpack and hurried to my next class. Math. Yuck.

"Mom," I cried into the phone, "how do I get coffee out of a white shirt?"

"Slow down," she said with a chuckle. "What happened?"

"There's coffee on this white shirt and I've been scrubbing it for an hour but it's not coming all the way out!"

"Well, sweetie, you can try using dish soap and vinegar. That works for a lot of stains."

I panicked as I looked around, hoping I had those two ingredients around. Seeing as I was in a dorm room and I didn't make more than raman or mac and cheese in my room, I didn't have vinegar.

"Darn it!" I called again, which made Mom laugh.

"Bring it to the dry cleaners," she finally said.

327

The thought sparked as inspirationally brilliant in my ears, and I was out the door before even saying thank you to my mother.

"You're a genius!" I told her, already out of breath from going down my two flights of stairs.

There was a dry cleaner just down the street, and they were going to save the day.

"Are you sure you're ok?" she asked me, listening to me panting into the phone.

"Yeah, it's just kind of an emergency. I need this shirt perfect by tomorrow afternoon."

Something in my stomach refused to admit that this was my ticket to the TA position. I wanted to earn it, but this wasn't exactly how I'd planned on wowing Professor Harlo

Mom and Dad were crossing their fingers for me to get the position because they knew how much it meant to me, but this felt a little too much like luck, and that curdled my guts a little.

"Ok sweetie. Let me know if you need anything else. Are you still planning on coming for the weekend?"

"Of course," I blurted. "I gotta go, Mom! See you Saturday!"

I clicked off the phone as she said goodbye and stumbled into the drycleaners.

"I need this stain out," I gasped out, shoving the shirt at the attendant behind the counter.

They looked at me like I was crazy, but simply shrugged.

"We can have it ready by Saturday morning," they said, blinking at me.

I just blinked back.

"I need it by tomorrow afternoon."

"Sorry, we're too busy. We're backed up for a few days. Until Saturday, exactly."

"Dang it," I grumbled, snatching the shirt back from them.

What was I going to do?

"You know they sell white button ups like that across the street at Walmart?"

A new shirt? Was I really stuck trying to pass off a new shirt as 'cleaned'?

"Or you can wait until Saturday."

"Thanks!" I called, already heading out the door.

Walmart was a bit of a walk, and it happened to be over ninety degrees in our Mississippi humidity, so I was sweating my rear off before I stepped through the air conditioned sliding doors. If I was smart, I would've taken my car, but frantic insanity had me running on foot while I talked to Mom.

Taking a few steps in, I had to pause and orient myself, because let's be honest, I had no idea where the men's section was. I mean, I'd gotten my fair share of clothes there, not too proud to sport Walmart brand while I was trying to save for tuition, but I'd never had a real boyfriend and I didn't have a brother, sooo...

Right, the men's section.

I went to the women's section first, positive that the men's clothes couldn't be too far.

And I was right. In the process of giving myself a pat on the back, I strolled through each section, looking for button up shirts. There was a tiny area, only maybe three feet wide, that was full of shirts. In that section, was a singular white button up in several sizes.

Oh shit! What size was he?

I frantically opened the stained shirt, finding only a 'Proper Cloth' tag on the neck. Further down, I saw another tag on the seam down the side and saw an odd set of numbers there. Holding it out, I assessed it against what my dad's shirts looked like, and it seemed darn close. Large? Ok, I could manage that. Crossing fingers that I was right

The shirts in front of me were also singularly marked small through XXXL. I grabbed the one marked L and hightailed it toward the register. Then I remembered that I needed some more bread, so I turned myself right back around and got the groceries I needed since I was at Walmart, anyway and I didn't want to come back anytime soon.

By the time I got home, I gave myself a little bit of breathing room, happy that I'd gotten the chore done. My roommate Clea was there, going through a thick textbook when I walked into our apartment.

"Girl, I was wondering when you'd get back. It's your night to cook," she said without looking up.

I grinned.

"Don't worry, I got this. I stopped by the grocery store and picked everything up."

"What're you making me?" she asked, finally tapping her highlighter against the page as she looked up at me.

"Your chef de cuisine shall make you a well loved special," I told her, enlisting my horrifyingly bad French accent. "Fromage on top of perfectly toothsome noo-dawls."

Clea giggled at me, then sighed.

"Mac and cheese again?"

"Sounds better when you say it with an accent," I tried.

Yeah, I was bored of the same old stuff as she was, but it didn't matter. Neither of us had the money for good food, nor did we have the kitchen to cook anything worthwhile.

"Extra milky?" she asked.

My roommate liked her mac with extra milk until it was practically mac and cheese soup.

To each their own, but...yuck.

"I'll milk your bowl, but I'm not ruining the whole pan of it!" I told her, like I always did.

She just waved her hand in dismissal before going back to her homework.

Shoot, I needed to work on my homework, too. Right after I took a shower to get rid of all that sweat.

I pulled the white shirt out of the bag and removed all the little pins and tissue, then I laid it over a chair to try and get out the little fold lines all over the thing. Hopefully he wouldn't notice. And even if he did, he got a freaking brand new shirt out of it.

"Do I want to know?" Clea asked while I ran my fingers over the rough cotton.

"Nope," was all I answered with, and it was good enough for her.

I'd have to play it off a little bit, but I was going to make the most amazing TA, and Professor Harlo was going to love me.

Refusing to think of that stupidly sexy body, I shoved him out of my mind for a little while and got writing to my latest paper from my English class.

Chapter 2

-Mia-

I waited outside Professor Harlo's office after my ten o'clock class let out. He wasn't around when I arrived at eleven, so I sat there for over an hour waiting for him to return from his own class. Then noon passed, and no Professor Harlo. He'd told me noon on the dot, and there I was, ten minutes past and he wasn't there.

Another almost half hour dragged by and I started tapping my foot. People were staring at me like I was a psycho for standing there so long, and my feet were aching something fierce. Genius I was for wearing thin, foam flip-flops.

Finally, approaching twelve-forty, Professor Harlo came meandering to his office, nose in a book and briefcase tucked under his arm while he dug through his pocket. He retrieved keys and finally lifted his face out of the pages long enough to look at his door, and consequently, *me*.

"Oh, good. You're here," he said, all chill and nonchalant, meanwhile, I was fuming.

"You told me to meet you at noon," I practically growled, my legs achy and stiff from standing at his door for so long.

He lifted a brow before closing his book with a perfect little 'thwack'.

"I told you to be here at lunch time, not noon. This is my lunch time."

I took a deep breath and tried to banish the sudden thought of beating him across the head with that book he'd been reading.

"I've been waiting here since eleven," I informed him.

"Well, why would you do that?" he asked dismissively, going into his office and leaving the door open.

"Because you said lunch time and I have no freaking idea when a professor's lunch time is. So I came between classes. My next one starts in twenty, actually. So I guess it's a good thing you decided to have lunch. *Eventually.*"

He sat behind his desk and leaned back, and that was when I finally got a good view of him in his perfectly pressed white shirt beneath another one of those old man sweaters. It even had the little patches of leather on the elbows.

With a sigh, Professor Harlo took off his glasses and rubbed at his forehead and eyes.

"Well, it's a shame you waited so long. That wasn't my intention. I suppose I should have been more specific with a time period for you to come.

That was almost an apology, and I'd take it. Hell, I'd cling to it, because I really, *really* wanted that job.

Suddenly, I tossed the shirt I'd been holding at him and he caught it, without his glasses on and all.

"What's this?" he asked, then reached up for his spectacles and put them on. "Oh, right. You got the stain out?"

I nodded, hoping he didn't read the lie written all over my face.

He didn't look too hard at it before he shoved it over to the side of his desk.

"Very good! "

"So the job is mine?" I asked, needing to hear the words.

"Yep. You'll start today."

I stuttered, staring into his caramel eyes through those stupid sexy glasses.

"We're actually having a test tomorrow, and I want you to take roll, time, and gather the tests at the end of class. You need to watch for cell phones and cheating."

I nodded, dropping my backpack to pull out my notebook.

333

I wouldn't need the notes, but I wanted to have them, just in case.

"Wh-what class?"

He blinked.

"You don't even know what classes you're TA-ing for?" He lifted a disbelieving eyebrow at me.

"It's more a matter of *who* I'm TA-ing for, not what class."

"So you specifically wanted to work for me?" He sounded even more skeptical then.

"Not you specifically... I mean, I've been aiming for this job since sophomore year. Professor Kingsley just never hired me..."

"So I'm the...rebound?"

The man certainly had a way about twisting my words.

"No," I said finally, folding my arms over my chest, tucking my notebook close. "You're certainly an accomplished professor and I'm excited to learn from you. I have faith that you'll be a great replacement for Professor Kingsley. Plus, a TA job will look amazing on my resumé."

His face relaxed at that.

"That's the most honest thing you've said to me yet," he said finally, shoulders slumping as if he was finally letting down his guard. "Let's get this straight. You're the only student I considered for this job, because Professor Kinglsey had nothing but good things to say about you, and I've been impressed with your writing so far, or, at least what Dora showed me. I think that the students in my class could definitely use some of your creative skills, and maybe you'll pick up a thing or two in the process."

Professor Harlo leaned forward in his chair, clasping his hands as he looked up at me with a stern face.

"I don't like polite bullshit, and I expect you to be early to every class. Not on time, but early by at least a few minutes so you have time to settle in before my students arrive. I also expect you to spend office hours here, in my office, between your classes where you'll grade papers and help prepare tests. I'll send you an email with a complete list of my expectations."

334

Well, this Professor Harlo was a total asshat, and I...liked that. I could appreciate the no-nonsense atmosphere. At least I'd have a compiled list of what he wanted me to do, so I wasn't left guessing like I'd been with the whole coffee shirt debacle.

"Wait," I paused him, putting my hand up. "If you only considered me for the position, why did you have me clean your shirt?"

He grinned.

"Why?" he asked with the slightest tinge of a British accent. "Because I'd spilled coffee on my shirt. Why else?"

"With all due respect," I told him, frowning. "You're an asshole."

He laughed.

"Good. There's that straightforward attitude I was missing," he said, seeming pleased. "Now, you've got a class to get to, and I've got a lunch to scarf down before my next class. If you don't mind, close the door on your way out."

Just like that, he dismissed me.

"What class, Professor Harlo?" I asked, needing to know what classroom he expected me to be at.

"Creative writing, of course," he said as if I was an idiot. "It's the evening class, so you shouldn't have an issue attending, correct?"

"Correct," I agreed.

"I'll send the room number and class details in the email I referred to earlier. Now, toodaloo."

The man was probably, at least a little bit, insane.

And oddly enough, I liked it.

Without another word, I left his office and made my way toward my next class, sore feet and all.

Well, even if I didn't learn anything, I was at least in for one heck of a semester with Professor Harlo.

Find Teach Me on Amazon

BoyFrenemy

♡

By L. L. Ash

— Preface —

Ivory

Three Years Ago

His hot breath on my cheek, sputtering from kiss-swollen lips just made me pant even harder.

"Fucking hell," he gasped, hips battering into mine in the dark closet of my best friend's basement.

Seven minutes in heaven had turned into something a little more than...uh...seven minutes.

We'd ignored every attempt to get us out and the subsequent catcalls that followed until we were just left alone to our erotic fairy-tale that wouldn't last past midnight.

It had started as angry, frantic kisses, then light petting, then I was smothering my face in a puffy winter coat while he ate me out with that cocky smirk on his face. He knew damn well what he was doing, and I both loved and hated him for it.

Now I was naked from the waist down, with a high heel under my back and buried into my ribs. My head banged on the wall with every thrust and huff of effort grunting from his lips.

But I didn't care.

I wanted him, and for the first time ever, he wanted me, too.

With a strangled little growl, he quietly finished inside the condom that he 'so happened' to have on him. Then again, what

338

eighteen year old boy didn't have a condom with them at all times?

In the quiet stillness of the dark closet, I tried catching my breath and digging the shoe out from underneath me while he pulled out and started buckling up his pants again.

"Thanks babe," he said, voice hoarse, but like silk to my ears.

I know what his orgasm voice sounds like now.

I grinned at the thought, then felt around for my panties, laying somewhere on the closet floor.

He stood and helped me up, then pressed a fierce kiss to my lips.

"What now?" I asked, elated that we were actually having contact instead of the regular cat and mouse game we'd played for years.

"Nothing."

Just like that, pantyless and baffled, I stood there while he slipped out of the closet and left me there.

Hunter Hayes had dipped in and shipped out, leaving me with dampness between my legs and a broken, bleeding heart.

Again.

Ivory

If I bit my lip any harder, I'd make a hole and would have a brand new place to put a lip ring. Not that I wanted one. They reminded me too much of *him*.

Instead of giving myself an inadvertent piercing, I started chewing on the inside of my cheek until I could taste the sweet and briny flavor of blood on my tongue.

"I can't wait until you come home, honey," Dad said to me over the phone. "I've been seeing someone. I really like her, and I want us to all have dinner together while you're home."

I grimaced at the idea of Dad dating.

Mom had divorced Dad more than five years ago. He'd just recently gotten back into the dating game when, all of a sudden, he was dating this mysterious woman who he fell instantly in love with.

Was it weird to remind my dad that he shouldn't fall in love with the first woman he dates? That seemed like the kind of advice that he should give to *me*.

Looking around my little shitty dorm room, I gave a wide grin to remind myself that, no matter who the woman was, I was an adult now, and I had my entire future ahead of me. I could endure some holiday dinners with any woman he chose, as long as she made Dad happy.

"I wouldn't want it any other way, Dad. Of course I want to meet her."

He sighed with relief.

"We planned it around the end of the semester. Her son will be there, too.

"That's nice," I said absently, not interested in this new woman or her son. Hopefully the guy wasn't a complete asshole.

"Oh! Pen's calling. I'll let you know as soon as we've cemented our plans. Love you, hun!"

"Love you too, Dad," I said, but he cut me off halfway through to switch to the new love of his life.

Blinking down at the phone, I frowned.

New love of his life.

All through high school, it'd just been Dad and I. Through boyfriends and breakups, proms and winter formals, Dad was right there as my right hand man while I managed to wade through it all. Now it was his turn, and I couldn't help but feel a little...left out.

I wasn't his number one girl anymore.

"Finally," my roommate growled, staring at her Ipad. "Next time, take your phone calls outside."

"This is my room, too," I reminded her.

God, I really hoped I got a new roommate next year.

"The year's almost over. Pretty sure you can deal with a couple calls until we don't have to see each other again," I told her, opening my American Economics textbook to go over today's chapters.

I hated the course almost as much as I hated my roommate.

She just lifted her hand to me and stuck up her middle finger as she popped gum over her own thick textbook.

Yeah, the feeling was mutual.

Not feeling like doing homework at all, I shut the book a little too loudly, just to piss off my roomie, then slipped my flip flops on while texting Hillary to meet me at the beach.

"You're going to have a *brother*?" Hillary asked while we sipped iced coffees on our favorite bench in Palisades Park.

It wasn't as busy as Santa Monica Pier and it gave us the calming sound of the ocean without the bustle of tourists and beach bums.

"Is he hot?"

I shrugged.

"I don't know. Never met the guy. He's probably a total geek. Or worse, a beef head."

"There are worse things than a beef head to look at across the Sunday dinner table for the rest of your life." My friend laughed, as if the situation was so fucking funny.

She tossed her bleach blond hair and it shimmered with whites and golds in the mid-afternoon light. And for the millionth time, I felt a pang of envy.

Hillary was everything that I ever wanted to be. She was curvy, blond, big breasted, and she had a smile that could light up a room. Not to mention her personality was a bombshell in and of itself. My bestie was just easy to look at, and easy to love. We'd been friends since freshman year in high school, and started UCLA together last fall.

"Enough about my new 'maybe' in-law. How's your roommate?"

Hillary gagged.

"I swear. I want to throttle the person who put me with someone other than you. I mean, we get along great! My roommate cooks freaking nasty shit in our room and the smell lingers *everywhere*. You know what it's like going to a party smelling like garlic, anchovies, and perfume? Well, I do, now."

I giggled.

"Oh, shut the hell up. All you have is some idiot who hates it when you talk. She doesn't stain your clothes with permanent funk!"

"Next year," I told her. "I know the person who helps sort rooms now, so I'll try and pull a couple strings with her. She thinks my hair is awesome."

Hillary pouted.

"Your hair is pretty awesome. I keep thinking I want to do something else with mine. You give me so much inspiration!"

I touched the magenta and cobalt stripes in my dark hair and smiled at her.

"Your hair is too perfect to mess it up with box dye. I'd kill you if you messed with that work of art."

She just blushed like the awesome person she was and stuffed a clump of the shiny strands behind her ear.

"Any call from Jason?"

I shrugged.

"Nope. I think one date was enough for both of us. It was an epic disaster. You know that."

"Well, yeah but he's been so into you. Maybe it's because finals are around the corner. I'm sure you'll hear from him over summer break."

"Maybe. What about your Greek cutie?"

Hillary's blush got darker as she grinned.

"I talked to him yesterday after our dance class. He's so freaking cute, Ivy! Like, the dark curls and his olive skin... God, I just want to lick him!"

"Oh my God!" I laughed, pressing my hand over my mouth when a nasty snort echoed out. "Lick? You want to lick the guy?"

"Hey, if you saw him, you would want to lick him, too," she countered, that adorable pout back on her face.

"Whatever. I don't like my guys delicious; I like them hot."

"Oh, I know, Ivory. You like them like Hunter Hayes."

She rolled her eyes while I shot her a glare.

"We do not mention the name of that asshole unless we're in the process of cursing him."

Another eye roll.

343

"Ooo! Speak of the devil! Is that him?" she sounded way too excited.

My head shot around and my eyes immediately found him.

Just up ahead, I could see him on the beach with his buddies, wearing nothing but board shorts that were riding low on narrow hips while they played around with their surfboards.

"Welp, I'm done here," I told Hillary.

"He's such a jerk," she agreed, standing with me so we could throw out our empty cups. "Why don't you just give him a piece of your mind and get it over with? This whole avoiding him on campus has gotten out of hand. The guy is freaking *everywhere*."

"'Cause he's a total manwhore that really gets around," I ground out between clenched teeth. "And no. I have no intention of ever talking to him again for the rest of my life. My time is too precious to waste it on him."

Hillary sighed and just followed me back to our cars.

"I've gotta get back. Thanks for meeting me for a drink," she said, looking at the time on her phone.

"Always. But I was the one to call you, remember?"

She shrugged.

"Same difference."

I just let myself smile a little before hugging my bestie and soaking in her sunshine a bit before going back to my depressing dorm room.

"Remember," Hillary sang as she sank into the driver's seat of her pink Volkswagen Bug. "Hate makes you ugly and bitter!"

"So does Hayes!" I called back, and she laughed before shutting her door.

Yeah, just thinking about stupid Hunter Hayes made my blood boil, even two years after 'The Big Mistake'. Twenty minutes in a dark closet with the asshole had turned me from a blossoming romantic to a bitter teen. One day, one mistake, was all it took for life to lose a little bit of its shine.

Shoving all thoughts of the jerk out of my head, I got back into my truck and started back to campus while Hillary went back to her job at Sephora.

Yeah, she was so cool that she got a job like *that*.

Slipping my sunglasses on, I wondered briefly if maybe I could get away with a moment of insanity of just driving over the dropoff and crashing into Hunter and his cronies. Not enough to really *hurt* anyone, but just to ruin their day like he'd ruined so many of mine.

No. I'd likely get a ticket at the least, or maybe jail time. That wouldn't look good on my record while I was trying to get into psychology and family therapy. I'd just have to get over it and move the fuck on.

Forgiveness wasn't for the other person, it was only ever for ourselves.

— 2 —

Ivory

Thirteen Years Ago

"Ivy?"

It was him. It was always him.

"What, Hunt?" I asked, frowning over my bologna sandwich.

"Wanna trade?" he asked.

He was holding out his deviled egg sandwich, which was my absolute favorite.

It was his favorite, too.

Mom didn't really care what I ate for lunch, and rarely got around to making me anything. Dad had managed to throw a sandwich together for me with what we had left in the fridge and stuck it in my backpack with a bruised banana for my lunch.

"Yeah," I told him, holding out the mangled Wonder bread and pink lunch meat.

I hated bologna, not that Mom cared. She bought it because it was cheap and easy. Hunter's Mom actually cared about him, so he got what he liked every day for lunch, unlike me.

"Hand it over," Hunter said, wiggling his fingers.

His hand was bigger than I remembered. He had just reached a growth spurt over the summer and Dad said he was going to be tall as a tree by the time we were grown up.

I gave it to him and he slapped the homemade bread with mayonnaise and eggs into my hands. It smelled like butt, but tasted awesome because his mom used Miracle Whip in it instead of just plain ol' mayo.

"Thanks," I told him.

He just smiled at me, then sat down next to me to open up the plastic baggie, taking a massive bite of the sandwich.

I was more careful with my sandwich, and I savored each bite of the stinky, delicious concoction.

"You see the new kid?" Hunter asked after a while, pointing to the new girl sitting by herself.

I nodded.

"They moved in next door to us. Mom says they're from Missouri."

"Where's that?" I asked, scrunching up my nose.

He shrugged.

"Dunno."

We ate the rest of our food in quiet companionship.

Yeah, Hunter and I had a lot in common.

He had a terrible dad, and I had a dud for a mom. We would hide at each other's places sometimes, when our parents would argue. Mom hated it, because she hated Hunter's mom so much, but I didn't really care. Mom would always shove it aside and drink, or go on a shopping spree until she felt better.

"You think we should say 'hi' to her?" I asked eventually, licking off any last remnants of sandwich filling from my fingers. "I was lonely when I moved in. I bet she's lonely, too."

Hunter frowned a little, but eventually he nodded and started getting up from the sticky cafeteria table.

Together we went to talk to the new girl, my hands a little greasy from my lunch, but it was a nice feeling to be full of good food.

"Hi," I said immediately when we made it to her table. "I'm Ivory Bell. Hunt calls me Ivy though, 'cause he's a dumb boy and he can't say my name right."

Hunter elbowed me in the side and I grunted, but grinned. He didn't like being called a dumb boy, that's why I did it.

"I'm your neighbor," Hunter said. "And Ivy has cooties."

The girl just stared at us like we were aliens coming down to take her away.

After a long bet of silence, I waved, then turned and went back to the table I usually shared with Hunter.

"I don't think she likes us," I told him.

"She just didn't like you," was his response.

I glared at him for a second, then we busted up laughing.

Find BoyFrenemy on Amazon

Other Reads By L. L. Ash

Sophisticated Seductions Series

HIM.

Teach Me

Wolf Series

Genesis

Friction Envy

Triage

Swan Song

Minutemen Series

Boyfriend By The Hour

Bullseye

Rock God Series

Phoenix

Crash

Fret

Standalone Novels

BoyFrenemy

For The Money

Heart Ink.

Novellas and Short Stories

Hitchhike

The Horror Of Our Love

About the Author

L.L. Ash is a Washington-born writer who has traveled and lived across the western coast of the US.

Ash has been writing fiction since she was a pre-teen, and while her writing has improved since then, her love for literature has not changed. Oftentimes you can find Ash reading an indie romance or enjoying a historical fiction. Dabbling in culinary arts and music, Ash has been an artist for decades but found her true love and passion in romances.

Find me at
llashmedia.com
Goodreads
Facebook
Instagram
Amazon

Made in the USA
Monee, IL
27 June 2023

37793532R00206